"CONGRESSMAN, WHAT ARE YOU TRYING TO DO TO ME?" SHE DEMANDED.

"Break you," he stated flatly.

"Why?" she whispered. "I've already been broken. Shattered. You must be the cruelest person living—"

"Living. Exactly my point, Rhiannan. You need to learn to open yourself up again to life."

"Open myself up? Great idea, Congressman. Then I can become a sitting duck for sadists like you. You should be quite pleased with yourself. I've definitely reacted to you. Well, I'm sorry, Kiel Whellen, never again. I prefer being a robot."

"No, you don't, and the more time you spend with me—"

"There will be no more time!"

"Wrong, Mrs. Collins, because I will plague you—"

"I hate you!"

"Good. That's a start anyway. And by the time I finish with you, you'll either love me or despise me. But at least you'll be feeling again—and living."

<u>BOOK YOUR PLACE ON OUR WEBSITE</u> <u>AND MAKE THE</u> <u>READING CONNECTION!</u>

We've created a customized website just for our very special readers, where you can get the inside scoop on everything that's going on with Zebra, Pinnacle and Kensington books.

When you come online, you'll have the exciting opportunity to:

- View covers of upcoming books
- Read sample chapters
- Learn about our future publishing schedule (listed by publication month *and author*)
- Find out when your favorite authors will be visiting a city near you
- Search for and order backlist books from our online catalog
- Check out author bios and background information
- Send e-mail to your favorite authors
- Meet the Kensington staff online
- Join us in weekly chats with authors, readers and other guests
- Get writing guidelines
- AND MUCH MORE!

Visit our website at
http://www.zebrabooks.com

QUEEN
OF
HEARTS

Heather Graham

Zebra Books
Kensington Publishing Corp.

http://www.zebrabooks.com

ZEBRA BOOKS are published by

Kensington Publishing Corp.
850 Third Avenue
New York, NY 10022

First Zebra Printing: September, 1997
10 9 8 7 6 5 4

Printed in the United States of America

*For my sister Victoria Graham Davant,
with love and thanks for always
being there.
And of course for Davis, my one and
only brother-in-law, and for D.J.—my
one and only nephew.*

Prologue

SEPTEMBER 22, 7:00 P.M.
WASHINGTON, D.C.

Congressman Kiel Whellen's steps were long and staccato as he hurried down the corridors of the White House to the Oval Office. He was accompanied by two Secret Service men. When he entered the room, there were several men hovering near the President as he sat at his desk—the secretary of the interior, the secretary of state, the speaker of the House, and the Vice-President.

The President, his age and the strain of office clearly revealed in the haggard lines of his features, stood at Kiel's entrance, offering a handshake as the others nodded in quiet greeting.

"Sit, Mr. Whellen, please," the President said.

Kiel, aware now that something was drastically wrong, took the chair in front of the President's desk. He had had a gnawing feeling in the pit of his stomach ever since he had been summoned an hour earlier. Now, glancing around at the esteemed personages gathered in grim silence, that gnawing feeling was turning into gut fear.

The President wasted no time. "Congressman, we have a crisis on our hands. Are you aware of the activities of the Red Hawks—the Red Liberation Army?"

Kiel frowned, his sandy brows furrowing over his sharp gray

eyes. "Red Hawks, sir? They're a terrorist group, I believe. Many of their members have had tactical training in North Africa. They comprise many nationalities, and their goal is an international government—by the people, or so they claim."

"Right." The speaker of the House stepped toward Kiel and sat on the corner of the President's desk to face him. "The Red Hawks are led by a man called Lee Hawk, who is something of a fanatic or lunatic and, unfortunately, a bit of a genius. He believes that only by violence can violence be stopped." The speaker shook his head with a bit of incredulity. "He claims the Bible condones his tactics and God understands his methods. His ultimate goal is total cessation of the production of nuclear arms and products for chemical warfare."

Kiel listened quietly to the explanation, his fingers laced over his lap. He wasn't particularly surprised that the Red Hawks were causing problems; they were renowned international terrorists.

Kiel felt increasingly uncomfortable, and the gnawing fear he had felt was intensified by his sense of confusion. What did they think that he, the junior representative from Virginia, with his limited power, could do? And whatever it was these prestigious men were implying had to be critical.

"Yes," he said quietly, his eyes scanning the speaker, then the President, "I've read a bit about Lee Hawk. And I agree: It seems the man is a genius but borders on being a lunatic. His goals are idealistic; his methods of achieving them are tragic."

The President stood up and stared out the massive window to the serenity of the sloping green grass beyond. He turned back to Kiel. "The last we had heard—and the last that our intelligence reports had been able to give us—is that Hawk and his group had been slipping from one European country to another." The President paused. "Our reports were faulty or tragically out of date, because two of Lee Hawk's agents are aboard a 747—the flight from Charleston to D.C."

Kiel's stomach was suddenly attacked by a pain as sharp as

a knife wound. Ellen was on that flight. Did the President know he was expecting his fiancée? Was that why he had been summoned?

He doubted it. A 747. The lives of two to three hundred people would be at stake. He had not been called so that these men could sympathetically hold his hand. A chill of terror unlike anything he had ever experienced seized him, and he fought it. It was nothing like the fear he had known in the service; this was different. It was a feeling of horrible fatality, as if he were trying to grab the reins of a runaway horse, only to discover that his hands had been tied in knots.

There was no visible change in the congressman's face as he watched the others in the room. He remained calm when he spoke, his gray eyes narrowing as he asked, "What do they want?"

"Demands we can't possibly fulfill," the speaker answered with a worried sigh. "Two of Hawk's men were taken by the West German government when they attempted to assassinate the minister of defense. They're in jail for killing ten German civilians in the explosion, and the German government refuses to release them."

What about the hundreds of people aboard that plane? Kiel wanted to shriek out, but he didn't. "What else are they demanding?"

"A large sum of money and the plane. They want to take it all to North Africa, where they can find asylum."

Kiel hesitated a moment, rolling his thumbs in circles, his lashes lowering as he stared at his fingers. He needed to clip his nails, he thought abstractedly. He directed his steady gaze at the President. "Why have you called me?"

The President paused only a second. "Hawk is up in that plane with his two agents. We have radio communication. He's refused to negotiate unless he can do so with you."

"Me?" Kiel lifted a startled brow.

The President shrugged. "He respects a number of your political stands. He wants you, Whellen. Says if he can't talk to you, he'll blow up the plane."

The weight of fear and massive responsibility suddenly seemed to clamp down on him, making it difficult for him to breathe. It was worse than the personal horror of knowing Ellen was aboard the flight. Maybe she wasn't; maybe she had missed it. . . . She hadn't missed it, Kiel thought with pained surety. Ellen was always precisely on time.

Kiel took a cigarette from his breast pocket and tapped the filter against his thumb. He reached for his lighter, but the speaker of the House was quicker, lighting Kiel's cigarette with the monogrammed lighter from the top of the desk.

Kiel inhaled, and his eyes were once more on the President. "What do I tell this Lee Hawk?"

"We're working with the Germans right now. And the secretary of defense and the aeronautical boards are all on this thing, too, now. Just establish communication, and for God's sake, stall him a bit. The plane is circling Richmond."

"When do I start?"

"Now."

The President flicked a switch on a two-by-three-inch speaker that sat next to his blotter. Kiel stood and approached the desk, absently noting that his hands were shaking. He glanced at the President, who nodded to Kiel.

"Lee Hawk?" Kiel said. "Hawk, are you there? This is Congressman Kiel Whellen. I understand that you want to talk to me. That's great. I want to talk to you."

SEPTEMBER 22, 7:15 P.M.
RICHMOND, VIRGINIA

Rhiannan Collins frowned as she glanced into the refrigerator. She was sure she had put the dip for her next-door neighbor's poker party on the second shelf, but she couldn't find it. She sighed. It was like starting a great quest every time she tried to find something in the refrigerator. It was simply too small. There were cans of the baby's formula, boxes of Ryan's school pudding, half-eaten bananas, half-consumed sodas, and containers of orange juice and sugar-free Kool-Aid and . . .

"Eeeekkk!" She let out a startled scream as she was suddenly grasped around the waist and pulled from the refrigerator into Paul's arms.

"Passion!" he exclaimed cheerfully, tilting her over his arm. "The kids are both asleep!" He adjusted his hold on her to check his wristwatch. "We have, ah, exactly four minutes and twenty seconds to be alone before the sitter is due!"

Rhiannan laughed, shaking her head as she met his sparkling brown gaze. "Forget the passion. We haven't got four minutes. I was supposed to have my stuff over at June's fifteen minutes ago. What kind of an offer is that?"

"What?" Paul demanded indignantly. "You're turning down this wonderfully romantic offer to walk cheese dip across the street!"

Rhiannan chuckled and ran her fingers through his dark hair. "Sorry, the honeymoon has been over for seven years. I'm not up to breaking my back on the floor!"

"No spirit!" Paul groaned with mock despair. "Ah, well." He grimaced as he pulled her to him and released her with a quick kiss on the mouth. He brushed back his hair and glanced at her mournfully. "Go easy with the stuff, will ya, kid? It's falling out by the combfuls!"

Rhiannan laughed again as she stuck her head back into the refrigerator. "It is not falling out, and you're not going bald. You're merely acquiring a little distinguishing gray around the edges."

"Yeah?" he asked her hopefully.

"Yeah," she replied, emitting a happy sigh as she finally found the cheese dip behind a gnawed granola bar in a baggy. "Here it is! I've got to run. Thanks, Mr. Executive Husband, for helping out this old-lady housewife! If you hadn't bathed the kids, I would have never been dressed on time."

"I don't mind bathing them," Paul said, grabbing a piece of celery to dig hastily into the disappearing dip. "Snow White as a bedtime story for the two-hundred-and-second time gets a bit heavy, but the baths, that's nothing! A father should give his kids their baths."

Rhiannan paused for a minute, slipping her purse from the counter into her laden arms. She glanced at Paul, feeling a tenderness well up within her. They had their arguments, but they also had, she thought, the most wonderful marriage she could ever have wished for.

She had everything! A beautiful home in the suburbs, two sweet, healthy, beautiful children, an immense, overlovable German shepherd, a fat tabby cat, and two yellow canaries that actually sang every morning.

But most of all, she had Paul. He left each morning in his tailored suit, handsome and neat, determined to become the sharpest market analyst in existence. But then he came home every night and he was just Paul, a man who loved to roll on the floor with his children, who cheerfully took out the garbage, who ate off paper plates without a word and instinctively knew when the role of housewife and mother had been a bit too much for her and insisted that they needed a dinner out.

She placed her purse, the dishes of fresh vegetables, and the spicy cheese dip back on the counter. Smiling mischievously, she threw her arms around him. "I promise a whole pack of passion tonight! How about it?"

"Sounds good!" He tapped her lightly on the rear. "I'll see to it that you have two margaritas and I should be all set."

"You think I need margaritas to be passionate?" Rhiannan demanded indignantly.

"It's all downhill after thirty," he teased solemnly, his brows jiggling warningly. Then he hugged her. "No, my love, you're still the most passionate, sensual, beautiful vixen I've ever met!"

Rhiannan smiled, patting his trim gut. "You're not so bad yourself, Casanova! Except that I get the strange feeling that

that compliment was a little flowery. You must really want something."

"I do!" he replied mournfully, snatching another celery stalk from the counter. "Passion!"

"You're hopeless!" Rhiannan charged him with a mock sigh. Her eyes lit on the large-faced kitchen clock and she groaned. "Almost seven thirty! June is going to kill me. I promised to help her set up the buffet table—"

"Well, get on over there!" Paul commanded, shaking his head with exasperation as he procured a large bag for her various Tupperware containers. "Much easier to carry this way. Go on over. I can wait for Cindy to get here; I can even give her your speech on what to do if the kids wake up. Since we'll be all the way across the street—"

" 'Across the street' is a hundred yards!" Rhiannan reminded him, containing a smile. He was right: She did harangue their regular sitter with a speech every time she came. And tonight they would only be at the Herberts' house.

"Okay. I'm just going to blow the kids kisses and I'll be out the door!"

Rhiannan tossed back her feathered black hair and hurried up the staircase to the second floor. Jenny was in the first room to the right. Rhiannan tiptoed up to the cradle and smiled. At six months Jenny had a full cap of curling brown hair. With her tiny fists beside her chubby cheeks, she was adorable. Rhiannan stretched over the crib bars to kiss her daughter's peach-soft face. " 'Night, precious!" she murmured.

Her next stop was her son's room. Five-year-old Ryan was sound asleep with his stuffed E.T. doll clutched tightly in his arms. He had kicked off his sheets. Rhiannan smiled as she replaced them, dipping to kiss his forehead. "Love you, sweetheart," she murmured.

She turned off the hallway light and left the bathroom light on, just in case Ryan should wake up and have to go. Then she hurried downstairs and back into the kitchen, where Paul was still crunching celery. "Did I do okay?" he teased, his eyes sparkling.

"You did perfectly," Rhiannan informed him imperiously. She took the bag and her purse from him. "Come right over soon as Cindy gets here. June wants to impress her boss with her sophisticated neighbors!"

"Oh, no!" Paul laughed. "It's a good thing she warned us to dress up!"

Rhiannan made a face and kissed him quickly, then hurried out the kitchen door. It was a gorgeous summer night. The sloping lawn looked beautiful as it curved to the roadway, and the Herberts' lawn looked equally as nice, rising far across from theirs on the cul-de-sac.

As she walked along in the moonlight she glanced up at the sky, frowning as she heard the droning of an airplane. It was strange, because planes never flew low this far from the city. She shrugged, dismissing the sound.

SEPTEMBER 22, 7:28 P.M.
WASHINGTON, D.C.

Kiel was staring out at the peaceful beauty of the brilliantly lit White House lawn. He was on his fourth cigarette, but other than that, his tension was barely visible, except for his tense pacing back and forth in front of the window.

"I like you, Whellen," Lee Hawk was saying over the speaker. "I've heard a lot of your speeches. No garbage in them—for a politician, that is. And you seem to fight for what you want. I was in the House that day you fought for the bill on cleaning up the nuclear waste."

Kiel's eyes were riveted on the President. Was security that bad?

They heard Hawk chuckle. "Yeah, man, I was there. Hard to believe, isn't it?"

"Yeah, hard to believe," Kiel replied. He crushed out his cigarette, wishing he could pitch his plea to Hawk in person instead of through a little box. "Listen, Hawk, you know that I respect your stand on germ warfare and nukes and the like. But what can you accomplish by killing three hundred people?"

"Two hundred and eighty-seven, to be exact," Hawk said calmly. "I don't like killing, Congressman. But sometimes some have to die so that others can live. But if you get me what I want, then this bird can sail right on into Dulles Airport. And then I'll just hold these people while you get me my men back from Germany, and the arms I've requested. I'll even let your pilot fly back as soon as he's gotten me where I want to go."

"We're negotiating with the German government right now," Kiel answered solemnly.

"Oh, by the way, your fiancée is doing real well, here, Whellen. Just thought you'd like to know."

Kiel gritted his teeth and swallowed. He felt the eyes of the other men on him and he made a stern effort to loosen his clenched fists. "Thanks for telling me, Hawk. How about the rest of the passengers?"

"So far, so good, Congressman. Just one problem."

"Oh? What's that?"

"I think we've got a couple of government men in the back. Maybe because we have one of your brother lawmakers aboard. Law-keeper, I should say. Justice Banes of the Supreme Court."

Again Kiel's eyes soared to the President's, accusing and angry. The President nodded slowly and Kiel felt his helpless fury grow. They had handed him an explosive deck to play, and they hadn't even given him all the cards.

"So what's the problem?" Kiel asked evenly.

"I just hope we don't have any heroes aboard."

"I agree." Kiel stared at the other men in the room, one by one. "Okay, Hawk, let's see how we're doing. We have the arms you want, fuel ready at Dulles, and a new pilot. But you've got to understand, it isn't our government holding your men. We don't have the power—"

"Keep talking to the Germans. We have several aboard."

"We *are* talking to them."

"I believe you, Congressman, I believe you. Let's just pray you get a few answers before this bird runs out of fuel. These nice people might live long lives thanks to you, Congressman. We might be—Dammit! Damnation!"

"What? What? Lee? HAWK? HAWK?" Shouting into the box, Kiel leaned over the desk, his fingers clawing into the wood, the broad muscles of his back and shoulders bunching with anxiety and tension. "Hawk?"

His only reply was a deafening report that might have been a gun—or an explosion.

SEPTEMBER 22, 7:30 P.M.
RICHMOND, VIRGINIA

Rhiannan paused at the Herberts' doorway, glancing curiously back up to the sky. The droning grew louder, suddenly stopped, and then became a deafening whistle as a silver missile streaked toward the ground.

Her mouth opened in horror and disbelief. The sound grew and grew. The silver streak approaching the ground came closer and closer, and then the world before her quaked and trembled and exploded into a red wall of flame.

Her scream escaped her and rose high on the air, defying the cacophony of whirling, clattering debris. Things flew around her; the air was as hot as a furnace, but she noticed none of it. Across the road from her the velvet green lawn was singed and pockmarked. Her home—her street—was no more. It had become an inferno.

"No!" she raged, choking on the billowing smoke that blew her way. *"No!"*

She started running toward the holocaust, but the Herberts were out by then. Bill Herbert caught her before she could run into the flames, tackling her to the ground.

"They're in there!" she shouted. "They're in there! Have to get them. The baby, Ryan . . . Paul . . ."

She was fighting, scratching, kicking at Bill Herbert, who wept as he held her. He didn't try to tell her it would be too late. He just kept weeping as he allowed her to rain her blows on him until the night came alive with sirens, until someone finally came to inject her with a long needle that offered the peace of oblivion.

The newspapers and magazines carried the story for weeks. Thirty people on the ground, as well as 281 of the passengers aboard the plane, were killed. Only six people survived the crash, making it the worst air disaster in history. The 747 tore away three full blocks of homes when it crashed. Ironically the body of Lee Hawk was never discovered, despite the tedious search through the debris. It was considered lucky that the plane had crashed in the suburbs, or the fatality rate would have been even higher.

Bullets were found among the wreckage, but they were so mangled that not even the world's best ballistics experts knew by whom they had been fired. No one ever knew exactly what had gone wrong in the air. The last words recorded by the plane's black box were those same words spoken to Kiel Whellen.

Publicly, Congressman Whellen took complete responsibility for the incident. He left Washington for an extended vacation in a remote cabin somewhere in the Blue Ridge Mountains. Despite what his supporters considered an appalling indifference to his campaign, he was reelected to office. It seemed that his constituents did not consider him responsible. Not many people did.

But Rhiannan was not one of them. To bear her grief she needed someone to hate, someone to blame. She didn't know Congressman Whellen; he was one of those distant men who sat in a pristine office and played with the lives of others. She blamed him. And when she shook herself out of her lethargy, she was aware enough to know that she harbored an intense dislike for the congressman.

When Kiel Whellen returned to Washington to begin his new term, he resumed all his duties with the fury of a man possessed. Fighting for legislation was an antidote for his pain. He was a strong man, a mountain man, as rugged as the cliffs and peaks of the Blue Ridge, and time slowly but surely healed his wounds.

Rhiannan Collins didn't fare quite so well. She was in shock for weeks, and then, when she accepted the situation, she spent hopeless days when she could do nothing but cry. She wondered why she hadn't been in the house to die with all that had been her life; she railed against God for leaving her and taking her children, her baby.

And when she could finally function fairly normally again, she discovered she couldn't bear the kindness of her friends, for as much as she tried to appreciate what they did, they were all reminders of all she had lost. Life went on for them. Bill Herbert would play golf; Paul would never hold a golf club again. Her friends' children would ride the school bus, their mothers would make lunches, the babies would fuss and gurgle and laugh from their strollers but all of that was gone for her. She would never hold her baby again.

Six months after the tragedy, her brother, Tim, fearing for her sanity, contacted a college friend who was the perfect person to remove Rhiannan from the surroundings that weighed on her heart so heavily.

"Don't be ridiculous, Tim," she laughed hollowly to her brother. "Pa-Paul . . . left plenty of insurance. I don't need a job. And I can't do anything! Tim, all I've ever been is a wife! And . . . a mother. I can play poker and mix martinis and serve nice canapés! I'm not qualified to do anything else."

"Rhiannan!" Tim tried to laugh. It was hard to when she still appeared so pathetically haunted. "That's the perfect part of all this! You have to do something; you have to go on! And Donald Flagherty's offer will make you do that! He is one of the most affluent men in the world; he doesn't need a secretary, or a file clerk, or a brilliant assistant! He needs a bright and attractive hostess. 'Annan, it will take you away." Tim bent down to take his sister's hand. " 'Annan, I know you feel you should be dead; I know that Paul and the children were your life. But I love you, Rhiannan, and Mom and Dad . . . For us, you have to keep going. . . ."

Tears flooded Rhiannan's eyes. She knew that losing their grandchildren had been almost unbearable for her parents, but at least she was alive. As much as she had bitterly wondered at first why she hadn't died with her husband and children, she knew that her life had been the single ray of hope to her parents and her brother. Dear Tim, staring at her now with tears glazing his eyes as he empathized with her pain.

"Okay, Tim," she managed. "If this rich friend of yours wants to employ someone to mix martinis and play cards, I'll take the job."

A month later she was glad she had taken the position. Donald Flagherty was a wonderful man, a philanthropist, intelligent and sensitive. Flying and yachting around the world was interesting. She still lived with her pain, but she learned to exist, and after a year she actually learned to smile again, and sometimes she could laugh. Her job called for the perfect hostess, and she was. Beautiful, aloof, and completely, distantly, charming.

To Don Flagherty and his associates, friends, and employees, she quickly became a beloved fascination. They called her the Queen of Hearts.

One

"Wait till you see her with her sails unfurled! That one there, she's the topgallant, and when she fills with the wind, this ship will seem to fly across the waves. What a beautiful lady she'll be then. Nothing on the seven seas will be able to compare with her, Rhiannan!"

Rhiannan smiled at Glen Trivitt, the ship's doctor for this first run of the *Seafire* since she had been purchased and refurbished by Donald Flagherty. It was impossible not to be enthused by Glen's wistful excitement, just as it was impossible not to be excited by the *Seafire*.

They had been standing together at the bow of the old sailing ship, one of the last privately owned square-riggers in the world, staring at the busy port of Miami for almost an hour. They had watched as the passengers prepared to board, and then Glen had turned with renewed enthusiasm to acclaim the grace and majesty of the proud masts once again.

"She *is* a beautiful ship, Glen," Rhiannan agreed, turning to follow Glen's arm to the point far above them where the masts of the ship seemed to challenge the sky. "It will be exciting to see her under full sail."

Glen grinned. "I wonder how much of our sail I'll be able to see. With our passenger list, I'll probably be busy from dawn to dusk, appeasing little old ladies who are convinced they're dying from seasickness."

Rhiannan laughed. "Just make sure you ladle out plenty of

Dramamine before we get started. That should solve your problems. Besides," she added, a faint sparkle touching her eyes as she turned toward the boarding plank once more, "it doesn't appear to me that our passengers are old ladies!"

"Oh, yeah?"

Quirking a brow high, Glen gripped the rail and stared once again at those boarding. He laughed and whistled softly at five young women laughing and chatting together and adorned in some of the most elegant casual wear ever designed: short, short skirts, wide-brimmed hats, knit sailor tops, and pearls. Rhiannan couldn't criticize their attire, for she felt a little ridiculous herself in a white skirt-suit. Logically jeans or shorts would best serve the sail to the Caribbean islands; whimsically, flowing silk would complement the beauty and grace of the clipper. But neither whimsy nor logic was allowed at the moment. Donald had ordered that all his employees—crew and personal servants—dress "with dignity" as the *Seafire* prepared to leave port.

"Well . . . I won't mind dishing out Dramamine to that group," he said lightly, "except they all look like fluff." He looked past the group of affluent young women and murmured, "The high and the mighty."

Rhiannan watched as a definitely distinguished-looking group of men approached the plank, all in business suits, all carrying briefcases.

"Congressmen?" she asked Glen.

"And senators and diplomats," he replied.

They both watched in silence for a moment. Although the *Seafire* had just recently been purchased by their employer as a public cruise ship, they both knew that this, her first passenger voyage in twenty years, was to be an extremely special occasion. Berths had been rented out, but the majority of them were being filled by invitation only.

Donald Flagherty belonged to a number of organizations, some charitable, some political. One of his number-one interests was a world free of nuclear arms. And so, to launch his newly purchased toy, he had invited a number of friends from around the world to hold a WWON—World Without Nukes—conference aboard his ship. The passenger list was therefore impressive, to say the least. Dignitaries were coming not just from England, France, Germany and western nations but also from the People's Republic of China and the Soviet Union. There were at least three U.S. senators involved, and probably half a dozen congressmen.

"Ahhh . . ." Glen sighed. "Think of it! They'll all be sailing and sunning, and alas, the two of us will be drudging servants to their elite whims!"

Again Rhiannan laughed. Glen Trivitt had the ability to make her do so. She was often remote and often cool, despite all her attempts to be more than polite to others. She didn't mean to be; but although she had mastered the mechanics of living again, she hadn't managed to learn to feel much of anything except for her deep affection for Donald. And since she had met Glen a month earlier, when he had come into Donald's employ, she had discovered that it was possible to laugh again. She liked Glen whom she guessed to be about forty and who was of medium build and nondescript features. His eyes were a pale, almost colorless blue, yet they looked at one with a deep and innate understanding. She was certain he knew her history—everyone did—yet, he never mentioned her past. He was just always pleasant and easy to be with. She felt that there was a deep wisdom beneath those colorless eyes—intelligence and a judicial mind.

"Glen," Rhiannan said, feeling the smooth, sun-heated varnished rail beneath her palms, "neither of us is likely to suffer much drudgery. It's possible no one will become sick. And don't think that anyone could call dealing cards or mixing drinks true menial labor, especially when you're doing it for Donald. If I didn't know that he had more money than most accountants could possibly keep track of, I'd feel guilty for being paid."

"Ah, 'Annan!" Glen objected, "you would be worth your weight in gold just standing on the deck!"

"Thanks, Glen," Rhiannan murmured, feeling just a moment's discomfort upon noticing the light in his eyes. She knew that he was attracted to her, and it bothered her. She would have liked to have felt something for him—a reaction to his touch, a stirring within her to the sound of his voice. But she felt nothing except a gentle liking, and she was so afraid she would lose the tenuous link of the undemanding friendship he offered.

"Look!" Glen interrupted her thoughts, pointing toward shore and smiling, dispelling her discomfort. "That short, portly bald man with the steel-gray hair. Do you know who that is?"

Rhiannan shook her head. "Who is it?"

"For shame, Mrs. Collins! That's Wilhelm Stroltz of West Germany, a diplomat assigned to his country's embassy in Washington, and a well-known negotiator."

"I'm very impressed!" Rhiannan laughed.

"And that's Pierre Jardineau of France."

"The tall man?"

"Yes."

Rhiannan stared at the cluster of distinguished visitors. She recognized a number of U.S. senators who had been serving for years, and then her attention was taken by a tall, dark-haired man. He appeared younger than the others at first sight, somewhere in his mid-thirties, and he looked more like an athlete than a politician. His shoulders were broad, his waist and hips trim and tapered. He moved with a litheness and grace, and seemed attuned to everything about him.

"Glen?"

"Yeah?"

"Who is that? A Secret Service man?"

Glen followed the point of her finger to the cordoned waiting area before the ship. He shook his head and pointed farther beyond to a semicircle of about thirty young, muscular-looking men. "Those guys are the security force. That"—he hesitated a moment, his voice taking on a deeper, peculiar note—"is Congressman Kiel Whellen."

A wave of cold chills seemed suddenly to wash along her spine. Whellen. The man who had been in contact with the plane when it crashed. . . .

She started to shiver beneath the hot Florida sun. She had heard the tapes of those last few minutes aboard the ill-fated flight; she had heard them again and again. For weeks after the accident the news programs across the nation had run little else. . . . She blamed him; she couldn't help blaming him. And seeing him brought it all back to her.

Why hadn't Donald thought to tell her that Whellen would be aboard the *Seafire*? Why hadn't he warned her? Had he reasoned that there wouldn't be any real contact between them and therefore wouldn't matter?

"Rhiannan? Are you okay?"

She pulled her gaze from the tall congressman and redirected it at Glen, forcing herself to smile. "Fine, Glen. I, uh . . . Who is that beautiful blond woman?" she asked.

"Let me see. That's Joan Kendrick. Fabulously wealthy. Her father made a fortune in paper products. She *is* attractive, isn't she? And it looks like she has an eye on the congressman. . . ."

Yes, the tall, well-built blonde did seem to have her eyes on the congressman. But then it seemed that she also looked up at them.

Rhiannan stared at Glen, but he was watching the people. Did the blonde smile at him as if in acknowledgment? And did Glen return her smile? No, of course not. Glen knew Joan Kendrick only from pictures, and she certainly wasn't looking at Glen anymore. She was smiling again at the congressman and sauntering over to speak with him.

Glen continued to point out prestigious people to her, but Rhiannan wasn't really seeing anything but the tall man who looked more like an athlete or a well-dressed bouncer than a powerful politician. All she wanted to do was get away and hide, grab whatever respite she could. Donald had asked her to handle the blackjack table in the private room of the casino, but she wouldn't have to start until they were out at sea.

"Excuse me, Glen," she murmured, pushing away from the rail, "but I think I'd better go change. It's black gowns for the casino, you know."

"Um, I guess I'd better go get out my Dramamine supply. See you later, 'Annan."

As Rhiannan turned from the rail, she noticed that the passengers had now begun to board. Donald, along with several members of the ship's crew, were greeting them as they stepped onto the highly polished planks of the deck.

The bow section was elevated above the promenade deck by a single story—the pilothouse was beneath her feet—and Rhiannan bit her lip in indecision as she realized that she had hesitated too long. To reach the mahogany stairway that would carry her to the cargo hold, where crew and employees had their cabins, she would have to pass through the crowd now boarding.

Glen had already swept through the *Seafire*'s guests, politely maneuvering his way to the first set of steps with their new guard rail.

Suddenly loathe to join the reveling passengers, Rhiannan decided to circle around to the port side and hopefully avoid the confused mass. Almost fifty of the passengers were dignitaries; another fifty were Secret Service. Another fifty were guests, such as the blond paper-products heiress, who were wealthy enough to pay the price to join the dignitaries.

It was an interesting assemblage and fit Donald's calculations perfectly. Don knew how to mix those with the power and charisma to affect international policies with those who could sponsor them financially.

There had been a time for Rhiannan when such an impressive guest list might have frightened her. But one of the benefits of living in a shell was the protection it gave her. Not much could jolt or affect her; she would be able to handle

Don's guests smoothly. Except for one—Congressman Whellen. Which was why she was really running around the deck.

She reached the port-side stairs and hurried down, but already passengers had milled around the promenade deck. She couldn't blame them for excitedly looking around. Unlike the pristine paint and newness of the majority of cruise ships, the *Seafire* offered a totally different atmosphere. Ropes, rigging, and sail—the entire workings of the ship were in plain view. Walking the deck, one milled with the sailors and stood a chance of being ordered to draw a line. The *Seafire* had begun her life as a clipper ship, for a time transporting lords and ladies from England to their holdings in America, and then for a time she had housed the brave and stalwart who had gone to sea in search of whales in the northern seas. But steam had come of age, and the beautiful *Seafire*, with her graceful planes, majestic sails, and classic figurehead, had become outmoded. She had sat in a shipping museum and almost rotted, then been purchased by an old captain who couldn't afford to renovate her but couldn't watch such history and beauty dissipate before his eyes.

Donald had purchased the ship from the old man's son, who had cruised her along the East Coast in order to keep her seaworthy, and had restored her to all her grandeur. The captain's cabin and master's cabin were almost identical to what they had been a hundred years ago. The beautiful figurehead of a proud woman with long, trailing hair had been lovingly restored by a New England woodcarver. Everything and anything that could be preserved had been. But Donald had also made concessions to modernization. Guardrails had been installed to prevent injuries; sparkling new baths—and lounges and casinos—had been furnished in the most elegant taste.

Rhiannan was proud of her employer's success in combining the old with the new. Nothing, nothing half as lovely as the *Seafire*, would ever roam the Caribbean again.

Paul would have loved to sail on this ship, she thought sadly. Tears blurred her eyes and she tried furiously to blink them away. She had avoided such thoughts for so long, and now they were threatening to overwhelm her again.

For a moment the world seemed to spin around her. She clutched desperately at the stairway banister but it eluded her grasp. Stumbling, she sought to regain her footing and did, but discovered that her impetus had propelled her against another body.

"Excuse me," she mumbled, instinctively steadying herself against a broad, strong chest. She looked up in embarrassment and confusion, then found that her gaze was strangely locked with a smoky gray one. Congressman Kiel Whellen's.

She should have murmured her polite excuse once more and hurried past him. But she seemed frozen in time as she stared at him, studying his features. He was young, somewhere in his thirties. But his gray eyes—large, wide-set, framed by heavy lashes and dark, arched brows—were, if not old, deep and perturbingly wise. There was no way that he could know her; yet, she felt as if he knew something about her . . . inside. He grinned, his full mouth a pleasant slash against his strong, square jaw, and she felt a rush of heat unlike anything she had ever experienced swell inside her.

"Perhaps I should be offering the excuses," he murmured, steadying her with a powerful but gentle grip on her elbows. "There's so much commotion here."

"Yes—yes, there is," Rhiannan murmured breathlessly, longing now to jerk away from him. She blinked and broke the commanding spell of his eyes. "But if you'll excuse me . . ."

He released her arms and she pushed away from his chest. But when she tried to sweep by him the hem of her white leisure suit caught on the curved claw at the end of the banister. She tried to walk, but her skirt pulled her back, sending her into his arms once more.

A slow flush spread across her features as he laughed pleasantly and reached for the hem in order to release her. His fingers brushed lightly and briefly against the flesh of her thigh like a breath of fire.

Mustering what little dignity she felt she had left, Rhiannan tilted her chin to meet his compelling gray stare once more.

"Thank you," she said curtly, then turned about and this time managed to make good a swift but smooth escape.

But by the time she reached her cabin she was angry and impatient with herself. She didn't like the congressman—she had decided that long before meeting him today—and she didn't like the way his presence unsettled her.

The American people might have forgiven their golden boy, but they had not lost everything that they loved because a man sitting in an office had not been able to fulfill his responsibility.

She sighed, tossed herself on her narrow bed, and stared bleakly up at the paneling. She had learned to hide the past away in a corner of her mind; she had learned to function and even to be pleasant. Life had taken on an aimless but comfortable drift, and the congressman, by being there, by speaking in his husky, authoritative tones, by touching her, was eroding the wonderful shell she had created.

No, she thought, standing up to shed her casual wear and head for the tiny shower. She wouldn't allow him to remind her of her misery or to touch her and make her shake.

She would avoid him. With two hundred people on board, it wouldn't be too hard.

When she stepped under the hot shower spray, she started to shiver.

She knew why she had been affected by the brief encounter with the congressman. She had felt as if he had stripped her of all her defenses and left her naked and vulnerable, body and soul.

Clutching her towel against her, she left the tiny shower and vigorously dried off, vehemently calling herself a fool. There was no reason for the congressman to seek her out. There were, as she had already seen, a number of rich and attractive—and young—women aboard the *Seafire*. Things were simple, as she had decided earlier. All she had to do was stay out of his way. He would never seek her out.

Rhiannan realized suddenly that she was just standing by her bed, staring sightlessly at the pleasant light blue spread. She dropped the towel and dressed hurriedly, then swept her hair from her eyes and clipped it with a pair of small silver barrettes. A slight movement of the ship caught her attention and she frowned, glancing at her travel alarm.

It was almost four P.M. They should be well on their way out to sea. And if she didn't hurry, she would be late opening the private blackjack room in the casino.

She actually forgot all about Congressman Whellen as she hurried back to the stairs. The casino was on the main deck, right below the promenade. She would need a minute or two to breathe once she got there, to cloak herself once more with her cool composure.

She liked to deal blackjack. It kept her mind busy as her hands deftly shuffled and dealt the cards. The betting moved quickly, the playing even faster. And she was good at the game. Very good. It was work, of course, but it had always been said that work was a buffer against memories.

One-armed bandits cranked, clanged, and occasionally shrilled in the background, but in the private room off the ship's main casino, where high-stakes gamblers sat with intensity over a game of blackjack, the bets were quietly spoken, quietly registered. The elegance of the small, exclusive room suggested hushed tones. The carpet was a deep, plush maroon, the walls were papered in soft beige brocade, and the chandelier was of delicately fashioned bronze. The woman who dealt the cards for the *Seafire* was as elegantly decked out as the room. She wore a black floor-length evening gown that was smooth and sleek and sophisticated.

Two men stood in the doorway, surveying the scene.

"So, what do you think, Congressman?" Donald Flagherty, with a broad grin and a definite tone of pride, asked his old friend.

Kiel scanned the scene once more with the sharp charcoal-gray eyes that were famous—or notorious—on the House floor. His features, which sometimes appeared to be chiseled out of stone—handsome features, nicely proportioned but often severe—remained ruggedly stern for only a moment. Then a broad grin broke out across the face of the young representative. He turned to the friend he had known since they were both kids in Fredericksburg.

"I think she's beautiful."

Donald frowned. "She?" He looked around the room, trying to see to whom Kiel might be referring.

"Oh." Donald let out a long breath. He looked at Kiel with foreboding, his sense of gaiety and wonder over the *Seafire*'s maiden voyage draining from him as if a tide had cleanly sucked away his happiness.

"What's the matter with you, Donald?" Kiel demanded, taking in the pallor of his friend's face.

"I asked you what you thought of the casino," Donald said, trying to joke, "and instead you're womanizing on me."

"I'm not womanizing," Kiel said lightly, curious at the reaction he had drawn from Donald. "The casino is marvelous, the epitome of elegance, and it's a damn good thing for the taxpayers that you've taken on the expense of this junket yourself." Kiel leaned casually against the high leather-covered back of one of the chairs by the doorway and studied Donald. He inclined his head toward the woman who had caught his attention. "Why did you go pale when I happened to single out a certain blackjack dealer?"

Donald ran a finger nervously beneath the rim of his collar. "Let's go back to my suite for a minute and I'll explain."

As they left the casino and headed toward the luxury suites they were met by numerous greetings. Kiel was not particularly known as a smiling politician, but whereas his competition thought of his gravity as a drawback, his often stern, sometimes severe countenance didn't hurt him at the polls. His constituency trusted his serious, no-nonsense approach to government and the issues. His beliefs were cut and dry and out in the open. If he promised to fight for a bill, he fought, no holds barred. His promises were never empty ones.

He would probably be the president of the United States in another ten or fifteen years, Donald thought. And he would be what the nation was looking for—a levelheaded but incredibly dynamic leader. Capable of thinking on a different level from most men, Kiel Whellen could put aside personal problems for the good of his constituents; he could even set aside tragedy. . . .

Even Donald seldom knew what Kiel was thinking or feeling. The young congressman from Virginia might be drawing the curious eyes of the country, but none of those curious eyes would ever see more than the congressman wanted to be seen. What went on in Kiel's heart and soul was privy only to Kiel. Which was why Donald was so nervous now. He didn't know how Kiel would take the strange coincidence of the "Queen of Hearts" being on board the *Seafire*. Nor for that matter, how happy Rhiannan was going to be to discover the congressman from Virginia on board. Donald hadn't spoken to her about Kiel; he had convinced himself that the less said, the less that would be dredged up from the past that might be painful. And Rhiannan never spoke about the past. Donald tried to convince himself that Kiel's name might not even mean anything to her. He sighed inwardly. How foolish a hope. Rhiannan had probably read and heard everything that had been written or said about the tragedy.

Donald pushed open the door to his plush suite. Velvet drapes were tied in loops and held away from the wide portholes, which gave a view of the emerald sea. "Want a drink, Kiel?"

Kiel politely lifted a brow. "Sounds like you think I'm going to need one. What on earth can the mystery be about this lady?"

Kiel spoke casually, but he was surprised at the strength of the impression left in his mind by the sight of the blackjack dealer. Perhaps it was simply because she was so striking. Sleek, fluid, sophisticated. Her hair was as dark as the handsome floor-length gown that hung simply down the elegant length of her straight spine. The sleeves of the gown were long and tapered to small, stylish points over her wrists. The Mandarin neck slit at the throat bared no more than a hint of her ivory throat and finely molded collarbone.

No, he told himself impatiently, it had nothing to do with the way she was dressed. She had entranced him when he had run into her on deck, and she had been clad in a casual suit at the time.

It had been her eyes that had fascinated him then. They were green. No, deeper than green. Brighter than green. Emerald . . . with perhaps a hint of blue. Like a cut diamond, they contained a multitude of shimmering facets and were framed by thick spiky lashes as black as the beautiful, sleek trail of her hair.

He smiled suddenly. She was elegant in the long black gown, but she had been equally elegant in the white skirt-suit.

But more than her impeccable, elegant beauty, it had been the quasitragic aura about her that had remained implanted in his mind. Her smile had been slight, polite. Not an arrogant smile, merely a disinterested one.

Donald had expertly poured two martinis, handed one to Kiel, and walked over to the porthole, his free hand in his pocket as he idly stared out the window. "Rhiannan," he murmured.

Kiel frowned, thinking Donald had been working a bit too hard. "Rhiannan?" he murmured in confusion. He shook his head. "Donald, what are you talking about? 'Rhiannan' is a song. Fleetwood Mac, mid seventies, I believe."

"No, no." Donald shook his head. "Rhiannan is a woman. The woman you were watching."

"Oh?"

Donald stopped looking out the window and turned with a

worried grimace to Kiel. "I haven't seen you look that way at a woman in a long time, Kiel, not since. . . . And she's not the woman you should be looking at that way."

"Donald," Kiel said impatiently, draining half his martini, "would you cut this great mystery bit and tell me what you're talking about? To begin with, all I've done is look at a beautiful woman. If she's special to you, say the word. I've been reputed to have my share of affairs, but I've never been accused of wedging in on a duo."

Donald shook his head so sadly that Kiel really began to think he was ready for a year's R&R.

"It's not me, Kiel; I wish it were. It isn't any man. Oh, she's sweet to me in her way—she appreciates having the job—but she wouldn't dream of anything remotely serious. Not that I didn't try. She has this way about her. . . . A hand inching too far and she simply catches it and gives you a stare with those incredibly wise green eyes, and you feel like an adolescent caught attempting to play spin the bottle. And that was *me*, Kiel, and I have no connection with her past. . . ."

"Donald, what are you getting at?"

He exhaled a long breath and looked at Kiel unhappily. "Remember the crash?" he said softly.

Bad phrasing, Donald thought. Kiel would always remember the crash. Not only had he been the man in communication with the plane at the time of the tragedy, but Ellen had been aboard the flight. . . .

Donald watched now as Kiel's mouth narrowed to a grim line. "Of course I remember the crash, Donald. Now, just what are you getting at?"

"Rhiannan," Donald said miserably, knowing he had botched his explanation pathetically. "Her, uh, husband and two kids were among the ground victims of the crash."

"What?"

The whisper was one of the most horrible Donald had ever heard.

"She lost everything, Kiel. Husband, home, family. She was

close to . . . well, she stopped caring about anything. I met her brother at the University of Virginia, and he told me part of the story at an alumni meeting. Maybe he knew my connection with you; anyway, it all came up. He was telling me how worried he was about her, how he thought she should get away, do something entirely different. But she had been a housewife and mother for seven years and didn't do anything except make marvelous martinis and deal a great hand of blackjack at Friday-night poker games. So I gave her a job. She's been with me as my hostess for almost two years now. I probably should have mentioned one of you to the other but . . ." Donald shrugged. "Rhiannan tends to keep quiet about the past. I tried to ignore the fact that seeing you might upset her, and I didn't think that you . . . I mean . . . well, hell, Kiel! You have a nation of beauties ready to hop in bed with you."

"I wasn't going to attack the woman, Donald," Kiel said wearily. He sat on the sofa below the portholes and extended his long legs over the coffee table, rubbing his forehead over his temple. "Donald, I didn't cause the plane crash. I did everything in my power to save those people."

"I know that, Kiel. It's just the way I saw you look at her. Most men skip a few heartbeats when they see her, but you're not most men, my friend, and it looked as if you'd been hit by a brick wall for a few seconds, there. You're going to try and see her again and again. She'll barely have cocktails with other men, and she certainly won't have anything to do with you. You're a link to her tragedy."

"Donald," Kiel said, his voice quiet and dry, "I might have a bit of a reputation, but I've never been accused of forcing my company on any woman." He was silent for a moment. "And I know what pain is."

"I know, Kiel. I didn't mean that. It's just that you did have your share of tragedy with Ellen, and you have been gaining a reputation for bedding every beauty on both sides of Dixie. You're a hard man to read, friend, but I've known you a long time. You're combatting the past in your own way. If you gave a woman half a chance, Kiel, most of those ladies you loved and left would have given one hundred percent to make a relationship with you last forever. But, Kiel, this woman will give you nothing. And, Kiel, you *want* her. I saw it, man, in your eyes. It was almost primeval, the way you were looking . . . I'd even say *savage* if I didn't know you better. And she's not the type to have a fling with, Kiel, or anything else. She's healing. At the moment she has nothing left to give. She sails the seas to exist—nothing more. The Queen of Hearts is not for you."

"Queen of Hearts?"

Donald blushed. "It's our name for Rhiannan," he said softly. "She, uh, well, she's captured all our hearts. Mine, the crew's—from the head bartender to the captain. And she has this uncanny ability to deal the queen of hearts to herself when she's holding an ace."

"Blackjack, twenty-one," Kiel said.

Don blushed uncharacteristically again.

Kiel finished his martini and set the glass on the mahogany coffee table. He swung his long legs to the floor and stood, half smiling at his friend as he stuffed his hands into his tux pockets.

"Tell me something, Donald, is it possible to beat the house in your casino?"

Donald frowned a little indignantly. "Of course, Kiel. You know me better than that. The house makes money on odds, but my games are run legitimately. There's no cheating involved."

"Then," Kiel said lightly, "I'll chance the odds. I play a decent game of blackjack myself. You've warned me, Donald, but I'm a big boy. I'm a congressman, remember?"

For a moment Donald grinned. "Yeah, and the way you've been carrying on in the last year, it's a wonder."

Kiel shrugged. "I don't ask people to vote on my sex life,

only on my performance in office." He turned and started toward the door.

Donald sighed. "You're going back to the casino?"

"Yeah. You should be glad. I'm going to go throw some money into your coffers!"

"Kiel . . ."

"Hey, Donald, ease up. I'm not too sure who you're more worried about here, me or Rhiannan. But quit worrying. There's a possibility that I can win in your casino—and beat the Queen of Hearts at her own game."

Kiel closed the door on Donald's "Kiel—" Caught between the flash of pain that always came to him with the memory of that long-ago night and a certain wry amusement with Donald's paternal manner, he started walking down the plush corridor.

If he could have, he would have stayed away from her. She would probably not welcome a man associated in any way with her past, but he couldn't stay away. Threatened with eternal damnation, he still wouldn't be able to keep his long, resolute strides from carrying him back to the casino, because it was as if he had been hit by a brick wall. Or perhaps been struck by a bolt of lightning. He was seized by a compulsion stronger than any he had ever known, and he had to see her again—just see her.

He had never experienced anything like this before. Even Ellen, whom he had come to love slowly, had not affected him like this.

Of course, he wasn't in love. He was in . . . something else. "In compulsion," he labeled himself with dry and slightly bitter amusement. Why this one woman, who despised him, had touched him this way didn't really matter, because Donald was right! He had felt something very elemental when he had seen her—an almost savage obsession. He wanted her. Beyond reason, beyond all cool and logical facts, he wanted her. She had become, with the simplicity of a distant smile, a tempest of fire and ice that raged within him.

His thoughts, his feelings for her, were alien to him. He genuinely cared for people, but never with this intensity. He had never in his life lost his sanity over a woman before.

His sanity? he taunted himself. Maybe he was very sane because he had known from the moment he first saw her what he wanted. But now, now that he knew who she was, it was something more. He needed to talk to her, to apologize. Why? He didn't know, since he had already gone before the public and explained what had happened. He didn't owe her anything, but he still felt the need to apologize.

It was imperative to him that he try to make her understand what he didn't really understand himself, he thought with a soft sigh.

Kiel was so engrossed in his thoughts that he barely noticed those passengers he passed. He automatically scanned faces as he walked, acknowledging those who greeted him. He had a superb memory—photographic when it came to faces. A real plus in the political arena.

He stopped suddenly at the casino door, a chill crawling down his spine. A face in the crowd stood out. One he had barely noticed at first; a totally innocuous face. Oblong, plain. Tepid blue eyes, a vacant half-smile. A face one could easily overlook. Not handsome, not ugly, not old, not young. But to Kiel, the face was familiar or uncannily similar to a face that he knew.

Kiel gave himself a mental shake. His "photographic" memory was giving him negatives. He definitely didn't know the man who was wearing a white uniform with bars on the shoulders.

Kiel exhaled slowly. It was the ship's doctor. It was only normal that the face should appear familiar. He had probably been in Donald Flagherty's employ before.

The image of that face was swept from his mind as quickly as it had come, because there was another image before him. Another face. Rhiannan's face. As beautiful, as delicate, as intriguing, as the name he could now give it. As lovely as carved ivory, as pure, as perfect. Framed by a wave of ebony hair, highlighted by those stunning eyes of shattering emerald.

She absorbed him; she filled his senses. She beckoned to him, purely unintentionally, but with threads that were almost tangible. The feeling was new to him, one he couldn't deny.

Kiel moved through the milling, bejeweled, and bedecked crowd and entered the private room. Taking a seat at her table, he threw down his cash for chips. He was ready to gamble against the Queen of Hearts.

Two

He sat as she was dealing out a hand, so Rhiannan's first glimpse of him was of his hands. Nice hands, longer rather than broad, the nails clipped evenly, the fingers strong and slender. Despite her mechanical concentration on the game, her mind registered those hands. They belonged to a man with confidence and had seen their share of work. They were obviously powerful, and yet, they left one wondering about the possible gentleness of their touch. . . .

Shocked by her own thoughts, she met his eyes as he laid down a handful of bills to exchange for chips. They were the same pair of gray eyes that had met hers when she had bumped into him on the deck. The ones that had unnerved her, that had made her feel that strange quivering sensation that she hadn't felt in years, hadn't even recognized at first. And all from a look. A simple touch. The lightest brush of his fingers. . . .

She hadn't recognized him at first when Glen had pointed him out. For one thing she had been away from Virginia for almost two years. And of course, when she had first seen his face, it had been in newspapers. Even if she had seen a newspaper recently it was unlikely that she would have recognized him. Black-and-white photos could never do justice to such a man. No camera could ever capture the essence of suave composure about him, the subtle force. But thanks to Glen Trivitt, she knew who he was.

Why did he have to be aboard? Although she had never met him, he was too much a part of her life, her past—part of the tragedy she had spent the last two years not trying to forget but merely to live with.

"I'll start with a thousand, please." The voice fit the man— low, husky, as soft as velvet but with a hint of a touch of steel.

Smoothly, expertly, she counted out the man's chips as she pointed to the rules boldly printed in white on the red felt along the inner circumference of the table. "Dealer must hit at sixteen, must hold at seventeen."

"Thank you," he said softly.

"You're welcome," she replied.

There was no more small talk as the bets were placed.

The cards were all dealt faceup. Rhiannan dealt out a seven, a four, a jack, and then, to the darkly handsome man, an ace, and to herself an ace. The first three players busted immediately. She dealt the jack of spades to the stranger, the queen of hearts to herself. She swept the other chips off the table and left the man's. When the cards were even, neither the player nor the house won.

The game continued. Players came and went. The man with the dark hair and stormy eyes remained. The card shoe was empty. Rhiannan shuffled the cards, offering them to a stylish matron to cut. As she dealt she smiled when her players won, enjoying in a distant way the hushed conversations that often went on with spouses urging on their playing mates.

As the game continued Rhiannan became aware that the man was watching her with more interest than he watched his cards, although he was keeping an edge on the game. She would meet his eyes when she needed to know whether he wanted another card, and she would sense a hesitation a split second longer than necessary, as if he were thinking. . . .

She knew that he wasn't thinking about his cards. The second his first card was down, he knew what he was doing instantly.

There were many scents about the table—Parisian perfumes, the most expensive men's colognes—but she knew beyond doubt which was his: a light after-shave, hinting at the attributes she had automatically given to him. It was a scent of both sea and earth. He would be perfectly at ease in the most plush contemporary office, but he would also be at home in the woods, happy on a small sloop with the wind tossing about those locks of dark hair, easing the lines of tension about his eyes and mouth.

She suddenly dropped a card, something she never did. She was extremely competent with cards; Tim had once joked that she should have been a magician. But the ace of spades suddenly slipped from the grasp of her slender fingers, sailing away despite a desperate attempt by her long, red-glazed nails to grasp it as it hit the carpeted floor.

He retrieved the card for her, and as she took it she realized she was blushing. She quickly turned to the others at the table to apologize. She dealt a new hand.

Suddenly she realized she was playing more than a game of blackjack and that she was losing control.

It wasn't the congressman's apparent interest in her that bothered her; men often tried to attract her, some for shipboard entertainment, some for more serious involvement. Lascivious old men, earnest young men. Some very handsome and expert at the role of seduction.

Rhiannan had never been offended or interested. For the most part she had watched most of the men's efforts with dry amusement and a certain sadness. She wished desperately that she could be interested; she would love to meet a man who could give her a night of forgetfulness.

But now, although he had not said or done anything, she was aware that she was being seduced subtly, thoroughly, and she was reacting to him. Her fingers kept losing their grip on the cards. She could feel the tiny beat of her pulse in her throat, and a strange breathlessness invaded her each time she caught his eyes.

He was the one man in the world she wanted to avoid at all costs; the one man who had been directly involved in the tragedy that had eventually disappeared from the front pages of the newspaper but remained forever on her heart and soul.

Rhiannan found herself pushing back the long satin sleeve of her gown in an attempt to gaze unobtrusively at her watch. The dealers were spelled on the hour every hour. It felt as if she had been playing forever. The air in the casino was growing hot and stuffy but he remained, impervious to the smoke, to the milling, the soft whispering, the occasional hoot of a big winner.

Five minutes. She had only five minutes to go, and then Lars would come to relieve her for a half hour.

She caught the man's eyes as she dealt his first card. An ace again. If she were cheating, she couldn't have planned to deal him better cards. "Hit me, please," he told her quietly. The king of diamonds fell next to his ace. Blackjack—twenty-one again. . . .

Rhiannan felt as if in the space of seconds they had exchanged the most absurd of messages through simple eye contact.

"You've won again."

"I play to win."

"We all lose on occasion."

"Only if we allow ourselves to do so."

There seemed to be a warning, or a threat, in his words. *Don't be insane,* she warned herself. It was foolish for her to feel threatened. But was it? The man was a threat in himself. She tried to remember things she had read about him. He had been engaged to be married and his fiancée had died. She had been aboard the plane. . . .

A card almost slipped through her fingers. She swallowed, then tried to concentrate on the game. She couldn't. Things she had barely registered when reading the newspapers after the tragedy came back to her. He had withdrawn from Washington after the incident, but then he had returned for a second term. The newspapers had hinted at his various affairs, but he had always been discreet if determined. Voters or no, he had announced that his personal life was his own.

Once, when she had been talking with her brother, Tim had mildly suggested that she was being illogical in blaming the congressman. Tim had pointed out that it was understandable that the thought or mention of the man made her uncomfortable: He was a reminder of her pain. But to blame him personally . . . well, he hadn't been in that Oval Office alone; God alone knew what other factors he had had to deal with. But, Rhiannan had argued, Whellen had been the one in contact with Lee Hawk, the one who had lost control.

Maybe it was illogical, she admitted to herself. But she couldn't help her feelings and she didn't want him on the ship. She didn't want him near her, reminding her, unnerving her.

Please, someone come relieve me. Please, please, she prayed just as Lars Tuftsun, a strikingly good-looking Norwegian, slid behind her at the table.

"Break time, Rhiannan," he whispered, putting his arm around her shoulder affectionately.

"Thank God!" she whispered.

Rhiannan finished playing the hand. She stood, feeling giddy with relief. "Thanks, Lars."

He smoothly took her position and dealt the next hand as she started out of the casino.

At the doorway Rhiannan found herself pausing to stare back into the flash and elegance of the casino. Her heart seemed to falter, ridiculously skipping beats. Congressman Whellen was no longer at the table. He had risen and was striding out of the casino.

Rhiannan would never be able to explain to herself or anyone else the terrible urge that struck her to run, as if she were running for her life. She turned and left the casino quickly behind her.

She should have sped down the four decks to her tiny cabin; she made her first mistake when she didn't. She had the uncanny feeling that he was behind her, and her survival instinct had ridiculously taken over. She wasn't about to lead him to her personal quarters. But beyond that, she simply wanted to escape him; exactly why, she would have to fathom later.

The *Seafire* boasted four fine lounges with continuous entertainment. The Manhattan was on the same deck as the casino and had intimate lighting. Jason and Mary, a brother-and-sister duo who performed relaxing cocktail music, would be on stage. Rhiannan decided she could hurry and slip into the lounge, find a back table, and still the disturbingly erratic beating of her heart before returning for her last hour of work.

The dance floor was full, as was the lounge. But there were empty tables in the far back, perfectly positioned for Rhiannan to feel as though she could disappear into the woodwork. She threaded her way carefully among the cocktail tables and sat, leaning against the soft, cushiony booth, inhaling deeply as she closed her eyes.

"May I join you?"

Her eyes flew open as he stood towering over her. His hands were in his pockets, splitting his jacket back, and she thought strangely that she had never seen a vest worn with more casual élan, or charcoal gray eyes smoldering to a smoky gray.

"I'd like to buy you a drink if I may."

"I'm, ah, sorry. I'm not really through working. Donald asked me to keep the blackjack table going until dinner."

He sat down, sliding into the curve of the booth. He was a respectable distance away, but she felt as if she had been scorched by the contact with his kneecap. It was a shockingly nice feeling.

"I most certainly do understand! Only the bettors should be inebriated when gambling!" He chuckled huskily, and the sound seemed to encompass her. "I'll amend my question. May I buy you a soda?"

Belatedly, Rhiannan realized she had made a mistake. She had assumed her explanation would send him away; instead he had sat down. She should have told him she was trying to relax, that she wished to be alone.

"I—" she began, but he had already summoned one of the waiters.

"Two Cokes, please." He glanced at Rhiannan. "Or would you prefer a Perrier?"

"A Coke is fine," she heard herself say.

She had had drinks with men on board before; exasperation had led her to it. She had been able to lean back, to listen, to respond occasionally. At the end of a conversation she had politely excused herself, returned to her work, to her cabin, whatever, without a second thought. Why was this casual encounter different?

He leaned back in the booth and watched her as he extracted a pack of cigarettes from his inner jacket pocket. Rhiannan noted the brand. She could easily see him in one of the customary ads for the cigarettes. He would be sitting on a horse, ostensibly out on a cattle drive. And he would look as ruggedly assured in a pair of blue jeans and Western shirt as he did in his black formal wear.

He offered her the pack. She accepted a cigarette, watching him in return as he lit it for her. She found her gaze attracted to his hands, which cupped the match against the subtle flow of the air conditioning. They were, as she had thought before, nice hands. Perfect hands for a man: clean, no-nonsense hands. . . .

Kiel wasn't surprised that she had accepted his presence; he had given her little choice, and now, as he sat beside her, he found himself becoming more and more intrigued by her cool beauty. She was in no way snide, nor was she flustered. She put on no pretensions. He thought with a bit of amusement that she was tolerating him, merely accepting with resignation a situation she couldn't avoid without a scene.

"My name is Kiel," he told her quietly.

"I know your name, Congressman," Rhiannan snapped unintentionally. Yes, she knew it well, just as she knew his slightly cultured accent. It was a Virginian accent, one clearly identifiable by another Virginian. *Yes, I know you,* she wanted to scream, but she suppressed the urge.

"I'm Rhiannan Collins," she murmured, lowering her lashes over her eyes and forcing a soft, cool politeness to her tone.

"I know."

Rhiannan glanced back up at him, surprised to see that he smiled as he spoke. It was a riveting smile: a half curl of his lip. She noticed that his teeth were white and even, startlingly attractive against the weathered tan of his features. He inhaled from his cigarette and then exhaled.

"I'm a personal friend of Donald's," he explained. "He told me your name."

She frowned, wondering why Donald had given Kiel Whellen any information at all about her. Surely Donald would have known that she wouldn't want to exchange two words with Whellen.

He misconstrued her silence for confusion and added, "Donald Flagherty—your employer."

"I know who Donald is too," she murmured, momentarily sweeping her lashes over her eyes once more in an effort to hide her hostility and sarcasm. She didn't want to be rude; Donald was a wonderful employer, sensitive to his vast army of employees, and he expected his help to be as cordial to the guests as he was, with special emphasis on his friends. He would be the first to defend an employee against abuse, but she could hardly say she had been abused by the congressman.

But she had learned enough about men to recognize those with animal magnetism and the lusty passions that went along with that natural charm. And although the congressman hadn't made an improper move or even voiced an innuendo, she was certain that he had decided he wanted her. He was young, he was healthy, and he had a certain reputation.

Wrong woman, Congressman, she thought. *And the amusing thing is, I wouldn't care if I were a passing fancy for this cruise. I would love to be just that—but not for you.*

Their Cokes arrived and he thanked the waiter, then stared at her once more, smiling.

Rhiannan couldn't resist the temptation to snap at him once more. "Congressman, you say you are a personal friend of Donald's. If that's so, then you probably know who I am. Surely you can understand when I tell you that I want nothing to do with you."

"Why?" he queried politely.

A tangle of emotions wound so fiercely inside her that she was tempted to throw her Coke into his face. "Congressman Whellen, we were both involved in a terrible tragedy. Perhaps you have been able to forget—"

Suddenly his hand shot out across the table, enveloping hers in a cruel grasp. She almost cried out with the surprise and pain, but the stonelike coldness of his gray eyes silenced her even before he spoke harshly. "Wrong, Mrs. Collins, I have never forgotten a thing that happened. Not a word, not a second."

For a moment she stared at him, held by his eyes, startled by the strength of his grip. A flush of fever rose to her face despite the knowledge that of all times to keep cool, this was it.

She wanted to be irritated, to sound annoyed, but her voice was a pained whisper when she challenged him. "Then why are you plaguing me?"

He released his grip on her wrist and on her eyes, turning to stare broodingly at his Coke. "I don't know exactly," he murmured, then again met her eyes. "And actually, I don't believe I've 'plagued' you—yet. But I will."

"Don't you understand?"

"I wonder if you do."

"Congressman, you're speaking in riddles, and I'm not in the mood. I've told you why I don't care to talk to you; my reasons should be obvious to you, of all people. I can't believe you would be so rude—"

"And I can't believe you have buried yourself so deeply that *you* refuse to accept what is obvious."

"And what is that?"

"That we are attracted to one another, Mrs. Collins."

"Oh, really, Congressman? I think you're growing too accustomed to making campaign speeches."

"No, I don't think so, Rhiannan," he said calmly, ignoring her less-than-subtle thrust. "Nor do I believe you would care to enter into a political debate. An attack on my public life would be completely unwarranted, and I think you know that."

"A lily-white politician?" she queried skeptically, fighting the urge to leap from the table and fly back to her cabin.

"Politicians don't come in lily white; they're human, like everyone else. I've never tried to pretend otherwise."

Rhiannan managed to keep her eyes steady on his as she sipped her Coke and offered him a humorless smile. "Which brings us right back to the point, Congressman. I'm not really sure what you're after, but your personal life has made the news a number of times. You certainly don't need anything from me. There are at least a score of young beauties on board who would love to entertain you through the Caribbean. I would just as soon not set eyes on you again. Can't we just leave things at that?"

"No."

How could a single word sound so determined, so threatening? Rhiannan wondered.

"Congressman—"

"My name is Kiel."

"All right, Kiel, you're wrong. There is no great attraction. I have no interest in going to bed with you."

"I don't remember asking."

"Then just what *do* you want?" It wasn't a scream, but he had cost Rhiannan her composure. Her words were a vehement hiss, a display of aggravation she dearly wished she might have taken back when she saw a subtle smile work its way into his features once more.

"To get through to you. To give the feeling a chance."

"There is no feeling."

"Why are you fighting me like this? Are you afraid? I'm really not as bad as my reputation. I don't run around seducing reluctant widows into my bed for overnight affairs."

Rhiannan was able to laugh lightly. "Congressman, you are way off track. I would love to feel the urge to indulge in a quick, overnight affair. But it simply isn't there. I have nothing to offer you. You would be the loser."

"I'm willing to take my chances."

"You're gambling on poor odds, Congressman."

"Not really. I weigh the odds, Mrs. Collins. I think they're in my favor. And . . . you've gambled with me. I have a tendency to win."

Rhiannan stood abruptly. "This is really an absurd conversation. I don't want anything to do with you."

"That's going to be hard to manage, isn't it?" he inquired softly, still smiling with open amusement. "You're Donald's hostess and I'm one of his best friends."

"Donald Flagherty would never dream of forcing us together."

"You're right. He's already warned me to stay away from you."

"Then—"

"It could be a long cruise, Mrs. Collins." He stood, too, and she noted again how tall he was. Relaxed in his tux, comfortable, assured in any surroundings. He bowed with a brief inclination of his head. "See you at dinner, Mrs. Collins."

He turned, threading his way through the crowd. He was stopped by a portly man and quickly gave his attention to the question asked, his gray eyes growing dark with intensity.

Rhiannan saw that his attention was already turning elsewhere when another man joined them, and she faintly heard the dialogue switch to French.

The fate of the world, she thought wryly, was probably being decided. And when she turned to leave the lounge, she noted again the amount of Secret Servicemen aboard. They had pulled a pleasant duty, she decided.

Feeling a bit like tightly strung wire, she left the lounge and hurried back to the blackjack table. Lars, deftly handling the cards, barely looked up as she returned.

"Mr. Flagherty was just by. Told me to ask you to meet him in his cabin."

"Fine," Rhiannan murmured. "Thanks, Lars."

The master's cabin was on the promenade deck. She was glad to feel the cool sea air against her warm face as she left the lower decks. She paused, seeing that the sails were now unfurled; as Glen had promised, the sight was beautiful. Several sailors were moving about, tightening the rigging, pulling the huge canvas sheets to capture the wind.

And a number of couples, delighted with the old but graceful *Seafire*, were strolling beneath the sails, sometimes getting in the sailors' way, sometimes snapping to quick attention when asked to hold a line. It was done with good camaraderie, and a soft smile curled Rhiannan's lips. Donald had done a beautiful job with the *Seafire*. If only he hadn't invited a certain congressman aboard, she might have really enjoyed the voyage. Maybe she still could if she didn't take his flattery seriously.

Suddenly, for a shattering second, she had a mental image of him—naked. He would be beautiful, all muscle and taut, agile masculinity. And his shoulders and torso would be as darkly tanned as his handsome features, as powerfully resolute as his character. She could see his eyes, that charcoal gray, dark and probing with desire and the relentless determination to draw her to him. . . .

"No!" she murmured aloud, the vision clearing away by a stabbing jolt of memory as she saw Paul in his place.

Rhiannan gave herself a mental shake and made the final steps to Donald's door, then knocked firmly on it. But her mind continued to wander in memory. Paul. There had only ever been Paul, and Paul was dead. But to think such thoughts about another man still seemed to be . . . adultery.

She was shivering. She couldn't lie in bed with another man. She simply wouldn't be able to do it.

"Oh, God . . ."

"Talking to yourself, young lady, is a sure sign of senility."

She started, flushing to see that her hand was raised to knock again on a door that was no longer closed. Donald was smiling boyishly at her, apparently delighted to see her flustered.

"Oh . . . Donald . . . I . . . uh . . . I'm sorry," she murmured, moving past him into the immense and beautiful cabin. "I was just thinking aloud, I guess."

"Uh-huh," he said, a chuckle in his voice as he closed the door. "Have you been drinking?"

"Only a Coke."

"Maybe you'd better start drinking."

"You know," she murmured, spinning about to meet his eyes, "maybe I will. What have you got?"

"Anything you want," he replied, grinning broadly as he indicated a carved rosewood bar that was part of the master's sitting room. "It's fully stocked and that's why I called you. We're having a private dinner in here tonight."

"We are?" she asked uncomfortably. "For whom? Why?"

"Senator Sanders wants to make a plea for a special children's center to be privately funded. So we're having ten of our more affluent guests."

"Which ten?"

She almost breathed easily as he rattled off nine names that meant little to her, but then he added, "Oh, and Kiel. He can talk a dog into buying fleas and can make a fair contribution himself."

Rhiannan busied herself behind the bar, putting far more vodka into her Bloody Mary than she had intended. She gave her full attention to a celery stick as she asked, "You mean Congressman Whellen?"

Donald paused so long that she at last looked at him. He seemed troubled as he returned her stare. "You've talked to him, haven't you?"

"Uh . . . yeah."

"Rhiannan . . ."

"Ah, listen, Donald, I know that you've talked to him, too. He told me that you kind of warned him to stay away from me. Thank you. I appreciate that. But don't worry about it: I can handle myself. And I really don't want to come between two friends—or between a man who can help and a project that may save dozens of children. You don't need to come to my defense any longer."

Donald was silent for a moment, then burst into laughter. Rhiannan stared at him as if he had taken leave of his senses. He waltzed across the room and gave her a quick hug and a kiss over the narrow bar.

"I have no intention of putting my nose into this any further at all!" he proclaimed mischievously. "I intend to throw you right to the wolf if I can!"

"What?" Rhiannan demanded, startled. "That's not exactly what I meant."

"But it is what *I* mean. I think I'll put him beside you at dinner."

"Now, wait a minute, Donald. You know that I dislike him—"

"I don't think that you do." Donald paused, lowering his eyes for a second, then raising them again, and she saw that a serious quality had replaced his streak of impishness. "Rhiannan, if you were only honest with yourself . . . ! You don't dislike the man: You dislike the image of the man that you've set into your mind. It's not fair and not right for you to blame Kiel. God knows, he's had to endure enough guilt that he cast on himself."

"I see," Rhiannan murmured bitterly. "That's right, you're his friend. He's convinced you that—"

"He never convinced me of anything, Rhiannan. He doesn't like to talk about it, and Kiel would never go to anyone, whining for sympathy. Publicly he took the blame. But I'll tell you this, Rhiannan, because I know politics and politicians: He wasn't to blame. Not alone, I assure you. He wasn't alone up in that office, calling the shots. A time bomb was thrust into his hands. He did the best damned job that he could."

Rhiannan hesitated uneasily. Donald's words were so similar to her brother's, but it didn't really change anything. Kiel Whellen had been the one handling the negotiations.

"His best wasn't good enough," she said quietly.

"Okay, Rhiannan," Don sighed, "you do dislike him."

"Thank you. So please, skip the plans about throwing me to the wolf."

"Not on your life."

"Donald!" Rhiannan wailed.

He smiled, his eyes and friendly features tender and wistful. "You may dislike him, Rhiannan. You may even hate him. But in a matter of hours he's managed to do something that neither I nor anyone I know has accomplished in months."

"Oh?" Rhiannan lifted her chin defensively. "And what might that be, Mr. Flagherty?"

"He's made you angry. He's made you flustered. In short, my little Queen of Hearts, he's made you join the living. Yes, I think I'll seat the two of you together. That should keep the sparks flying and the meal an exciting affair!"

Three

Food in itself was amazing when served at Donald Flagherty's table. Fresh fruit had been followed by salmon mousse; the Caesar salad was delectably seasoned, and the main course was a puffed pastry shell designed to resemble a grinning piglet. The top of the pastry lifted away to reveal medallions of pork embraced by spinach stuffing.

It was all served with a vintage white burgundy, and admittedly Rhiannan was consuming far more wine than she normally would. But, short of resigning her position, there had been no opposing Donald once he had made up his mind. She was seated at the end of the long table with its snowy white cloth, across from Donald and next to Congressman Whellen.

Not that she was called upon to carry on much of a conversation with the congressman: The blond paper heiress to his left kept quite a dialogue going. They discussed everything from vitamins and minerals to the space program, and both appeared quite content with one another's company.

A charming but staid English lord was seated to Rhiannan's right. Throughout the entire meal he kept her busy replying to his dissertation on the pollination of summer roses.

Occasionally she caught Kiel Whellen's eye; she saw the blue sparkle within the gray that clearly informed her that he found her plight amusing, but she had brought it all on herself by snubbing him, of course.

She hadn't actually snubbed him. She wasn't about to let her own tensions ruin Donald's dinner. Kiel Whellen, arresting beyond reasonable measure in a pleated blue shirt, black tie, and tux, had made no effort to detain her over drinks. But long after she had handed him his martini with a twist and an olive, she had felt his eyes on her. Not obtrusively, for he carried on pleasant, intelligent conversations with those around him, but continually. She would move and feel his gaze on her, a warming sensation that began at the base of her spine and moved upward until it engulfed her cheeks in flame.

He had been there to pull out her chair for her; he had solicitously inquired how she was enjoying her meal. But after her curt "Lovely, thanks" he had smiled with wicked assurance and turned to the blonde.

And for no explicable reason Rhiannan felt little barbs of jealousy. It was a painful sensation, one she hadn't felt in years. Her marriage had been solid and she had trusted Paul explicitly. Now, when she was certain she could never really love again, she was feeling this horrible discomfort over a man with whom she definitely wanted no involvement.

But then, maybe it was because the paper-products heiress was so very beautiful and young. Twenty-five to Rhiannan's thirty-three. Joan Kendrick might have been a princess straight out of a fairy tale. Her hair was the color of the proverbial spun gold, and her eyes were not so much brown as they were the shade of honey. Her gown was a white strapless affair with long slits up either side, occasionally revealing long, shapely thighs. She was just perfect, giving off hints of seduction and possibly taunts of the unattainable.

Next to the glittering creature, Rhiannan felt like an aging Morticia, straight out of *The Addams Family.* That, too, was discomforting. It had been a long time since she had felt jealousy; it had been even longer since she had felt threatened by another woman.

"I still prefer red. Don't you agree, Mrs. Collins?"

Rhiannan set her fork down with its uneaten morsel of pork medallion and turned to her left. "I'm so sorry, Lord Nevill. What did you say?"

"Roses! Roses, my dear! My gardeners tell me that yellow are now the rage, but I say that red is—and always will be—the color for a rose. Don't you agree?"

Agree? At the moment she really couldn't care less!

"I'm sure you're quite right, Lord Nevill. Yellow and white can be very pretty, but I think the poets agree with you. Think of all the beautiful lines—"

"Lips like roses?"

Rhiannan broke off to turn to her left. Kiel Whellen had offered the comment with a very statesmanlike guilelessness. Only that blue sparkle within the charcoal gray of his eyes gave any indication that he was doing more than adding to the conversation.

"Quite right, my boy!" Lord Nevill agreed enthusiastically.

"Do you ever wear red, Mrs. Collins?" Kiel asked politely.

"Seldom," she replied shortly.

"You should do so more often. But then, black does become you beautifully. Perhaps one of Lord Nevill's roses could be worn . . . tucked so . . ." Deliberately he lifted a bronzed hand, carefully letting it hover near her breast, then reached for his wineglass. ". . . or perhaps in your hair."

She forced herself to smile politely. "I'm sure you must be extremely eloquent on the House floor, Congressman. You have quite a way with words."

"Only when necessary, Mrs. Collins."

Joan Kendrick asked Kiel a question, and he excused himself to turn away. Lord Nevill began a new discourse on orchids. Rhiannan caught Donald's eye down the long length of the table and he lifted his wineglass to her. Dryly she returned the salute. She vaguely heard Lord Nevill rattle on, but then he, too, excused himself to speak with the senator's wife on his right.

"Here! Ask Mrs. Collins, Kiel. I'm sure she'll tell you the same."

It was Joan Kendrick who had spoken, linking a graceful

arm with Kiel's to speak past him to Rhiannan. Kiel's eyes also turned to her with curious amusement.

"Well, Mrs. Collins?"

She smiled sweetly. "What are *we* speaking about?"

"Gravity!" Joan Kendrick exclaimed with a wide-eyed laugh. "Kiel is such a dear. He was so surprised when I told him I spend several hours a week at a gym. But I explained that unfortunately gravity gets to us all. The older a woman gets . . . well, it seems the more she has to fall! Do you work out, Mrs. Collins?"

Rhiannan exercised great muscular control and kept her smile lightly plastered to her face. "Not often, I'm afraid, Miss Kendrick. But then, working for Donald Flagherty can be a workout in itself."

She wondered if her intentional innuendo would affect Kiel in any way. It didn't: His smile remained, naturally.

"You do seem awfully busy, Mrs. Collins. Perhaps I can prevail upon our mutual friend to see that you have more time off."

Her smile slipped. That wasn't at all what she wanted.

Thankfully dessert and espresso were served, and the conversation finally turned to the point of the dinner: the children's project. She was surprised to see how quickly the glimmer of amusement could leave Kiel Whellen's eyes as plans were discussed, and she had to admit that he had a number of knowledgeable points to make. Money could only be useful when channeled properly, and he would be more than willing to offer his support—political and financial—if he could be assured that careful management would be maintained.

He was supported by everyone at the table. The pledges were staggering. They made the outrageous price Rhiannan was certain Donald had paid for the dinner and wine more than worthwhile.

Rhiannan managed to escape the group when the table was cleared and brandy and cognac were served. She slipped out of the cabin, assuming that Donald wouldn't miss her now that the meal and business had both been completed.

She closed the door behind her and leaned against it, inhaling deeply of the fresh sea air. Glancing up, she saw that the sails were still billowing in the wind, silver wings against the velvet black panorama of the night sky. The breeze that swept across them was crisp and cool, but she reveled in it. It felt wonderful to stand on deck, as if the wind and sea could clear away the dark corners of her mind.

She pushed away from the cabin door and sauntered idly toward the rail. It was strange how she had felt that she couldn't quite breathe within the cabin. And stranger still that all through dinner she should have felt so hot and then so cold and now a little dizzy. A result of the wine, she thought dryly.

But the sea wind seemed to be sweeping her dizziness away. She wondered if the sea air at night always had such a cleansing effect, or if it was just the clipper with her regal rigging and sails?

Rhiannan rested her elbows on the rail and stared out at the unfathomable darkness of the water. White foam rose like silver in the ship's wake, matching the silver luster of the sails and greedily reflecting the moon, too. Staring out was like looking into infinity. If one stared long enough, the mystery of time could be deciphered. . . .

"Watch out for gravity, Mrs. Collins. This is one place where it could really hurt."

"What?" she gasped, startled as a pair of strong arms came around her, pulling her back from the rail. She spun about angrily, recognizing the husky voice—and the touch.

"You were leaning out too far," Kiel Whellen told her harshly, his face a saturnine mask in the moonlight, his eyes hard.

"I was not—"

"You were. Tell me, are you suicidal?"

"No, and will you let go of me, please?"

He did instantly, moving past her to lean over the rail himself. "You might as well be, you know."

"Might as well be what?" Rhiannan asked irritably.

"Suicidal."

"Thanks."

"Oh, no insult intended. But you certainly aren't making any effort to live."

He spoke casually, staring out at the sea. The breeze lifted his dark hair off his forehead and sent it waving back again. In the moonlight she noticed a myriad of tiny creases around his eyes, and she felt a strange twinge of conscience for the ill feelings she bore him. The intensity of his job and his life was evident in the harsh lines that gave the deep character to his handsome features. Was it possible that she had been judging him too harshly? To find him disturbing because he reminded her of tragedy *was* understandable, but was it just to lay the horror of almost three hundred deaths completely on him?

She didn't know; she just didn't know. And her pang of conscience was rather absurd when he had just told her she might as well commit suicide, that she wasn't bothering to live.

She leaned against the rail, studying him. "I don't know what you mean, Congressman. I live quite nicely, thank you. Ask your friend Donald. I assure you that working for him keeps me hopping."

"Ah, yes. 'She walks, she talks. She even smiles occasionally.' So do the robots at Disney World. That isn't living. Living is taking chances."

"Wonderful. I'll take my chances at roulette when we reach Nassau."

"You've a sense of humor at least," he murmured, "even if it is caustic."

"It can be much worse, I assure you. So, Congressman, why don't you make us both happy and trot back into Donald's cabin and entertain Miss Kendrick? She's such a charming girl, and she's handling her gravity so well."

Kiel laughed easily and straightened, reaching into his vest pocket for his cigarettes. He offered one to Rhiannan. She hesitated, then accepted it and leaned forward as he cupped **his hand around the flame of his lighter. She noticed his hand** again, and another little chill made her tremble as she couldn't help wondering what that hand would feel like on her. She drew back abruptly, exhaling shakily as she leaned against the rail for support.

"Miss Kendrick does seem to have a nice handle on gravity. But then, so do you."

"I'm thirty-three, Congressman Whellen."

"I'm thirty-six."

"How nice for you."

"You do have a wicked sting to that tongue, Mrs. Collins. Tell me, did you browbeat your husband?"

Rhiannan drew her breath in sharply, feeling as if she had been slapped. How could anyone be so cruel? "No!" she hissed venomously, fighting waves of weakness. "And how could you—"

"Because you have no right to spend your life feeling sorry for yourself. Because you owe it to your husband to cherish your memories, not bury them with sorrow." Suddenly he tossed his cigarette into the ocean and gripped her shoulders, his fingers biting cruelly into her flesh, his features harsh, his eyes a smoldering furnace as they seared into hers. "You are not the only one to have lost someone you loved, Rhiannan. My fiancée was killed the same day as your husband."

"It wasn't just my husband!" she shrieked, shaking within his grasp and not caring that she was losing all control as tears sprang into her eyes. "It was my children . . . my son . . . my baby. . . . She was only—" She broke off as a horrible sob caught in her throat and the tears cascaded down her cheeks. She closed her eyes and tried to slip out of his hold, but he refused to let her go. Instead he shook her vigorously until her head snapped back and she was forced to meet his eyes once more with the tears still streaming from her own.

"That's it," he muttered, and there was no apology to his tone. "Talk about it and cry. Yes, it's unfair. Yes, it's terrible and unjust and you wind up believing that there can't possibly be a God, because if there were, healthy, beautiful children couldn't die. But we don't know the scheme or reason, Rhiannan—"

"You knew the scheme and the reason! *You* were there! *You* determined that some obscure principles were more important than the lives of a few individuals and that—"

"What?" His features went white; his jaw clenched as he shook her once more, furiously this time. "Bitch!" he whispered, and she vaguely realized that she was digging into him as deeply as he was digging into her. "What the hell do you think I felt?" he demanded in the same hoarse whisper. "The feeling, the knowing, the total helplessness and then the hopelessness . . ."

Rhiannan struggled to break his grasp. She didn't want to see the pain in his eyes; she didn't want to feel empathy for him. All she wanted to do was escape him. "Please let me go," she whispered to him.

He didn't release her, but his grip loosened. He took a deep breath, smiled with grim ruefulness, and hid his anger and emotion from her as he started speaking again.

"None of us is ever given a true knowledge of the future, Rhiannan. We all like to believe that tragedy happens to others, not to ourselves. What happened was a personal tragedy, Rhiannan, to many people. But *you* didn't die—"

"I wanted to die!" she interrupted in a hoarse wail.

"But you didn't. And the greatest disservice you can do to those you loved is to make a mockery of their lives with your own."

"A mockery? Out of two small children? You tell me, Congressman, what was it all for? Why? Why didn't you save them?"

She broke free from him and pounded furiously against his chest, gasping and sobbing out her words. What was the matter with him? Surely he was a sadist. All the pain was with her again, flooding her heart with grief.

"Dear God, Rhiannan, I wanted to save them! I would have sold my soul to the Devil just to have had the power to save one of those lives lost! I'll never really understand why it had to happen, and no one will ever be able to really tell you why. But loving is a part of living, and your family taught you how deeply you could love. You should never lose that love. It can give to you; it will always be a part of you. And if you can come to terms with it, it can enhance everything that the future can give."

"The future can give me nothing," Rhiannan said dully. Suddenly she felt no vengeance against him. All that she felt was exhaustion. Confusion and exhaustion. "My children are dead," she explained tonelessly.

"You're young. You'll have other children."

"No! They can't be replaced!"

"Not replaced—never replaced. Every love we give is special and unique."

"Congressman, what are you trying to do to me?" she demanded, jerking away from him and attempting to dry her eyes with the sleeves of her gown.

"Break you," he stated flatly.

"Why?" she whispered. "I've . . . I've already been broken. Shattered. You must be the cruelest person living—"

"Living. Exactly my point, Rhiannan." His hand came down on her shoulder and remained there stubbornly when she attempted to shake it off.

"Please!" she whispered.

"Rhiannan, you need to talk about it. You need to feel the rage, and the horror—and the pain and despair. That's the only way it will begin to heal, bit by bit."

"It will never heal."

Kiel swallowed, knowing her pain, knowing his own. He

wanted to ease her pain so badly. Who better than he knew how she felt? He would never forget the long days and nights of loss. Awakening from nightmares, thinking about the people who had been aboard the 747, counting on him. The nights when he had lain awake thinking about Ellen, thinking that she hadn't deserved to die, and certainly not because of him. Time. Time could never fully erase the guilt, the pain, the loss, or the continual ache of missing Ellen. But time had helped to blunt the edges, to make him accept what had been. To allow him to begin to forgive himself and admit that he was mortal. To know that he had truly done all that had been in his power to do.

"You're wrong. The past shouldn't be completely forgotten, but *time* does slowly heal all wounds," he told her softly. "Even the scars can be obscured. But you have to allow time to help you. And you have to learn to open yourself up again."

She pushed away from him and stared into his eyes accusingly. "Open myself up? Great idea, Congressman. I can become a sitting duck for sadists like you. You should be quite pleased. I've definitely reacted. Well, I'm sorry, Kiel Whellen. I prefer being a robot."

"No you don't. And the more time you spend with me—"

"There will be no more time!"

"Wrong, Mrs. Collins. Because I will plague you."

"I hate you!"

"Good. That's a nice start. But by the time I finish with you, you'll either love me or despise me. But at least you'll be living. Walking, talking—and *feeling*."

Her tears had at last dried with the night wind. She tilted her chin back and challenged him with the silvery moonlight creating a shimmering storm of fury in the green of her eyes.

"You overrate yourself, Congressman. I find you to be cruel, rude, and abrasive—nothing else. Now, if you'll excuse me, I'm going to bed."

She spun around to leave him but gasped as she found her wrist clamped and her body spinning back to crash against his. Before she could protest she again found herself locked in his embrace, staring into his probing gray eyes, which burned with a fathomless intensity. "I am more than cruel, rude, and abrasive, Mrs. Collins. Much, much more. And you're going to find that out."

She opened her mouth to rail against him, but the sound never left her mouth. His lips descended on hers, stealing her words away and taking brutal advantage of having her in his arms. He wasn't harsh, just determined . . . and relentless. His mouth was firm and masterful, molding hers, forming it to his will. His tongue delved deeply, and he tasted faintly of brandy and tobacco. His scent, so subtle, suddenly seemed overwhelming in its manliness. She didn't respond; she was simply too startled, too stunned, and then too aware of sensation to protest. She felt his ragged breath, the beating of his heart, and in a purely elemental physical way it all felt good—so good that it added to the hypnotic effect he had on her. He was male, so very male, hard and firm and compellingly strong, yet warm and giving. His kiss was experienced, creating a riot of sensation, coercing, ravaging, but so heady that it didn't seem to matter. All she could do was follow, knowing that his hands splayed against the small of her back, allowing no quarter.

It was he who broke away from her, smiling, his whisper still a caress against her lips as he spoke lazily. "There definitely is a future, Mrs. Collins."

She had never felt such fury. Her first reaction was to slap him, except he held her wrists behind her back. He must have sensed her desire to strike him because he laughed. "Ah, a nice spurt of temper, Mrs. Collins. That's good, too, except you should refrain from violence. Especially with me."

She stared at him, then emitted a string of oaths that would have done any man aboard proud.

"The Queen of Hearts does break and explode. Things are going to be nicely exciting when you come around to my way of thinking."

Rhiannan kicked him as hard as she could in the shin.

He must have felt pain, but her only reward was another laugh, one that was disgustingly pleased.

"Will you please let go of me!" she shrieked.

"As you wish." He released her hands and broke the body contact between them. "Run to your cabin, Mrs. Collins. Run away. Retreat is the better part of valor. Just remember that you can't run away from yourself."

She stepped irritably past him, heading for the staircase. "I don't want to run away from myself, Congressman. Just you."

"You'll be able to run away from either of us for just so long, Rhiannan."

"Please don't gamble on that, Congressman." She passed the rigging and gripped the banister to the stairwell that led below before turning back to him. "And, Congressman . . .

"Yes?"

". . . I'm a Virginian. You'll never get my vote again."

"I'm willing to give up a vote. Can I see you to your cabin?"

"No!"

"To one of the lounges?"

"No!"

"Too bad. I'm in the mood to dance."

Go dance with Miss Kendrick."

"Not a bad idea. I think I'll do that. Good night, Rhiannan."

"Good riddance," she muttered audibly, starting down the stairs. But his laughter followed her, and it haunted her.

Rhiannan was tired. She felt as if she had been run over by a cement mixer. But when she had changed into a nightgown, turned off her lights, and crawled into bed, she found it impossible to sleep.

It was that damn congressman. He *was* the cement mixer, and he had certainly run over her. He had ripped into her like a shower of knives, but she had made him bleed, too, she reminded herself. She couldn't forget that ashen look on his face when she had accused him of the tragedy. Nor could she forget the pain in his voice when he had told her that he had tried to avert it.

No, she thought with a little tremor, he hadn't been alone in the Oval Office. He had taken the blame for the others. He had offered up his own career, possibly to save others. Or to cover up? She didn't know. Somehow tonight he had made her feel that she should forgive him, but she didn't want to forgive him. She had worked so very hard to be numb. And now . . . now she was exhausted, drained, but unable to sleep because her mind was wide awake.

She rolled onto her side and hugged her pillow to her chest. The smooth cotton case was cool, the coolness of an inanimate object.

Once she had been able to sleep with her arms curled around a man, touching warm, giving flesh. And she had hugged and embraced a little boy and a baby, and the feeling of tenderness that had swept over her had been the greatest, sweetest emotion of life. Now she was hugging a pillow.

She squeezed her eyes tightly together, but it didn't matter. She was all cried out, restless, and lonely. Lonely for the touch and feel of a man.

Paul! she cried out in her heart. To think of someone else seemed so terribly disloyal. But painful as the admission was, it would be nice to sleep with her arms entwined around a someone rather than a something. It was always the nights that were the worst. And darkness could create a dreamland. If she were to hold someone real, she could close her eyes and pretend for a few brief moments that nothing had changed, that everything in the world had not been taken from her.

Rhiannan clutched her pillow more tightly. She could feel the ceaseless roll of the ship in the water. It should have been soothing. Instead the sea seemed to roil and churn with the tempest of her mind. She wondered vaguely if a storm was forming. If so, she fervently hoped that Congressman Whellen would dance his way right off the deck and disappear into the darkness.

Unwittingly she drew her forefinger to her lower lip. His lips against hers had felt good. So had his arms wrapped so strongly around her, his hard-muscled body crushed against hers. He had just been so male.

Rhiannan groaned softly and tossed about. There was no denying that he stirred her, created a simmering heat in her blood. He caused the exact attraction she had wondered if she would ever feel again. But he was exactly the wrong man.

Why? she asked herself. Because she still blamed him? Or because she was afraid of her own feelings if she decided to forgive him. Maybe there was nothing to forgive him for. Maybe he had done the best that could have possibly been done.

Rhiannan didn't want to think too deeply, to reason. It was easier to build a wall, to tell herself that she disliked him.

He would have been just what she needed: an attractive, virile, but intelligent adult male with whom to share a brief affair . . . a reentering to the real world for her. He would have been perfect. A man who wanted no commitment, no real emotion, in return. After all, Whellen had been linked with a dozen women in the last year and a half, and his affairs were always described as discreet and dignified and brief.

But he was behaving completely contrary to his usual form. She felt as if she were being stalked by an experienced playboy when there were other, more delectable women about. Why?

He wants my forgiveness, she thought suddenly. She pictured his face again as they had spoken on deck. She remembered his anger and his pain and how he had lost control, almost as if he had said more to her than he had said to anyone else before. Perhaps that was why he was so determined to haunt, to rip her apart and claim that she would either love him or despise him.

"I do despise you, Congressman!" She swore aloud vehemently, plunging a fist into her pillow. "We don't need to go the length of the cruise to reach that conclusion."

Or did they?

She didn't really know what she felt. Her mind was a simmering caldron of confusion.

She tossed onto her back, unaware that she nervously plucked at her sheets as she determinedly closed her eyes once more.

He was dancing somewhere, more than likely with Joan Kendrick. Miss Gravity Defiance. Blonde and beautiful and slim and young.

Rhiannan rolled onto her stomach once more, wondering why she was allowing thoughts of the pretty young woman to bother her. She had told Whellen to go dance with her and she had meant it. But now she could see the two of them together. Whellen with those smoky gray eyes—eyes that sometimes appeared like granite, sometimes like a misty sky, sizzling with the wicked dazzle of a mischievous sun—staring down at the radiant blond head of Miss Kendrick. Miss Kendrick meeting his gaze and edging ever closer against his hard, muscular body. Rhiannan could see his hands, broad and work-roughened but fastidiously clean, resting on the blonde's curvaceous hips. . . .

"Dammit!" she exclaimed, springing up in her narrow bed and sliding her legs over the edge to rest her feet on the floor. She raked her fingers through her hair and squinted across the room to stare at the luminous hands of her travel alarm clock. It was past two A.M. She had been trying to sleep for over three hours.

Impulsively she stood up and ripped off her nightgown and dug through a drawer for a T-shirt and a pair of jeans. She wouldn't look much like Donald Flagherty's hostess if she was seen by any of the elegantly dressed passengers, but all she wanted to do was slip into one of the lounges and slip out again with a small—no, not small: *stiff*—brandy. She had to relax or she was never going to sleep. And they were going to spend the next day anchored off Cat Island, which meant she was going to be busy at the blackjack table and running around, supervising whatever meetings, social or business, that Donald had privately planned. And then she wouldn't be clocking out at five o'clock, so it might be a long night, too.

Things were quiet as she crept along the halls of the old clipper. She could still feel the sway of the ship. It was probably beautiful up on deck with the wind whipping the white sails. Maybe she would venture out after she stopped by the lounge. She hesitated. Which lounge? She didn't want to run into any of the ship's crew. For a moment she thought rapidly, then smiled with relief. The Pirate's Cove, just below the promenade deck, would be closed. It was the first to open, the first to close.

Quickening her footsteps, Rhiannan hurried for the central stairway. There was no one around. Some passengers would still be awake, trying their luck in the casino or dancing through the night; but the majority would be asleep in preparation for a full day of sea and sun. The day-shift crews would be sleeping and the night shift would be working. If she was lucky, she wouldn't encounter a soul.

A few seconds later she reached the old oak lounge, which had once housed a weighing-in station. She breathed a little sigh of relief to discover that the door was unlocked, then slipped inside.

It was a bit eerie in the lounge with the moonlight streaming through a window with the original panes. The lounge was set up something like a pirate's den, with crossed swords on the paneled walls and gold-foil-encased mints resembling pieces of eight strewn in the candle dishes that sat in the center of each table. Rhiannan moved fluidly around the tables to the bar and slipped beneath the service flap. She occasionally relieved the bartenders, so she knew the order of the service rack without the benefit of decent light. Vodka, gin, rum, whiskey, bourbon, sweet vermouth, dry vermouth, and brandy. Only the brandy wasn't there. She made a quick search of the bottles once more, then was startled as a voice suddenly rang out in the room.

"If you're looking for the Christian Brothers, Mrs. Collins, it's over here. On the table."

She almost screamed with the ripples of fear that accosted her at the sound of a voice in the seemingly deserted lounge. Somehow she caught herself and merely stiffened rigidly, dismay and anger sweeping through her system. She knew the sound of his voice. She would know it until the day she died.

Narrowing her eyes, she stared into the darkness. She could vaguely see him. He was still in his tux, but his posture was ridiculously relaxed. He was leaning lazily against the back of his chair, his legs comfortably stretched before him on the table. She could see a steely sparkle in his eyes as he returned her gaze.

"What are you doing in here?" Rhiannan snapped. "This lounge is closed."

"I have an in with the management," he said, not moving. "And I'm here for a nightcap, the same as you. And by the way, since we're throwing stones, does your boss know that you prowl his ship at night to tip the bottle?"

She smiled and replied through gritted teeth, "Congressman, I assure you my employer would have no argument with me. I have my own in with the management."

"Then come have your brandy."

Rhiannan hesitated, then noted the white flash of his teeth as he smiled. She wasn't afraid of him and for some reason found herself being drawn to him.

Rhiannan smoothly lifted a snifter from the rack and ducked beneath the bar. She moved casually past the tables until she reached the far corner of the room. She lowered her lashes against the eyes of the man, who didn't move as he watched her. Then she reached for the brandy bottle.

His legs swung to the floor and he clutched the bottle. Rhiannan at last looked at him. He lifted his brows, then stood to pour a stiff portion of the brandy into her glass.

"Sit down, Mrs. Collins."

"I'd really rather return to my room."

"I couldn't allow you to do that. It's quite unhealthy to drink alone."

She smiled sweetly and sat in the chair across from him. "If I'm not mistaken, Congressman, *you* were drinking alone."

"You're right, I was. It was nice of you to come along and save me from my own company."

"That was hardly my intent."

He shrugged, sat down, and again made himself comfortable, stretching his legs out on another chair this time.

"For a lady who went to bed long ago, you appear to be quite awake," he told her pointedly.

"Thanks to you, Congress—"

"Dammit!" He exploded suddenly, kneading his temple tiredly with his fingers. "Will you please stop that? You know my name. I'd appreciate it if you would quit addressing me as if I were an object."

"But that *is* your name. Congressman Whellen. That is the way one addresses an elected representative, isn't it?"

He didn't respond to her flippancy.

"Do you always press your luck, Rhiannan?"

"Press my luck?" Somehow she retained the sweet innocence in her voice—an innocence just hinting of sarcasm—even though she was trembling so much that she was certain he could see the quivering of her fingers holding her glass. She held the glass tighter. It wasn't exactly fear that made her shiver. She felt a bit as if she were playing with fire. There was a very basic, very male sense of danger about him.

"The Queen of Hearts," he murmured, pleasantly enough. But she saw that the lashes half closed over his smoldering eyes hid a glimmer that was completely alert. "A good card," he added. "But a queen can always be beaten by a king. And then, the ace of spades can take anything."

"I take it you consider yourself to be the ace of spades . . . Congressman?"

His feet hit the floor again, and his fingers were suddenly squeezing her wrists, drawing her attention to the warning thunder clearly in his face even in the soft moonlight.

"Kiel. Very easy. One-syllable name. Try it."

Again his words were level but husky. She was tempted to ignore him, ignore the steel bands of his fingers, their searing touch. She was tempted to drive him to the limits of his temper, to test his every reaction—and he had no right to insist she do anything.

She stared coolly down at the hands that held her, then into his eyes. Her look usually quelled any question but now it merely caused the grim line of his mouth to tighten.

"You're hurting me," she said curtly, then paused, finding she had to moisten her lips. Then, without real intent, she blurted out the word he wanted to hear. "Kiel."

He released her. "See how easy?"

She picked up her snifter and sipped the brandy, feeling her heart beat like thunder within her chest. What had been the matter with her? She didn't want to run around taunting this man over petty absurdities. She wanted to stay away from him. He did strange things to her; he ripped her to pieces.

"What were you doing in here?" she asked casually, watching her brandy glass. "I thought you were going dancing."

"I did go dancing."

"But you called it an early night. Was Miss Kendrick tired?"

He chuckled softly. "No, I believe Joan and Donald are still enjoying the night. I'm afraid the music didn't hold my interest for long."

"I'm surprised. Donald's performers are quite talented."

"I'm sure all his employees are quite brilliant at their tasks." An innuendo—meaning what, she wasn't sure—was there, but he continued smoothly. "Perhaps it was the company that didn't quite hold my interest."

"How amazing. Miss Kendrick is lovely."

"Yes, she is."

"Then—"

"She lacks a certain maturity that I find I look for in a woman. And the sensitivity that accompanies it." He leaned back once more, slowly assessing her, then his fingers entwined with hers once more, gently, but allowing no opposition. "Besides, Rhiannan, any of my constituents can tell you that I am a determined man."

She wanted to draw her hands away but she couldn't.

"Anyone could tell you, Kiel, that I cannot be . . . reached."

He smiled faintly, then stood, pulling her to her feet. "Then I would say that the evening was a draw. Come on. Toss down that brandy and you should sleep like a child. This time I will walk you back to your cabin."

"I hardly think it's necessary on the ship," Rhiannan protested in a murmur. "I doubt if we have any muggers aboard."

"You never know," he answered with a shrug. "And it's always better to be safe." He plucked her snifter from the table and handed it to her. "Drink up."

She obediently consumed the remaining brandy in a gulp. It burned pleasantly from her throat to her abdomen. She watched his eyes on hers all the while. He took the empty glass from her fingers, set it back on the table, placed his hands on her shoulders, and turned her toward the door.

"Come on, now. You have to work tomorrow and I'm having breakfast with a Chinese statesman. I want to be very diplomatic. We're discussing nukes."

She glanced at him with interest. "Red China? I didn't think that the Chinese were that advanced in the nuclear age."

"It depends on what you mean by advanced. Any high school chemist with the right ingredients at hand could create an atomic bomb. And when China gets moving, she moves. Want to have breakfast with us?"

"No, thank you."

"Too bad. Chou Lou is a charming man."

"I work for Donald, remember?"

"Ah, yes. I will keep that in mind."

They were silent as they left the lounge and started down

the central stairwell. Kiel put his arm around her waist as he escorted her, and although she stiffened at first, she didn't protest. It was a gesture as casual as one Donald might have made, and as basically polite. What's more, there was something about it that felt strong, secure and warm.

Rhiannan clamped her teeth together. She was doing it again. But the light scent of his after-shave was still stirring and pleasant, and she was sorely tempted to stop and lean her cheek against the material of his jacket and feel beneath it the muscular hardness of his chest and the even deeper warmth of being enveloped in his arms.

He seemed to know that her cabin was on the lower deck, and he halted at her door.

"Where's your key?" he asked.

"I didn't lock it."

"Great," he muttered sarcastically, pushing open the door. To her dismay, he walked in. She followed hastily, noting first that he seemed extremely tall and broad-shouldered in the small cabin, then frowning as he abruptly opened the door to the shower and briefly checked it, then did the same to her closet.

To her annoyance she blushed as his eyes quickly scanned over her rumpled bed.

"What are you doing?" she demanded.

"Just making sure that you're alone."

"Why? I'm an adult."

He sighed with exasperation, his irritation showing in his face as his eyes flashed to hers. "I'm trying to make sure you're safe."

He meant it. She saw that immediately and felt annoyingly contrite. "Kiel, there are dozens of security men on board."

"I know," he murmured, looking quickly away from her. "But do me a favor: Keep your door locked when you're out."

"All right, but—"

"Just do it, okay?"

He gripped her shoulders and planted a quick kiss on her

cheek before she could argue, then made the distance to her door with two long strides. "I'll see you tomorrow, Rhiannan."

"Kiel!"

He paused and turned back to her.

"I think it's only fair to warn you, I plan to avoid you," she said quietly.

He smiled, and she was struck by the way he looked, his granite features softening, his frame so tall and sinewy in her doorway.

"I think it's only fair to warn you, there's no way in hell you're going to be able to do that!"

The door closed behind him.

Rhiannan stripped off her jeans and T-shirt and donned her discarded gown once more, wondering all the while how she would manage to sleep now.

But in the morning she could barely remember closing her eyes. She could recall bits and pieces of her dreams. They had all centered around a gray-eyed man with wonderfully strong arms that had imprisoned her with tenderness.

Four

"How was your breakfast with our Chinese friend?" Donald Flagherty asked cheerfully, joining Kiel as he leaned idly against a mast and stared out at the calm aqua waters of their anchorage off of Cat Island.

Kiel lifted his sunglasses from his nose for a moment to glance at Donald and grinned. "Good. Chou Lou is a very diplomatic man who abhors violence. If we had a world full of Chou Lous, we'd be in good shape."

Donald was silent for a moment. "Think we're going to do any good out here, Kiel?"

Kiel paused, then shrugged, crossing his arms over his chest and leaning back to stare out to sea again. "Sure. Anytime you bring intelligent men of many nations together who can actually talk, you've done some good. But sometimes I wonder what I'm trying to do to begin with. I don't think it's the leaders, per se, of any nation who plan on pushing any buttons. It's the fanatics in the world who scare me."

"True," Donald agreed with a sigh, then brightened. "But we did raise quite a sum for the children."

"Yep."

"By the way, how's my hostess?"

Kiel straightened and stared at Donald. "What do you mean? She's your hostess; haven't you seen her?"

Donald chuckled softly. "Cool down, my friend. I haven't seen her this morning, but I know she's okay. She didn't answer the steward's knock, so I told him to open up and check on her. She was sleeping so soundly, I decided to let her sleep. And it just so happened that when I was running a check on the ship last night, I heard voices—your voices—coming from the lounge. That's why I'm asking you, how's my hostess?"

Kiel slipped his glasses back into place and slid down to the planking, stretching his legs out as if he were reflecting carefully on his answer. He was dressed in a knit sports shirt and cutoffs and looked more like a tanned and hard-muscled surfer than one of the nation's most promising politicians, Donald thought. "Can I get you a beer or something while I'm waiting?" Donald joked.

"You know, that does sound good."

Near the bow, a steward was delivering frosted island drinks to a party of sun-lovers. Donald lifted a hand and the man was at his side. "Can you get me a beer, please, George? Make that two."

"Sure thing, Mr. Flagherty."

Kiel laughed as George walked swiftly away. "You remind me of a king, Donald, with loyal serfs running about to serve you."

"Kiel . . ."

"Hey, I say that as flattery. You are truly an unusual individual. Completely unselfish."

"Ah-ha! Are you telling me I've worked on the campaign committees for a selfish congressman?"

"You bet."

George returned with the beers, and Kiel and Donald thanked him.

"Now," Donald said after a long swallow, "what about Rhiannan?"

"You sound like a father. Are you asking me what my intentions are?"

"You bet."

Kiel was silent for a moment. He thought of his feelings for her, that instant attraction and all the other emotions that haunted him. The need to reach her, to protect her, to hold her and swear that there could be a brighter tomorrow. He felt that he was the only man in the world who could ever really understand her completely, and he knew beyond a doubt that she was the only woman who could ever touch and understand all the facets of his heart. He knew his answer was going to sound ludicrous, but it was true.

"I want to marry her."

"Oh, come on, Kiel, you just met her."

"Hey, you were the one who said I looked like I'd been hit by bricks."

"That's lust, and you fall in and out of lust like a damned basketball."

Kiel shook his head, smiling ruefully. "I'm dead serious, Donald. There's something about her . . . or maybe it's everything about her. She's beautiful, a little mysterious, and that slender spine of hers is so damned straight. But I think it's deeper than that. We're living in an age in which great achievement is supposedly the 'in' goal. Getting ahead, being on top. That's not bad. I enjoy seeing a bright woman reach a position she deserves. But too often it's as if the real goals in life—like loving a child, enjoying the simple things that most people can have for the asking—are lost. Rhiannan is not like that. She loved her husband; she loved her children. Completely. And she wasn't afraid of having that love be the main focus of her life. It has nothing to do with working or not working. I . . . I think that Ellen had that same quality. Maybe I've been searching for it ever since. All I really know now is that I do want her in the forever sort of way. I think, too, that she needs me."

"Needs you?" Donald asked dryly. "She's a strong lady, and strongly against you."

"We all need someone."

"Including Kiel Whellen?"

"Yes, including Kiel Whellen." He was silent for a minute, as if he were digesting some inner revelation. "I need her."

"I can just imagine the lady's opinion," Donald muttered. "Kiel, she blames you for the crash."

Kiel grimaced. "So I've discovered. But give her time."

"Confident, aren't you?"

"Politicians have to be."

"So why is she so tired? Just how long did you keep her awake?"

Kiel laughed. "You can cut the growl, Papa Bear. I wasn't in her bed. I wouldn't be in hers anyway. I would have brought her to mine. That's a tiny place you have for a key employee, Donald."

Donald shrugged. "She insisted on it. She wants to be treated just like the others—says her position has too many benefits to begin with." Donald noticed that Kiel was suddenly frowning.

"How much influence do you have with your employees?"

"Why?"

"Because I want you to mention to her that she keep her door locked."

Donald was surprised and took a moment to digest his friend's words.

"Why? There's security crawling all over this ship."

It was Kiel's turn to be uncomfortably quiet. "I don't know exactly, Donald. Haven't you ever just had a feeling about something? That day with the plane . . . from the moment they called me, I knew something was terribly wrong. And I had a terrible feeling about it. There was a moment when I knew that I hadn't been given all the crucial information, and the sense of fatality, of dread, was almost overwhelming. I wanted to strangle someone because I was so frightened. That was the past, but now I feel that same strange sense of unease that touched me as soon as I entered the Oval Office. As if something isn't right, as if something is going to happen. . . ."

"On my ship? My clipper? A graceful old clipper I just spent a mint refurbishing, with scores of dignitaries aboard? Thanks a lot, old friend!"

"Sorry," Kiel said sheepishly. "I could be wrong. I mean, I haven't got a damn thing to go on. Just a . . . a dumb feeling. Getting paranoid in my old age. But just the same, remind her to keep her door locked, will you?"

"Hey, you're the one who's going to marry her."

"Yeah, but she doesn't know that yet." No, she didn't know him, nor did she understand the depth of his feelings, his absolute need to touch her, to give her back the ability to feel, the beauty that was also life . . . love. His love, his protection, all the tenderness that welled in him when he saw her, along with his desire. He shrugged. "It's definitely going to take some convincing. At the moment I think she'll take any suggestion much more kindly from you."

"All right. I'll talk to her. But, Kiel, be gentle with her. You're my friend, but she is very precious to me, too."

"I intend to be gentle." Kiel stretched and stood, pressing his now empty beer can into Donald's hand. "Thanks."

"Where are you going?" Donald demanded.

"Diving."

"You're not going to pursue your future wife?"

Kiel grinned. "I *am* pursuing her. There are times to attack the bull head on, Mr. Flagherty, and then there are times when you let what you've already said stew in the mind for a while."

"Got it."

"I'm going to attack head on when we reach New Providence."

"Yeah?"

"Yeah. Don't you feel like taking bikes around the island?" Donald grinned slowly. "With Rhiannan along, I take it."

"Well, you are her employer."

"Employer, yes. Not a tyrant king."

"She'll come along if you ask."

"You think so?"

"Five dollars."

"You're on."

To Rhiannan's surprise, she wasn't bothered by Congressman Whellen at all during the day. She wasn't sure whether to he relieved or insulted.

She had awakened terribly late and rushed to find Donald to apologize. He had waved away her stammerings. "I would have gotten you up if I really needed you." He had outlined her duties for the rest of the day, then casually asked, "Have you ever been to Nassau before, Rhiannan?"

She hesitated a moment, then said, "Yes, I was in Nassau once."

"With your husband?" Donald queried softly.

"Yes." She forced a light smile. "It was a long time ago, before we had the kids. We went on one of those weekend cruises. We weren't there long, and we didn't get to do too much. We just strolled along Market Street and bought a ton of straw souvenirs."

"Would it bother you to go to Nassau again?"

"Ah, no, not really. Not any more than anything else. I knew we were going to Nassau when you planned the cruise, Donald."

"Good, because we're going to have a lot of fun. I want to escape all this for the day—no meetings or business. You can rent scooters and drive around the island in a matter of hours. See the fort and some of the more out-of-the-way places. I'd like you to go along."

"Of course," she said automatically.

"Can you drive a scooter?"

"I never have."

"Can you ride a bicycle?"

"Sure."

"Then we're all set."

It didn't occur to her until later to ask who else might be coming along, and by that time she was too busy.

Donald had a pair of cruise directors to handle most of the passenger entertainment, but he also had so many special arrangements going that Rhiannan spent the afternoon moving about with little time to breathe. She was all over the ship, and although she didn't want to admit it, she continually had an eye out for Kiel Whellen. He didn't appear, and she wasn't about to ask Donald what his friend was up to.

She had a brief break after dinner before she had to put in her two-hour stint at the high-stakes blackjack table. Rhiannan had assumed she would enjoy spending the time in her cabin, resting, but she discovered that she was too restless. She changed into her black gown—her "Morticia" outfit, as she was coming to dub her evening outfits—and left her small cabin well before she was due in the casino.

With twenty minutes to spare she decided to go and sit in the back of the Manhattan lounge. Jason and Mary were on stage again, and as she neared the room, she could hear their rendition of "Every Breath You Take." She slipped through the back door and took the far corner table in the back of the room, smiled at the waiter, and thanked him when he automatically brought her a Coke.

A moment later she realized with annoyance that she was nervously playing with her straw. In another minute, she thought, she'd be biting her nails. Then she started to wish she hadn't come into the lounge, because she couldn't help remembering that the last time she had been in there, Kiel Whellen had appeared to join her. Had she come purposely, hoping that he would appear once more?

He hadn't been around all day, and it was more than possible that he had decided to seek greener pastures. Joan Kendrick? But he had said that Joan didn't interest him, that she didn't possess the maturity that he sought in a woman, or the sensitivity. But he didn't have to be madly in love with Joan to spend time with her, to make love with her.

Sitting alone, she felt her face flush with warmth. Her feelings about the congressman were paradoxical. She really didn't want to be involved with him. He was too intense, too passionate a man. He was shades of the past.

But she didn't like imagining him with another woman. Talk about immaturity! she mused. She didn't want him, but she didn't want anyone else to have him.

But still she blamed him for all the misery in her life. . . . Or did she? Hadn't she begun to see reason, to believe what he had told her? Perhaps he hadn't gone down on bended knee to beg her forgiveness, but he had tried to tell her, to swear that he had done everything that he could. And wasn't it true that, no matter how she fought it, she was seeing him as a man, and she couldn't believe that the man who was the real **Kiel Whellen wouldn't have done everything in his power?**

She didn't want to change her feelings. There was a realm beneath them that was frightening. Because on the one hand she did want him. She wanted him badly. She longed so intensely to touch him that it was frightening. She would have the courage to only if his vocal cords were cut and a blindfold was placed over his eyes. She would like to meet him in the dark, with no identity, and discover just what it was that drew her to him. She would enjoy a night outside of herself, a time to curb the loneliness she had begun to feel more and more.

Exhaling a long breath, she sipped the last of her Coke and was about to stand, when suddenly she froze in her chair.

Jason and Mary had begun a new number. It was one she knew extremely well, although it was an old song: "Rhiannon."

She had never heard the duo play it before. In fact, she hadn't heard it in years. Paul had teased her when the song had first come out. "Are you sure you don't have friends in Fleetwood Mac?" he would ask her. But then he would tell her it was a beautiful song, and that it just fit her, and someone had written it just for her. . . .

As she listened to the beautiful words she felt as if she were quivering all over, as if great sweeps of dark waves were cascading over and over her. And before she turned to the opposite corner of the room, in a jerky slow-motion twist, she knew that she would see him standing there.

He was, his eyes dark and fathomless in the dimness of the lounge, but probingly on her. He was in a dark suit, his shoulders filling out the jacket nicely. He stood by the rear wall, his hands in his pockets. He made no move to come toward her; he just watched her, and she found that her eyes locked curiously with his. And for a moment, as the song swept over them, with no rationale about it whatsoever she felt as if they shared a special understanding. It was as if he knew her inside and out, knew the tumult of her heart and mind, and gave her a unique empathy that was not in the least pity. But that was ridiculous. He was the man who had lashed her into tears with his brutal queries. But maybe, just maybe, he did understand her, she thought as she steadfastly returned his gaze, a strange ripple of pleasure touching her. Because she knew him too. She knew him as few other women ever could. He was a fighter who would never be down; any battle lost would make him more determined to win the war; any heartache would touch him deeply, but he would keep it all inside, and from it he would grow in caring, in wisdom, in quiet strength.

The song ended. Applause filled the room.

Rhiannan shook herself and the spell was broken. She stood, tore her eyes from his, and left the lounge.

Rhiannan worked for an hour and a half, then was given a fifteen-minute break by Lars.

She didn't go near the lounge but ran up to the promenade deck. She could see the lights of the yacht club and marina on Cat Island; she could even hear the faint sounds of laughter and music. She knew a number of the passengers and crew had gone to the island for the evening.

Wistfully she wished that she had been one of them. It would be nice to dress up and go out for the night with all cares forgotten—enjoy a candlelit dinner with the sound of the surf behind her and the breeze a soft caress against her skin. The sky seemed made of velvet. The stars were out in abundance, and the moon was full. It would be a beautiful night to walk along the sand and inhale the fresh scent of salt and sea.

Rhiannan squeezed her eyes closed and gripped the rail tensely. For the first time she did not imagine herself on Paul's arm as she walked along the sand. She pictured Kiel Whellen.

Rhiannan released the rail and rubbed her temples with the palms of her hands. *Damn that man!* she thought. If he had set out merely to torture her, he was doing a damned good job of it.

"What's the matter, 'Annan? I didn't think I'd ever see it, but you appear a bit flustered."

Rhiannan turned quickly, then smiled as she saw Glen Trivitt walk up beside her. "I'm just enjoying the view."

"Are you?" Glen teased.

"Umm. And how are you doing? Did you get a break in the Dramamine handouts? I haven't seen you since we sailed."

"Oh, I have been busy. This grand old lady has a lot more rock and roll than her modem counterparts. The passengers drink a bit too much and stay confined in the lounges, and— *voilà!* Seasickness. I toss them some pills and tell them to get out on deck, in the air. But it's nice and calm now, and queasy stomachs are adjusting. I've been free all night. In fact, I saw you earlier."

"Really?"

"Yeah, in the lounge, but you were busy staring at a certain congressman."

"Oh," Rhiannan murmured.

"You didn't notice another soul in the room."

"I was annoyed."

"Because of the song?"

"I suppose."

"You didn't look annoyed."

"Glen . . ."

He laughed softly. "Sorry. I was just about to express my approval."

"On what?"

"Well, you know I've languished after you myself, 'Annan, but to no avail. Still, I'm capable of being a good loser. And if the Queen of Hearts is at long last about to relinquish her own, then I can see no better candidate than the congressman."

"Oh, Glen, I'm not about to relinquish anything. The congressman has become a thorn in my side, nothing more."

He shrugged but smiled. Rhiannan stared out at Cat Island

again, but her curiosity got the better of her. "Why did you say that?"

"About Whellen?"

"Yes, about Whellen."

"Because I like him—more than I do most politicians, anyway."

"I didn't realize that you knew him."

"Oh, I don't. But I follow politics and I read. Whellen may not always go by the rules, but he doesn't do anything that everyone else doesn't. The difference is that he doesn't hide anything. He's got his problems," Glen said with a dry sniff. "Oh, yeah, he's got his problems. He's on a leash up there in Washington, just like the others. He takes orders. But if I were going to pick a man to reason with, it would still be him."

"Good," Rhiannan muttered dryly, "you reason with him."

Glen laughed. "Definitely flustered."

"Flustered and out of break time," Rhiannan murmured, glancing at her wristwatch. "I've got to get back. See you later, Glen. I hope the sea remains calm!"

"So do I!" he called after her as she left the rail and headed toward the stairwell. "I'm fond of leisure time."

Rhiannan smiled and started down the stairs, then paused, staring up at the night sky one last time. She was going to warn Glen teasingly that there was a full moon out and he should watch himself, but the words died on her lips as she started up the few stairs she had descended.

Glen was already talking to another woman—Joan Kendrick.

Rhiannan frowned, thinking it strange that the ship's doctor should be in conversation with the heiress. But then again, it wasn't strange. Joan might be feeling sick and, seeing Glen, thought to ask him for medication.

But Joan Kendrick didn't look sick. She was laughing, apparently teasing Glen, leaning against him, almost as if she were taunting him.

Rhiannan frowned again, but then she shrugged. Joan could

play around wherever she wanted. It was her business, and at least Rhiannan knew that Joan wasn't with Kiel.

Oh, stop it! she chided herself silently. *I refuse to act—or think—like an adolescent! I've told Whellen I don't want anything to do with him, so he's definitely free to be with whomever he chooses!*

But the vision she had imagined of herself walking barefoot along the sand on Kiel Whellen's arm remained with her as she deftly changed places with Lars and began to deal out the cards. As usual, her table was full. She wondered a little irritably how there could be so many people who could lose such vast sums of money and think nothing of it. Half of India, she was certain, could be fed for a week on the money dropped at the blackjack table alone.

She had been dealing for another half hour when her fingers almost faltered again. She didn't have to look up to recognize him this time: She knew his hands. The long, capable fingers, bronzed and calloused. No rings. Clean, neat nails. And she knew the subtle, masculine scent. Despite its light, light fragrance, she could recognize it through a field of perfumes and stronger colognes.

He was at the end of the table. Despite her feeling of hesitation, her fingers barely missed a hit. She dealt out his down card, then her own, then started around the table, wanting to kick either herself or the cards when she gave him an ace.

Her own card was a nine. Below it, an ace.

"Dealer stays at nineteen," she said.

The five other players asked for hits. All busted.

She started to draw in the chips as Kiel's hand came down upon hers.

"Twenty-one," he said softly, deftly flipping over his bottom card. His lips curved slightly at the corners as he met her eyes. "It seems I've drawn the queen of hearts."

Hiding behind an impassive facade of both annoyance and the quivery sensation that filled her at his quiet words, Rhiannan paid him.

He stayed at the table another fifteen minutes and kept winning hand after hand. The other players jokingly commented on his luck, and he returned their comments as lightly.

Rhiannan kept her eyes on the cards but knew he was gone when his powerful bronze hands were replaced by those of an older man. Absurdly she felt a sense of loss, and the time seemed to drag interminably.

At last Lars reappeared, and she was off for the night.

Tonight she didn't bother going straight to her cabin. She stopped by the Manhattan lounge once again and delighted the waiter by ordering a decaffeinated Irish coffee. She wasn't—really wasn't—looking for Kiel, but she did notice that he wasn't there. It was a big ship. He could be anywhere. He might have even decided to go on into Cat Island.

In her cabin she showered and changed into a nightgown, then picked up a magazine to read as she sipped at her drink. She stared at one page until she had consumed the hot liquid, then sheepishly admitted that she didn't remember a word she had read. She scrambled out of bed to brush the sugary taste out of her teeth, then turned out the lights and curled up with her pillow, wondering if sleep would elude her again.

But she was pleasantly drowsy, drifting in a way that would soon result in a sound and restful slumber.

Where was he now? she wondered vaguely as she drifted nicely into a semi-doze. In one of the lounges? Out on deck? Who was he with? Was he in bed? Whose bed?

The questions whirled in her mind and she tried to will them away, but it was impossible. She could control her behavior and her facial expressions, but it was impossible to control her rampaging thoughts. She couldn't help thinking about what he'd said.

He claimed an attraction to her, but tonight they had barely exchanged two sentences while she was working. And in the lounge there had been that special something in the long stares they had exchanged. She was almost certain he had asked the performers to sing that song.

Special . . . she couldn't let anything become too special. She didn't want special. She didn't want a future, but she was still wondering where he was, even as she drifted into her dreams.

She would have been surprised to know that Congressman Kiel Whellen was also in bed—his own. He had spent the afternoon with a diving party, and so he was pleasantly tired.

And he wasn't in the mood for company, not even Donald's. The trip was already proving to be a wonderful success—not that anything agreed upon would mean immediate changes of policy, but some important foundations were being laid in many directions. He and the senior senator from Utah had gone to the Island for dinner with the representatives from Yugoslavia and East Germany—followed by a half-dozen security men—but things had still gone extremely well. A number of private projects had been started, and who knew? Maybe some kind of real success would be attained with the nuke discussions.

And it would have been impossible for a more pleasant, more relaxed atmosphere to be created. Warm winds, the hospitable clipper, a benign sun. Working was easy. . . .

But tonight he didn't want to be involved with the world. He wanted to be alone with his nighttime daydreams. Rhiannan . . . it still amazed him that he could feel what he did for her so quickly. But it was there, that incredible fascination. He would have wanted her no matter what, and learning who she was had cast him heart and soul into deeper dimensions. He did need her, and he wanted her to need him. He longed for her, and yes, for both of their sakes, he needed to love her.

Jerking his tie from around his neck, Kiel moved about the large, elegantly decorated room to extinguish the lights. His windows were above the outer deck, and if anyone thought of stopping by, he hoped they wouldn't if they saw his cabin in darkness. The cream-colored drapes were moderately heavy, but moonlight and the night-lights from the ship filtered through, casting an eerie glow on the dark paneled walls of the cabin. He could see well enough to strip down to his briefs and throw his clothing over the back of a cream-colored brocade chair.

Then he lay down on the queen-size bed, pulling the spread up to his waist. He laced his fingers behind his head and thought how ridiculous he was to have felt so confident about making Rhiannan want him.

He didn't seem to be getting terribly far with his objective.

She had fascinated him so much at the blackjack table that he had been tempted to applaud her aloofness. There had not been a blink of her eye, not a flicker of expression on her face, just her lovely eyes with their dark sweeping lashes meeting his, cool, distantly challenging.

A frown creased his forehead. He had been independent so long. He had enjoyed dating, enjoyed companionship. But he had never met anyone who made him think on any kind of a deeper level.

Admit it, he told himself. *You were as licentious as most men, but most mornings you wanted to wake up alone.*

Until Ellen. He had realized slowly with her that he wanted more, much more. He wanted to see her gentle smile each morning, hear her quiet advice, and with that went all the other things. Lifelong commitment. Children. He loved her sharp mind, cheerful wit, and oh-so-feminine touch; but in the end he hadn't been able to protect her. At the moment of her death, he had been totally helpless. . . .

Kiel squinched his eyes closed. He remembered Hawk's voice telling him that he hoped there were heroes on the plane. He remembered looking around the Oval Office, accusing the other men with his eyes. *"You should have told me!"* he had wanted to scream. If he had only known, he might have asked Hawk to put one of the other men on the radio before the tension had grown to such a point that there was no stopping it.

Kiel opened his eyes with a sigh. What sense did it make

to blame the others? He knew the terrible complexities of the situation. The President carried a horrible weight on his shoulders. He had done everything humanly possible. Human. They were all human, nothing more. But because they were human, Kiel had been a part of Ellen's death and, at the last moment, totally helpless.

He had racked his mind for days, for months, after. Surely he could have done something. With the agony of loss came the agony of self-blame. He knew now that it hadn't been his fault. He didn't torture himself anymore with "What if . . . ?"

He still thought of Ellen. But the pain had a soft blur to it. He could never regret her; she had given him so much. She had taught him what love could be, that he had a great capacity for giving and needing and feeling.

Rhiannan was different. Lightning, a thunderbolt—a ton of bricks. But the feelings she brought out were the same, only stronger. He wanted to shake the cool green from her eyes and toss her on a bed, but he also wanted to hold her, and cherish her, and promise her that he would do all that was earthly possible to make it better for the rest of her life. . . .

Was he wrong? Did he sense something there that simply wasn't? No. . . .

This kind of an attraction was indescribable, but it did exist. Somehow he just knew. She was what he had been looking for. He was as sure of that as he was that the sun would rise in the East. The problem was, he told himself dryly, getting the lady to realize what he already knew.

He shrugged, grinning to himself in the darkness. He was good at presenting his case, and he would. He was also good at fighting. Damned good. If one method of attack didn't work, there was always another. Gently, roughly, fair means or foul.

Luckily it was a long cruise. He'd have plenty of time to implement his strategy.

Kiel frowned again, wondering why he felt a little shiver in his blood at the thought.

What was with him, he wondered with annoyance. Why did

a feeling of concern about Rhiannan and the ship come over him at the strangest times? There was probably no place safer to be, not with all the brilliantly trained security men aboard. But it was there with him, a feeling that nagged him. It was dormant most of the time. But then it would reach out for him again, the same feeling that had touched him on the day he had walked into the Oval Office. A growing, gut fear. A sense of fatality. The horror of being helpless again, unable to stop the wheel that was in motion. . . .

Kiel gritted his teeth, silently begging his mind to let him be. He rolled onto his stomach to sleep.

His was a stupid fear, totally ungrounded, and he was going to shrug it off before he really stepped on Donald's feelings. And it shouldn't be too hard, because he was constantly thinking of the woman. And wanting her. There. In that bed. Her magnificent hair spread out on the pillows, a tangle of ebony contrasting the sheets and her creamy satin flesh.

He would want the light on to see her. Nothing glaring or rough. Perhaps a candle to lend its soft glow to the perfection of the shadows and curves of her body.

Kiel sat up with a sheepish grin, then bolted out of bed. He was glad that Donald had had nice forceful showers installed. He needed a long, long cold one to clean up his dreams to the point where he wasn't driving himself crazy.

But long after he took his shower, he was still awake. And still thinking about her.

Rhiannan.

A woman like the wind.

And the sun.

And the mystery of the night.

Five

They were docked in Nassau Harbour when Rhiannan awakened to the shrill of her alarm. She had barely groped for the button when her phone rang. She picked it up to find one of the cheerful crew directors on the line, reminding her that she was going into town with Mr. Flagherty. She tried to thank the cheerful voice politely, but there was nothing she hated as much as cheerful voices when she had just gotten out of bed. Rather than be rude, she hung up quickly.

Stretching, she decided to lie down and close her eyes for just a moment longer, but just as she did, the phone rang again.

It was Donald, and he was disgustingly cheerful, too. "You awake, 'Annan?"

"Yes, Donald."

"Great. Breakfast, my cabin, fifteen minutes. Bring a bathing suit, but wear jeans."

"Jeans?" she mumbled.

"Yeah. Just in case you topple over on the motorbike."

"Just in case," she told him dryly.

"Fifteen minutes."

The phone clicked in her ear and she closed her eyes. They flew back open with alarm when she realized that her fifteen minutes were probably down to only fourteen. She jumped out of bed and raced into the bathroom, dousing her face with cold water.

Somehow she was ready in less than ten minutes. She had time enough left over to wonder why such a crowd had formed on the promenade deck when she reached it. Probably just because they had docked at Nassau, she thought. From the deck the straw markets were in view with the industrious natives already prepared for a day of bargaining. But the passengers weren't looking toward the island. They were all staring up at the rigging. The *Seafire*'s sails had all been drawn and furled, and the naked masts appeared almost skeletal against the unbroken teal blue of the morning.

At first Rhiannan could see nothing but the sun's glare. But as she stared quizzically upward along with the others, Mary Keller, of the Jason and Mary singing duo, tapped her excitedly on the shoulder. "Isn't this wonderful? There's always a show!"

Rhiannan smiled vaguely. "It's great, but what's the show?"

Mary laughed, her hazel eyes flashing with excitement. "Watch!"

Shielding her eyes from the brilliant morning sun, Rhiannan stared up again just in time to see a graceful young black man skim from the main mast to the beam and then execute a perfect dive into the harbor. For a split second Rhiannan's breath caught in her throat; she hadn't seen any way that the man would not hit the deck.

But as Rhiannan edged to the rail along with the others, she was relieved to see his head appear, his eyes twinkling merrily with pride and a sense of adventure.

"Thank God!" Rhiannan whispered.

Mary laughed, running her fingers through her tawny curls. "Don't sound as if it's a miracle, Rhiannan. These men do this for a living. Jase and I worked aboard the *Emerald Seas* once; you should have seen them diving from *that* deck! Oh, look! There's another man ready to dive!"

Another superbly athletic native was atop the rigging, taking a moment to weigh his distance. Then he, too, was soaring, easily clearing the deck of the *Seafire*.

Rhiannan felt compelled to watch for his head to surface from the harbor. Despite Mary's words, she breathed another sigh of relief.

She was so busy watching for the native that she missed seeing the first diver climb back aboard the ship. And she didn't see that two of the ship's passengers, barefoot and dressed in bathing trunks, were in laughing conversation with the Bahamian.

"Wow!" Mary murmured.

"What?" Rhiannan asked quickly.

"They're going to do it."

"Who's going to do what?"

"Erich Friegholt and Congressman Whellen! They're going to dive!"

Rhiannan spun about so quickly to stare up at the rigging again that she felt dizzy. But Mary was right. Erich Friegholt, a charming young West German, was climbing just ahead of Kiel toward the mast beam. They were laughing and joking with one another as they climbed, and pausing to listen to instructions from the Bahamian on deck below them—far below them.

The mast had never looked so tall before. . . . "No!" Rhiannan whispered.

"Aren't they something!" Mary stated with excited awe. "They're both just beautiful! So broad-shouldered and trim! I'd take either of them in a flash! But then, it seems that Whellen is already hung up on you. Gee, Rhiannan, I swear I would have given my eyeteeth for a shipboard romance with him. Oh, look! He's going first. But you know, Erich is such a dynamite man, too. He's just wonderfully polite and complimentary every time he comes in the lounge. . . ."

Mary was still rattling on, but Rhiannan definitely wasn't listening. Her eyes were riveted on Kiel Whellen as he moved along the beam, balancing himself carefully. Rhiannan felt a scream rising in her throat.

It was true that both Kiel and the German were in excellent shape. But the broad shoulders that Mary had commented on were just what terrified Rhiannan. The native divers were almost wire-slim, much lighter than either Kiel or Erich. And it wasn't that either Kiel or Erich was heavy; they were just more muscular, their frames more solid. They couldn't possibly have the same agility as the Bahamians.

"No!" The scream suddenly tore from her throat as Kiel stood at the end of the beam. With horror she saw his head twist. His eyes, so dark in the distance, scanned the crowd with anxiety, breaking his concentration. He staggered for balance suddenly, then gave a swift, running leap into the dive before he could lose the equilibrium he had so scarcely achieved.

When Rhiannan saw his body fly through the air like a golden streak, she let out another horrified scream and closed her eyes. The world seemed to be spinning fiercely. Black dots appeared before her eyes, obscuring the deck—the people who rushed to the rail. But she heard the applause, the laughter, the vehement, singsong praise of the Bahamian divers. . . .

"Rhiannan!" It was Mary, her eyes bright with pleasure. "Rhiannan, he made it! But if I were you, I'd get out of here! I wonder if he knows who screamed. Wow, honey, you messed him up pretty badly there. I'd be as mad as a hornet. You really should run!"

He was alive. He had made it. Relief flooded over her. Then guilt washed through her. She had almost caused him to have an accident.

But then anger took hold of her. Damn him! He shouldn't have even been up there! He had acted like some stupid kid in high school with his daredevil pranks.

"I'm not going anywhere," Rhiannan said, ripped apart by both her guilt and her anger. "I'm going to stand right here and apologize."

She was shaking like a leaf. She vaguely heard the encouraging shouts as Kiel asked Erich to dive. She didn't even hold her breath as she heard Erich walk out on the beam. She was both numb and shaking. A huge splash informed her Erich had made the dive.

"Aren't they both just gorgeous!" Mary said cheerfully.

"They're coming out of the water! Congressman Whellen is laughing. I guess you're in the clear. Oh, thank God nothing happened."

"Thank God," Rhiannan echoed.

I am not going to run, she thought. I am not going to run. I am going to face him. In spite of the fact that she had almost caused him to teeter, that he could have been crippled or killed, she wasn't going to run. She was going to stand right there and tell him she knew exactly what she had done and that she was very sorry. Then she was going to run.

No, no, no. Not run, but make it clear to him that more than ever she wanted nothing to do with him.

While she was standing stiffly beside Mary, planning her speech, Kiel and Erich accepted the towels that were handed to them by an enterprising young steward and chatted together. Rhiannan stared at Kiel. She noticed the tiny lines about his eyes, more apparent with his wet hair sleeked back from his forehead, and that in contrast, his smile, with his white teeth flashing, made him appear exceptionally vibrant and youthful.

It was the first time she had seen him in something as scant as bathing trunks. And just as his smile made him seem young, the flurry of short dark hair that covered nicely the bronzed breadth of his chest gave him a distinct maturity.

A man really is in his prime in his thirties, she thought vaguely. His legs were nicely shaped, long and firm, well-muscled without being thick. Only along his shoulders and arms was the buildup of power visible, and it was very handsome. . . .

What am I doing, she wondered suddenly. *I have to apologize, then get away from him! I'm so sorry, yet I want to strangle him for terrifying me. And any minute he'll turn this way, ready to break every bone in my body.*

But to her amazement Kiel Whellen never came toward her. His eyes flickered at her briefly, yet still with a smoldering thunder. They moved quickly, very quickly, as he laughed and answered a question put to him by Erich.

But no matter how brief the contact, it had been enough to tell her that he knew exactly who had screamed, exactly who almost caused him to falter. The stormy gray had filled with anger and contempt and—what else? A fervent desire to bound and gag her and cast her over the side?

Rhiannan blinked, and Kiel Whellen left Erich to walk on past her to what was apparently his cabin, the large one just beyond Donald's. He hung the towel around his neck as he slipped his key from a pocket in his trunks and inserted it in the old lock. He never turned around.

A disturbing thought swept into her mind. Did he think that it had been a twisted form of revenge? Rhiannan felt dizzy. *Please, no,* she thought, *don't let him believe that I would be capable of hurting him because I wanted revenge.*

"Looks like a reprieve for you," Mary said cheerfully. "We'd better get going or we'll be late for breakfast." She chuckled softly. "I'm sure the congressman can get away with being late, but not the hired help lucky enough to be asked along for the day's outing."

Rhiannan instantly snapped back to the present. "What?"

Mary took hold of Rhiannan's elbow and started leading her along the deck. "Mr. Flagherty said he'd received so many compliments about us that he'd like to do something special for us. He said that he and Congressman Whellen, Erich, Joan Kendrick, and Senator Tyson's daughter Julie were going to rent bikes and explore the island for the day and asked if we would like to come along. I can't tell you how stunned I was! And frightened! But he must have known the company scared me, because he told me that you would be along, too. And you always make everyone feel at ease, Rhiannan. Isn't he something? Asking Jase and me along with such important people. But then, Mr. Flagherty is like that, isn't he?"

Rhiannan smiled stiffly, earnestly trying to hide her dismay. Why didn't Donald tell her that he had asked Kiel along? Why hadn't she thought to ask? "Donald is great," she told Mary.

"I mean, I guess you're used to it all. You're his hostess;

you're special. Jase and I are just plain working folks. But he's a strange man. I mean, he's worth all that money, but he makes you so comfortable!"

"I'm not special, Mary. I work for him, the same as you do."

"But it's still different. You don't have to work. You're on the same social level."

Rhiannan had to laugh. "Mary, I could survive without working, but I'm far from wealthy. Donald Flagherty is simply not a snob. Money doesn't make people different, Mary. Donald is an exceptionally nice person."

Mary laughed. "Oh, money does make people different! Maybe not Mr. Flagherty, but Joan Kendrick reeks of money. Her nose is always so high in the air, I'm surprised she doesn't catch birds in her nostrils!"

"Mary!" Rhiannan laughed.

"It's true. Hey, hit me if I eat with the wrong fork or something, will you?"

They had reached the door to Donald's cabin. "I will not hit you, Mary. I'm sure breakfast will be casual, and Donald would never judge anyone by the fork they use, so don't worry."

"But stay by me, will you?"

Rhiannan hesitated. She had decided to give Donald an excuse for backing out of the day. How could she have been so stupid? She knew Donald had decided that Kiel was good for her. It should have been dead obvious that he was planning on throwing them together.

"Please, Rhiannan? If I make a fool of myself in front of Joan Kendrick, I'll just about die of embarrassment!"

Rhiannan sighed. She had been looking forward to the day out and they would be on bikes. If Kiel took the lead, she'd take the rear. How much contact could there be?

"Let's go in before we're any later than we already are," she replied lightly to Mary.

The drapes in her employer's cabin had been drawn wide and

the sun shone through the windowpanes in crystal brilliance. As Rhiannan had guessed, breakfast was casual. Juice, coffee, eggs, bacon and sausage, rolls and muffins, had been set on a table drawn up to the window. It was a serve-yourself-style buffet, and Donald was dressed casually in worn jeans and an old Grateful Dead T-shirt.

"You're late," he said cheerfully after ushering them in.

Rhiannan's eyes quickly scanned the room. Julie Tyson, a bright, nice young woman with enormous brown eyes, gave her a friendly wave from the corner of the room where she sat with coffee. Jason, Mary's attractive older brother, was sitting beside Joan Kendrick on the edge of Donald's bed. Poor Jason looked a bit like a nervous terrier being patted on the head by a master he craved to please. Joan, as always, looked fresh and lovely and fully aware that she had acquired another adoring fan. But Mary had been, in a way, astutely right: It was evident in Joan's bored features and sulky posture that she considered Jason a waste of her time. After all, he was only a musician.

Rhiannan frowned suddenly, remembering how she had seen Joan in the tight tête-à-tête with Glen. It had been dark, but Rhiannan was sure Joan hadn't worn that superior expression then. She shrugged. Joan probably considered doctors to be a cut above musicians. It would serve her right if Jason and Mary became fabulously rich and famous. Jason was in his late twenties and striking in a dark, slender way. Rhiannan would love to see the day when Joan floated on over to Jason and Jason dismissed her with polite boredom!

"You've been oversleeping frequently, eh, 'Annan?" Donald inquired.

Rhiannan turned her gaze to him and gave him a dry smile. "I didn't oversleep; I talked to you, remember? And we're not as late as two others, Donald, if Mary gave me your guest list correctly."

"Oh, I did!" Mary said innocently.

"Kiel and Erich will be right along. They went out diving.

They've both eaten already." Donald echoed Mary's innocence. Rhiannan wondered if Donald knew he had come very close to having to fire her. "Have something to eat, girls. I'd like to be off the ship by eight."

"We saw them diving!" Mary said excitedly. "They were just marvelous! That's why we're late, Mr. Flagherty."

Donald smiled at Rhiannan once more, then looped his arm through Mary's. "Let me fix you a plate, young lady. What will you have? Eggs with ham or cheese. Or both?"

Rhiannan started to follow behind them when a sharp tap sounded at the door. " 'Annan, that's either Erich or Kiel. Let in whoever it is, will you?"

"Of course," she murmured briefly. She was, after all, his hostess, but it had seemed lately that he wasn't letting her handle many of his social affairs.

She was annoyed to note that her palms were damp with nervousness when she reached to open the door. And she was even more annoyed to realize that she was praying that she would open the door to Erich rather than Kiel. She had her hand on the knob when a sharp rap sounded again and she drew the door open quickly.

It was Kiel. His hair was still damp, but a comb had been run through it. He had changed to worn jeans, and his T-shirt was an advertisement for Busch Gardens in Williamsburg.

His eyes swept over her as he stood there, and she couldn't begin to read the emotions in them. It was almost as if he could make them grayer at will. Deep gray and dark, and fully shielded.

"Excuse me," he said at length. "I was invited. May I come in?"

"I—" Her tongue seemed to be sticking ridiculously to the roof of her mouth. But suddenly "I'm sorry" seemed totally ludicrous when she might have cost him his life.

He started to sweep by her, but she stopped him, feeling something like a little electric shock as she placed her hand on his bare arm. "I . . . I realize that this isn't sufficient, but I'm . . . I'm sorry."

He stared at her hand on his arm and then into her eyes. "You should be," he said briefly, and walked on by her.

He couldn't have drawn a more purely physical reaction from her had he slapped her or doused her with cold water. The anger that swept through her was very tangible; from head to toe she felt as if she burned. Her fingers were shaking like blown leaves as she closed the door in his wake. It was all she could do to keep from spinning about and shouting that he was a pigheaded, reckless bastard.

When she turned around, Kiel was drinking a cup of coffee and smiling as he talked with Mary. Julie Tyson and Jason were drawn into the discussion; Joan had latched on to Donald.

There was another tap on the door. Knowing that it was Erich, Rhiannan opened it with a winning smile. "Hi, Erich."

"Hello, beautiful lady." Erich's voice was slightly accented in a way that made his greeting all the more complimentary.

"Thanks," Rhiannan murmured. "You were a little bit beautiful out there yourself this morning. You can certainly dive."

"*Ja?* Thanks." He politely took hold of her arm as they moved into the cabin. "I'm afraid I still don't surpass my friend Kiel."

"Still?"

"We met at the '68 Summer Olympics," Erich told her with a pleasant chuckle. "I took the bronze, but my American friend took the silver."

Oh, great, Rhiannan thought, an Olympic diver. Why hadn't she ever read anywhere that Kiel had been an Olympic diver? Why didn't she remember his name? Because in 1968 she had still been in high school, she told herself dryly. And truthfully she didn't know who the current Olympics champs were.

"—because someone screamed right before he plunged. It was lucky that he wasn't too distracted."

She hadn't paid attention to the beginning of Erich's statement, but it was impossible for her to ignore the end.

"That was me, Erich."

"Ach! How nice for Kiel. Tell me, would you have screamed for me?"

"Of course," she said quickly. "I was terrified that someone was about to kill himself!"

"Ah, Erich!" Donald said, coming forward to greet his last guest. "I hear you guys managed to keep up with the natives. Great. Well, since you're here, I guess we're all set. Shall we go, everyone?"

A chorus of agreement was his reply. As they all began to file out Rhiannan wished that she had been able to grab a quick breakfast rather than having been on door duty. But at least she had been close to the door, close enough to be the first one out and avoid Kiel.

Captain Knutson, a distinguished-looking man, was at the gangway to see them off. He tipped his hat and wished their party a pleasant day. Donald paused to speak with him briefly, then caused Mary practically to pass out with pleasure as he grabbed her hand and swung it easily as he led the way along the straw market toward Market Street.

The street was fun, full of life. Gaily dressed Bahamians offered their wares in cheerful singsongs, and all about them everything was bright and languidly pleasant. But as they moved past the stalls of woven straw hats, bags, T-shirts, and carvings, Rhiannan realized uneasily that the group was perfectly split—four women, four men. Donald was walking with Mary. That left him out to hide behind—not that he would have helped her anyway, she thought sourly. This whole thing reeked of a planned affair.

And she was now at the head of the group. She needed to stop, turn around, and pair up with Erich before someone else did.

As she turned around she found that Joan Hendrick had already approached the West German. Had she given up on convincing Kiel that she was not yet and never would allow herself to be the victim of gravity? No. She had chosen Erich because Kiel was walking between Julie Tyson and Jason.

Please stay attached to Julie! she thought silently. *Please!* She felt as if her temper were going to break any second, and she was dangerously near a blowout in front of six other people who thought her the epitome of poised equanimity. Maybe she'd better just keep walking as fast as possible.

"Hold up, 'Annan!" Donald suddenly called to her. "Julie and Joan want to stop for some perfume, and Erich wants to buy one of those little Scottish dolls for his niece."

Rhiannan slowed her pace and reluctantly turned back, but she couldn't bring herself to join the others in the shop. She saw that Mary looked anxiously about for her, and waved with a very false but very broad smile to assure her that she was near.

Through the shop window she saw that the coupling seemed to be mixing. Julie Tyson was helping Erich pick out a doll. Joan Kendrick was with Kiel, pointing out various bottles of perfume. Kiel made a purchase, and the little stab of jealousy that touched Rhiannan made her even more furious with him, but mainly with herself.

" 'Annan, don't you want anything?"

She started when Donald appeared beside her on the sidewalk. "No thanks, Donald."

"They have Oscar and Opium, and I know you like them both. I'll run in and get you some of each."

"No! I mean, thanks, Donald, but I still have the bottle of Opium you gave me for Christmas. Scout's honor—I don't need anything. Where's Mary?"

"Right here!" Mary exclaimed, appearing behind Donald. Rhiannan looked at her starry eyes and hoped she wasn't falling desperately in love. Not that Donald would ever purposely be cruel, but Mary was so fresh and sweet that she could be too easily crushed, and Donald had remained a bachelor for almost forty years.

Donald locked his arm in Mary's once again and looked

behind him, where the others were filtering out of the shop's doorway. "Are we all together again? Good. The bike rental is just ahead in the Sheraton parking lot."

Moments later Rhiannan had to admit that Joan Kendrick's efforts to keep gravity at bay had kept her nicely coordinated. She had never operated a motorbike before, but she got the hang of it as soon as she sat down. Mary looked a bit apprehensive, but Donald quickly suggested that she ride behind him; Mary just as quickly agreed.

Julie Tyson made one stab at riding the bike, then laughed and said "No thanks!" Jason nervously asked her if she would like to ride with him, and was rewarded with a soft and brilliant smile.

That is one nice girl, Rhiannan thought of the senator's daughter. But then she gave Julie and Jason no more thought, because the rental agent was bringing up her bike.

"You can ride, missy?"

"Yes," she said, certain she could master the small vehicle. Rhiannan straddled the seat.

"If we're all set," Joan called out, "let's go!"

The others started out of the lot before Rhiannan could figure out how to start the bike.

"What you doin', missy?" the rental agent asked with exasperation, scratching his head with a sigh as he watched her.

"If you could just tell me—"

"Here," he said. "Lookee here. Twist the right handlebar for gas, yes? Let go to slow down. You have a brake at your foot and on the bar. Your gears, see, are on the left handlebar. You know?"

"Yeah, I know," Rhiannan mumbled, then looked at him guiltily. "I'm sorry. Thank you."

"Now try."

She got the bike started, but she would have felt more secure riding a pterodactyl. Her legs were wobbling and the bike was wobbling.

"Watch out!" the agent called. "You must stop for the traffic on the street!"

Somehow she slowed the bike down at the end of the driveway; luckily nothing was coming. She moved out to the road. The agent was shouting again, but she couldn't really hear him. Something about the left. The left handlebar? She had gotten it straight. Her power was on the right, her gears were on the left, and a rickety old pickup truck was coming straight at her—on *her* side of the road.

"Oh, God!" she shrieked as they came closer and closer to a collision. The truck driver had a look of absolute panic on his face. She was certain it mirrored her own. He couldn't maneuver the heavy truck away from her in time.

She jerked her motorbike viciously to the side and just wobbled out of range of the truck as it swept on past. But she had completely lost control. Thankfully she was not on the main drag of the town. The motorbike sheared into an embankment and toppled her over on a mound of dirt.

And then she realized what the agent had been saying. *Drive on the left-hand side of the road.*

Everything hurt. Her hands, her head, her whole body. Cursing her own stupidity, she staggered woefully to her feet. She grabbed the handlebar of the fallen bike, then dropped it with a wince. Her palms had been scraped ragged.

As she stared down at them she sensed a movement nearby and looked up sharply. With arms crossed over his chest and a look of irate impatience etched into his features, Kiel stood watching her.

Ignoring her palms, she reached for her bike. "I had a little spill," she said quickly. "What are you doing back here? Go on, I'll catch up."

"The hell you will," he said angrily, striding toward her with a sure stalk that caused the bike to slip from her suddenly slick fingers. "Some 'little spill': You almost killed yourself."

"Don't worry about—" Rhiannan began, but she broke off

because he had gripped her shoulders, and his eyes were boring into her with lethal intent.

"Don't be ridiculous. You're not getting back on that thing. Leave it to a damned woman driver to be on the wrong damned side of the road!"

"I'm a good driver!"

"Maybe in a car, but you're a walking death wish on a motorbike. Now, madam, you're going to sit down right here and watch my bike while I return yours."

"I am not—"

The pressure on her shoulder suddenly increased and her knees buckled beneath her. Like it or not, she was sitting.

"Uh-uh, don't open your mouth. I mean it. You be here when I get back. I don't care if you want to ride with me or not. I swear, if you've moved an inch, I'll thrash you like a bratty child. And don't doubt it for an instant. I won't feel the least bit sorry about tanning your hide rather than facing the possibility that we might have to peel you off the road!"

Rhiannan closed her mouth, allowing only her narrowed and sparking eyes to tell him exactly what she thought of his form of chivalry. She knew he was right; admitting it was bitter, bitter gall.

She didn't have the nerve to move. At the moment, with tension evident in every ripple of his sleek and powerful muscles and in eyes that had darkened almost to black, she was certain she would wind up facing physical abuse if she did attempt to rise.

He gave her a last warning stare, then plucked her motorbike from the ground with such a vengeance that she was afraid he would actually throw it in the air. A second later the small motor coughed and then purred to his command, and he was swiftly taking it back down the street on the left-hand side of the road.

Humbly, Rhiannan stared at her smarting palms, wondering how it was possible that she could be so miserable on her day out.

It seemed that Kiel had barely gone before she saw him walking back. He didn't approach her, didn't even look at her, but walked straight to his bike, parked on the side of the road. Only when he had straddled it did he turn to her. "Get on."

"This is not the damned Army!" she snapped.

"Get on!"

Rhiannan assured herself that it was only because she knew deep down that she was in the wrong that she stiffly obeyed his last command. She sat, bracing herself on the rear of the seat rather than put her arms about him.

She should have known better.

His voice was the closest thing to a bear's growl she had ever heard from a human being. "Hold on *properly!*"

Biting her lip, she realized that she was only turning embarrassment to humiliation. She slipped her arms around him.

The motorbike coughed into action and they were back on the road. Rhiannan had to admit that it was easier and much less taxing on her nerves and body to ride behind him. But then again, it was more taxing on her circulatory system. She had to press her face against his back to avoid the wind, and she could feel the heat and the steel hardness of his stomach muscles beneath her hands.

Of course, it wasn't so bad as long as they were riding. She could feel the wind whipping by her, playing havoc with her hair. The sun was warm, the freshness of the day exhilarating. And he was very strong and very secure.

But they would stop, and she would have to face him. The others would be around then, and both of them might be exploding inwardly, but neither of them was the type to create a scene and make the day unpleasant for anyone else.

The bike suddenly veered. Rhiannan anxiously pulled her face away from the shield of his broad back to see what he was doing. Surely they hadn't caught up to the group already. They hadn't. The road that encircled the island had the sea to its left, and Kiel was now pulling alongside what looked like a deserted stretch of beach.

"What are you doing?" she asked softly as he stopped the bike and kicked down the kickstand.

"Your hands are a mess," he told her curtly. "For lack of antiseptic, a little seawater may help. Come on."

Rhiannan followed him down to where the azure sea lapped gently against the sandy shoreline. Hunching down, he gripped her wrist and dragged her down beside him.

She winced slightly as the salt burned her cuts, then bit her lip to control her reaction to the pain and keep her features impassive. His hands were surprisingly gentle, considering the state of his temper as he carefully washed her palms, assuring himself that all the tiny particles of dirt and grit had been cleaned away. Then he sat back in the sand, bracing himself with his arms. She knew that he watched her, and she couldn't raise her eyes to his.

"Why did you lie about the bike?" he demanded.

"I didn't really lie. I do know how to ride a bicycle. I assumed it would be the same."

"You're lying again. You did it so that you wouldn't have to ride behind me."

Her eyes widened as she looked at him. "Well, if I did, I certainly had reason enough."

"Because of this morning?"

"You were rude and hostile."

"And I had a damned good reason to be. I might have been killed!"

"I tried to apologize, so I had a good reason not to be with you on—"

"You *are* a brat! You had no right trying to drive that motorbike!"

"Well, you had no right crawling around the rigging like a high school kid who was dared to do some reckless, asinine stunt! There really is no difference—"

"There's a ton of difference! I know how to dive!"

"Oh, dammit, will you leave me alone? I think I would have

preferred being run over by the pickup than being torn apart by you!"

Rhiannan sprang to her feet and started walking toward the parked bike. She was too angry to realize he would stop her, and was stunned when he grabbed her by the arm, jerking her around to face him. A cry of surprise escaped her, but he didn't release her. He pulled her to him, her body pressed to his by the pressure of his other hand at the small of her back.

"*That* is exactly what scares me about you. You'd prefer being smashed by a pickup to facing life. Well, you listen to me, lady, and listen *well* this time. You don't have any monopoly on pain or sorrow—or guilt. And no one—no one living—has the right to hang it all up. Don't you think I know what it's like to wonder why I'm walking around and all those people are dead. I know what it's like to wish that I could die, too, or crawl into some hole where I could try to pretend it never happened. How the hell do you think I felt? *I was the one talking to him!* Maybe I'll never understand what it was to lose a child—two children. I pray to God I'll never have to. But you can thank God you never had to go through the days and months of torture, of wondering if there wasn't something, any small damn thing, that might have saved all those lives, including that of the woman I loved!"

He was hurting her. He had moved his hand from her arm to her nape, and his grip on her neck was so tight that tears were springing to her eyes. But suddenly it wasn't her own pain she was feeling; it was his. And despite all the tension and bitterness that had passed between them, she knew that he was an exceptional man, strong in character as well as body, but vulnerable, humane, and very, very human. For the first time she finally realized how he must have suffered.

"But it wasn't your fault!" she heard herself saying. "Surely you know that it wasn't your fault. You can't still believe that . . . think that . . . worry that you might have . . ."

Was it true? she wondered. Had she really forgiven him, come to believe that he was not guilty? After seeing him and hearing him, she could no longer judge him. Nor for the life of her could she keep herself from wanting to soothe his pain.

He closed his eyes for a moment and she felt him shudder as he at last regained his self-control. His hold on her neck loosened, as did the pressure on her back.

"I'm not a masochist," he told her, "and no, I don't run around daily torturing myself. But it was something I had to learn to live with." He released her completely, then casually put his arm lightly around her shoulders and began to lead her toward the bike.

"We'd better catch up with the others before they start worrying."

Rhiannan silently took her place on the motorbike behind him. She did not feel at all adverse to putting her arms around him, and as they rode it was strangely peaceful and comforting to rest her face against the warm expanse of his back.

They caught up with the others at a rustic native restaurant halfway around the island. The place looked like a patched-up hut on the outside, but it was fastidiously clean, and the aroma of the cooking food was deliciously scintillating. Their group looked up as they entered, and scooted closer together on their bench to make room for the late-comers.

"What happened to you two?" Donald demanded.

Kiel caught Rhiannan's eyes as he stared at her across the table. "Rhiannan had a little trouble with her bike. We decided to ride together." He turned his attention to his menu. "Turtle soup—that's for me. I always did want to try it. 'Annan?" His eyes met hers again. They were a light green. They echoed the polite query of his voice.

"Turtle soup sounds interesting," she replied.

"Looks like turtle soup all around," Donald, to Rhiannan's left, said cheerfully. "And I'm for a beer. That sun is hot as all Hades."

Rhiannan was still gazing at Kiel. He grinned and shrugged. She slowly smiled.

Six

Great Abaco, Eleuthera, Great Inagua. The *Seafire* made her way through the chosen islands. And as the ten days passed, bringing them from port to port, Rhiannan frequently found herself coupled with Kiel. She no longer fought the situation. A calm seemed to have settled between the two of them, as peaceful as the tranquil turquoise of the waters.

The majority of the time they were involved with groups much larger than that which had spent the day circling New Providence. There were diving parties and shelling parties and parties that dressed to the hilt just to go to an island club for an evening. And then there was the never-ending succession of functions aboard the ship. There were small, quiet luncheons and large dinners of mixed nationalities where the debates grew heated.

On the Thursday night when the *Seafire* left the Bahamian waters to sail for the Virgin Islands, the World Without Nukes group settled into the large Manhattan lounge for a full-fledged dinner and debate.

Rhiannan didn't attend. There was a storm brewing, and she was up on deck, enjoying the fierce lash of the wind. The crew were busy running about to trim sail, and were not particularly enjoying the thought of the storm. It meant a lot of hard work and very rocky seas. But there was something very exhilarating about the wind, something wild and dangerous and enticing. When the storm actually broke, Rhiannan knew that all passengers would be ordered to remain below deck. The *Seafire* had antiquated stabilizers, and it was very possible that a too-reckless passenger could end up overboard.

But for now she could luxuriate in the strange feeling of excitement. She could close her eyes and feel the wind blow through her hair and flush her cheeks. Then she could open her eyes and see the water roiling, black and angry.

She had spent some time grabbing and holding lines for the busy sailors, but when the canvas had begun to whip and crack amid the onslaught of the elements, she had been thanked and courteously sent away. But the captain was at the helm, and knew she was still on deck. He would send someone to ask her to go below when the weather became too fierce.

She was somehow deep within herself—and also outside of herself. Never had she felt so thoroughly the elemental power of the earth. Never had she felt as if she were so unimportant in the grand scheme of things, more like a grain of sand on an endless beach. The sea had the power of its waves, and the sky its forceful winds.

Yet, it was also possible for man to best the sea and the wind. They were doing that with the *Seafire*, as it moved among the swells, defying the wind, using the sea. It was dangerous and exciting to face the elements and take them on. It gave a sense of life and also the precariousness of it.

And there was a secret about her that lay within it all. There was an answer out there, and she was just about to touch it, but it kept eluding her. A flight of fancy, she told herself. There was no answer because she hadn't asked any questions. But still that sense was there, a sense of something to be learned from the night and the coming storm.

"Oh!" she gasped suddenly, the startled scream escaping her as a pair of strong arms slipped around her and locked her to the rail. She twisted to see Kiel's face, tense against the wind as he braced her.

"Feeling suicidal again?" he queried dryly, his eyes as dark and murky as the storm clouds.

"No. I like storms. You can let me go. I'm not planning on taking a dive."

"I like to think there's a bit of the cavalier in me," he replied, undaunted. "Call it a male quirk. I saw you standing here and wanted to think that I could offer a shelter if the wind became too rough."

Rhiannan kept her hands on the rail as she studied his features and his eyes curiously.

"Tell me, Kiel, do I remind you of Ellen?" she asked finally.

He laughed, and she felt the deep sound as it rumbled in his chest against her back. "No. Not in the sense you're talking about. Ellen was about five foot two, as blond as the sun, and as gentle as a kitten. Amiable and reasonable."

Rhiannan arched a brow. "I'm neither amiable nor reasonable?"

"Far from reasonable and as amiable as a prickly pear. But I'm glad you asked the question. It's nice to know you were afraid that I was making comparisons."

"I wasn't afraid of anything," Rhiannan retorted coolly. "I was merely trying to discover a 'reasonable' reason for your obsession."

Kiel chuckled softly, and again the sensation was warm and strong and nice. Rhiannan turned again to stare out at the sea, no longer objecting to the arms that braced her.

"How did your meeting go?" she inquired.

"What?" He dipped low to her ear to ask the question. The wind was tearing away the sound of their words.

She twisted to repeat the question, and her lips accidentally brushed his cheek. She pulled away quickly, confused by the pleasant sensation of the touch and the scent of his after-shave.

"I said how did your meeting go?"

He shrugged and instinctively moved more closely against her. "Fine. We have some good articles written and rallies planned. Letters to congressmen and senators and the like. We've been promised television coverage for all the major events."

Rhiannan was silent for a moment. Just as she had inexplicably thought there was something to be gained from the wind and the sea, she felt that there was something special about this moment. Kiel taunted her but didn't pressure her, and his arms around her now felt as good as the wind of the coming storm. There was danger in both but also excitement, that sensation of the elements and of learning.

She was a fool to be with him, just as much a fool as if she were to lean over the rail and plunge into the sea. Both could cast her about like a matchstick, tear her apart like a raging tempest.

She didn't hate him anymore; she didn't blame him anymore. But she still felt that she was half insane to be with him. He was so intense a man, so dominant, confident, and assured. Like the never-ending night sky and the sea around them, he was an endless strength that could too easily engulf her. But still, she didn't want the moment to end.

"Do you think you can ever really accomplish anything with your group?" she asked him, twisting her head just slightly and speaking loudly.

He shrugged and his arms tightened around her. His head inclined toward her ear and she felt the warmth of his breath where the wind had been cold.

"Yes and no. We can make people aware of the danger of losing our entire world, but we can't really control the government—our own, or any other."

"But *you* are the government!"

"A very, very small part of it! And it's a tricky game. I couldn't advocate that the U.S. alone stop production of nuclear weapons because we do have to maintain a balance of power. What the WWON is trying to do is create a forum for reasonable men from all parts of the globe. Reduction must be done simultaneously. We all know that—the major powers and the countries caught in between."

"Makes sense," Rhiannan murmured. She liked to hear him talk. There was something ridiculously soothing in his complete assurance and confidence—and reasonableness. "Reasonable," she added.

"What?"

She laughed and turned to him. The wind caught her hair again and lashed it in soft tendrils across his face. He chuckled with her and at last released her to untangle the ebony strands that encompassed him.

"I said you were reasonable!" Rhiannan proclaimed, joining with him to retrieve the wild strands of her hair and twist them into a knot at her nape.

"I think it would be reasonable to get inside!" he announced.

"I—"

At that second the rain began. It wasn't a soft, warning pelt; it came down in sudden torrents.

Kiel grasped her hand. "Come on!"

She could barely breathe as the wind robbed her of breath and the rain drenched her. But his hand was firm on hers, and she was being dragged along blindly. He was a shelter against the wind.

She collided with his back as they reached his cabin and he fumbled with the key, but a second later the door was open and he was shoving her inside to welcome relief from the rain. The ship took a sharp list as he closed the door behind him. Rhiannan, still catching her breath and balance, staggered, crashing against the bed and plopping less than gracefully upon it.

Kiel balanced himself by the door, then turned around to laugh at her. "Make yourself at home."

She was dripping all over the bedspread and quickly got to her feet. "Sorry," she murmured. "That last wave took me by surprise." *And I am suddenly very, very nervous,* she added silently. She glanced around at the cabin, which was approximately the same size as Donald's. Tasteful, uncluttered, simple, but elegant—and dominated by the bed.

Rhiannan brushed several strands of wet hair from her brow and grimaced. "I think I just soaked your bed."

"No problem. It's quite large."

"So I see." She felt a bit like a fly that had just discovered itself fully caught in the spider's web. "You know, I appreciate your rushing me out of the rain, but I just realized that, uh, I really need to get to my own cabin. Dry clothes, you know."

"It's still raining," he said, leaning against the doorway and watching her with amusement in his eyes. The corners of his lips strained not to curl. "And that's the one problem with Donald's deluxe cabins: You can't go from these to below without crossing the open deck. You'd be drenched worse if you walked out now."

"Still . . ."

"You're afraid of me."

"No. I'm not. Should I be?"

He allowed himself to grin and lifted his arms in an innocent gesture. "That's up to you." Leaving the doorway, he walked to one of the dressers and dug through a drawer. He pulled out a large football jersey.

"Here, why don't you hop into a hot shower and put this thing on. It should come to your knees—nice and modest."

Rhiannan hesitated. "The ship is pitching."

"Not anymore. Feel it. The wind has died down since the rain began. You should manage."

"I . . ."

His grin became annoyingly broader. "Rhiannan, the bathroom has a lock. Feel free to use it."

"I automatically use bathroom locks. But I just—"

"Feel funny?"

"I suppose. And what about you? You're drenched."

"I can hop in right after you, and I never use locks in my own cabin."

A blush rose to her cheeks. If she had any sense, she'd run back into the rain. Why did she always feel so determined to prove him wrong? She was afraid of him and she should be running like a hare. But she was irritated by her blush and angry with her fear. She was a mature adult, a determined one. She should be able to play an adult game and call the moves and also call it quits if it went too far. All he had done was take her into his cabin and offer her a hot shower and a dry shirt, and already she was running scared.

"I hardly think that you need to lock a door against me," she said, still without moving or accepting the shirt.

He threw it across the room so that she was forced by reflex to catch it.

"Does that imply that you do need to lock it against me?" he inquired, barely concealing his laughter.

Rhiannan gave him a dry, unamused smile. "You wouldn't dream of forcing a woman into anything?"

He was undaunted by her sarcasm. "No, I wouldn't. And I'm sure, despite your defenses, you aren't in the least afraid of being forced into anything. You are afraid of yourself, not me. So I'll make this easy for you. I never take what isn't given, but I'll be damned if I turn down an invitation. If you're afraid of yourself or the consequences of being here with me, go on, run. I'll even escort you back through the rain. If not, hop into that shower before I plop you in myself. One of us will end up with pneumonia."

Rhiannan issued a grunt of exasperation and spun toward the bathroom door, trailing the shirt over her shoulder. "You needn't worry about any invitations, Congress—" She broke off, her eyes opening with alarm as he suddenly appeared at the door ahead of her, opening it and cutting her off.

He laughed at the naked panic in her features, panic she hadn't had time to mask.

"I'm not attacking you, Mrs. Collins. Just thought I'd raid the refrigerator before you went in." He swept by her into what he called the shower stall and knelt before a small refrigerator set below the double sink. "I should have some champagne in here. Cheese and crackers are in the dresser, but ah—here! Pepperoni."

"Do you frequently entertain in your bathroom, Congressman?"

"Every chance I get," he replied lightly.

She'd asked for that, Rhiannan supposed, but she was hit by a sudden stab of jealousy again. Had he ever entertained Joan Kendrick in his cabin?

She glanced down at his dark head as he plucked things from the refrigerator, grabbing two ice trays from the minuscule freezer section.

"Don't bother on my account; I'm not hungry," she murmured.

"For shame, Mrs. Collins. You should never imbibe champagne without munching on something, especially when the sea is rolling like this."

"I really don't need any champagne."

"Dear Lord, you must think I'm a mad rapist or a seducer of innocents," he said, standing. The ample bathroom suddenly seemed very small. His damp shoulders seemed to fill it.

"I'm hardly an innocent," she murmured.

"A thaw in the Queen of Hearts!" he chuckled. "Watch it, lady, that sounded dangerously close to an invitation."

"Well, it wasn't. Could you get out of here, please? You were yelling at me about pneumonia."

"I'm going, madam. Have to set up the seduction scene."

"Don't you dare."

"I'm only going to break some of these ice trays into a bucket so that I can open the champagne. You'll be able to drink it, I'm quite sure."

He swept past her, raising a brow with a devilish intent that mocked her into another blush—but thankfully, one that he didn't see as the door clicked shut behind him.

She bit her lip, exhaling a long, exasperated breath. He hadn't touched her, except to slip by her, since they had entered the cabin. She was making a bit of a fool of herself, defending what he wasn't attacking.

Rhiannan turned around and clicked the lock. She listened,

half expecting to hear him laugh, but she heard only the sound of soft music as he inserted a tape into a recorder. Was he setting the seduction scene? Yes, but he had warned her to leave and his words had rung very true with her. He wouldn't want anything that wasn't given.

"Oh, who am I kidding?" she whispered to herself. "He does want to go to bed with me, and I would probably be insulted if he didn't want to."

Impatiently she began to undo the buttons on her blouse, tossing it on the tile floor when she finished. She stripped off her jeans, then paused self-consciously. In a minute she would be naked with him not more than twenty feet away at most. There was a door between them, she reminded herself. A locked door. But the door had nothing to do with her feelings. If only she could have her night of darkness with a total stranger! A lost moment in time—one she would never have to answer for when it was over. . . .

There was a large mirror over the double sinks. Rhiannan noted her wide eyes and pale face. She turned away from her reflection as she slipped out of her bra and underpants. She didn't want to see herself. She didn't want to know if "gravity" had already set in. Not that it mattered, she assured herself. She might want to have a secret night with Kiel Whellen, but logically she didn't want an affair with him. They were still antagonists on one level, but since the day they had gone to Nassau, they had also become friends. She knew that he did care for her, and she had to admit that along with being fascinated by him, she liked him. But she wanted no emotional involvements in her life. She didn't want to care again. She might have forgiven him and admitted that she actually liked him, but that was as far as she was willing to go.

Again she thought of Joan Kendrick and wondered if the young blonde had ever been in Kiel's shower.

Oh, God! She groaned to herself. What was the matter with her?

He had never displayed any interest in Joan other than a

casual friendship. Rhiannan decided that anything more than that she had to be inventing herself. He was always polite to Joan, but if he danced with her or escorted her on his arm, it was always at Rhiannan's suggestion.

It would serve me right if they were having a hot and heavy affair, she thought. *And it would probably be better for me. Damn! If the voyage would only end!*

Rhiannan wound her hair back and turned on the shower. The water was hot, the spray nice and hard. She didn't realize how chilled she had become until she felt the warmth seep through her body.

She closed her eyes again and let the water flow around her, steaming the world to mist as the boat rocked beneath her.

Tonight the shower brought Paul to mind, causing her to remember the times they had showered together. They had been so comfortably married, so accustomed to one another.

She remembered Paul counting off the days after the baby had been born, and then the night that Jenny was five weeks old. Rhiannan could remember it so well because Paul never shaved at night, and that night he had. He had decided to shave while she was in the shower. Then he had joined her in the shower with such a plaintive appeal in his eyes that she had laughed and they had kissed and teased one another beneath the water for so long that both had been on fire.

"Let's dry off quickly," Paul had told her. "Better yet, let's not dry off at all!"

They had giggled like teenagers all the way to the bed. Paul didn't like to make love in a tub. He was too tall and too angular, and the one time they had tried it, both had come out of the experience too bruised to call it ecstasy. Yet, they had laughed.

She had laughed. It had been so easy with Paul. She had known how much he had loved her, and if she was less than perfect, he had loved her anyway. She hadn't been afraid he wouldn't find her physically appealing after the baby. If her breasts were less firm, it was a small sacrifice for the beautiful baby, the sweet tiny life that was no more. . . .

"Hey! Are you alive in there?"

Rhiannan shook, then covered her face with her hands. How long had she been standing there, lost in memory? She turned off the water with a jerk. The bathroom looked as if a heavy fog had rolled in.

"I'm alive!" she called out, trying for a cheerful sound that fell flat. The water on her cheeks was salty. She had been crying again.

Kiel was strangely silent on the other side of the door. Rhiannan grabbed one of the huge snowy towels with *Seafire* stitched on it and wrapped it around herself, drying her face with the tip. "I—I'm sorry. I'm coming right out."

He didn't answer, and she searched around quickly for the jersey he had given her. She slipped it over her shoulders and noted with satisfaction that it did almost reach her knees.

She picked up her soaked shirt and jeans and hung them on the rack where the towel had been. When she noted her soaked undergarments still on the floor where she had left them, she plucked them up. Then she tucked the bra into the sleeve of her shirt and bent hastily to slip into the matching panties.

She hesitated as the material slipped over her foot. They hadn't been so terribly soaked to begin with, but since she had left them on the floor and dripped all over them, they were wet now.

I have to have something on! she told herself. Why? She planned on keeping her legs discreetly together. How would he ever know? Even to make the run back to her own cabin when the rain stopped, she would be okay. The jersey was definitely modest. She rolled her panties into a little knot and stuck them into the sleeve of her shirt, along with her bra.

Before he could call out to her again, she threw open the bathroom door, only to find him standing right outside. The steam followed her out like a rush of smoke.

Kiel stared at her curiously, then at the bathroom, and then at her again. "Maybe I should have forced the issue and showered with you," he told her. "Think there might be any hot water left?"

"I really am sorry. I should have gone to my own cabin. I—"

"I was joking," he said quietly, catching her chin in his hand and lifting her face gently so she could meet his quizzical eyes. "You forget who owns this ship. Donald can't stand cold showers, even when it's roasting outside. I'm sure his hot-water tanks can go forever."

He released her and turned back to the dresser to rummage around again. "Would a pair of cutoffs offend your sensibilities?" he asked idly, his back to her.

"No. It's your cabin. Make yourself comfortable."

"That's leading."

"It was intended to be polite."

"All right, it's taken politely. I poured you a glass of champagne. It's on the bedside table."

Rhiannan wandered over to the little table, then perched on the edge of the bed beside it. The top of the nightstand held a brass lamp, a clock radio, and a little tray set up with two glasses of champagne—one half consumed—and a plate with the cheese, crackers, and pepperoni artfully arranged. The champagne bottle was on the floor beside the little nightstand. She noted the brand, a French name a cut above Dom Pérignon, and glanced over to Kiel. He had stripped off his tie and damp jacket and had placed his cuff links in a small upper drawer of his dresser.

She smiled, knowing that her question was probably offensive, but would not be taken so. "Are you as rich as Midas, too, Kiel?"

He laughed. "No. I'm not poor, but I'm not filthy rich."

"Where did you meet Donald?"

"Believe it or not, we grew up on the same street. His folks owned the mansion on the hill; the rest of us were just street bums. We used to like to tease him to death; you know how kids are. But Donald slugged the hell out of one of my brothers one day and I had to challenge him to a fight. We both came out of it pretty well messed up, but neither of us dared call pax. We both wound up on the ground, staring at each other. Donald finally told me that we were both making monkeys out of ourselves and wouldn't I rather come up to the house and have an ice cream than give him another black eye and get one in return. I was ready to agree. Then he invited us all up to swim one day—the Flahertys had a fantastic Olympic-size pool—and we all became friends."

"That sounds like Donald," Rhiannan said, not without a touch of pride for her employer.

"He never changes," Kiel agreed. He stripped off his shirt, and Rhiannan picked up her champagne quickly, suddenly shy about staring at his muscular chest with its wealth of crisp dark hair. She almost gulped down the full glass.

"I'll be right out," he told her, walking toward the shower. He paused just outside the door, glancing her way, a slight smile on his lips, his brows drawn and puzzled. "Unless shower hypnotism is contagious."

Rhiannan lowered her eyes quickly, plucking a piece of pepperoni from the tray.

When the bathroom door closed, she stood and prowled the cabin restlessly. It occurred to her that she had been in Donald's cabin—so similar to this—dozens of times. But it had never seemed so intimate. Tonight she noticed all the little things that made the cabin uniquely Kiel's. The half-open closet doors with its row of neatly hung suits and jackets. The dresser with his comb and brush, cuff-link box, and watch. His tie flung carelessly on it . . . over a small note and a bill. Rhiannan stared at it from a distance, reminding herself that anything sent to him was none of her business. She didn't pry. She had never opened mail, even junk mail, when it had come addressed to Paul.

She ate another piece of pepperoni. Sat. Stood. And then

gave up. She walked over to the dresser. She didn't touch the tie; she didn't need to. The note was brief and in Donald's scrawl.

"The five bucks I owe you! Keep forgetting. Dumb bet! I set it all up against myself! Anyway, this is your official five for Rhiannan."

She felt her reaction from head to toe. Anger was like liquid fire, beginning in the pit of her stomach, spreading through her limbs, rushing to her face. It was so strong that she couldn't think, only react.

She plucked the note from the dresser and sailed toward the bathroom door, barging in fiercely with the strength of a prize-fighter. She still didn't stop to think. She ripped the curtain open and waved the note beneath his nose.

"What the hell—?" he began.

"That's right, Congressman. What the hell is this? A bet? I'm a five-dollar *bet?*"

The water kept running as he stared at her, his eyes narrowing as they flashed from her to the note in her hand.

"You *bastard!*" Rhiannan exclaimed furiously. It didn't seem enough. She dropped the note and, still without thinking, tried to slap him.

He caught her arm in midair. "Wait a minute, Rhiannan—" he began, his voice menacing. But the physical contact between them was a jolt that drained her of fury and forced her to think at last. She had just slammed into the room and attacked him—in his shower.

Inadvertently her eyes slipped down his frame, bronze and slick with wetness, as hard and trim and as male as any woman could possibly desire.

She jerked her wrist from him. "Oh, never mind. I'm getting out of here." She spun on her heels and started out. She was ready to run with rising panic when she heard his voice thunder out behind her.

"Oh, no you're not."

The shower continued to rush and roar as he heedlessly

stepped from it, catching her shoulders and spinning her around to face him.

"You're not going anywhere until you give me a chance to explain."

"No! I don't want an explanation! It's all clear!"

"No, it's not—"

"You're not dressed!"

"I seldom am in the shower. Surely you suspected that when you came stomping in."

"Let me go. I want to get out of here." Why was it so hard to keep her eyes fixed on his? And why couldn't she stop trembling, shaking?

"I'll let you go as soon as you're willing to listen."

Rhiannan tossed her head back and managed to make her voice faintly cynical. "I thought you never forced a woman, Congressman. You're forcing me to stay."

"Only long enough to listen, Mrs. Collins," he snapped in return. "And if you can burst into a shower, I can force you to hear what I have to say."

Rhiannan swallowed and closed her eyes. She had to get out of there. He made her do ridiculous things. Anger, pride, and fear all took control when he was around. She didn't behave normally around him at all.

Use your wits, she warned herself. They should have been in abundance, because she hadn't used them once so far.

Rhiannan went limp beneath his grip.

"All right," he said quietly. "I'll just turn off the shower and dress quickly if you wait one minute."

She nodded and waited until he had released her and turned around to switch off the water. Then she turned again and made a dash for the door.

It was a foolish venture, over before it had begun. She was still running when her feet left the floor. She was gasping with the breath knocked from her, flat on her back on the bed, and to her utter devastation he straddled her, pinning her wrists to her sides.

"This is——" she began.

"Don't give me any of your speeches about force or brutality—not when you pull tricks like that."

Rhiannan went perfectly rigid, gritting her teeth and closing her eyes. The jersey had been hiked up almost to her waist and the embrace of his thighs over hers felt as hot as a brushfire. She was afraid to move, to breathe, to open her eyes. To admit even to herself that more than anything she would love to reach up and ease the anger from his features and ask that he hold her and promise that she would never have to lose him.

"Now, listen to me . . ." he began coldly.

"You said you'd get dressed," she hissed.

"That was before you decided to play at being Secretariat. That bet didn't mean a damn thing."

"This is chauvinistic, macho, brute force, and——"

"And if you don't shut up, you're going to be the first woman who has received anything resembling brute force at my hands. The bet involved Donald more than it did me; I had forgotten all about it. He was sure you would refuse to go into Nassau if you knew I was coming along. I said you wouldn't. That was the whole damn thing. I swear, I'd forgotten all about it until I saw the note he left me!"

She opened her eyes. His features were hard, strained, and tense. His eyes were dark, as gray as the storm pounding about them. They were angry but also pained and wistful. "Why?" he asked her in a hoarse whisper.

"I don't know what you're talking about," she said.

"Yes you do. You keep fighting yourself, not me. Why, Rhiannan? Just let it be."

She swallowed again, then spoke. "You said you wouldn't seduce me."

"I said I wouldn't force you."

"You *are* forcing me."

"Only to talk. Anything else is your decision."

He held her eyes, impaled by his own. With a little cry she

managed to break the contact while a tug of war went on inside of her. She could feel him so thoroughly, the hands that held her firmly but not hurtingly, his knees hugging her torso, his bristly hair through the jersey. She could feel his bare flesh exuding controlled power, tension, longing. He ignored his state of arousal, but she couldn't. She felt him pressed against the soft flesh of her belly, making her vulnerable with the longing to know rapture once again. A different rapture. A different man. She couldn't hide as she so longed to do. She couldn't escape the elements or the truth. She would have to face him again, in full light, both knowing the other for all that he or she was. . . .

Tonight, just this once she'd give in to her desire, because she was flesh and blood and needed to feel loved, even if that love was a stolen illusion.

"You don't understand!" she lashed out with sudden vengeance. "If I were to stay with you, if we were to . . . to . . ."

"Make love?" he supplied harshly.

"Yes, make love!" she sputtered. "If we were to make love . . . it wouldn't be fair. It wouldn't be right. I would only be using you."

He stared at her for a long, tense moment. He didn't laugh or smile, but studied her turbulent eyes, the struggle and fear within them, the confusion.

He wasn't angry. He betrayed no emotion whatsoever. Slowly he released her wrists. He lightly cupped her cheek and chin with his calloused palm.

"Then use me, Rhiannan. I'll take my chances. Use me."

Seven

"Illusion is often grander than truth, Congressman. I . . . I hope you're not going to be disappointed."

At last he smiled and shifted his weight beside hers. He leaned on an elbow and bent his head over hers, taking possession of her mouth slowly, gently, savoringly. But the tender assault was resolute and sure. His lips covered hers in a persuasive caress, then the tip of his tongue softly rimmed them until they parted. He moved more heavily against her and his tongue slipped into her mouth, filling it, giving her an exotic preliminary to all that was to come of delving into all her secret places, tasting and exploring with the greatest leisure.

He was making her want more and more of him, intent on fusing her mouth to his, returning the seeking thrust of his tongue with her own, reaching to touch and savor and enjoy, to feel the shiver of desire begin within her, fan out. His scent was so pleasant, the clean smell of soap and something deeper yet tighter, pleasantly, uniquely male, like the strength and warmth of his hard-muscled chest, the teasing of his coarse hair, the intimate feel of his leg angled over hers. . . .

If only they were in darkness . . . if only she could hide, she could let the hunger grow. She could reach out and take all that he had to offer. She could let her inhibitions and fears drain away with the fading of the telling light.

He pulled away from her and traced the dampness of her lips with his forefinger. "I prefer reality to illusion anytime," he murmured huskily. "It is far superior in every way."

She tried to smile. She wanted him so badly, but suddenly she felt awkward.

He leaned to kiss her again. She stopped him, moistening her already moist lips to whisper, "The lights, Kiel."

He paused, then stiffened, and the tenderness within him swelled as surely as the fever of his desire for her.

It would be so easy to oblige her, to rise and cast the room into darkness, to let her mix her dreams of the past with the reality of the present. She would come to him as sweetly as a kitten, and then return his love with reckless passion and all the daring sensuality he had always sensed within her. It would be easy to still the haunted fear within her eyes. But although he couldn't let her know it, he loved her, and he couldn't allow her the easy way out.

He shook his head and smiled ruefully. "I want you to know who you're making love with," he told her softly.

Her eyes widened. "I do know, but . . ." Her lashes lowered halfway over the stunning green. "Kiel, it's been . . . a long time. I'll be so self-conscious, lying here with you. . . ."

Her voice trailed away and he allowed himself to chuckle softly. "I promise, I'll make you forget all about covering up."

Her eyes grew wide, a spark of defiance within them. "Sure of yourself, aren't you, Congressman?"

"Uh-huh," he murmured. "I'm sure I've never wanted anything in my life as I want you. And I'm also sure that you are all done stalling!"

This time his kiss was not so gentle. It consumed her with unleashed passion. It swept her away. His arms locked around her and drew her to him, and in seconds she was breathless and dizzy—and eager for more and more of him. She was glad of the naked flesh that touched her, of the hard male body she hadn't dared to appreciate. Where skin brushed skin she was on fire; yet, even through the jersey she could feel him with every nerve. She was alive as she hadn't been for so long, and like a sleepwalker awakened to the brilliant light of day, her senses were acutely honed, almost painfully so.

Did every man have cheeks that felt so wonderful, clean-shaven yet telling with their lightest brush against the softness of her own chest that he was overwhelmingly male to the core.

And his hands. . . . His right hand threaded through her hair, his left moved to her knee, grazing upward leisurely over her hip, rounding her waist, pulling the hem of the jersey along, higher and higher.

She started to shake at his touch, her inner being opening up to him. Her last defenses were down, but it didn't matter. Not when she had the taste of him. Not when her fingers skimmed along his back and felt the delicious ripple of hot, hard muscle beneath them. Not when her eyes were closed and she hungrily returned his kiss. Not when his hand continued its subtly erotic movement, spanning the curve of her waist, sliding to her hip, the fingers drawing lazy circles that teased and teased, igniting an ever brighter flame deep in her secret center, but didn't touch, letting the need rise and skyrocket until she groaned deep in her throat.

Then they were rolling together, still locked in the embrace. The jersey was a knot about her waist. He cradled her buttocks, pressing her against him, enjoying the firm roundness, the soft texture of her skin.

He broke the kiss, raising her above him. His eyes were both smoldering gray and blue fire as they burned speculatively into hers. She quickly lowered her lashes, somewhat ashamed of her ardent response. She wanted to bury her face against his shoulder, but he wouldn't let her.

"Take off the jersey, Rhiannan," he said passionately.

She hesitated. Maybe he should have made it easier for her, but he wanted everything from her now. His senses were pounding like a drumbeat; his nerves were as tight as piano wire. His desire for her had become torture, but an exquisite torture. She was sitting over his waist, and the soft embrace of her thighs was almost more than he could bear. He had the strange feeling that he could toss her onto her back and take her with no protest from her. He could ease the building explosiveness inside of him now, but he wanted more than to have her. He wanted to hold her. He wanted her to need him with more than desire.

"Rhiannan," he whispered, and his fingers brushed her lips and brow, his knuckles grazing her cheeks. "Give to me," he murmured.

She crossed her arms to reach for the hem of the jersey and pulled it over her head, extricating her arms and allowing it to fall beside her. Her eyes met his.

He reached up to touch her, his open palms lightly brushing her nipples; then slowly his fingers moved around to cradle her full breasts. They quivered to his touch and swelled, and she swallowed, then closed her eyes, pressing against him. But he was content to go slowly for the moment, savoring her with his eyes. His fingers stroked her gently as his eyes devoured her.

"Look at me for a moment," he told her hoarsely, and her thick lashes flew open, allowing him to delve into the emerald green of her eyes. She was so exotic. The waves of ebony hair streaming down her back, framing and cascading over her creamy skin. She sat tall and proud, her features fine, her throat long and graceful, her shoulders slender and straight, her collarbone dipping to hollows that tempted a man to touch. And then her breasts, firm, full, and mature, with dark pink nipples, beautiful crescents over the sleekness of her rib cage, the narrowness of her waist.

"Kiel . . ." she suddenly pleaded, and he laughed with pleasure at the sound of his name on her lips, threading his fingers through her hair once and cradling her neck as he shifted to sweep her to his side. He planted a flurry of light, impassioned kisses over her face, her brow, her cheeks, while avoiding her mouth. Then he pressed his lips against her throat, running the tip of his tongue down its length, finding the hollow at the juncture of her collarbone. His mouth moved downward again, his face buried reverently between her breasts.

His hands slid beneath her to cup her buttocks as he shifted again, his lips grazing over a nipple, his teeth nipping lightly. A shudder rippled through her as he drew the full nipple into his mouth and teased it with the length of his tongue. He felt her jerk; he heard a strangled gasp from within her throat. Her nails raked across his back, and his entire body echoed her shudder.

"Like this?" he demanded throatily after repeating the moist caress on her left breast. He lifted his head to find her eyes once more. They were wide and unflinching.

"Yes," she said softly.

His eyes lowered to her breasts again. "You're perfect," he murmured, bending to kiss her ribs.

"No," she whispered breathlessly, "I'm not. Please don't expect perfect."

"But you are perfect to me. All my expectations have been met."

She shivered but did not deny him as his lips roamed to her waist, as his tongue laved the soft flesh of her abdomen. "You taste like the sea and the sun and the wind," he murmured. "Rhiannan . . ."

Low on her belly, along the angle of her hip, was an almost invisible silver line. She jerked when his tongue traced it.

"I told you I wasn't perfect!" she rasped suddenly.

He could have kicked himself. The line was a tiny stretch mark. Proof that she had been a mother. A reminder of the children that she had lost.

She was withdrawing from him into her heart, into her secret self, regretting that she had made herself vulnerable to him. And maybe she was even afraid. A younger woman, a woman who had never borne a child would not have such a mark.

But he could not retreat, not when their future hung precariously before them. Not when it felt as if his blood boiled like lava, setting a shrill tempo for every nerve in his system.

"Kiel!" she gasped, her fingers digging into his hair, dragging at it. He ignored the harsh pull on his scalp and lifted her buttocks slightly, purposely kissing the line again. And before she could vent another protest, he slid his fingers down her thighs to her knees, parting them with a swift, fluid movement that was firm enough to prevent any objection.

He raised his head to look at her, and when he spoke it was harshly. "Don't shrink from me, my love, ever. Everything about you is beautiful to me. Even the line, Rhiannan. It's part of you, just like the years and events gone past. The good and the bad, Rhiannan. Everything that has happened to us is what makes us, and I could not want you the way that I do without you being what and who you are."

Her eyes stayed on his without wavering, but a mist of tears was forming over them. Her lips, beautifully puffed and dampened from his kisses, were quivering.

"Maybe we should wait—" she began.

"Wait, hell!" he exploded.

Suddenly his hands were in her hair and his mouth was on hers, fusing with it almost brutally but also so givingly. Again she felt his hand along her side, his fingers touching and cherishing, stroking her hip, her thigh. She could feel him, the wonderful firmness of his body, already between the shivering length of her legs.

She wanted him and she wanted him to want her, wanted him to believe that she was perfect.

But she was so frightened, for now she was not searching to recapture the past. She was completely embracing the present—and that present was him. Everything else dimmed when he touched her, kissed her, overwhelmed her with his demanding, taut, sinewy body. She was pliant and needy as he touched her and wedged his hips against hers.

He lifted his lips from hers at last and stared demandingly into her eyes. He shifted to stroke her upper thighs with his fingers first, to search out her center, to stroke her again until she cried out and then to bring himself fully into her, thrusting deeply, opening her to him. For a second she panicked. She was so vulnerable and so completely his. The muscular length of his body, his firm hips, his long legs, possessed her.

But the panic subsided almost instantly. He possessed her, yes, but he filled her with desire and life. He was strong and potent, and she felt him inside her, demanding, giving, starting the fire again, stoking the flames. All that she had needed was being given to her. All that had ached for his touch was being touched. And beneath his skillful hands she could give in return. She could arch to meet him with joy, taking him into her more deeply, embracing his ardor with her own. As passion consumed them she met his lips again and again, locking her arms around him, thrilling to the sporadic tension of his muscles beneath her fingers.

The fire grew ever greater within her, and there was nothing for her except the warmth of his skin, the whisper of his breath, the demanding stroke of his heat and strength within her. Their lovemaking was so good, it was almost unbearable, and it kept climbing, soaring, as they moved in perfect fusion, embroiled in their passion, seeking one another with lips and tongues again and again until she felt him pause, move into her with his whole being, shudder, and release into a new blaze of fire that brought about her own shuddering peak with the pure deliciousness of pleasure and pride in her sex and being.

The wonder, the sweetness, enveloped her. She suddenly felt the soft rocking of the ship and heard the wind outside the cabin. But he still dominated her body and mind. His bronzed skin was slick with perspiration. His hand lay lazily upon her breast. His hair teased her cheek. His breathing slowed with hers, as did the pounding of his heart.

She couldn't remember feeling so wonderful. Nor could she completely accept that he had been hers. Only now did Rhiannan realize completely how essentially masculine he was—how trim, how strong. His body was sleek and powerful, but his masculinity was more than a physical thing. It was in his thoughts, in his sensitivities, and in all the little things that added up to his great strength of character.

She was afraid to open her eyes, afraid to let him go before it could all fade away—the drowsy sense of completion, of fulfillment, of intimacy and total sharing and now, sweet relaxation combined with a little bit of awe.

"Stay with me tonight," he said suddenly.

She opened her eyes. His head was on the pillow, close to hers, and his eyes, as usual, were dark and fathomless.

But even as they lay there, even as she wondered if she could lose him when he wasn't with her, when he wasn't a part of her, she felt a new intimacy. It was good just to lie beside him naked. His nudity gave her a strange sense of power. She could still reach out and touch him, feel him, explore him. He was, despite his obvious strength, vulnerable to her, as she was to him.

"I—"

"Don't run," he told her, lifting himself up on an elbow to splay her hair out over the pillow in wild splendor as he spoke. "Don't run away from me now. I want to hold you as I sleep. I can't let you go, and I can't let you do it to yourself."

Rhiannan reached up and touched his cheek, following the line of his brow with the nail of her forefinger. There was wonder in her eyes, in her touch. "I'll stay," she said softly.

"Every other Sunday we spent the day at my mom's. And every other Saturday she and Dad kept the kids. Mom was convinced that the flare went out of most marriages because it's hard, especially in this day and age, to make ends meet, take care of children, and have the energy left over to be romantic. She and Dad were great."

Rhiannan looked from the pillow to Kiel. He had poured more champagne and pulled the covers down so that they might slip beneath them, and he had opened a dresser drawer to produce a battery-operated video machine with a dozen game tapes. As they munched on the cheese and leisurely drained the champagne, he had challenged her to a game.

Now they lay comfortably together, and he had begun to

ask her questions about her past, and to her surprise she had wanted to answer them.

It still hurt so badly, but by the same token it felt good to talk about her past. It made Paul more real and brought the children back to her. That they were gone was hard to bear, but until tonight she hadn't realized that her hiding from the truth and pretending that they had never existed was even worse. They had lived, and they had been special, beautiful, and unique. To bury herself and the memory of the love that had been hers was the greatest disservice to herself—and to them.

But what was she doing? she wondered with a little shiver of horror. Lying naked in bed with another man, a man with whom she had just made passionate love, and talking easily about the man who had been her husband, and the little boy and infant girl who had been her whole life up until about two years ago.

She shouldn't be talking about her husband when she was indulging in an affair with a man who could stalk about with naked grace while she was lying in his bed, still flushed with the feel of his body against hers. A man who, with or without blame, had had a hand in the death of her husband and children. It shouldn't have felt so right. . . .

And the virile congressman was probably bored to tears with her reminiscences. If this was just an affair, he should want no more from her than what he had already gotten. Unless it was to hold her in his arms again and enjoy the undeniable chemistry once more.

Rhiannan wanted to make love again, and she was certain that he did. She was suddenly just as certain that he wanted her to be relaxed, to talk, to feel completely comfortable with him, without having to be in the throes of passion.

He was smiling at her, and the curve of his lip was gentle, his eyes warm. He didn't look bored; he looked comfortable. He looked like Paul had when they had talked at night.

"Your parents sound like very wonderful people," he told

her, smoothing a strand of hair from her forehead. "They must miss you. When were you last home?"

"About a year ago. Yes, I guess they miss me. I miss them. But I think they understand that being away is best for me."

"Maybe," Kiel murmured, "but perhaps you should think about going home more often. Sometimes when you stay away you make it worse."

Rhiannan looked at him curiously. There were times when he had hurt her terribly, but only because he was trying to reach her. Then his words and suggestions had been to help her, to reassure her, and only once, on that day in Nassau, when she had realized the truth herself, had *she* ever offered *him* any gentle words.

"Kiel," she said suddenly, "I—I don't know if I'm saying this right, but I'm very sorry about Ellen."

He didn't look at her but he smiled, his lashes closing over his eyes as he drew a finger idly along her inner arm. "Thank you. I think that after the sorrow, the worst is the rage. You think of someone young and beautiful with a wonderful, gentle spirit to offer the world. And you think of the waste. Then you have to believe that there is a grand scheme to things, that there is a God, and that He has His reasons for what He does. For a long time I couldn't go near the Smithsonian or the National Zoological Park or a dozen other places that we used to go to a lot together. I did leave Washington, but"—he looked at her, grimacing, and shrugged—"I'm afraid that congressmen have to spend a lot of time in Washington, and in time I learned to like remembering. I would think of something she had said, something incredibly wise or funny, and I would start to smile, realizing that I was glad that she had touched my life."

Rhiannan was silent for a moment. "That's lovely," she said at last. "But . . ."

"But what?"

She found herself nervously smoothing the sheet. "Well, you've acquired a bit of a reputation since then. Are you trying to find her again? In another woman?"

"No. Not the way you mean."

"Then—"

"Then why the reputation of going from woman to woman? For one thing, it's vastly exaggerated. For another, there just hasn't been another serious involvement. There are things I'm looking for, but not things that make a woman 'like Ellen.' We all have things we look for in a person; things that are important to our own makeups. Maybe we don't really understand it. Maybe it's in the way we want to live, in the things that are priorities to us. Not a perfect match; that would never work. Too dull. But you need the same commitment to loving, to making the other person important in every way." He laughed suddenly. "I don't really think I can explain exactly what I'm trying to say. Feelings can be too nebulous."

He rolled over suddenly, rising up on his elbows and stroking the line of her cheek with the back of his forefinger. "Rhiannan . . ." he murmured. "I love the name, and I thought it only existed in a song."

Rhiannan smiled. "It's existed for centuries and centuries. It's an old Welsh name."

"Your father is Welsh?"

"My mother."

"Ahhh."

"And actually it was a name generally given to males way back when."

"Males, huh?"

"Yes."

"Never again. You are far too female to even imagine such a thing. And the name—"

"Fits me?"

"Uh-huh. Because you're as beautiful and elusive as the wind. But I'm sure your husband told you that."

"Thank you. Sometimes he did."

"What was he like?"

"Paul?" Rhiannan thought for a moment. "Gentle. Tall, lanky, easygoing."

She was surprised when he picked up her hand almost idly, then kissed the back and then the palm. "He must have been very special. He had you."

But then Rhiannan began to wonder if she had imagined the moment, because he shifted suddenly, reaching over to the bedside table to pour them each more champagne, then pressing her glass into her hand. "Sit up now and drink this. I'm trying to have a night of decadent pleasure and I can't get you even slightly inebriated."

Rhiannan sat up, dragging the sheet along with her over her breasts. She accepted the glass from him and smiled. "Why do you need me inebriated?" she asked.

"I don't, but I do need you awake. There's nothing like making love to a woman who falls asleep when you kiss her. Devastating on the male ego."

Rhiannan studied the lines of his face. They were somehow handsome and also very rugged—clean lines, hard lines, but his smile could always soften the harshness of the contours.

She liked the way he looked against the sheet and pillow. His flesh very dark, the taut expanse of his chest very broad. His hair was tousled, and again she felt a special feminine power from just being with him. She knew that he had had a number of women. He was too expert a lover not to be well experienced. But the past didn't bother her, perhaps because she felt she couldn't have a future with him. The moment was enough for her. She had something no other woman did. She had him in bed, and she could share this intimacy with him as a prelude to the moments to come.

She smiled. "I can't believe any woman ever fell asleep during one of your kisses," she told him dryly.

He grinned. "I'll never tell." He reached over her again and plucked a piece of cheese from the tray, offering it to Rhiannan. She bit the cheese, then felt his finger run over her teeth. A little tingle swept through her, especially when his eyes met hers, heavy-lidded, sensuous.

"Donkey Kong Junior," she said quickly.

"What?" he queried with a raised brow and puzzled frown.

"You asked me what I'd like to play. Donkey Kong Junior."

"Oh." He nodded solemnly and lay back against his own pillow. "Okay." He fumbled with the little cartridges at his side, then hopped from the bed to insert one into the small computer. Rhiannan watched him, admiring his graceful, un-self-conscious movement and his body. He was built like an athlete—muscular, broad-shouldered, with a very trim waist and hips. His legs were long, and well shaped from strenuous use. His buttocks were round but firm. And the thick dark hair on his chest tapered nicely down his chest, thinning provocatively at the waistline to flare again below.

More than the hair was flaring, she thought with a little flush.

"Donkey Kong Junior!" he proclaimed, getting back into bed. He handed her the small black control mechanism. "They call this a joystick, you know."

"Decadent, isn't it?" Rhiannan laughed.

"What they teach children these days!" he sighed.

"I can't believe we're on a century-old ship with a video game."

"You know Donald," Kiel said with a grin. "Maybe he thought I would need to entertain myself."

"Heaven forbid."

"Hey, I've been practicing. I'm good. Okay, you're player one. Move the stick to go up or down, and push the little button to jump. Go."

A little monkey appeared at the bottom of the luminous screen. Rhiannan pushed the jump button and made it swing from vine to vine, hitting little bunches of fruit to hit the little alligators that were after the monkey. In the next few seconds she had the key to release Papa, and the game moved to the second level.

Kiel watched in amazement as her little monkey escaped the birds and alligators of the second level and went on to the third. And the fourth.

She was on the sixth level before she lost her first monkey. His eyes were on her, sharp and accusing.

Rhiannan laughed. "Hey, I came from a red-blooded American household. Actually, this is one of my weaker games. Have you got Missile Command or Tron?"

"We'll stick with this one, I think," Kiel said. He plucked the joystick from her hand and made an admirable showing. He smirked at her after making his way through the first level, but then they both laughed as the first bird got him on the second.

It was Rhiannan's turn. This time little bursts of blue and gold color were after the monkey. She didn't get zapped until she almost reached the key.

"You have to look out for that little gold bugger," Kiel warned, mockingly solicitous. "It will eat you all up."

"Congressman!" Rhiannan protested. "Watch it!"

He glanced her way and tsked sadly. "Really, Mrs. Collins, the remark was perfectly innocent. It's your own mind that is in the gutter."

"Really? Am I slumming, then?"

"Hm, I'd have to think about that."

"Well, don't think now: It's your turn."

"Is it? Well, then . . ."

His smile broadened as he tossed the joystick over the side of the bed, ripped the sheet away, and pounced on her. "Definitely my turn. And I intend to get to all the levels."

She smiled, reaching to embrace him as he came to her, loving the feel of his body next to hers. He whispered things that made her laugh, and thrilled to his touch.

"First level . . ." he murmured, drinking long and savoringly from the nectar of her lips.

"Second level . . ." His kisses wandered to her earlobe and along her throat.

"Third level . . ." With light flicks of his tongue he taunted her nipples, making her breasts throb and ache to be touched.

"Fourth level!" she exclaimed, tugging at his hair, bringing him to her. Pressing him down on his back, she showered his chest with the butterfly touch of her mouth, with gentle bites and the soft curve of her tongue.

He clasped her hair with his strong hands, cradling her neck, forcing her eyes to his. "Go on," he told her huskily. "Fifth level. And sixth."

She rained her kisses over his hips, explored the length of his legs, took all of him until he groaned in shuddering desire and delight.

His arms came around her, dragging her to him. His hands possessed her; his lips caressed her flesh until she was quivering with desire for him. And again she was lost in the spiraling heat of his impassioned demands, adrift in his sea of sensation, and yet totally secure in the surrender to his possession.

At one point they turned the lights off, and sometime late in the night they slept. But even as she slept, Rhiannan knew that she was beside him, and the feeling of contentment was exquisite.

Sometimes she awoke in drowsy contentment, and she would note every little detail of his body. The rough hair on his legs that scratched as they entwined with hers, the way his fingers dangled as his hand rested around her waist, below her breast. She twisted and watched his face as he slept, and saw how the lines eased about his eyes. She watched the pulse in his throat, and she stored away each little detail in a special corner of her mind.

It never really became light in the cabin. The drapes were too heavy to let in the dawn sun. But somehow she knew it was morning.

Then, as she twisted in his arms to absorb him with her eyes once more, the pain began. Even after she had forgiven him, she had thought herself a fool for being with him, realized why she had wanted to build a wall, why she had been afraid. She was falling in love with him. No, she loved him already.

He was strong but caring, fierce but caring. The world was

his battleground, and he met it head on. He could blanket her
with the tenderness of his words, draw from her what she
thought she no longer had left to give. He could ease her heart
and fill her soul, and she couldn't take it. Just couldn't endure
it. Not again. He was the type of man who could become her
life, and her life had already been shattered into a thousand
pieces once.

Rhiannan closed her eyes, feeling the warm touch of his
flesh against hers, the absent caress as he held her in his sleep.
Tears slipped unbidden from beneath her lids, caught in her
lashes, slid down her cheeks. Carefully she disengaged herself
from his hold. He mumbled unintelligibly under his breath and
rolled to his other side.

Rhiannan leaned over to brush a kiss against his back. She
smiled, noticing the splattering of freckles across his shoulders.
Then she rose from the bed.

Her clothes were still damp, but she donned them anyway,
then tiptoed quietly to the door. She had to look back, fill her
senses with him one last time, because she couldn't see him
again. The risk to her heart, to the facade of strength it had
taken two years to build, was far too great.

He hadn't offered her real love, he hadn't offered her any
kind of a commitment, and he was known for his affairs. But
he did care for her. What he really wanted she couldn't tell
for sure. She did know he wanted to move her, to shake her,
to make her feel again.

He'd never understand that he had made her forgive him,
but she still didn't want to feel again. She couldn't allow it
because there was something so deep that still hurt so bad.
She had lost too much—Paul, her children—and she couldn't
risk having all that again, only to lose it. Kiel would want a
family, something she couldn't give him. But he would go on;
one day he would have everything . . . everything she had already had—and lost.

She couldn't change the emptiness and pain inside her. No

matter what he wanted from her, she just couldn't gamble anymore.

But, she thought as she looked at him, *I thank you, Congressman. So much. I just can't see you again. I love you too much already. . . .*

Rhiannan slipped outside the door and closed it quickly behind her.

When she stood outside the cabin, the radiance of the orange glowing sun almost blinded her, but she saw that the crew were about, raising the sails to catch the wind. The *Seafire* hadn't changed. Only she had.

Eight

Exotic. It was more a feeling than a word, Kiel thought, drifting pleasantly awake from the deepest sleep he had enjoyed in ages. He stretched lazily, and the thought became more focused on Rhiannan.

She could be completely chic; her features were nothing less than classic, fine, and delicate. When she walked, talked, and moved, it was with grace; she was often reserved, sophisticated, cool. But it made the transformation all the more fascinating when her ebony hair waved about her in dishevelment, a wild and beautiful contrast to the fairness of her skin.

He would never be able to erase the picture of her above him, her eyes as green as a spring meadow, her lashes darker than the night, her shoulders and spine straight and proud, her breasts full and firm and enticing. . . .

He stretched luxuriously once more, smiling like a sleek and contented cat as he reached for her. His smile quickly became a frown. His eyes opened and his mind rid itself of the shadows of lazy contentment and he became instantly alert—and annoyed. She was gone.

"Damn her!" he muttered aloud. *Damn myself,* he added silently. How the hell had he slept while she was getting ready to leave? He could usually hear a pin drop, and he usually slept lightly.

He had been drugged with her, driven to a storm of passion to match that which had coursed the seas, set adrift in a sweet misty web of sensuality that robbed his mind of reason. Then he had been left to bask in the most comfortable contentment, in lulling ease, in complete peace, and she had walked out.

Kiel sighed. He wouldn't trust her again. He'd allow himself the luxury of drowning in sensation with her, but then he'd keep a tight hold on her slender waist or tie her to the damn bedpost before closing his eyes. If he got her into his cabin again, he thought, a frown furrowing his brow as he thought of the implications of her departure.

She was running again, and it was so damn foolish. It made him want to jump up and storm around the ship until he found her, then shake her until her head rattled. He smiled suddenly, wondering what her expression would be if he were to tear after her stark naked and haul her over his shoulder back to the cabin. It was a pity that elected officials were not supposed to do things like that. Besides, he could never hold her that way.

He was holding a pat hand, but if he didn't play his cards right, he could lose everything. Maybe she needed a little distance. Not too much: just a little breathing space.

Oh, Rhiannan, he thought with a flash of overwhelming empathy and tenderness. He couldn't give her back what had been taken, but he could promise to give her all that was within his power for all the years to come. And he knew that pain fades when it is accepted and when one allows oneself to open up and live.

Kiel closed his eyes for a moment, and a soft smile touched his lips. He could never say that it didn't hurt to think of Ellen, that there weren't moments when he felt he would go half insane at the injustice of the waste of all the sweet beauty of her life. He could remember her smile so clearly, the dazzle of her eyes, the delightful melody of her laughter. And for all of his life he would love her with a part of his heart, but because of her, he knew that he needed to love—and be loved in return.

Yet, not even Ellen had touched him as Rhiannan had. She evoked his most ardent passions and also his greatest tenderness. His body could heat at the sight of her across the room, and he could find ultimate happiness in just feeling her near, hearing her talk, watching her fluid movement as she walked with natural grace.

Kiel groaned aloud to himself and threw off the covers. Thinking of her could drive him up a wall, and he had just spent the night with her.

It was going to be a rough day, especially when he was going to have to play it a little bit cool. He would set the trap and she would have to walk into it and hopefully find herself too firmly ensnared to escape.

Kiel walked silently into the bathroom and turned the shower on hard. He was supposed to meet with Dr. Picard, a French scientist, for lunch. Picard was alarmed with the growing interest of private American concerns in the development of germ warfare. It would make for a great lunch discussion, Kiel thought dryly. But it was an important topic that he needed to learn more about, and Picard was a sincere man who had dedicated himself to the curing of diseases.

Although Kiel made a point of doing a mental rundown on Dr. Picard and his government-subsidized clinic, Kiel was continually scowling as he shaved, and nicked his chin half a dozen times. Still frowning, he dressed in a leisure suit while wishing that the good French doctor was a little more casual. There was a breeze on the open sea, and the *Seafire* was air-conditioned below deck, but Kiel would have been infinitely more comfortable on the square-rigger in a pair of cutoffs and a T-shirt at all times.

He was surprised when he lingered unaccountably at the door of his cabin, compelled to turn back. His bed looked as if a cyclone had hit it. Rhiannan was like a cyclone, a storm, as tempestuous and as beautiful as the wind.

Kiel chuckled suddenly, amusement crinkling his brow. The steward was going to wonder what had hit the fastidious congressman. A ton of bricks—wasn't that what Donald had said.

Still grinning, Kiel walked out his door, then paused to lock it behind him. As he inserted the key in the lock he felt a slight chill shoot up his spine. He turned around curiously. The sun was blazing; the sails were billowing white and full against a cloudless blue sky. It was a stunning crystal-clear day. The water was reflecting the sun as if it were composed of a million prisms, radiant, fresh, and innocent. What could give him such a ridiculous chill?

"Hey, there, Congressman! You're up late!" Bill Thayer, one of the *Seafire*'s chipper young sailors, waved and shouted from the rigging.

Kiel laughed, but the sound rang false to his own ears. "I overslept, Bill."

"Wish I could have! That storm last night made me as seasick as all hell!"

"A seasick sailor?"

"Yeah, it's embarrassing."

"I wouldn't worry: We've all been seasick at one time or another."

"I think that half the ship was last night," Bill replied with a good-natured grin. "Hey, the ship's doc was even seasick! But I guess he's all better now."

"Oh, yeah?" Kiel queried, frowning again. That strange feeling had returned. An uncomfortable feeling. Just like the one he had experienced when Rhiannan had left her door unlocked. A feeling that made no sense at all because the ship was swarming with security men. The passengers had all been checked over with a fine-tooth comb; papers had been checked; all past associations had been reviewed for the slightest unorthodox leanings.

"Yeah!" Bill grinned from the rigging. "I can see him up ahead by the pilothouse, talking with that Joan Kendrick again." Bill exhaled a long, envious sigh. "She doesn't even look at crewmen. This is the first time in my life I ever wished I'd gone through medical school!"

Kiel laughed, but once more the sound was harsh and strained to his own ears. He waved to Bill, then started for the stairwell. He suddenly made an about-face and started aft, toward the pilothouse. When his long strides took him around it, he saw Joan Kendrick standing at the starboard rail, staring out to sea.

" 'Morning, Joan," Kiel said, walking up to join her at the rail.

She turned, startled at first, and then offered him a dazzling smile. "Kiel! Good morning." She linked an arm through his and stared up at him mischievously. "It's a pleasant surprise to see you unattached, Congressman!" She issued a dramatic and coquettish sigh. "Here I was at last, on a Caribbean cruise with the dashing rogue and heartthrob of all Washington, and you haven't given me the time of day!"

Kiel smiled, wishing he could disengage himself but thinking better of the notion. He flashed her an insinuating smile in return. "Joan, from what I understand, you haven't spent a moment of this cruise alone. Where's the good doctor?"

"Pardon?"

Did he imagine it? Or did her smile fade for a brief moment?

"Dr. Trivitt. I understand you've been gracing him with your company. Where did he go?"

Joan tossed her blond hair and fixed her vision on the sea again. "I'm sure I don't know what you're talking about. I'm certainly not having any kind of an affair with the ship's doctor. I barely know the man."

"Sorry, I just heard that he was up here—with you."

"With me? Oh, yes, you're right. He just stopped by to ask how I was feeling."

"I'm sorry again," Kiel murmured. "I didn't know that you had been feeling ill."

"I wasn't. I mean, not really. I had a, uh, touch of seasickness last night."

It was reasonable. It was logical. Why didn't he believe her? Worse still how could he possibly feel that there was something sinister about the pouting blonde on his arm? If anything, the young woman could best be classified as a brat. He'd met her a few times in Washington when she'd come with her father, who often worked on government contracts. She was a flirt and a tease with the attitude that Daddy's money could buy her anything on earth. But she needed a swat on the rear, nothing more. She was hardly dangerous except to some poor young fool who might fall for her blond beauty and not realize that the lovely shell was hollow inside.

She twisted suddenly, edging closer to him and lifting her perfectly manicured fingers to straighten his tie, which he knew perfectly well was already straight.

"Now that I've finally gotten you alone, Kiel Whellen, I don't want to discuss the cruise physician. It's a beautiful, beautiful day. . . ." She laughed low and huskily. "That was your cue to suggest we spend some of it together, Congressman."

He smiled, at last disentangling himself as her arms curled around his neck. "I've a meeting that I'm probably late for already, Joan."

She pouted again, resting her hand lightly on his upper arm. "Surely your meeting can't last all day." She closed her eyes for a moment, then opened them slowly, their sparkle as brazenly flirtatious as the curl of her lips. "Congressman, you do fascinate me. I just love muscle. . . ."

"I'm sure you do," Kiel said dryly. He wondered why he was hesitating. He should just tell her firmly but politely that he had to go and walk away before she had her octopus arms about him again.

She was a shell, maybe, but a very pretty shell. Someone you might have a good time with for a brief, uninvolved spell. But he had been touched by Rhiannan, and everything and everyone else paled when compared to her. And he had touched her, lain with her, and was determined to have her again. Forever.

But although he wanted nothing to do with Joan, he felt for a reason he couldn't begin to understand that she was up to something, and he wanted to find out what it was.

"How about an early dinner?" he heard himself ask her.

Be sure to visit our website at www.kensingtonbooks.com.

To start your membership, simply complete and return the Free Book Certificate. You'll receive your Introductory Shipment of FREE Zebra Contemporary Romances. Then, each month as long as your account is in good standing, you will receive the 3 newest Zebra Contemporary Romances. Each shipment will be yours to examine for 10 days. If you decide to keep the books, you'll pay the preferred book club member price of $15.95 – a savings of over 20% off the cover price! (plus $1.50 to offset the cost of shipping and handling.) If you want us to stop sending books, just say the word… it's that simple.

BOOK CERTIFICATE

Yes! Please send me FREE Zebra Contemporary romance novels. I understand I am under no obligation to purchase any books, as explained on this card.

Name _____

Address _____ Apt. ____

City _____ State _____ Zip _____

Telephone (____) _____

Signature _____

(If under 18, parent or guardian must sign)

CN091A

Thank You!

PLACE
STAMP
HERE

Zebra Contemporary Romance Book Club
Zebra Home Subscription Service, Inc.
P.O. Box 5214
Clifton , NJ 07015-5214

"Stretching late into the night?" she queried in a kitten's purr.

"Sorry, I've a late meeting too," he lied. "But . . . at least we can have dinner."

"All right. I can wait for my dessert."

He smiled and extricated himself a last time to walk away.

Before he reached the stairwell, he was wishing he could give himself a good right to the jaw for stupidity. He had just made a date with Joan Kendrick. Sure, she had been lying to him. So what? She probably didn't want it known that her taste had run to a mere cruise doctor.

If rumor held any grain of truth, Joan Kendrick did like "muscle." She was supposed to have had affairs with a dozen young electricians and carpenters, a few football players, and a prizefighter or two. But she never admitted her associations. She made it plain to friends, reporters, and anyone who would listen that she would never engage in a serious relationship with anyone "who hadn't the capacity to maintain himself in the socioeconomic sphere in which she was raised."

Glen Trivitt probably made a decent income as a doctor, but not the millions that were her accustomed style. Kiel laughed dryly. He sure as hell didn't make millions. She must have been considering him "muscle."

Idiot! He groaned. Now he was stuck with her for dinner. Maybe it was just as well. It would keep him away from Rhiannan, and he had to give her a little room. But after dinner he would find her.

Kiel said a number of hellos as he passed casual friends and closer associates. He offered Dr. Picard a genuine smile as he found him in the Manhattan lounge. But just as he sat down to his drink, he knew what bothered him. Bill . . . Bill, from his vantage spot in the rigging. He had said that Joan was with Glen Trivitt again. *Again.* She was lying; definitely lying. So she was having a secret affair with the doctor. Who the hell cared? But it just didn't fit. Trivitt didn't have great wealth *or* muscle. He just wasn't Joan's type.

"—and it should be of very grave concern to you, Congressman Whellen," Dr. Picard was saying gravely. "The blame belongs to no one in particular and to all of us as one. But just as you work with the nuclear issue, I wish that you could make the strong American populace aware that all over the world men are working with microorganisms . . . germs . . . viruses. Look yourself, Monsieur. Smallpox. We now have a vaccine. But see all the diseases for which we have no answer. They can be cultured, Congressman. Newer, stronger organisms can be bred from them. It is, I assure you, as frightening as any missile. . . ."

The business at hand at last took precedence. Kiel listened intently to all that Dr. Picard had to say, and promised to look further into the situation in the United States.

"I will send you all of the documentation that I have," Picard promised as they moved to the dining room for lunch.

"I'll appreciate that," Kiel said, and then Dr. Picard went on to lighter matters, describing his home in the countryside on the outskirts of Paris. And Kiel again began to think of Rhiannan as he politely asked the doctor questions about his family and leisure time in France. What was she doing now? Was she thinking of him? Didn't she realize that he would will himself to be stronger, that he was determined to have her at all costs?

She could be as cold as a steel blade when she wanted, but even a steel sword could be broken. And he would see that she broke, because he loved her. A wistful smile curved his lips as he wondered again what she was doing, and whether she was thinking of him and the night they had shared together.

She was and because of that she had decided movement—a lot of movement—and a lot of work might keep her reasonably sane. And it had proven to be a good day for an industrious attitude.

Rhiannan had rushed down to her cabin and plunged hurriedly into a steaming shower, trying not to mind that she was washing away his touch. It was for the best.

But her every movement was a reminder. She was stiff and sore from the unaccustomed activity. The hot water helped somewhat in easing her muscles but it couldn't steam away her memories, nor could it stop her from shaking, even with its heat.

She had wanted Kiel so badly, and it had been the most wonderful night. She couldn't remember ever feeling so attuned to sensation, ever being lifted so high that she soared above the elements, forgetting everything around her except the sight and touch and scent of the man. She couldn't remember ever feeling so alive or so in love.

She began to shudder, and it was like a black wall had descended over her heart. This feeling had touched her many times after Paul's death, frighteningly, engulfingly, sweeping around her. It held her heart in check, allowing her to feel no more pain, because love had become pain, the love that had been severed with death.

Kiel was alive and she loved him, but she could only allow herself to care just so much, because the black wall had become the terrible fear of loss. And so loving Kiel could never be for her, because the blackness would shut down over her. It was a wall she couldn't penetrate. She had to stay behind it, hide behind it, seek the refuge it offered. She didn't want to be in love, and the wall wouldn't allow her to reach out.

She should have never taken the night with him she had wanted so desperately, because now it was going to be harder. He might know that she had meant never to be with him again by the fact that she had left. But he had uncanny perception, and he might still try to face her, to challenge her, and she would have to maintain a pose of total, brutal, indifference.

How could she be indifferent? Every time she saw him now she would remember the touch of his hands on her, the breadth of his naked shoulders, so bronze against the crisp white of the sheets.

She couldn't bear to think about him anymore. She had to get out of the cabin so she wouldn't be alone to think or worry anymore. She'd find Donald and see if he needed anything done. She had to stay busy.

She threw on a knit shirt, a pair of shorts, and her deck shoes, and hurried back to the deck. She tried not to look past Donald's door to Kiel's next door as she tapped on it. She tried to smile radiantly when he opened it immediately and swept her inside.

"Oh, Rhiannan, am I grateful to see you! I tried your cabin earlier, but there was no answer."

Praying that the wash of blood that reddened her face didn't give her away, Rhiannan mumbled, "I took a long shower."

"I knew I should have had you in a cabin closer to mine. Oh, it doesn't matter; you're here now. First I need a favor. You know Sally Fitz, the pretty little sports director? She got awfully sick last night and she's still under the weather! Half this ship was sick last night! What a storm we hit! Anyway, did you have coffee yet?"

"Ah, no."

"I'll get you some. Sit. You can drink it while I fill you in for the day."

Rhiannan sat down in an upholstered chair facing the bed. Donald brought her a cup of steaming coffee and sat across from her on the edge of his mattress. He was wearing a soft yellow knit shirt with a pair of darker shorts that made him look closer to twenty than forty. Something about his worried expression made him look more like an anxious youth than a mature and responsible, if sometimes eccentric, multimillionaire.

"What's the favor?" Rhiannan asked.

"Oh, as I just told you, Sally is still sick. This isn't exactly your job, but she has an exercise class with some of the women each morning."

Rhiannan grimaced. "Donald, I'm not worried about anything not being exactly my job, but I've never run an exercise class."

"Nothing fancy, 'Annan. I'm sure you can fake it. Just do some jumping jacks or something. Run up and down the decks."

"Your sailors will just love that."

" 'Annan—"

"I'm sorry. I'm just a little nervous about it. I don't remember the last time I did jumping jacks."

Donald waved a hand in the air. "You'll manage. You're thin enough so that they'll all believe you exercise."

"Thanks," Rhiannan murmured dryly.

"It's only for half an hour. Then I need you back here right away. We're having that captain-and-crew luncheon today, for all those interested in the actual sailing of this square-rigger. I want to check over a few last-minute details here, then you can shower and change. The luncheon will be in the Pirate's Cove, and I need you to welcome everyone and see that things run smoothly, and— Hey!" He interrupted himself, leaning forward to give her an assessive stare. "Are you feeling all right?"

"Yes, fine."

"Well, you don't look it. You've got shadows that almost match the color of your eyes. Were you sick last night, too?"

"No," Rhiannan said hastily. "I . . . uh . . . I guess I just didn't get enough sleep."

She lowered her lashes and sipped her coffee again, praying once more that a blush wouldn't give her away. Maybe she should have just told the truth. Would Kiel tell Donald where she had been anyway? Did men tell each other things like that? Worse still, had there been another bet on the possibility of her falling into Kiel's bed?

It didn't matter. Kiel could tell Donald what he wanted. But then again, maybe he wouldn't. Men didn't gossip. Hah! she thought dismally. They were probably ten times worse than women!

"You've got to catch up on your sleep. I can't have you getting sick on me. Tonight you can— Oh, no. Damn. I promised that you'd take the blackjack table for a few hours. Do you mind? I know: You can sleep in tomorrow morning. That should help."

"Don't be silly, Donald, of course I don't mind. I work for you, remember? I've almost forgotten myself. I've hardly done anything this whole trip."

"Don't you be silly. I could have never kept all this social stuff straight without you."

Rhiannan smiled. "Thanks. What a nice liar you are, Donald. When's this exercise class?"

"Ten fifteen."

"I guess I'd better get going." She started to rise but he stopped her, his voice suddenly shy.

" 'Annan, I've got another favor to ask of you."

She raised a brow curiously. "Yes?"

"I'm having an intimate little dinner in here tonight. What should I serve?"

Rhiannan stared at him, puzzled. Donald Flagherty was one of the smoothest men she knew. Nothing ruffled him, and he had been dating—and seducing, she assumed—dozens of different women through the years. Why he should suddenly be asking her advice was a mystery to her.

"I'm surprised you're asking me such a question," she told him honestly.

"Well, the lady is a friend of yours."

"Mary?" Rhiannan queried with surprise.

"Yes. Should I start out with that special Finnish caviar and go to duck pâté and—"

Rhiannan smiled as she interrupted him. "If you're trying to give Mary a special evening, Donald, keep it light. She doesn't need to be overwhelmed or awed; she already is. And she enjoys the pleasure of your company, not any special thing that you can supply. She's fond of shrimp. Why don't you take a simple seafood route with a nice white wine?"

"Sounds perfect. Will you check with my chef and arrange it all?"

"Sure. What time do you want to have dinner?"

"It doesn't matter. This is her night off from the lounge. Let's say about nine."

"Gotcha, Chief, and have a nice night."

"I think I will."

"Great. Well, I'm going to go on out and meet my hefty demons."

They weren't a pack of hefty demons. Four of the women were the wives of American congressmen and senators; the fifth woman was a lovely and graceful Chinese lady, a Mrs. Chou. All five were trim and svelte and had apparently joined each morning's exercise session just for the sheer enjoyment of fresh air and stretching muscles to keep them lithe and youthful.

Jumping jacks, huh? Rhiannan thought, but she did start out with stretching, then running in place.

At first it was agony. She was sore in places she hadn't even known existed, and again each movement reminded her of Kiel. She had to keep a smile on her face, and in a while the exercises began to feel good. She was watching out for "gravity" at last, she told herself ruefully.

But what did it matter? Kiel Whellen was probably the only man she could allow to touch her, and she could never allow herself near him again because the black wall was between them. Even thinking about him made her dizzy with that torrent of fear that cascaded over her.

She clenched her jaw and put greater effort into a set of leg stretches. In fact, she exercised with an astounding vehemence and energy.

The ladies were exhilarated and enthusiastic in their praise of her abilities when the session ended. Rhiannan was exhausted and winded. *I've been smoking too much lately,* she told herself, trying to smile and disappear before they could see her gasping for breath.

She headed for Donald's cabin, then decided she didn't want him to see her gasping either. A few of the sailors called greetings to her as they let out more canvas, and she waved in return. She decided the bow of the ship, past the pilothouse, would offer her the greatest privacy, and crossed portside by the mainmast to follow the rail to the bow.

But she had barely started forward when she stopped in her tracks, gripping the rail as she inhaled sharply. Kiel was there, bronze and sleek and handsome in a light-colored leisure suit. The breeze was rippling his hair across his forehead, and despite the suit, or perhaps because of it, he looked exceptionally rugged.

He was talking to Joan Kendrick. More than talking. The blonde was adjusting his tie, stroking the white collar of his shirt. Something ripped through Rhiannan that was so violently hostile that it made her literally see through a red mist. She wanted to rush up to the pair, grab Kiel, and slap the blond woman's hands away. *No,* she thought sickly, *walk away, walk away.* But she couldn't. She didn't want Joan Kendrick touching Kiel. The night spent with him was too fresh in her mind. She should be the one touching his cheek, feeling the coolness of his collar, adjusting his tie and seeing his eyes stare down deeply into her own.

She couldn't be jealous, she assured herself, because she did not want him. Furthermore, she couldn't have him. She wouldn't allow herself to love and lose a second time.

Her fingers gripped the rail so tightly that her knuckles went white, but she didn't notice. She was glad to see that Kiel disengaged himself from Joan's grasp, but Joan merely set her hand on his arm while Kiel kept smiling.

How could he have forgotten so fast? Rhiannan's mind seemed to screech inside her. Not that long ago, their naked legs had been entwined. She had felt his heat, his heartbeat. He had held her. His long-fingered, rough-palmed hands had comfortably rested about her bare waist, and, she thought with a rising, perverse indignity, she hadn't even had a chance to make it totally clear to him that she couldn't see him again. . . .

Kiel at last broke away from Joan, but he turned back and

said something with another smile. Then he walked away, heading starboard around the pilothouse.

They hadn't spent more than a few minutes together, but Rhiannan could still see Joan Kendrick's self-satisfied expression. Joan had just received something she had wanted. Was that something Kiel Whellen?

"No!" Rhiannan exclaimed to herself in a weak whisper. She closed her eyes and shook off the paralysis that had gripped her. No? Why not? She had to tell him that she wouldn't see him ever again, and Joan was welcome to whatever made her happy.

Rhiannan was furious with herself because of her reaction to seeing Kiel with Joan when she finally convinced herself to turn around and head for her cabin once more to change for the captain-and-crew party. But her anger stayed with her, bubbling and boiling, all through the afternoon. Every time she poured a glass of champagne, she wished she could take the bottle and crack it on Kiel's bronzed temple.

Nine

There was little action in the casino that night. Rhiannan assumed that most of the heavy gamblers had already lost their money. And it was a pity, because the time seemed to drag unbearably.

Her temperament had gone from bad to worse because she had stumbled upon Kiel and Joan Kendrick once again in the main dining room. He had invited Joan Kendrick to dinner! Of all the rotten nerve!

Rhiannan had been certain that Kiel would seek her out during the day. She had rehearsed the words she planned to say in a dozen different ways, but he had never looked for her. She had fumed all through the afternoon after seeing the pair at the bow rail while trying to convince herself all the while that it was for the best.

Even now, hours later, reflecting on the sight of the couple made her dizzy again with anger. Joan Kendrick seemed to have had the arms of a giant squid as she sat across the table from Kiel at dinner. If she hadn't been so mad, Rhiannan might have grudgingly granted that Kiel seemed politely aloof to the situation.

It was a feat of the greatest willpower for Rhiannan to shut her mouth after she had seen the two, regain a calm expression, and turn smoothly to exit the room from the same direction she had entered—through the kitchen—without being seen by either.

If Joan had seen Rhiannan, she wouldn't have noticed her.

Her eyes were fixed on Kiel, along with her hands. He had been in a black dinner jacket again. And somehow, even the material of the jacket became more masculine as it stretched across the breadth of his shoulders. The white shirt had looked so clean and touchable. His tie had been perfectly straight, but just as Joan had earlier, Rhiannan had longed to reach out and run her fingers over it, to place her cheek against the faint scratchiness of the fabric that clothed his chest. Right after she had tossed the contents of a soup bowl over his head, of course. *How could he?*

She needed to throw or break something, Rhiannan thought now, idly shuffling the cards at the empty table. She felt like a keg of dynamite about to be detonated.

How could he? How could he chase the blonde after the night they had spent together? It was humiliating, insulting. It was unbearable!

Joan Kendrick just didn't have the right to touch him. But she did, Rhiannan thought dismally. Because she had to go to him and tell him that she wouldn't be seeing him anymore except when she must aboard the ship.

Rhiannan glanced at her watch. Thirty minutes more. Then Lars would take over for the rest of the night. She could run to her cabin and throw pillows around until she could sleep from the sheer exhaustion of the effort.

I've been taken, she thought, *taken by an experienced womanizer.* She had fallen for every word, then gone into a panic because she was so afraid of caring too much, of facing his determination.

"The casino is still open, isn't it?"

"What? Oh, yes, I'm so sorry, Mr. Ledges. . . ."

The slender, middle-aged man who sat down to play was a construction mogul but a mild-mannered, nice man. He loved blackjack and certainly helped support the operation, because he had a tendency to lose. He placed a number of bills on the table and Rhiannan exchanged them for chips.

"Seems lonely down here tonight," Mr. Ledges commented.

"Uh, yes, it is a quiet night," Rhiannan murmured. She shuffled the cards again and set them before Mr. Ledges to cut. Normally the dealer was supposed to refrain from conversation and the players were generally dead quiet. But tonight there was just the two of them, and it seemed ridiculous to follow the rules so strictly.

She dealt the down cards. "How are you enjoying the cruise, Mr. Ledges?"

He chuckled. "It's wonderful. All these charities! I've come up with a half-dozen darn good tax breaks that make me feel great! And all beneath the sun. I hope Donald plans a charter like this every year. I'll definitely be aboard."

"That's wonderful, Mr. Ledges."

"And how about you, young lady?"

"Pardon?"

Rhiannan dealt him a seven. Her own card was a nine; beneath it she had a jack. She paused, glancing into his eyes at his question and awaiting his call.

"Are you enjoying the cruise?"

Enjoying it? Yes, just last night, it had been the greatest enjoyment she had ever known. But it always seemed that anything that was good, that was a dream, was destined to bring pain in its wake.

"Ah, yes, very much, Mr. Ledges."

He studied his cards thoughtfully. "Hit me."

She gave him a card.

"Damn—busted! Why do I like this stupid game so much?"

Rhiannan laughed as she swept in his chips and cards and began to shuffle again. "I don't know, Mr. Ledges. But if it makes you feel any better, I'm a slot-machine addict."

She began to deal the cards again. From a corner of her eye she saw another man entering the room. She didn't have to look directly at him; she knew his body, his height, his movement, the subtle scent of his after-shave.

The cards automatically seemed to stick to her fingers.

"Is this a private game," Kiel joked lightly, "or can anyone join in?"

"Hi there, Congressman. Certainly, join us. Perhaps you can win a few hands against this young lady."

Kiel laid his money on the table's velvet-covered top. "Oh, I intend to win more than a few hands."

She could sense his eyes on her and hear all the undertones in his casual voice. He was amused and angry.

The bastard! What did he have to be angry for?

"I'm sorry, Congressman Whellen," Rhiannan managed to say without shrilling out the curses on the tip of her tongue. "We're in the middle of a hand."

"I can wait." Again there was that undertone.

Mr. Ledges studied his bottom card. Rhiannan met Kiel's eyes. *You can wait till hell freezes over, Congressman,* she thought.

"Hit me, young lady," Mr. Ledges said.

His second up card was a nine.

"Busted again! Oh, Kiel, get your chips now," Mr. Ledges suggested quickly.

"Just waiting on the dealer," Kiel said coolly.

Grudgingly, Rhiannan exchanged his money for chips.

"You have to watch out for beautiful women in black, Mr. Ledges," Kiel warned the older man with a smile.

Mr. Ledges laughed. "Black widows, all of them," he agreed.

Rhiannan found it difficult to maintain her "employee" smile. "Are you ready, gentlemen?"

Mr. Ledges grunted. Kiel said nothing. She ignored him and began to deal.

Three hands went around. Mr. Ledges kept losing. Kiel kept winning.

"How do you do it, Kiel?" Mr. Ledges asked as Rhiannan began to deal the fourth hand.

Kiel laughed. "I'll let you in on a little secret, Mr. Ledges:

The first couple of hands are luck. After that, you can count the cards."

"Count the cards?"

"Yes. You can't do it many places, because in Vegas and most casinos they play with more than one deck at a time. But Donald has set it up to give you a better chance. You just remember what's been played and count on the law of averages."

"But how do you remember?"

Kiel shrugged. "I've got a good memory."

"Photographic?"

"More or less."

"Do you want another card, Congressman Whellen?" Rhiannan said irritably. She had dealt him an ace.

He glanced at his down card and stared at her. "No."

She had a five and a nine and had to take another card. It was a six. She smiled at Kiel. "Dealer has twenty."

He returned her smile and flipped over his down card. "Queen of hearts," he told her. "Twenty-one."

She wished she could throw his winnings at him and tell him that he surely knew what he could do with them.

Mr. Ledges chuckled delightedly. "Congressman, you do have a knack for this game! But I'm out of chips. I think I'll call it a night and leave you two to battle it out alone."

"Good night, Mr. Ledges," Rhiannan murmured.

"Good night, sir," Kiel added quietly.

Rhiannan tensed as Mr. Ledges left the room. Her deck of cards was down low, and she nervously began to shuffle them.

Kiel's hand suddenly closed around her wrist. "What the hell is the matter with you?" he demanded sharply.

"Nothing is the matter with me," she snapped back, then met his eyes with her own, bland and cold. "Would you release my wrist, please, Congressman? I'm working. If you wish to sit in that seat, I'm obliged to deal out the cards."

She felt his hand tighten and she gasped at the painful pressure. His eyes narrowed to slits, and she felt them impale her like steel shafts.

"You can get off your high horse now, Mrs. Collins. And remember who you're talking to. Me: the man you spent the night with."

Rhiannan hissed, "Let me go, Congressman."

"Not until we have a little talk. And if you call me Congressman in that tone of voice once more, I swear I'll drag you out of here and make you wish you hadn't."

She believed him. The tension, that energy that was always about him, seemed to be at an explosive level.

"There is nothing to say. Surely you realized this morning when I was gone that I had decided it was all a mistake."

His fingers relaxed slightly. "I realized this morning that you were running, that you were acting like a complete coward. You have a chance to grab at happiness with both hands and you won't allow yourself to reach—"

"You're presuming way too much from a one-night stand, Con— *Kiel*," she interrupted, swallowing when she felt his fingers tighten on her wrist again. The bones would snap in another minute, she thought vaguely.

He shook his head. "Not from one night. I'm going to marry you."

To her amazement she began to laugh. "You're going to marry me? The philandering congressman wants what he has already had badly enough to marry me? How benevolent, sir! Except you have to excuse me if I turn down your magnanimous offer. I will never marry again, Congressman. Never."

"And you don't give a damn about me, right?"

"Right."

"Then why the protestations? I'm looking for more than a night in bed. I need a hostess, too, and I sure as hell can't afford the salary Donald pays you. Mutual benefit."

"Mutual benefit? What on earth would I get out of such an arrangement?"

"A stable life. A man who you apparently don't find too repulsive to sleep with. A home. Children . . ."

"Stop it!" The anger rose in Rhiannan so swiftly that she managed to jerk her wrist from his grasp. "Stop it! I don't want a home, a man to sleep with, or children! Ever! Don't you understand? Doesn't anything ever penetrate that thick skull of yours? Where is your photographic memory, Whellen? Because I want you to memorize this: *I don't want anything you have to give!* No home, no marriage, and definitely—*definitely!*—no children!"

He arched a brow at her coldly, apparently undisturbed, seemingly impervious to her anger. "I thought you were working, Mrs. Collins. My chips are on the table. Deal the cards."

Gritting her teeth, Rhiannan reshuffled. His comment was not what she expected; the cards were all she had to draw her scattering defenses tightly around herself once more.

Two down, two up.

"Do you want another card, *sir?*" His up card was an ace again. Damn him! How she would love to see him lose!

Where was Lars? Surely she should he off by now.

"No."

She flipped over her own bottom card, a seven to go with her eight. She gave herself a card. A five.

"Dealer has twenty."

He turned over his own card. The queen of hearts. "Twenty-one," he said coldly.

Silently she passed over his chips, then stood stubbornly, still seething.

"My bet is on the table. Deal."

"Surely you have better things to do than sit at a blackjack table, Congressman."

"I'm winning, Mrs. Collins. Keep dealing."

"You aren't winning a damn thing, Whellen. You're having an uncanny string of luck."

"Deal, please."

She wasn't going to be able to deal much longer. She was

going to snap and the cards were going to go flying all over the room.

"Tell me, Mrs. Collins, do you make an occasion like last night a common experience?"

How she would love to hit him! Whack that arrogant tone right out of him. "That's none of your business, Congressman. My nights are my own concern."

She was totally unprepared for his sudden movement. Abruptly he stood; the stool fell to the carpeted floor and his hands gripped her shoulders.

"I asked you a question!" he snapped.

"And I don't owe you any ans—"

She broke off with a wince as his fingers dug into her shoulders.

"You do owe me an answer, and I want it *now.*"

She could scream. Someone would come. Of course, by then he might have decided to snap her neck or rip her in half. He seemed angry enough.

"No, Congressman, I do not make a habit of spending my nights out."

He released her, righted the stool, and sat down again.

Rhiannan closed her eyes for a moment and took a deep breath. "Kiel, this is absurd. I'm not paid to be manhandled."

"That's nice to hear. Deal."

Where the hell was Lars?

"No. You're being obnoxious. And I don't have to—"

He was up again, catching her chin between his thumb and fingers, smiling as he gazed warningly down at her.

"Oh, but you *do* have to, sweetheart. Face life and face me. They're one and the same right now, where you're concerned. Now, do you want to deal the cards? Or would you rather take a little walk."

"I'm working."

"Then deal the cards."

Rhiannan snapped the cards down on the table.

They played a round in silence. She had never been so pleased when the house won.

He set his chips up again. She dealt.

When he spoke next, it was in a cool, level tone. "I'm curious to know," he murmured, lifting his bottom card to read it, "why a woman who doesn't indulge in frequent affairs would be on the pill."

"I'm not—" She stopped, her words freezing in her throat. She had started to answer him! "Again, Congressman, I can only tell you that what I do or do not do is not your concern."

"I told you not to call me Congressman again in that tone of voice."

"I don't take orders from you."

His eyes darted up at her again. They held a deathly glitter. "Lady, you do know how to push a man's patience. But if you're not on the pill, tell me what precaution we had last night?"

"Precaution?"

"Against a pregnancy. Against having one of those children you're so vehemently against?"

She blinked quickly, thinking rapidly, then kept staring at him, hoping her sudden confusion was not apparent. *Composure!* she warned herself. She flipped over a card. "Congressman Whellen, if I'm not concerned, why should you be?"

"Because I am."

Rhiannan uttered a sigh of exasperation and annoyance. "Please don't worry on that account, Congressman. I assure you, instant pregnancies only occur on soap operas."

"Do they really? I'm sure I could introduce you to a score of unwed mothers who could tell you differently, Mrs. Collins. It can have little to do with frequency of relations. Shall I explain it scientifically? Once can be enough; it just depends on the fertility of the woman at the time."

"I do not need any scientific explanations!"

"But perhaps you will need a husband."

"I'll look one up in the Yellow Pages."

"The hell you will."

Rhiannan slapped down another card and narrowed her own eyes as she returned his heated stare. "Really? And just what are you going to do? Marry every woman who might get 'scientifically' involved with you? Bigamy is against the law, Congressman."

"What are you talking about?"

"Well, you seem so certain that you're Mr. Fertility. But no problem, to your way of thinking, it appears. What the heck, we'll just call the captain in. He can marry you to me and then to Joan Kendrick."

He looked positively lethal for a moment—so tense, she almost cringed. But then, to her utter amazement, he laughed. "So that's the crux of this whole thing. I had dinner with Joan Kendrick."

"There is no 'crux' to anything. I don't care who you have dinner with."

"Obviously you do. But don't worry about Joan Kendrick: I promise you she isn't pregnant. Not by me at any rate."

"Oh?" Rhiannan inquired with super-sweet sarcasm, desperately wishing she could just shut up, but stupidly unable to do so. "Did you ask Joan first if she was on the pill?"

"What a wonderful wit," Kiel muttered coolly in return. "I have no idea if Joan does or doesn't take pills. I only know that she definitely isn't pregnant—not by me at any rate. You're overreacting to a dinner, don't you think?"

"And you're overreacting to one night in bed."

"Maybe. But maybe I'm just considering all the possibilities."

"There are no possibilities. Can't you understand that?"

"No, I can't. Not when you run from me, then turn around and have a temper tantrum because I had dinner with another woman."

"Oh, God!" Rhiannan groaned. "Kiel, can't you please go away? You entertained yourself with Joan all day; go do so now! Then you won't have to worry about my so-called temper tantrums. All you have to do is leave me alone."

"I'll never leave you alone. We both know that last night was more than a quick affair."

"Then I'm astounded, Congressman, because you certainly hopped from bed into her arms."

"I did not. I ate dinner with the woman."

"Why?"

His puzzled expression, and then his shrug, completely startled her, because she knew it was honest.

"I don't really know," he said. "Just a hunch. I can't explain it. I can't explain a lot of things lately," he added in a soft mutter that was more to himself than to her.

Then his eyes fixed on her again. "How soon are you off duty?"

"Fifteen minutes ago, or so I thought. But as soon as I can leave here, I'm going directly to my cabin. Alone."

"I swear to you, all I did was have dinner with Joan, and I didn't really want to do that. Come on, Rhiannan, don't be absurd! You know I could hardly care less about Joan Kendrick."

Tears started to sting her eyes, because she believed him. But she was back behind the black wall, and she couldn't let anything get past it.

"Damn you!" she raged suddenly, and at last the cards flew from her fingers, scattering all around them like a sudden snowfall. "I want you to leave me alone!"

He was on his feet again, reaching across the velvet-covered table, gripping her shoulders and shaking her.

"And damn you, Rhiannan Collins! Damn you for being a coward! But I won't let you run! And I won't let you lie to me. I've been with you! I know that you are a heated, passionate, warm-blooded woman and that you need to be loved. I know what lurks behind your black gowns and pretense of dry-ice chastity. You need to be trounced around on a bed a lot more."

"By you, I assume?"

"Yes, by me, instead of a ghost!"

She exploded with pent-up anger, jealousy, frustration, and pain. She jerked from his grasp, delivering a sharp, stunning blow across his cheek with such swiftness that he couldn't avert it. The sound rang over that of the occasional distant slot machine. Then there was dead silence, except for the dull buzzing that began to cloud her ears as she stared at him, terrified for one long moment that he was going to retaliate with ruthless fury.

He didn't touch her. He didn't move, but it took him another long moment to speak. "Don't . . . don't give me an excuse to lay my hands on you, because I have this feeling that keeps trying to fly out of control—a feeling that I could take you and slap and shake some sense into you, force you to realize that you're a fool."

She was shaking inwardly, wishing desperately that he hadn't goaded her into violence. But she couldn't allow him to see that. Her throat was so dry. She swallowed and it was still dry, but she lifted her chin, and her voice was only slightly tremulous if little better than a whisper when she spoke. "You've already shaken me, Kiel, and forced me to be with you, to listen to you. It can't work. If I wanted it to work, it couldn't. I was angry about Joan, but I didn't have the right to be. You owe me nothing. My ego was bruised and maybe you were right: Maybe I just wanted the chance to tell you I couldn't see you again. It doesn't matter. Nothing matters. It all boils down to the fact that I simply have nothing left to give."

"You have everything to give, and I plan to take it all."

The room seemed so tiny, so tight. She could feel his tension. The table was between them, but she could feel the heat of his body, the strength of his will.

She wanted nothing more than to brush past the barrier that separated them and hurl herself against his chest, feel the ripple of muscle, the power of his arms around her. It was almost as if an inner strength exuded from him, compelling her to break to his will. The tension was static in the air between them, charged.

"No. . . ."

"Kiel! Rhiannan!"

The feeling was broken; she was released. She had barely mouthed the word before Donald charged in on them. He glanced her way but then ignored her and the mess of cards and chips all over the table as he strode straight for Kiel and gripped his shoulders.

"For Pete's sake, Kiel, I've been looking all over the ship for you!"

Rhiannan saw Kiel's frown, then felt a strange chill ripple along her spine. She had never seen Donald so agitated, and neither, apparently, had Kiel.

"What's the matter?" Kiel asked quickly.

"I've got to talk to you."

As if remembering that she was in the room, Donald glanced toward Rhiannan. "Outside for a minute," he told Kiel. Then he glanced back to Rhiannan. "Lars won't be on tonight. We're going to close down. Stay here for just a minute, then one of us will walk you to your cabin."

He turned his back on her, leading Kiel to the door of the private room.

"Wait a minute!" Rhiannan suddenly shrilled. "Donald, what's going on? Something is definitely very wrong—"

"Damnit, Rhiannan!" Donald said with annoyance. He had never spoken to her like that. "I asked you to wait! Now, please! Do it!"

She stood there staring as they stepped outside the door and leaped into a quick, rapid-fire discussion. She could see amazement registering on Kiel's face, and then a deadly hard frown that sent the chills running furiously along her spine. Something was wrong—very, very wrong.

At last the door opened again and the two men stepped back inside. Kiel grimly walked around the table and took her arm.

"Come on. I'm taking you up to my cabin." His tone was frightening, ruthlessly determined, and detached. He was ordering her about and he wasn't even thinking about her.

"I want to go to my own cabin if I have to go to a cabin."

"No, you're right," Donald told Kiel, interrupting Rhiannan. "She should be up on deck. The air-conditioning systems are different. I don't know much, but that could mean something."

"What is going on?" Rhiannan demanded, her voice rising again as the chills along her spine turned into quivering panic.

"We'll explain as soon as we know more," Kiel said briefly, his fingers on her arm tightening. He was going to drag her to his cabin and she was going to have to go along, because there wasn't anyone who would stand in his way. Donald and Kiel were both looking as grave as if the world were ending and talking about her as if she weren't even there.

"You get Picard," Kiel told Donald as they moved toward the casino doors again, Kiel pulling her along and not even noting her resistance. "I'll take her up and then meet you."

"Damn you two!" Rhiannan exclaimed. "Kiel, I will not be taken to your cabin."

He finally turned to her, irritation clearly etched into his face. "Stop it Rhiannan. I'm not going to attack you. I won't touch you again. But you are going to my cabin, because it's the safest place for you to be."

She opened her mouth to protest, then shut it, realizing that Kiel had practically announced that they had been sleeping together and that Donald hadn't even batted an eyelash. Whatever was going on was so serious that where she had been sleeping was totally inconsequential.

"I can carry you there over my shoulder, or you can walk."

She brushed past him. "I can walk, and I can walk on my own. You don't have to waste your time." Rhiannan turned blindly and started for the outer casino, which was empty. Donald had already ordered it closed. Dear God, what was going on?

Donald left them on the deck on which the Manhattan was

located when Kiel informed him that Dr. Picard was in cabin 207.

The chills multiplied along her spine and spread throughout her body. Dr. Picard. Dr. Picard. . . . Who was he? She closed her eyes briefly and placed him. He was the slender, sincere Frenchman. Some kind of a scientist. . . .

They were up on deck. She didn't even see any of the sailors. The *Seafire* was anchored, her sails furled.

Kiel fiddled briefly with his key, then pushed his door open and prodded her in. "I'll be back soon," he told her briefly. Then he was back out the door.

"Kiel, wait! Please, wait. Tell me—"

The door snapped closed, practically in her face. Then she heard the key grate in the lock.

She frowned for a moment, too stunned to realize the implications. Then it hit her: He had locked her in! Rhiannan furiously slammed a fist against the solid wood. She bruised the side of her hand. Absently she brought it to her lips. Then she tried the door. It was definitely locked.

Confused and frightened, she wandered into the room and sat on the bed. What was going on? What could possibly make two grown, mature men behave the way Kiel and Donald were behaving?

Picard. Picard. The little French scientist. Who specialized in diseases. That was it. Germs. Viruses. Contagious diseases. . . .

Sitting on the bed where just last night she had known the sweetest ecstasy, she began to shiver, and wish that no matter what, Kiel would come back and hold her and tell her that everything was going to be all right.

Ten

"Bubonic plague! Trivitt has to be wrong—has to be wrong!"

"Calm down, Donald. Picard will know. This is his specialty," Kiel said quietly.

Donald's hand suddenly crashed hard against the paneling. "And Mary! Why Mary? How could she possibly get so pathetically sick?"

Kiel sympathized with Donald; he had never seen his friend care so much about a woman. But his worries were stretching further. They were going to have to move quickly once they knew what they were dealing with. Trivitt had said it was the plague. If he was remembering his history and science correctly, it would spread like wildfire. They would have to make an announcement to the passengers and hope against panic. They were going to have to call in one of the disease centers, and surely they would have to float on the open sea for weeks, because no government would allow a plague-ridden vessel to dock.

The two men stood anxiously outside Donald's door, waiting. Occasionally Donald would pace a few steps. Kiel was stiff and still. At last the door opened and Dr. Raoul Picard stepped outside, followed by Dr. Glen Trivitt.

"How is Mary?" Don demanded tersely.

Picard replied swiftly. "I'm afraid, gentlemen, that Dr. Trivitt has been most astute in his observations. It most certainly does appear as if we have a case of the bubonic plague. But the lady is holding her own for the moment. I will need more specific medications than I have at the moment, but it is a disease that we can treat."

"How?" Donald whispered incredulously. "Oh, my God! Mary . . . has bubonic plague!"

"You must not panic, Monsieur Flagherty," Dr. Picard said soothingly. "We will control this situation."

"But a plague? *Bubonic* plague? How?"

"Donald," Kiel said quietly, placing a hand on his shoulder, "I think we need to find a place to talk. Mary is in your cabin; Rhiannan is in mine; but I don't suggest we go anywhere public."

"No, monsieur," Picard said in vehement agreement. "This must be our first concern. I suggest that the proper authorities be contacted immediately and that all efforts he directed toward the control of what could be an epidemic."

Donald struggled to control himself, then squared his shoulders. "There is an office around the corner from the pilot-house. We can go there. We've a radio connection in the office, too, so we can contact the States from there."

"I'll stay with the patient," Glen volunteered.

"Fine, Glen. Thank you," Donald murmured, then stared at his ship's doctor with vehemence in his eyes despite the control he had managed to hold over his voice. "As soon as we've taken all appropriate action, I will stay with her."

"Monsieur Flagherty," Dr. Picard said, "we are talking about a communicable germ here. Those exposed—"

"I've already been exposed."

"We've all already been exposed," Glen said. "The entire ship has been exposed. Mary should, of course, be isolated, but it's highly likely that the organism has already spread. If you'll excuse me, I'll tend to Mary, and Dr. Picard can explain the situation."

Just moments later Kiel and Donald sat at Donald's desk, both staring at Dr. Picard with their disbelief and incredulity still apparent in their grim faces.

"I'm sure you know, messieurs, that the bubonic plague, or

Black Death, is the disease that swept Europe in the Middle Ages, decimating over a quarter of the population."

"I had thought it disappeared in the Middle Ages too," Donald said in a stiff whisper.

"No, no, the disease has never entirely disappeared." Dr. Picard lifted his slender shoulders. "There were several outbreaks through the 1800's, and even in our century. New York . . . San Francisco. Seattle had an outbreak at the turn of the century. And just last year there was a minor epidemic in Arizona. But in developed countries, especially the United States, the disease has been kept well under control. British scientists discovered in 1907 that the germ was carried by rats and the fleas that inhabited them." Again, Picard gave them an eloquent shrug. "You control the rats and you control the plague. Hygiene, extermination, and quarantines have kept our society relatively safe."

"Doctor," Kiel murmured, hunching his broad shoulders, "I do not question your capabilities, but are you quite certain that what Mary is suffering from is the bubonic plague."

Picard stiffened. "Quite certain, Congressman Whellen."

"My apologies, Doctor. Under the circumstances, I want full assurance. Before we do any more discussing, I think we'd better get a hold of the authorities. Donald, shall I do the talking?"

Donald waved his hand helplessly in the air. "Pick up the phone," he whispered. "Our radio engineer can get you through to the States. Just tell him what you want."

Kiel hesitated a few moments, then decided he had better go through the government first. Considering the passenger list of the *Seafire*, it was going to be imperative that the situation take number-one priority.

His call was put through to the States as an emergency, and he was connected with the Vice-President.

"Bubonic plague? Are you sure? I mean, quite sure, Congressman?"

"Yes, sir. We've Dr. Picard, the French expert, on board. And, sir, I'm sure you know who else is on board."

"Of course, of course," the Vice-President mumbled, and even over the static Kiel could hear the deep anxiety in his voice.

"All right, Mr. Whellen, I'll take care of things from here; you'll have to handle the situation at that end. I'll contact the disease control center immediately. You'll have help as soon as they can get a helicopter in the air. This is incredible. Bubonic plague—"

"Sir," Kiel interrupted, "there have been no reports of any type of an epidemic from any of the ports at which we docked, have there?"

"To my knowledge, no, Congressman, there have been no reports of bubonic plague anywhere in the *world* at this time!"

"Then . . ." Kiel hesitated, then said, "Sir, I realize the security of this voyage was tight, but could you go over our passenger list one more time with a fine-tooth comb?"

"What are you suggesting, Congressman? Plague is surely an act of God."

"I don't know what I'm suggesting, sir. But could you have that done for me, please?"

"Wait a minute. I've Dr. Gutton from the Atlanta center on the other line. He wants you to keep the passengers separated and calm. They have a vaccine. You've only one case of the disease so far?"

"As far as we know, sir. But it's three in the morning."

The Vice-President's sigh could be heard over the airwaves. "Yes, Kiel, it's three A.M. here, too. But I'm going to have to wake up the President. You've got top-flight diplomats aboard that ship. Dear God, I hope we've caught this thing in time. Put Dr. Picard on the line, please. Dr. Gutton wishes to speak with him. He says they can get out with a chopper in two to three hours, and in the meantime, Kiel, you've got to keep those people separated without causing a panic."

"Yes, sir."

Kiel grimaced and turned the phone over to Picard. Apparently, Dr. Gutton also spoke French, because the conversation switched to that language.

Kiel stared at Donald, who had sunk into his chair, his hand resting over his brow.

"How?" Donald repeated, bewildered.

Kiel shrugged. "Donald, it's surely not your fault. Rats—"

Donald came to life, smashing his fist against the arm of his chair. "There were no rats aboard this ship! She was gone over by the best extermination companies available. She was cleaned to the bone. It's impossible!"

"Donald, she's an old ship, and even the most luxurious new ocean liners can get rats down in their holds. It's an old tale of the ocean and ships, I'm afraid."

Donald eyed Kiel sharply. "No, not this time, because you tell me, Kiel, from where? We were docked in Miami and Nassau. I heard your question. No one else has reported an outbreak of the bubonic plague."

"Well, we're not actually reporting an outbreak, Donald. We've only one case."

"We'll have more. That's why they call it a plague," Donald said wearily.

"But it can be treated, Donald."

"Yes, it can be treated. But to what avail?"

Picard, finishing his own discussion, replaced the phone receiver and turned to Donald.

"With excellent results, monsieur. I believe that we have caught this plague in its embryonic stage. This young Mary is in the very early stages and Dr. Gutton has the finest antibiotics available. I promise you, monsieur, we will not lose the young lady. But if you gentlemen will excuse me, I will tend to my patient. Congressman, may I suggest that you take the necessary measures to keep the rest of our passengers and crew separated?"

"Yes . . . we have to do something." He turned to Donald. "Have we a P.A. that reaches all the cabins?"

Donald waved his hand. "Just pick up the phone. They'll arrange it from communications. But we've crew on deck."

"They'll have to stay on deck, it seems. No change of shifts. Everyone stays where they are."

"I am going back to Mary," Donald said determinedly.

Kiel didn't say anything. What difference would it make? Donald had been with Mary all night already. He had been with her when she had first told him she thought she was getting a cold. It was Donald who had realized she was burning up with fever and that she had very swollen glands.

Buboes, the glands after which the plague had been named, Trivitt had told them briefly. A plague with an enormously high death rate. . . .

But it had been caught in the early stages. It was a freak incident that could all turn out well, Trivitt had assured him before slipping back into Donald's cabin with Dr. Picard. His last piece of advice was to keep it as isolated as possible.

Kiel reviewed the possibilities of doing that. Mary was a singer who had been singing just the night before in a lounge with God alone knew how many of the passengers. He had been exposed himself—exposed to Donald. They had all been exposed. It was unbelievable that in the twentieth century he could be a victim of a medieval disease. It was definitely ironic. Too ironic?

Picard was handing him the phone. "Congressman? You must tell our passengers something. They must stay put, at least until representatives from the center arrive. They will handle control from that point."

Kiel held the phone for a moment and willed his body to release its tension so that it would not be revealed in his voice. But then he shook his head ruefully. "I've got a better idea. As soon as I get on that speaker especially at three A.M., I can guarantee we will have a panic. This may seem a little high-handed, but I suggest we run around and lock everyone in. Is that possible, Donald?"

Donald nodded. "But what happens when they all realize that we've locked them in?"

"Then I make the announcement. The only people we want walking around are crewmen, and only those necessary to keep her floating. Hopefully help will arrive before the majority of the passengers awaken."

"All right," Donald said slowly as Picard nodded his approval.

"I'll need to see the captain, and then I'll speak to the crew on deck," Kiel told him.

"All right," Donald agreed again. "It's your show, Kiel. I'm going back to Mary. Dr. Picard? Are you coming?"

"Wait," Kiel said. "I'm going to need Dr. Picard in case someone else comes down sick. Can Dr. Trivitt take care of Mary?"

"Yes, certainly," Picard said with assurance. "Most certainly. I was quite impressed with his diagnosis. He will keep her fever down and give her what medication we have available until we receive the sulfadiazine and streptomycin that we need."

Kiel rose, along with Donald, and glanced at Picard. "You watch the lines for the moment, please, Doctor. I'm going to speak with the captain and crew and see Donald back to his cabin."

Donald stood with Kiel for a moment after the captain had been ordered to alert the crew.

"I still say it's impossible, Kiel. If I heard Picard correctly, the plague is carried by rats with fleas. The fleas bite people and carry the germ—*Pasteurella pestis,* as he called it. I say that my ship has no rats." He lifted a hand before Kiel could interrupt him. "Even if we did pick up rats in port, where did we get *infected* rats? There's no plague in Miami, no plague in Nassau. Only *my* rats are infected? On a ship that was picked absolutely clean in the process of restoration? I don't believe it!"

Neither do I, Kiel thought. But then where else did bubonic

plague come from? From rat fleas. That was the only answer
Then why did he feel like Donald? And why did he have tha
uncomfortable feeling that had plagued him since they had lef
port. "Plagued" him? What a turn of speech. What an irony
Even more ironic was that he had been so concerned abou
Rhiannan keeping her door locked. Locked doors meant noth
ing to the Black Death of medieval times. . . .

Get ahold of yourself, Whellen, Kiel warned himself. *Thi.
is the twentieth century. We will have this thing under contro
in no time.*

"Go on in and sit with Mary, Donald," Kiel told his friend
"I think you'll feel better keeping an eye on her."

Donald nodded and left him, striding quickly to his own
cabin. Kiel thought briefly of Rhiannan, still locked in there
probably about to claw down the walls by now. But he couldn'
go to her. He didn't want to see her again—not until the ex
perts arrived. He didn't know that much about the nature o
the disease and had been sitting with Donald, who had beer
with Mary, and he didn't want to take any chances of being
a carrier when, as it stood, Rhiannan might escape real expo
sure.

"She's just going to have to keep clawing the walls for a
while . . ." he murmured unhappily out loud.

And he had a lot to do—too much to worry about her re
action at the same time.

Kiel ground his teeth together and stared up at the sky. The
stars were out; the moon was a silver orb. There was a sof
breeze.

It was a stunning night. He suddenly raised a fist to the
moon. "God, don't let her come down with this thing. Don'
let her get sick. Don't you dare let her die. Don't you dare
You have already taken your toll from her!" Kiel paused and
let out a long sigh. He himself had also taken a toll from
Rhiannan, and man didn't barter with God. He'd already
learned that.

"Please, God. Please . . . not her." Not Rhiannan. He

couldn't bear it, just as she hadn't been able to bear losing her husband, her children.

"We've a chance, God. Dear God, give us that chance, and help me handle this thing now . . ." he prayed out loud.

He couldn't help thinking back to that day in the Oval Office when he had been called upon to avert disaster. The day that he had failed. All those lives slipping through his fingers like stardust.

He wouldn't fail again. This time he would be in charge. He had been given a second chance. He would be playing with a full deck. He'd have all the information he needed this time. He wouldn't—couldn't—fail. He was not a doctor; he could not cure the plague. But he could avert panic and disaster and get to the bottom of this.

He closed his eyes and clenched his fists. Prayers were for solitude. Right now he had to talk to the crew, and he had to be assured, calm, and certain. He couldn't let them know that he was scared. Gut scared.

"Congressman."

The captain was coming toward him, grave but calm. "I have the night crew together, and the other shifts have been ordered to sit still. My radio engineer has handled everything smoothly, but I think you need to say your few words now, especially inasmuch as we're going to start locking cabins and handling this thing like a military procedure. We've also got a man named Boswick up here. Says he's head of the Secret Service on board."

"Great," Kiel murmured. It was one time in his life when he was going to be damned appreciative of the Secret Service. They could help police the situation.

He took a deep breath and strode calmly to the bow and the milling crew members. "Gentlemen, we've got a bit of a problem. We're going to need your courage and your cooperation."

* * *

Rhiannan absently rubbed the tension from her neck as she watched Kiel's bedside alarm crawl to six. She had watched it crawl to three, then four, five, and now six. Where was Kiel? What was going on?

She stood and began pacing the cabin again. It was amazing, she thought, that she hadn't worn holes in the carpeting. It had been the longest three hours of her life. And if he didn't come back soon, she was going to throw herself against the walls.

The drapes! she thought suddenly. It was at last dawn, and she would at least be able to see what was happening on deck.

She shivered suddenly, realizing that she was terribly scared. She had thought since the plane crash that it wouldn't matter if she died, that she would be ready; but she wasn't—not anymore, because she loved Kiel. No matter how she hid from it or tried to deny it, she loved him. She wasn't ready to let go anymore. Not now. She wanted to live to see him, to touch him, to watch the planes of his face when he spoke, hear the caress of his voice. See his eyes as they changed. . . .

Rhiannan closed her eyes tightly, then opened them and drew back the drapes and frowned. All over the deck there were boxes wrapped in some kind of brown plastic, and the crew was running around to get them and arrange them. As she watched a rope suddenly fell from the sky. No, it wasn't a rope; it was a rope ladder, and the crew members were running around to steady it. A man with safety straps was descending it.

She suddenly realized that she was hearing a strange buzzing. Ducking down to peer upward from the bottom of the window, she saw that there was a helicopter in the sky, hovering above them.

The man hit the deck and was caught and supported by members of the crew. He was dressed all in white, a doctor? Another man was coming down. Another man dressed in sterile white.

Someone shouted. The man sprang to the deck, and the

buzzing increased as the helicopter moved away. They were shouting about the wind.

The helicopter made another spin about. U.S.A.F. Rhiannan read the large black initials on the side of the khaki-colored machine. Air Force. The United States Air Force was dropping men onto the *Seafire*.

The ladder fell toward the bow section again, out of the way of the masts, and another man came down . . . and then another. And then a woman. All dressed in the sterile white.

Rhiannan inhaled sharply as she saw Kiel and the little Frenchman, Dr. Picard, rushing to greet them. They all started talking hurriedly beneath the orange glow of dawn.

Then the ladder was lifted and the droning of the helicopter faded as it rose higher in the sky and flew away.

Kiel was leading the people in white toward the bow. Toward the pilothouse? No . . . toward Donald's small office.

The crew went back to work at their stations, keeping the *Seafire* motionless.

Oh, God! What was happening?

She paced back into the center of the cabin and sat nervously at the edge of the bed. She should have been exhausted. She had barely had three hours of sleep in the last forty-eight hours. She should lie down and try to sleep and she would quit worrying and wondering. She could seek release from the temptation to just start screaming as long and loudly as she possibly could.

She would never sleep. Never. No matter how exhausted she was. Rhiannan stood again. She hadn't been able to sit for more than a few minutes at a time all night. Kiel had left a pack of cigarettes on his dresser. She picked it up and noticed with a frown that there were only a few left.

She looked at the overflowing ashtray. She had already lit and discarded almost a full pack of cigarettes in just a few hours, and she usually went days without smoking at all. Her fingers shook as she tried to light another butt. She lit the middle of the cigarette, then tried to stub it out.

She almost jumped a foot into the air when the door to the cabin suddenly swung open and she saw Kiel, still in his black tux. There were deep grooves around his eyes, which were somber and sunken. His lips, too, were grim, a tired white line slashed across the bronze of his square chin.

She swallowed, wanting to run to him, afraid to. Then suddenly she did.

"Kiel—"

He caught her arms and held her back and she saw that one of the white-suited men was behind him. "Rhiannan, this is Dr. Trenton. He has a few questions to ask you." His grip on her arms was firm, hurtful, and his eyes were boring into hers like steel blades. "It is imperative that you answer all that he has to ask *totally truthfully.* Do you understand me?"

Anger ripped through her, spurred by fear, spurred by the ruthless domination of his tone. He was treating her like a child, refusing to tell her anything.

"Mrs. Collins," the doctor addressed her, smiling, speaking gently, "it really is important that you think carefully about what I ask and answer truthfully. Will you do that for me?"

He was a man of about fifty with salt-and-pepper hair, soft blue eyes, and an easy assurance that inspired trust.

"I—yes, of course."

"Have you felt at all feverish?"

"No."

"Any body aches or pains?"

"No."

"Chills?"

"No, I—"

"Any swollen glands, pain in the eyes?"

"No, and would you please tell what this is all about?" she finally demanded with impatience.

She was answered with the doctor's hand on her forehead. She would have drawn away with impatience, except Kiel held her steadily.

"It's all right," Dr. Trenton assured Kiel. "She's as cool as a nice, fresh cucumber. Now, Mrs. Collins, if you'll just allow me to check your throat . . ."

"Wait a minute! Why?"

She couldn't back up because Kiel was standing behind her, a solid wall, holding her. The doctor's hands felt her neck, her throat, with firm, expert fingers. "We've some illness on board, Mrs. Collins. I just want to assure myself that the vaccination will be effective." He smiled cheerfully. "Now, if you'll just give me your arm."

"Kiel—"

Rhiannan tried to swing about. Kiel caught her and began pulling up the sleeve of her black gown. "Give the doctor your arm."

"Kiel—"

"Now!" he shouted. "Dr. Trenton is a busy man. Don't hold him up."

"But wait—"

She couldn't have moved her arm if she tried. Dr. Trenton had already produced a small black bag and was calmly filling a hypodermic needle. Before she could finish her protest, he sterilized her arm with cotton moistened with alcohol and clutched her wrist to position the needle against a vein.

"Now, this will sting, Mrs. Collins, but only for a minute."

Sting? It burned like blue blazes. But she didn't jerk: Kiel's grip on her elbow prevented her from moving.

"Thank you for your cooperation, Mrs. Collins," Dr. Trenton said evenly, that cheerful smile on his face once more. He looked over her head to Kiel. "Congressman, you have a few minutes while my colleagues complete the rest of our preparation. Then we'll need you."

Kiel nodded grimly behind her. "I'll be right with you."

The doctor kept smiling. "We'll need that announcement over the P.A. before we proceed further, and I think your early risers will be starting to worry. You're the best man to assure them, Congressman. Mrs. Collins, it's been a pleasure to meet you."

She couldn't reply. She just stared at him as he exited, closing the door firmly behind him. Then she spun on Kiel. "If you don't tell me what's going on now, I swear I'll gouge your eyes out, and I do believe I have the strength to do it!"

He stared at her tiredly, closed his eyes, opened them again, and wandered back to sit on the bed, stretching. "Mary came down with a case of the bubonic plague last night. Dr. Trenton is from the Center for Disease Control in Atlanta. Since five A.M. we've had three more cases reported."

"What?" Her question was barely a gasp.

He cracked a dry, rueful smile that offered no humor. "Bubonic plague."

"That's impossible."

"No, I'm afraid it's quite possible."

"But—"

He rubbed his temple. "It is possible because it has happened. But it's really not as bad as it sounds. Thanks to Dr. Trivitt, it was caught very early. And with the immediate and expert medical attention we've received, there's every reason to believe that those who have caught the disease will recover. They've come a long, long way with the vaccinations. That shot you just received is one of the newest breakthroughs. It's safe, even if you've been exposed to the disease. But the doctors must be careful, because if any of the passengers have chills or other symptoms, they must be treated rather than be given preventatives."

She felt cold and stiff, like a mannequin, as if she couldn't quite walk right or talk right.

Plague. There was a plague aboard the ship. The same plague that had wiped out a quarter of the population of Europe centuries before. The Black Death.

For some reason she walked to the window and pulled back the drapes. The sun was shining more brilliantly, breaking through the sea mist of dawn. It looked calm on deck. Only one doctor was with the boxes, checking them in. And as she watched a sailor crawled back over the side of the ship, carrying another box with him. They must have dropped the majority of them into the ocean, Rhiannan thought vaguely. But the sailors looked calm. The doctor looked calm, but with the morning sun rising higher in the sky, passengers would awaken. There could be utter chaos soon. . . .

But there wouldn't be. The doctors were there in their sterile white suits, and they were going to give everyone vaccines and everything would be fine. Except that people were already sick, and it was doubtful whether any port or government would let them bring the ship in.

"Oh, God," she murmured, spinning around to face Kiel again. "Mary . . . how is she, Kiel? Will she really be all right?"

"So they tell me," Kiel murmured.

"And Donald? Donald was with her."

"Donald had no symptoms. They were able to give him the vaccine."

"And—" She stopped suddenly, unable to voice her fears.

He looked at her and smiled, and the weariness dropped from his features for a moment. "Were you going to ask about me?" he asked her softly.

She swallowed. "Yes."

"I had the vaccine, too."

"And is it . . . is it . . . ?"

"A hundred percent effective? No. But ninety-seven percent, or something like that. I don't think you should worry too much on that account. If it wasn't a good vaccine, I don't think these white-frocked saviors would be walking around quite so cheerfully. The problem is averting a widespread epidemic, and that's why they have to be so careful about the ship. They want us to stay on the open sea for a minimum of four weeks, and then we're going to have to transfer to another ship very carefully. They're going to exterminate the hell out of the *Seafire*, and Trenton also came aboard with some special soaps and shampoos that kill fleas and lice."

"Fleas and lice?"

"The plague is carried by rats. Rats have fleas. The fleas get on people, and there's your plague germ."

"Oh," Rhiannan murmured.

He stood, raking his fingers through his hair. "I guess I'd better get back and make that announcement. Communications are going to be a mess. All our diplomats and statesmen are going to want to contact their respective countries."

She could see his eyes darken with his thoughts. She could almost hear the ticking of his mind, careful, methodical.

He wasn't with her any longer. He was braced once more for action and decisions. He was going to leave her and fill his time with positive and productive procedures and she was going to be left to stare out the window and worry.

Was this what he had been like, she wondered, on the day that the 747 had gone down? So determined, concerned. Tense, straining to keep things on an even keel, his eyes dark and brooding, haunted.

"I think I'd like to go back to my own cabin—" she began.

"No!" he interrupted, his voice suddenly a whipcrack as he strode across the cabin to grip her shoulders with barely controlled violence. "You're going to stay right here where it's safe. I have no intention of worrying about you along with everything else!"

"Safe?" Rhiannan protested. "I've had the vaccine, so I'm safe, right?"

"Don't start arguing with me now. Don't even try. I just won't argue with you now. You're staying right here."

"But—"

"Just shut up for once, Rhiannan. I won't attack you," he said with bitter irritation. "I'm too tired now, so I can guarantee I'll be too tired when I get back."

"Let go of me, Congressman!" Rhiannan flared. She didn't want to tell him that despite all his assurances, she was still scared. Scared for Mary, for Donald, and for herself. And for Kiel. But activity was better than the horrible waiting any day!

'Maybe you're not the only one who can be useful! I work on this ship. I can probably help."

"Maybe you can help tomorrow. Not today!" Kiel snapped.

"I need something to do, Kiel! I need—"

"Take a shower. Take a nap. Read a book."

"I haven't any fresh clothes."

"Grab one of my T-shirts—and don't worry," he added, his voice bitterly scornful now. "I told you I wasn't in the mood to attack you. You can walk around stark naked and I won't notice."

He released her shoulders and headed for the door.

"Kiel—" She doubted that he heard her. The door slammed behind him, but then she heard the grate of the lock. Apparently he didn't trust her to stay.

She was shaking, she realized, shaking badly. She walked back to the bed and sank down on it, realizing suddenly that her arm was still burning. Bubonic plague. . . . Kiel was saying that it was really all right. They had vaccines; they'd be fine. But Mary . . . poor Mary. Was she really going to be all right? It was all so scary. The white-coated doctors being helicoptered in, the quarantine. . . .

And Kiel. He was so tired. Wouldn't that weaken his system?

Rhiannan clenched her hands together tightly. *How could they possibly have plague aboard Donald's ship? He was meticulous, careful. No one had come aboard ill, and bubonic plague had all but died out almost a century ago.* More frightening than the disease was the fact that it was aboard the ship at all.

Rhiannan started as she suddenly heard Kiel's voice again. She looked about the room in a moment's confusion, then realized that the sound was coming through a speaker system.

"Ladies and gentlemen, this is Congressman Kiel Whellen. The switchboard is getting jammed with your questions, so I think it's about time I assure you that things are under control but that we do have a bit of a problem. Those of you who awakened earlier know that you are locked in your cabins.

That's because we've picked up a bug. But we've already gotten help from the U.S., from the Center for Disease Control. Doctors will be going from cabin to cabin. Please stay calm and give them your full cooperation. We'll be at sea longer than we expected, but we should be back to normal soon. The ballroom on the Manhattan deck is being turned into an infirmary, so all those who haven't been feeling well should tell the doctors about it and they'll be taken care of immediately. And we'll be coming around with coffee and breakfast soon for all those who can't quite open their eyes." His voice went on and on, calm, unhurried, soothing and authoritative.

He was damned good in catastrophes, Rhiannan admitted grudgingly. Yes, he was damned good. He had probably been every bit as good that day in Washington.

She thought sadly then that she had once been guilty of maligning a truly fine man. Kiel had never been to blame. Somewhere judgment had been faulty, but not Kiel's judgment. She knew in her heart that he would never blame others, and perhaps no one had really been to blame. All of them were just people doing their very best, but losing anyway.

Kiel wouldn't lose this time. He couldn't. Eventually he would call the "bug" what it was. By that time everyone would be able to accept it—unless someone died.

Oh, God! She was so scared, and she wanted Kiel to come back, to soothe her instead of the ship's populace. To hold her . . . to love her. . . .

Tears sprang to her eyes and she brought her knuckles to her mouth and bit down hard on them. The black waves seemed to be attacking her again. She didn't remember ever being so frightened of anything or her feelings.

Kiel wouldn't let her go, and she couldn't seem to fight the urge to cling to him. What would happen if he did let her go?

The blackness yawned before her. It seemed that there was no way to keep from toppling into the pit of despair and fear that beckoned to her.

Eleven

It was four o'clock in the afternoon before Kiel wearily trudged back to his cabin. Until today, not even he had understood the full scope of the international representation aboard the *Seafire*. Communications had been jammed all day. Luckily the majority of those aboard the ship had handled it all with admirable aplomb. Repeating the same answers over and over again and trying to maintain a diplomatic facade had been the most tedious chores.

Donald had refused to leave Mary again, and so Kiel had found himself completely in charge and strangely alone. He was the liaison between the passengers, the shore, and the efficient doctors.

There had been those, of course, who panicked—some wives of officials and some officials themselves, who had insisted they be immediately allowed off the ship. That was impossible, Kiel had tried to explain. The ship was in quarantine. No one was allowed off. Surely that could be easily understood. On board the *Seafire* a disease could be caught and controlled, but if it were carried to land, to any major port, it would be a disaster. No port would allow it; it was that simple.

But things would be back to almost normal in another day or so, he tried to assure them all. And of course the ship would be under investigation and patrolled. After the vaccine had been in effect for twenty-four hours, those who were well would be welcome to move around the ship once more.

What a miserable, miserable day.

By now, he thought, the newspapers and T.V. channels across the world would be carrying the story. People would be tuning in to the afternoon and evening news and learning all about bubonic plague—its cause, its history, its effect. They would be marveling at the advances of medicine, because hopefully no one aboard the *Seafire* would die.

Kiel had started that rumor himself. The President had insisted on a press conference, and Kiel had taken all that Picard and Trenton had said and twisted it only slightly to avoid any kind of a true panic. It was really only a small lie. He had been told that the vaccines were almost foolproof, and that the drugs currently available for treatment were excellent.

He knew that he was laying everything on the line, that he was facing a potential disaster. His career was on the line. If disaster did erupt, he would be the scapegoat. But he didn't resent being the sacrificial lamb—he had taken that role once before with far less conviction—because he knew that they were all, including the President himself, merely mortals.

And this time, this time, he was the one drawing the lines. It would be his judgment alone that he relied on. He wouldn't allow any pertinent information to slip through his fingers. And if he failed . . .

"But who can give guarantees, Congressman?" Dr. Trenton had asked him with a resigned shrug that spoke of experience. "I've seen people die of the common cold. Of measles. Of the flu. I tell you, it's often strange, Congressman. We can put a man on the moon. We can kill millions of people with a single bomb. But microscopic germs . . . viruses . . . bacteria—there are dozens of them we can hardly touch."

"And if we were able to touch them," Kiel asked bitterly, "we would merely manage to breed new viruses that were stronger?"

"Don't ask me that question, Congressman. I'm not on that side of the line. The known plagues have been my specialty since I got out of med school."

"Sorry," Kiel murmured, unable then to forget his luncheon

with Dr. Picard and their discussion on the possibility of germ warfare. He sighed. "You're not to blame, Trenton. For the plague or my temper."

"You need some rest. Badly."

"That's an understatement. I feel like I could sleep for a week."

"Well, go and get a night's worth at any rate, Congre—"

"My name is Kiel, Doctor."

"Mine is Michael."

Kiel smiled. "I'm almost afraid to go to sleep."

"Don't be. You've done everything that can be done for the moment. You've handled everything on the ship and on shore. I don't think that anything we couldn't handle could crop up now, and if it did, we'd awaken you." Michael Trenton smiled. "If I had a lady like yours waiting for me in my cabin, I wouldn't be fighting the urge to get back to it."

Kiel chuckled for the first time in hours. "The lady isn't particularly happy to be there, Michael. I more or less stuffed her in there when I didn't understand what was happening."

Michael's lined face crinkled with laughter. "We haven't given any all-clears to move about the ship for another twenty-four hours. That gives you some time."

"Time I'll be too tired to put to good use." Kiel grinned.

"Maybe not," Michael Trenton told him, indicating two foil-covered packets he had given Kiel. "Maybe you can share your flea baths."

Kiel stared down at the packets. "A flea bath doesn't sound real romantic, does it, Michael?"

"Hey, life is what we make it."

"Yeah, I guess you're right, Doctor. I guess you're right."

Kiel inserted his key in the lock and then paused, wondering if he should knock. He decided against it. She might tell him to go away, which he had no intention of doing.

She was still in her black dress, leaning across the bed and playing with the video game. She didn't glance his way when he entered, although she obviously knew he was there.

Kiel dropped to the chair beside his bed and pulled his shoes off.

"Video games," he commented dryly. "Nice way to spend the day."

She shrugged, keeping her attention focused on the game. This time little flying saucers were scuttling across the screen.

"I've read," she replied almost tonelessly, "that when the Black Death struck Europe, nobility and servants alike ran about the castles and the halls, dancing and singing until they fell. This is the twentieth century. Why not video games?"

Something about her casual voice, about her disinterest in him—in the horrendous situation that had kept him running about all day like a chicken with its head plucked off—snapped his fraying temper. Emitting a sharp oath, he sprang from the chair, grasped the controls from her hand, and sent them flying across the room.

At last she looked directly at him, her eyes brimming with a green fire. "That was hardly necessary, Congressman. You're the one who locked me in here. I had little choice of things to do."

She leaned on an elbow as she stared at him; his spurt of fury had apparently left her undaunted. She was as cool as a winter wind, except for her eyes. And with her hair falling about her like a rich cloak of sable, she was unnerving him far more than he could hope to do to her.

"I told you to take a shower and a nap," he said harshly.

"I was about to take a shower," she replied, still completely poised and making him feel like an unruly adolescent. "But some of your white-coated friends walked in. Only these guys had masks. They were exterminators, or so they told me. Politely of course. These people are all very polite."

"You'd rather they were rude?"

"No, I'd rather that I didn't feel like a prisoner on death row."

"You're not on death row!" Kiel snapped. "For God's sake Rhiannan! The situation isn't that drastic—"

"If things aren't that drastic, then what the hell is going on?"

"Rhiannan . . ." With a sigh Kiel sank down to the chair again and stripped off his socks. "Try to pay attention to me. I've been going through this all day and I can't repeat any of it twice now. Infected rats generally cause bubonic plague. The rats get fleas. The fleas bite people. Now, modern medicine has given us a wonderful vaccine against the bubonic plague. The one we've been given was only perfected after the outbreak in Arizona not so long ago. But it's top-drawer—the best. And it's very, very unlikely that anyone else will come down with the disease. But disease control has to be very careful. Fastidiously careful. They have to get to the bottom of this—search out any rats and fleas. They have to keep the ship under a quarantine. They just can't allow the ship to come in and allow a plague to run rampant in port and possibly spread to other ships and other countries."

She just kept staring at him.

"Did you have anything to eat?" he asked her lamely.

"Oh, yes. One of those polite darlings in the little white coats came around with meals for me."

"Don't be hostile. Those 'polite darlings in white' are here to help."

Rhiannan lowered her lashes. "I know it," she murmured, then stared at him bleakly again. "How is Mary?"

"Sick," Kiel replied tersely.

"How sick?"

Kiel hesitated briefly. "They don't really know yet, but she is being treated with the best drugs available, and those drugs are damned good."

"When can I see her?" Rhiannan demanded.

"I'd rather you didn't—"

"I'm not asking you what you'd rather. I refuse to be locked in here helplessly much longer."

"No one is going to be free to roam around until the vaccine has had a minimum of twenty-four hours to be effective. There are side effects to the vaccine."

"And then there is that slim possibility that the vaccine won't be effective at all."

"It's a razor-slim possibility. Rhiannan, you're not going to die."

"I wasn't really worried about that," she said softly, and her eyes at last fell from his.

For some reason he was struck anew with fury. He bolted out of the chair again and dropped violently down beside her, gripping her shoulders and pinning her to the bed. "You wouldn't give a damn if you did or didn't die, would you? It would be justice to your warped little mind. Well, it isn't going to happen!"

"Kiel! Stop it, please!" She implored him as she met the violence and weariness in his eyes. It seemed that she had melted a bit when he had touched her, as if she had come back to him, become the woman once more whom he had known and loved.

"I . . . I don't want to die, Kiel. Really I don't. But I can't stop thinking about Mary. I know a little about the bubonic plague. I read a lot on European history when I was in college. Kiel, plague victims usually die by the fourth day. If Mary is bad now—"

"Rhiannan!" He rose up a bit to grip her chin between his palms, stroking it lightly with his calloused but gentle touch. "Way back then, they didn't have the drugs that we do. Mary is sick, yes. Very sick. But she has every chance in the world to recuperate. I promise you that."

"Every chance," Rhiannan repeated, but her eyes held his with bitterness. "So if she dies, it will be an act of God. Just like the plague is an act of God."

Her question left him feeling strangely uncomfortable, so much that he released his hold on her and rolled off the bed ostensibly to strip away his jacket.

"Mary isn't going to die," he said flatly. He remembered

the shampoo packets in his jacket just as he thought it was definitely a good time to change the subject. Kiel riffled through the jacket pockets and found the packets. He tossed one on the bed beside Rhiannan.

"What's this?"

"A flea bath."

"Kiel—"

"I'm serious. Want to shower first or second? Or better yet, let's think of the ecology. Conserve water—shower with a friend."

"I really don't see how you can be so flippant."

"Hey, you were the one playing the video games."

She rolled off the bed and stood gracefully. "I'll take the first shower, thanks."

"Fine. I'll guard the door from exterminators."

"Thanks."

Rhiannan stalked into the bathroom and closed the door behind her. She methodically stripped off her clothes, then tried to read the back of the packet, but all she understood were the words *U.S. Government Issue.* The rest was a jumble of chemicals. Just reading it made her feel itchy, as if she did have fleas.

"Oh, stop it!" she whispered softly to herself, reaching into the shower stall to turn on the water. It came out very hot, instantly steaming up the enclosed space.

She stepped beneath the shower with her little packet and doused her head beneath the water. What the power of suggestion could do to the nerves! Her whole scalp was suddenly driving her nuts.

She did not have fleas! she told herself, ripping open the foil with her teeth and grimacing as it gave. She stepped back and pinched out the creamy white liquid. It didn't smell unpleasant or too medicinal, and it was a generous supply. She was able to get her itching scalp foaming almost instantly.

But then her hands suddenly froze in her scalp. No, she didn't have fleas, and neither did Mary. Something was going on aboard the ship; she had sensed it, and now, although she didn't know what, she knew that something malicious was taking place. If only she could pinpoint what it was!

"Hey!"

The bathroom door swung inward and she heard Kiel's voice.

"Kiel, I told you—"

"I've been knocking for ten minutes, but you wouldn't pay any attention to me."

"I . . . I didn't hear you. What do you want?"

He was on the other side of the curtain. She could see his silhouette; she could feel his presence. She would always be able to feel him near.

He chuckled. "Do I detect a note of chaste outrage in that tone? Seems to me you were the last one to invade a peaceful shower. But actually, madam, I didn't come to assault your virtue but to preserve it. You walked in here with nothing to wear. I brought you a T-shirt that should cover your knees."

"Thanks," Rhiannan mumbled. She sensed him turning to go, and although it was probably foolish, she stopped him. "Kiel?"

"What?"

"You know, it was strange when the exterminator came."

He felt his heartbeat quicken. "Strange how?" he asked.

"Well, actually, it was the exterminator who said it was strange. He looked all around the room, and sprayed some stuff around. This was one of his last cabins, he told me. They had started below deck and worked their way up."

"Go on."

"What?"

"I said to go on."

Rhiannan forgot for a moment that she was in the shower. It was annoying that she couldn't see his face and hear him clearly above the roar of the water. She pulled the curtain back to see his face.

"Kiel, he said that it was the darndest thing: Almost all

ships carry rats, especially old ones like this. But they hadn't found a single rodent from the bottom up."

"That *is* strange," Kiel murmured, feeling a strange gnawing in his stomach. He didn't let on to her that Donald had given him the same information. He didn't want her feeling his sense of apprehension, so he shrugged. "Maybe our rat jumped ship. Or maybe he crawled away and died in a cubbyhole somewhere."

"Maybe."

He smiled suddenly. She was holding the curtain over her breasts, but she had managed to clutch only a part of it. One lean hip was left completely bare. And her hair! The majority of it was well sudsed and high on her head, giving her eyes a wide and temptingly vulnerable look. Very tempting. She had also left a strand of her long hair untouched.

"You missed a spot," he told her.

"Where?"

"I'll get it for you."

"No!"

In her haste to fix her own hair, Rhiannan dropped the curtain.

Kiel laughed. "You are being ridiculous. I assure you, I've already studied all your attributes very thoroughly."

"Very amusing."

He shrugged and grinned once more and started working on the buttons of his cuffs.

Rhiannan yanked the curtain back in place. "I don't know what you think you're doing."

"I'm not going to attack you," Kiel promised, but strangely enough, she could hear his shirt fall to the floor above the noise of the shower.

"Kiel . . ."

"But," he continued as if she hadn't spoken, "I am hopping in with you. That's medicated shampoo. It won't do you any good if you don't use it properly."

He was standing behind her as he finished speaking, and

although she assiduously kept facing forward, his was such a strong presence that she was achingly aware of him and inwardly ready to jump a mile away.

"I'm glad you gave me a choice about the shower, Congressman," she told him dryly, except that the sound of her voice didn't come out entirely dry. There was a husky quality to it that made her want to kick herself.

"I'm not going to allow the fact that you're behaving ridiculously to impair your health," he told her gallantly.

She did jump when she felt his hands in her hair expertly, efficiently, taking over the shampooing.

At first she was aware of nothing but his fingers, gentle and soothing on her scalp. The water was falling all around them, and if she closed her eyes, it all felt a bit like paradise. She was in a land of mist, lulled by the kiss of the heat and water and his touch.

Stunned is more like it, Rhiannan thought ruefully. She didn't dare move, because she was aware of much, much more. He was so close behind her that the movement of his arms caused the coarse hair on his chest to graze her back. And she could feel his thighs the same way, the hair . . . a rough grazing on the softness of her flanks. She could feel the strength and tension of his body, the hardness of his masculinity.

"I . . . I think I should rinse it out now," she gasped.

"Wait," he said. The massaging of his fingers moved along her nape, and both hands slid along her shoulders.

"It's for all over the body."

"All over? But—"

"All over," he repeated gravely, his voice tauntingly close to her ear. "Dr. Trenton warned that pests could seek out the most intimate places to hide."

"I think there's only one pest I have to worry about seeking out my secret places to hide!" Rhiannan retorted swiftly.

His laughter was spontaneous and husky. "But that pest, my lady, would never seek to hide. Now behave! I promise you, it's truly your well-being I have in mind at the moment."

He studiously scrubbed the lather along her shoulders and over her back, then slid his hands along her ribs, making her swallow and choke back a gasp when they cupped her breasts.

"My well-being, huh?" she demanded hoarsely.

"Yes, but don't begrudge my enjoyment of the assistance rendered."

"Tell me, am I supposed to reciprocate this assistance?"

His hands paused as they slid along her midriff, then moved to alight on her shoulders and spin her around to face him once more. There was a hunger in the deep gray of his eyes, a fiery demand, but also a disconcerting tenderness and sincerity.

"Only if you choose to," he promised.

She could give him no answer, nor did he seem to require one at the moment. He stared at her a moment, then fixed his attention on his efforts as he brought more lather thoroughly over her arms.

"We're out of lather here. I've got to get the other packet."

"That one is yours."

"But I haven't half as much hair as you. Besides, I'm counting on your being a Good Samaritan."

Rhiannan shivered as he stepped out of the shower. He was gone only an instant, but in that time she fought back a sudden rush of tears. There was no future for them. She loved him— she knew she loved him—but she couldn't keep herself from holding back.

As he stepped back into the shower he was ripping his own packet open with his teeth. Rhiannan continued to stand still as he poured a small amount of liquid into his palms and rubbed them together before placing his hands on her hips and pulling her slightly forward.

"You're getting too wet. Had to get you a little out of the spray," he explained.

His massage began over her hips, and then she was drawn even closer to him as his hands curved over her firm buttocks. Her eyes met his, but she could neither fight him nor come to him. He just continued to watch her until he slowly slid to his knees, bringing his gently laving hands along her thighs up to her hips once more, along her belly, to her thighs, and then between them.

A sound escaped her, a startled whimper. Unwittingly she reached for his shoulders for support. "Kiel, please stop!" she gasped. "You promised—"

"I promised not to attack you, and I won't. But neither will I stop until I'm finished."

She didn't dare say anything else; she was afraid to open her mouth lest she moan once more. She wasn't aware that she dug her nails into his flesh; she was barely even aware of the rippling muscle beneath them. She knew only that the deft ministrations of his careful fingers created a flood of sensations that defied everything. The slight roughness of his calloused hands, the firm strength that was determined and thorough but gentle, was rendering her totally helpless.

It took everything—her entire will—to stand still, to fight the field of mist and magic, especially when she didn't really want to fight it. But somehow . . . somehow she just couldn't give in to it. The magic, the mist, would become blackness.

He moved downward once more and she drew in a deep and jaded breath. If he noticed, he gave no sign. He fastidiously washed her calves and her feet, then rose before her once again.

Although she closed her eyes for a moment to steady herself, she felt him achingly near. Her breasts were brushing his chest, and it would be absurd to pretend that they didn't swell and that the pink crests didn't stiffen and long for the brush of his hands again. It was just as ridiculous for either of them to ignore his own reaction to his intimacy with her.

When she opened her eyes at last, it was to stare up into his. But they both knew that there was another brush of flesh against flesh of which they were both acutely aware. His masculinity was hard and taunting against her lower belly.

Rhiannan swallowed. "Can I . . . can I rinse out my hair now?"

He nodded. She turned and ducked her head beneath the steady stream of the water. But even then, without asking, he moved to help her, his hands rinsing her hair clean.

When she faced him again he moved her behind him so he could stand beneath the steady spray. Then, with the clinging droplets of water somehow adding to the rugged, masculine appeal of his features, he confronted her dryly.

"I don't suppose I'm going to get any assistance?"

No, she should have said, and she should have stepped out of the shower, wrapped herself in a towel, grabbed the T-shirt, and fled.

"Duck your head," she told him. "I can't reach it this way."

He obediently ducked and she enjoyed running her fingers through his hair. There was an intimate domesticity about the action. His hair was thick and sleek and nice to touch. She scrubbed it with definite purpose.

When she was done, she went on. Maybe she wanted an excuse to touch the broad expanse of his chest again, explore the pattern of his hair, the dips and angles of his lean muscle and strong bone.

She washed his arms just as he had hers. She ordered him to turn so that she might use both hands on his back. And she felt the constriction of muscle in his buttocks, hesitated only slightly, then scrubbed.

"Turn around again," she told him, and when he did, she could not meet his eyes. She watched her own hands with fascination as they moved over him intimately. She was slightly embarrassed, for she savored the heat and pulse and potency of the masculinity that came to full life in her hands.

His own hands suddenly fell on her shoulders, and, startled, she couldn't keep her eyes from flying to meet his. Nor could she keep from seeing the strain that now made his features tense and haggard.

"I made a promise to you, Rhiannan, but I'm hardly a saint,

and you've gone well past my breaking point. So step out. I appreciate your assistance. It was more than I expected, but if you're going to run, do it now. I can still turn the water on cold."

Rhiannan opened her mouth in misery. She wanted to explain to him how badly she wanted him, but she just couldn't reach out. Why couldn't he be a bit of a brute? If he forced her, if he carried her away, she could fall. There would still be the blackness, but it would pass, and she could rise above it.

"I see," he said coldly. But there wasn't any anger in him now, just weariness. "Out!"

He picked her up bodily, ignoring the water that cascaded to the floor as he carelessly pushed open the curtain, and set her down outside of the shower.

A paralysis seemed to come over her as he stepped back in and ripped the curtain back into place. She just stood there dripping, forlorn and rejected and wishing she could talk, wishing so badly that she could explain.

Vaguely she heard his movements. She could envision the agile stance of his athletic body as he studiously rinsed the lather from his hair and body. Then she heard the jerk of the faucets as he turned them off. The curtain slid aside.

Blindly she reached for a towel and, fumbling, wrapped it around herself.

He ignored her, grabbing a towel himself. He didn't even dry off before stalking from the tight confines of the bathroom and slamming the door behind him.

For long moments Rhiannan stood there, feeling the paralysis descend upon her once more. Paralysis and so much emptiness. Everything was going to hell all around them. Men were striding around the ship in white coats. Poor Mary was desperately ill. Donald was sitting by her side. Kiel had spent the day working with tension and fatigue, and he had been called on to handle it all. Yet, they had each other to give shelter to one another as they weathered the tumult and the storm. He could be so strong; he could give so very, very much. And she was denying him, denying herself, because she was afraid. It was all so ridiculous. It would be easy to fight the blackness. All she had to do was go to him, tell him that she needed his help. A few simple words and he would understand. *Go to him,* she told herself. *Oh, go to him now. . . .*

She didn't bother with the T-shirt. She shook off the lethargy of her soul and spun to the door, throwing it open.

He was lying on his stomach, naked on the bed. Rhiannan rushed over to him, kneeling down by the bed.

"Kiel, I . . ." Her voice trailed away as she saw that his eyes were closed. He was breathing deeply and easily. The fingers splayed over the sheets were limp and relaxed. He was sound asleep.

"Oh, Kiel," Rhiannan whispered. "Oh, Kiel, I do love you so very much." She leaned over to kiss his forehead, then stood. She was about to drop over herself.

But he had fallen asleep on the bedspread, and his bronzed body was still damp from the shower. The last thing he needed to do at the moment was catch a common cold. Rhiannan dug around in the closet and found a blanket and an extra sheet. She spread both out over him, then crawled into the bed beside him.

For several seconds she lay stiffly apart from him. Then she gave in to the temptation and the need to feel his strength. She edged next to him and slipped her arm around his waist and rested her head beneath his shoulder. She had lost her chance to talk to him, to give to him, but she could still sleep beside him, naked but warm and assured by the touch of his naked flesh, clean and fresh and sleek, touching her.

Sleep . . . it was overcoming her so easily. She would awaken beside him. The morning would come, and they would already be touching. . . .

"I'll make it up to you, my love, I promise," she said in a muffled whisper against his sleeping body. Everything had fallen on his shoulders, and then he had wound up with her. She didn't know what they could really have in the future, but for now he deserved so much more than to be saddled with a shrew. She would quit taking from him and give to him. She would support him, try and offer him the shelter that he had given her.

With such pleasant thoughts she closed her eyes, and her dreams were not full of the terror but full of him. Full of his optimism. Full of his assurance. The world could be a cruel place, but if you faced it and took it firmly in your own hands, you could fight the demons of death and of life. With love.

Twelve

When Rhiannan awakened, she was alone. It took her several minutes to rise out of the fog of sleep to assimilate the fact that not only was he no longer in the bed, but no longer anywhere in the room.

Absently she hugged his pillow to her breast and leaned back against her own, overwhelmed by a sense of acute depression. She had lost something very dear. A chance. A moment in time and space when, despite all else, she might have found a sense of peace and balance and plunged herself into a high-stakes gamble for life.

She started as she heard the key turn in the lock and instinctively pulled the covers more tightly about herself as she stared at the door.

It was Kiel. He was dressed in tan slacks and a knit navy shirt that made her blink and dream for a moment that the shattering disease that had befallen the *Seafire* had been an illusion of sleep and that they were still engaged in nothing more than a pleasure cruise.

He walked into the cabin and she realized that he was carrying a pile of her clothing. But before she could open her mouth and speak to him, he started talking to her, crisp, cool, distant.

"It seems you're going to achieve your desire for freedom this morning," he said, plopping her clothing down at the foot of the bed and meeting her eyes with his hands on his hips. "I'm not really happy about sending you down to our makeshift hospital, but then, I don't want Donald toppling over, either. And Trenton assures me that you should be fine—as fine as you're going to be anywhere on this ship, at any rate," he said, more to himself than to her, his eyes seeming to cloud for a minute.

"What are you talking about?" Rhiannan at last asked him in confusion.

"Donald refuses to leave Mary's side. He's been with her all this time. He won't trust Picard, Trenton, or even Dr. Trivitt. And he knows I'd be called away as soon as I sat down. The only one he'll trust so that he can get some sleep is you."

Rhiannan sprang out of bed, heedless of her nudity as she rummaged through the things he had brought. He was efficient as always, she thought. He had brought her jeans, shirts, bras, and underpants. She clutched a set of clothing and headed for the bathroom.

"Poor Donald," she mumbled, her concern and sympathy for her employer deep in her voice. "I can't believe he won't even trust her brother. Jason must be going crazy."

Kiel's silence stopped her in her tracks and she turned around to stare at him.

"Jason is in the bed next to Mary's," Kiel told her.

"Oh," Rhiannan murmured unhappily.

She closed the door to the bathroom, hurriedly washed and dressed, and was back to join Kiel in a matter of minutes.

They were silent as they walked to the Manhattan. The only people they passed on the way were the newcomers to the vessel—the medical team. All of them nodded to Kiel as they walked on by with brisk, efficient footsteps.

Rhiannan was amazed by the change in what had been a lovely and gracious lounge. Cots now lined either wall, each distinctly separated by a screen, and a number of the white-coated figures were also there, carrying water pitchers, trays with little white paper cups of medications, bowls of ice water, and sterile white cloths.

"Come on," Kiel said briefly. "Mary is at the end of the row."

Rhiannan felt her heart clutch and squeeze as she stared down at the pretty young singer who had been so full of life. Mary's eyes were closed. Her complexion was so pale that it appeared gray rather than white. Her breathing was ragged and shallow. She seemed terribly thin and fragile except around her throat, where it seemed that she had puffed and swelled and grown a double chin.

She looked strangely beautiful lying there, so very young, so very fragile, her tangled hair splayed across the pillow in sharply contrasting beauty.

Donald's head was bowed over her as he held her hand. Rhiannan felt her stomach tighten as she saw the dark spots beneath the fragile stretch of translucent flesh of Mary's hand.

Rhiannan felt Kiel hovering behind her, watching her. *Hold me,* she thought. *Hold me for a minute and I'll have the strength to reach out and help Donald.* But he wasn't going to hold her. She had decreed the distance in a moment's hesitation. She had thrown away the bond between them with both hands.

Rhiannan stepped toward Donald and placed her hands on his shoulders. "Donald, it's Rhiannan. I'm here, and I'll stay here until you clean up and get some sleep. I promise."

He looked up slowly. His bleary eyes seemed to take a moment to focus. "Rhiannan," he murmured, and groped with his free hand for hers. A tender pain tugged at her heart as she looked at him. A thick five-o'clock shadow covered his usually clean-shaven chin. He looked all of his forty years—and more.

"Donald," she urged him gently, "you're not going to do her any good if you keel over on top of her. Get up and go eat; take a nap and a nice long shower."

He nodded limply. "You won't leave her?"

"Not even for a minute. I won't even take a bathroom break unless Kiel can come back to spell me. I promise."

Donald nodded again, but he looked at her with pain glazing

his reddened eyes. "She's the worst, you know. Why Mary Rhiannan? She's so young. I wish it were me! I'm forty and she's barely twenty-five."

Rhiannan took a deep breath and swallowed. She knew what he was feeling. She knew exactly what he meant. She had thought the same thing when her children had been taken from her.

"Donald, she's going to pull through. Get up and stop sounding like a bleating sheep. Get yourself together so that you can be useful to her!"

His eyes blazed with a sudden anger and stared at her with outrage, but then he smiled. " 'Annan, I'm sorry. Of all people for me to cry to. . . . You're right. I'm going. I'll sleep a few hours and then I'll be back."

He stood and briefly kissed her forehead. Rhiannan had almost forgotten Kiel, but she suddenly felt the intensity of his eyes on her once more. She turned to see that he was indeed still staring at her. His expression denoted nothing—no approval, no disapproval. He appeared strained and detached, nothing more.

"Come on, Donald . . ." he began, but before the two men could move away, a nurse approached them. "Congressman, they want you on the radio. Top priority—it's the White House."

"Come on, Kiel," Donald said. "I'll walk you to the deck."

Kiel nodded at Donald but didn't glance at Rhiannan again. She watched the blue shirt that hugged his broad shoulders as he walked away. Then she sank down in the chair Donald had vacated and watched Mary, feeling as if her heart and soul were a void.

"Mrs. Collins?" It was the pleasant young nurse.

"Yes?"

"You could help us tremendously if you would keep these cloths cool and on her forehead. She has an I.V. going over here"—the nurse pointed out the tube running to Mary's right arm—"but if she asks for water, please give her some."

"Of course," Rhiannan murmured. "How . . . how are the others?"

The nurse smiled. "Not bad—light cases. We got here in time. In fact, this girl's brother—Jason? Is that it?" She paused until Rhiannan nodded, then continued. "Jason is giving us fits because he wants to sit with his sister." The nurse chuckled softly. "We had to sedate the young man to keep him in his own bed and out of trouble."

Rhiannan smiled. "When Donald gets back, I'll check in with Jason if he's awake."

"That would be very helpful, Mrs. Collins."

The nurse smiled and moved on to her other duties. Rhiannan began to wet the cloths and apply them to Mary's forehead. Mary didn't move. She didn't blink. Rhiannan noted the dark spots beneath the skin of Mary's hands again. Unknowingly she began to pray. *Please let her live, God. Please let her live. Please.*

Did God ever answer prayers? She wasn't terribly sure anymore. It seemed to her that God didn't know anything about justice.

"Kiel, I've done what you asked with a fine-tooth comb, although I still don't understand. From the toilet scrubbers to the diplomatic elite, I've rechecked everyone on that vessel."

"Thank you, sir," Kiel told the Vice-President. "And . . . ?"

"And there's not much, I can assure you. And then again, there's a little too much. Most of your statesmen, American and foreign, have been involved in nonviolent protests, which stands to reason. What can you expect when a quarter of the ship belongs to WWON?"

Kiel raked his fingers through his hair and gripped the telephone receiver more tautly with frustration. Was he a fool for thinking there was something where there was nothing? Or did he think he was becoming a psychic in a premature old age?

No, the discomfort was there. And that feeling . . . the feeling that went along with his near photographic memory. Somewhere he had seen something, something that should be clicking now. But it didn't make any sense and it was plaguing him to distraction. *Plaguing* him! Damn did he hate that association!

"Did you go through everything, sir? Everything?"

He couldn't hear the patient sigh that followed his question but he could sense it. "Kiel, believe me, we've got the expert to do the job here."

"Yeah, I'm sure you do. Sorry. But nothing?"

"Like I told you, Kiel, nothing and too much. Actually, Congressman, you've got the worst record of the lot. All those war protests! Good thing you wound up in the service or I'd call you suspicious at the moment—if I knew why we were being suspicious."

"They didn't find a single rat on board the ship, sir," Kiel said dryly.

"Rats come and go without worrying about customs."

"Still seems strange. Did you check up on . . ."

"Who, Kiel?"

"A Dr. Glen Trivitt. Not a passenger. He was signed on as the ship's doctor."

"Trivitt . . . Trivitt . . . that's a *T*. Yes, here. Glen Trivitt. Forty-three. He checks out fine, Kiel. More than fine. He graduated from Johns Hopkins—all kinds of honors. Member in good standing of the American Medical Association. All the right groups. No arrests. Nothing wrong. Why? I thought he was the one who identified the disease and kept the situation under control with his prompt thought and action."

"He is," Kiel said with a sigh. Trivitt was bright, quick, efficient, and pleasant. There was no reason to suspect him.

"Want more?"

"No . . . no, I guess not."

"How are things going?"

"Good, I guess. We've got a lot of very responsible people aboard. Intelligent and cooperative. Things seem to be calm."

"How many came down ill?"

"Less than twenty."

"Out of two hundred? That must be some vaccine."

"A great vaccine," Kiel agreed. "All those ill had the symptoms before the vaccine."

"Good, good. Keep me posted."

"Yes, sir."

Kiel was about to end the conversation when he paused. "Sir?"

"Yes?"

"You keep me posted, too."

"Of course."

Mary opened her eyes. They were dazed and unfocused, and her lips were dry and parched.

Rhiannan leaped from the chair to lean close to her.

"Water."

With trembling fingers Rhiannan ripped the sterile covering off a plastic cup and poured a small portion of clear, clean water. Supporting her friend's head, she brought the cup to Mary's lips.

"Not too much, Mary." Her warning didn't matter. Mary barely moistened her lips before falling limply against Rhiannan once more. Rhiannan eased her head to the pillow and sank back to her chair.

Dismally she looked about the room. Only the rich carpets and drapes were left to remind her that it had once been a place of laughter and dancing and music, and Mary's sweet voice. The band had stood not far from where Mary now lay.

"How's she doing?"

Rhiannan almost jumped at the question, then smiled ruefully as she saw Glen gazing at her from the end of the screen. Like the other medical personnel aboard the ship, he was clothed in one of the white coats.

"I don't know, Glen. You tell me."

Glen moved around the bed, excusing himself as he brushed by her to lean over Mary. He checked her heart with the stethoscope dangling around his neck, then looked into her eyes with a bright pencil flashlight. He placed his hands on her throat, forcing her mouth open.

"She's a sick little girl, but I think she'll pull through."

"Do you, Glen? Really?" Rhiannan asked anxiously.

"Yes, I do. Of course, we won't know for sure for another couple of days, but if she makes it past Friday, we'll be in the clear. So far, she hasn't gone into the pneumonic stage."

"And if she does?"

Glen shrugged. "Let's worry about that if it happens, okay? Things are looking too good right now for us to be pessimistic." He smiled at Rhiannan but then frowned. "But you, young woman, what are you doing in here?"

"Sitting with her."

"I can see that. But you shouldn't be here."

"I've had the vaccine."

"Still . . ."

"Hey, what about you, Doctor?" Rhiannan retorted. "You're lucky you didn't get ill yourself! You and Donald were certainly in very direct contact!"

Glen laughed, his features easing into pleasant lines. "I'm a doctor, remember? We probably get exposed to so much that we have a natural immunity, and I had the vaccine, too."

"Well, good," Rhiannan murmured. "I'd hate to think of you falling ill, too, Glen."

"Would you really?"

There was a strange, wistful quality to his question. Startled, Rhiannan met his eyes, but they told her little. "Of course. You're too good a man to suffer, Glen." His gaze on her still left her feeling strangely disconcerted. "And listen, Doc! If you want to give someone a hard time for helping out, look to our beautiful blonde."

"What?"

Rhiannan pointed across the room. Joan Kendrick was sitting at one of the bedsides, changing cool towels on an elderly man's forehead. "Our rich friend has been acting like a bona fide Florence Nightingale all day. Makes me feel a little useless, but I promised Donald I wouldn't leave Mary's side."

"Oh, Joan," Glen said dismissively.

Rhiannan frowned at his casual acceptance of the situation. Glen saw her frown. "What are you going to do?" he asked with a shrug. "Every once in a while the filthy rich who spend their lives stepping on humanity get on a guilt trip and decide to turn into angels of mercy. You can't stop them. Just ignore them." He smiled at her. "Seems like we're going to have little control over you, too, 'Annan. I can see that look in your eyes. You've been allowed into the sickroom. And if I don't miss my guess, you're determined to stay."

"I'm sure I can help," Rhiannan admitted defensively.

"That I don't deny. We've been given a fair share of doctors and nurses, but all of the patients need round-the-clock care."

"It's better to help than to sit around, worrying," Rhiannan said.

"Probably, for a woman like you."

Rhiannan barely heard his last remark. Far across the ballroom-lounge turned hospital, the door was opening. One of the white-coated attendants was on his feet, confronting the newcomer. But it was Kiel, and the man quickly became at ease, taking his seat behind a makeshift desk once more.

Kiel didn't come immediately toward her. He paused at the third bed—the bed where Joan Kendrick worked over her older patient. Both of them disappeared behind the screen, but Rhiannan could see the silhouettes close together. Joan's head was tilted up to Kiel's, her hand on his arm. Were they smiling? Whispering intimately?

She didn't have long to ponder the situation, because Kiel came back around the screen and started walking to her. He addressed not her but Glen. "Dr. Trivitt." He acknowledged the other man with a nod.

"Congressman," Glen replied.

"Think we'll have any new cases?" Kiel asked.

"No, hopefully not. Trenton, Picard, and I all agree that if we make it through the night, all those vaccinated in time are safe." He grimaced. "But it may be a tough night. I've just been visiting the cabins. A few of our passengers are overreacting to the side effects of the vaccine. They're having chills and some stiffness in the bones, and they're panicking easily—not that I can blame them. But we'll be busy tonight running around with reassurances. How are we doing on the diplomatic end, Congressman?"

"Good so far. I think we'll be doing even better once the passengers are free to roam around. They'll believe that the danger is really past then."

"You're probably right," Glen agreed.

Kiel's eyes alighted on Rhiannan so suddenly that she almost jumped beneath their silver-steel stare. "Go and get some lunch," he told her. "The Pirate's Cove has been turned into a doctor's lounge. You'll find coffee and sandwiches there."

"But—"

"Don't worry, I'll stay here with Mary. Unless the ship starts sinking, no one will call me away for at least fifteen minutes."

"Come on, Rhiannan," Glen told her. "I could use some coffee myself."

Five minutes later she was seated across from Glen at one of the plank tables chewing a piece of toast that seemed to have no taste.

"That's all you're going to eat?" Glen queried with disapproval.

"I'm not hungry," Rhiannan told him.

"Queasy?" he asked her.

"A little, I guess."

He patted her hand. "Don't worry. It's a natural reaction to the shot. All vaccines give you a touch of the disease, you know." He shook his head in wonderment. "That Trenton is one hell of a genius. You can't usually give a vaccine when people have already been exposed. Oh, well. Thank God for small miracles."

"Hmm," Rhiannan agreed with a murmur. She looked about the small lounge at the white-coated men serving the few other white-coated men and women who had wandered in to grab a bite to eat.

"Glen, how many people came aboard from Disease Control?"

"Let me see. Trenton and three other doctors. Ten nurse-assistants. And ten men who are experts in pest extermination. Why?"

"They just seem to be everywhere."

Glen chuckled. "Some of those in the white coats, such as the two gents serving lunch, are security personnel. They were already aboard and were called into active 'white-coat' duty."

"Oh," Rhiannan answered. "Well, that makes sense, I guess."

"I guess."

Just as she hadn't been looking at or really hearing Glen earlier when Kiel had stepped into the infirmary, she realized suddenly that Glen was not looking at her. His eyes were on the door to the small lounge, where Joan Kendrick was entering. Joan glanced in their direction.

Rhiannan began to frown, then saw that Glen was looking at her once more. "Our Florence Nightingale," he said with skepticism.

"She *is* helping."

"Yes, she is."

Rhiannan wondered why it should bother her that Joan's eyes fell on her and Glen. There were very few people in the room, and it was natural that anyone entering would look about. And she could truly care less what went on between Joan Kendrick and Glen Trivitt. Glen was a grown man, and he seemed to know Joan's type. If he chose to allow himself to be used, it was his own concern.

But it didn't gel. Rhiannan had seen Joan around Kiel. She

had seen the way Joan looked at him and touched him. Kiel was a man whom Joan wanted, not Glen.

Joan headed for their table. "May I join you two?"

"Certainly," Rhiannan heard herself say. "Please sit down."

Glen stood silently to slide back a chair for Joan. The blonde sat and smiled as she ordered toast and coffee, then turned her full attention to Rhiannan and Glen.

"These make for long days, don't they?"

"Very," Rhiannan agreed.

"Oh, well. It should all be brighter soon. Kiel was telling me that they're going to resume some activities tomorrow. Open one of the lounges, have a few games. Regular meals in the dining room. Maybe even send out a few diving parties, although we're really too deep for much enjoyment on that score. But it will be something to keep people occupied."

"That does sound brighter," Rhiannan said. She lowered her eyes to sip her coffee, then as she raised them she noted that Joan was staring at Glen, who hadn't said a word to her so far.

Was it a look that said *I have to talk to you?* Or was she imagining things? Rhiannan wondered. Whichever, she suddenly felt acutely uncomfortable, as if a dark wall were closing in around her, making her feel horribly claustrophobic. She drained her coffee cup and stood so quickly that she almost knocked her chair over.

"Excuse me. I think I should get back. I promised Donald that I wouldn't leave Mary alone, and you know how it is with Kiel: He gets calls to be somewhere else every other minute."

She was rambling on nervously, she realized, but hopefully both Joan and Glen would chalk her behavior up to worry over the plague. She offered them a tenuous smile and waved them a brief farewell.

"See you soon," Joan called after her.

Rhiannan paused at the door, compelled to turn back. As she had somehow known, Joan and the previously silent Glen were in deep conversation, their heads bowed closely together. A ripple of inexplicable fear shot along her spine as Rhiannan turned again and fled back through the halls to the hospital-lounge.

Kiel was helping the nurse as she changed Mary's I.V., but his eyes narrowed as she hurried back to the bed. "Did you eat?" he asked her, sounding more terse than he had intended before a third party.

"Yes," she said simply, taking the chair and watching the procedure.

"There we are!" said the perpetually sunny nurse, her round face creased into her usual smile. "Now, do keep an eye on those tubes, please!"

"Of course," Kiel and Rhiannan said in unison. But as soon as the nurse had moved on behind the next screen, Kiel scowled at Rhiannan openly.

"What's the matter with you?"

"Nothing!"

"You're as white as a ghost."

"Well, nothing is wrong," Rhiannan snapped.

"I don't think you should be here. Maybe you're having more of a reaction to that vaccine than—"

"Oh, Kiel, for Pete's sake, I'm fine! And you're not going to move me from this spot unless you want to drag me, and there are an awful lot of people around for you to pull any macho stunts."

It was the wrong way for her to have spoken to him. His eyes narrowed further until they were nothing more than points of piercing silver. Tension darkened his features until they appeared ruthless and harsh. "Don't tempt me, Rhiannan. If I feel you look any worse, I will drag you out of here over my shoulder, and I won't give a damn who is around to see my 'macho' stunt."

Rhiannan lowered her lashes swiftly, deciding it was a good time to retreat. "I'm fine, Kiel. I swear it, and I want to stay with Mary."

"All right," he said crisply.

Rhiannan didn't look up as she heard him spin about on his

heels. She didn't look up again until she was certain he had had time to leave the room.

But he hadn't left. Joan Kendrick had come back in again, and he had paused to talk to her once more. Chills touched her again. *What is wrong with me?* she asked herself wretchedly. She didn't like Joan talking to Kiel or to Glen. Now she must be going crazy. But she didn't feel crazy. She just felt terribly alone. Kiel had been telling Joan all about his plans, and he hadn't talked much to her at all. But, she reminded herself, he had been with her. He had cared. He had washed her hair and her body. Her whole body. He had told her that everything was up to her, and she hadn't been able to make the choice. But, oh, how she wanted to!

I am still the one sleeping in his cabin, Rhiannan assured herself. There was still time. . . .

But was there? She was learning more thoroughly every day that one didn't always receive a second chance.

"Rhiannan?"

"Mary! Oh, Mary! You know me."

Mary managed a very weak smile. "Oh, boy, Rhiannan, do I feel like hell!"

"I know, I know. But you'll be better soon. It won't be long. How about a sip of water, Mary?"

Mary nodded. She struggled to sip the water as Rhiannan helped her, then fell back on her pillow, exhausted. Her lips tried to form words again.

"What is it, Mary?" Rhiannan asked, bending close to Mary's lips.

"Donald?"

"He'll be back soon," Rhiannan promised.

Her answer seemed to appease Mary, as she closed her eyes and slept again.

Rhiannan sat holding her hand as the afternoon slipped into evening.

It wasn't until almost nine o'clock at night that Donald returned sheepishly and anxiously to Mary's bedside. He looked ten times better, Rhiannan thought with relief. He had shaved, changed to comfortable slacks and a light pullover sweater, and looked well rested.

"I'm so sorry, 'Annan!" he whispered fervently as he joined her by Mary's bedside, immediately clutching the young woman's hand. He stared at Mary a long while, then dragged his eyes from her to Rhiannan. "I was out like a light. I didn't mean to leave you so long."

"You needed the rest," Rhiannan said. Then she couldn't help smiling. "You're really in love with her, aren't you, Donald?"

"Yeah," he said softly. "I guess I am." He smiled a little crookedly. "The little songbird came into my life like a melody that stays with the soul. But . . ."

"But what, Donald?"

"She's just twenty-five. So young."

"You're not a doddering old man, Donald. You're forty and in your prime. She asked for you."

"Did she?"

"Yes."

Donald sank to his knees beside the bed, bowing his head slightly. "If she lives . . . if she'll just live . . . I'll give her everything."

Rhiannan touched his bowed head with warmth and tender affection. "Donald, I think you have already given her everything. All she ever wanted was your love."

Donald tried to send her back to Kiel's cabin to sleep, but Rhiannan was too restless to go. She wanted to talk to Jason, so she went to his bedside and spent an hour assuring him, with far more confidence than she felt, that Mary was going to be just fine.

Then, from a cot nearby, Rhiannan heard someone ask for

water. She was surprised when she realized that it was Lars who had called her, and after she had given her friend and fellow employee a drink, she stayed to change the cloth that gave comfort to his fevered forehead.

She lost all track of time until she heard a rough, commanding voice at her ear, one that sent shivers racing like quicksilver all along her legs.

"It's midnight, Mrs. Collins. Want to come along nicely? Or are you willing to gamble that I won't put on one of my 'macho' shows?"

She didn't dare look at Kiel. She folded the cloth over Lars's forehead once more and straightened.

"You needn't speak to me like that. I wasn't aware of the time, but I do have some sense."

"Pity you don't display it more often."

Rhiannan tilted her chin but didn't offer him the dignity of a reply. She allowed him to take her arm, but paused to inform the night nurse that she was leaving.

Silence reigned between them once more as they walked back to his cabin. Kiel stripped his knit shirt over his head as soon as they entered the room.

"Sorry if it's rude," he told her brusquely, "but I'm taking the first shower tonight."

"Go ahead," Rhiannan murmured.

She felt achy and tired and sore, too tired to argue with him. Now that she was out of the hospital, she could hardly keep her eyes open, but she had to. *I want to come to him tonight,* she reminded herself. *I want to touch him. I want to tell him somehow that I need him.*

Kiel wasn't bothering with any proprieties. He stripped off his pants and shorts in the doorway and headed for the bathroom. Rhiannan flopped onto the bed in exhaustion, but then found herself speaking her sudden thoughts aloud. "There's something peculiar about Joan Kendrick."

"Is there?" Kiel asked coldly. But it seemed to Rhiannan that he faltered in his naked trek to the bathroom.

"Yes," Rhiannan stated flatly. "There is. There's something going on between her and Glen Trivitt."

"Oh?" He stopped in the bathroom doorway, but turned to stare at her, leaning casually against the door frame. "I don't see where that is your concern. Unless you've appointed yourself the ship's chaperone."

"That isn't what I mean!" Rhiannan snapped. "She isn't after Glen in that way. She's after you in that way, and you seem pleased to oblige her every chance you get."

He shrugged. "That you're interested in me where Joan is concerned is certainly flattering but hardly justified, since you don't seem to be 'after me in that way' anymore."

"Kiel . . ." she began.

But the bathroom door had already closed, and she was certain that her weak and hurt whisper hadn't been heard. *Bastard!* she thought with dry resentment. But then her thoughts softened. She was too tired to feel angry.

Yes, he was a bastard, all right, but when he came out of the bathroom, she was going in. And when she came out she would be feeling soft and smelling delightful. And if his back was turned to her in the bed, she was going to caress him with her entire body and then see if he could sleep through that sort of temptation tonight!

Maybe she shouldn't wait. Maybe she should just barge into the shower and join him. They seemed rather adept at barging in on one another. Yes, she would do that. In just a minute . . . just as soon as she could open her eyes again. . . .

She never did open her eyes again that night.

When Kiel came out of the shower, his tensions and temper and worries somewhat eased away by the steam, he walked to the bed, determined that he would have her again that night, no matter what her feeble arguments were. But he stopped short when he saw her. Her lashes were thick crescents over the shadows beneath her eyes. She was hugging her pillow, curled against it. Her lips were slightly parted and her breathing was deep.

He bit his lip with a long and resigned sigh. He couldn't awaken her. He just couldn't do it. Still, he arched a brow. He couldn't let her sleep fully clothed like that. He slipped off her shoes, then her pants. To his chagrin she didn't wake up. Her body limply fell about as he maneuvered it. Not even when he pulled off her shirt did she do more than moan slightly and readjust her body to the pillow and the bed. And when he fumbled with her bra, all she did was mumble, then grunt that she understood what he was doing, and once again readjusted.

With a soft smile Kiel lay down beside her and took her gently into his arms. He would be content to hold her, to feel the satin of her skin, the velvet of her hair. . . . Well, maybe not content, but resigned.

Absently Kiel stroked her soft flesh, his fingers appreciating the swell of her breasts, the curve of her waist. Sleep was eluding him. His fears were not so vague now. They were still inexplicable, but Rhiannan was sensing the same thing. Something just wasn't right, and no matter how well the good doctor checked out, it all kept coming back to Glen Trivitt. And Joan Kendrick. What in bloody hell was it?

Thirteen

The man had to be part robot, Rhiannan thought a little bitterly of Kiel when she awoke the next morning and once again found him gone. He had to be battery-operated and set for instant energy by six A.M. at the latest. His bedside alarm informed her that it was still shy of the hour.

Another night had passed and another lost chance. And the distance was growing between them.

But as she swung her feet over the bed, she realized that he had taken her clothes off, and the realization made her smile. He might have acted with platonic concern for her comfort. Might have. She preferred to think that just like her, he wanted the intimacy of her naked touch.

Rhiannan showered and dressed quickly and let herself out of the cabin. She waved to the crew members on deck and stared down below, certain that Donald had spent the night beside Mary and determined that she would be able to send him back to his cabin once more.

She checked herself before heading for the infirmary, and made a detour. Coffee first. Then she would be better prepared to handle the long morning in the pseudohospital.

Almost able to smell the fresh-brewed coffee from beyond the doors of the Pirate's Cove, Rhiannan hurried toward them. But once she had placed her hands on the wood, she paused, startled by the muffled sound of an argument. She was about to turn away, not wishing to intrude on someone else's busi-

ness, but there was something familiar about the female voice
that was rising stridently. Rhiannan opened the door a crack.

"Just leave me alone and don't worry about things I might
say in my 'quest for a certain male'!"

A male voice muttered something Rhiannan didn't hear. She
pushed the door open a tiny bit more.

"Oh, stop it! You worry about your own relationships! My
staying celibate was not part of this deal! I'll go after Whellen
if I damn well choose. This has nothing to do with business.
This is all over that black-haired bitch in heat you moon over
like a sick calf! If she can't keep the congressman on her own,
that's her problem."

The male voice that answered her was low, yet it held a
deadly quality that made Rhiannan shiver. "You forget who
runs this show, Joan. And I think you forget that I can be a
very dangerous man."

Joan Kendrick laughed nastily. "Is that a threat, *Doctor?*"

"No, Miss Kendrick, an assurance."

Joan whispered something in reply. Rhiannan leaned closer
to the door, then froze in rigid panic as a hand clamped down
on her shoulder.

"Good morning, Mrs. Collins."

She breathed a sigh of relief as she swung about to face the
kindly Dr. Trenton. "After some coffee?" he demanded cheerfully.

"Ah . . ." She was still having trouble breathing. Her heart
was hammering viciously in her chest.

Dear God, what had she heard? What was the deal between
Joan Kendrick and Dr. Glen Trivitt, two people who could
have never met before the voyage. She was trembling as she
stared, ashen-faced, at Dr. Trenton, ready to blurt out that
something terribly frightening was happening, something more
frightening than the horror that had already struck.

She was being foolish. What could she say? Trenton might
challenge Joan and Glen, and they could very well make it
appear that she was a daft eavesdropper imagining what she

wanted to hear, distorting a friendly conversation. And then what would happen when those two knew that she had heard them?

"Are you all right, Mrs. Collins?" Dr. Trenton asked, suddenly concerned.

"Fine. Just fine," Rhiannan said swiftly—too swiftly, probably, because Dr. Trenton was still looking at her as if she belonged in an asylum.

"Well, then, let's get that coffee, shall we?"

Rhiannan nodded wordlessly. Dr. Trenton swung the door inward and ushered her inside.

Glen and Joan were sitting together, but both were guilelessly discussing the clear blue of the sky and commending the *Seafire*'s sailors for their calm and capable approach to the situation.

Good mornings were called all around, and both Glen and Joan gave Rhiannan brilliant smiles. Somehow she managed to return them without appearing sick. But when Dr. Trenton grabbed a cup of coffee and excused himself to hurry to the infirmary, Rhiannan felt a shaft of panic strike her again. She couldn't remain alone in the room with Joan and Glen. She, too, grabbed her coffee, murmured a lame excuse, and rushed out of the room.

She would have loved to throw her coffee in Joan Kendrick's face for the blonde's referring to her as a "bitch in heat." But even the temptation to avenge the crass insult couldn't cut through her feeling of real terror. They weren't playing games here. The insult was inconsequential.

But what did she know? Nothing! Just what she had been sensing since they had left port. Joan Kendrick and Dr. Glen Trivitt were dangerous, and they were definitely up to something. But what? Glen didn't like Joan flirting with Kiel. Why? Because she might spill something in the heat of passion? What? It all made no sense.

Oh, Kiel, damn you, where are you? Why do you have to be needed by everyone else in the world when I need you now?

Rhiannan realized suddenly that her feet had automatically led her to the infirmary. She stepped in and nodded to the white-coated man at the entrance desk. Obviously he recognized her, because he waved her in with a polite smile.

Rhiannan hurried on down to Mary's bed. As she had expected, Donald was still sitting beside it, his eyes closing, snapping open, closing again.

"Donald," Rhiannan whispered gently, "I'm here to spell you again."

His eyes flew wide open and he gave her a sleepy, somewhat confused smile. "Rhiannan."

"Donald, do you know where Kiel is?"

He shook his head. "Haven't seen him this morning. But bless you, 'Annan. They say that Mary is holding her own, but I still don't like to leave her alone for a moment. There could be a change. . . ." He trailed off with a long tired yawn and stood up, stretching.

Rhiannan thought that she would normally have been touched by his absolute faith in her. This morning she wasn't. She had been wondering if she could possibly talk to Donald—spill out her fears and terror and insist that he find Kiel immediately. But she realized dismally that she couldn't. Donald was barely coherent, barely standing. She wondered bleakly if he would even make it to his cabin. He sure wasn't going to comprehend a thing she tried to tell him in his exhausted and almost somnambulant state.

"I'll send him to you, 'Annan," Donald promised with a slur, "if I should see him."

He patted her shoulder and walked on past her—staggered past her, actually. The previous day's sleep hadn't been able to totally compensate for all the sleep he had lost.

At any rate, he was gone. She hadn't had the presence of mind to stall him, and she had promised to watch Mary. Could she leave Mary to go and find Kiel? There were plenty of nurses in the room, and Dr. Trenton was there examining Lars at the moment.

But what could she accomplish? she asked herself bleakly. Last night had proved that Kiel thought her suspicions an absurd form of jealousy. Would it be worthwhile to disappoint Donald and leave Mary just to have Kiel laugh at her and tell her that eavesdroppers seldom got things straight? And just what did she really have to tell him?

Mary whimpered and Rhiannan looked down at her with concern. She hurried around the bed and changed the cloth on Mary's head. Then she almost forgot the conversation she had overheard, because a thin trickle of blood leaked from the corner of Mary's mouth.

"Dr. Trenton!" Rhiannan screamed. "Dr. Trenton! Please come here. Quickly!"

All through the morning and afternoon, Mary fought a precarious battle for her life. Rhiannan, hovering near the doctors and nurses while still trying to stay out of the way, knew their concern. Once the patient had begun to throw up blood, the situation was critical. Worse than critical. The percentages for survival dropped almost to nil.

Trying to keep from crying, Rhiannan stayed by Mary's side. Dr. Trenton was always near, but it seemed that he had chosen to rely on Rhiannan in this case rather than the nurses.

"Keep her bathed," he told Rhiannan. "Keep the iced cloths on her. We can't allow the fever to get high."

Despite wonder drugs, the practice of medicine could still get down to basics: ice-cold cloths placed on Mary's chest. Then she had to be raised so that the cold cloths could be put on her back. Otherwise, one of the nurses told her, the heat and fever would continue.

Mary regained consciousness several times, screaming against the treatment. "I'm so tired," she told Rhiannan. "So tired of hurting. I wish I could just go to sleep and stay asleep."

"No, Mary, no!" Rhiannan protested. "Mary, you have to fight."

"I hurt so bad. . . ."

At five in the afternoon Dr. Trenton sighed after examining Mary again. "We're going to have to break the boils," he muttered. "It's our only hope."

Rhiannan bit her lip. She hadn't wanted to send for Donald; she hadn't wanted to watch him suffer along with Mary. But now she changed her mind.

"Dr. Trenton, would you send for Mr. Flagherty first?"

Trenton eyed her with a certain admiration. "You know, Mrs. Collins, you may have something. If she gives up, we'll lose her. Maybe Mr. Flagherty will be able to say something to her. . . ."

Rhiannan had never seen Donald Flagherty look as haggard as he did when he was led back to Mary's bedside. He looked down at the woman he had fallen in love with and swayed where he stood.

"Donald," Rhiannan murmured, "say something to her. I think that she will hear you."

Donald knelt down beside Mary and took her hand in his. "Mary . . . Mary, honey, you have to listen to me. You have to get well because . . . because I love you. Oh, God, Mary, I need you. I've searched for you all my life. Oh, God, Mary, you can't leave me. I . . . I talked to the captain today. He said that he can marry us out here at sea, Mary. Oh, Mary, can you hear me?"

Rhiannan didn't know if she was imagining what she wanted to see, but she could swear that Mary's lashes fluttered softly and that her blue lips attempted to curve into a smile.

Dr. Trenton looked at Rhiannan and then nodded toward Donald. Rhiannan went to him and gripped his shoulders. "We have to get out of here for a few minutes, Donald. The doctors have to help her."

Donald nodded and stumbled to his feet. Rhiannan led him out of the infirmary and to the hallway, and she held him as the tears began to slide down his cheeks. Donald, who was always so calm and suave and kind.

"Oh, God, 'Annan, she can't die. She can't. . . . I won't be able to stand it. It can't happen. She is so young and alive. . . ."

It can happen, Donald, Rhiannan thought. *It can. It won't be fair, but it can happen.*

As if reading her thoughts, Donald pulled away from her, his misery still dark in his eyes. " 'Annan," he said sickly. "I'm sorry. I'm so sorry. I can't cling to you like this, not when you lost so much. Oh, God," he groaned, "you must hate me. You must be thinking of how your children deserved to live. You must—"

"Donald! Please don't! I want you to cling to me, and I want Mary to live! Oh, Donald, I haven't become that embittered. I loved my children and I loved Paul and I lost them. But I haven't lost the capacity to love, Donald. I can still pray for Mary with my whole heart. Please hold me. Cry. Let me help you."

"Oh, 'Annan," he murmured, and he held her against him once again.

Rhiannan started shaking, thanking God that He had given her the strength to give to Donald.

An hour later Kiel at last came tearing down the hall, searching out Donald. Rhiannan could see the depths of the concern and pain Kiel shared with Donald, and she loved him for it.

Donald left her arms to accept Kiel's embrace. The bond of friendship between the two was naked and unashamed. Rhiannan stood quietly by, and when Kiel and Donald at last drew apart, she was overwhelmed with sweet gratitude as she felt Kiel's arm protectively and assuringly about her. The strain between them was forgotten, washed cleanly away as he gave her the support she needed, the strength that had been drained from her.

"How long have the doctors been with her?" Kiel asked.

"Over an hour," Donald said tonelessly.

Kiel nodded, then withdrew from Rhiannan to enter the infirmary. He came out almost immediately and offered Donald an encouraging smile. "They say we can come back in now."

Mary was still in the bed. A long white bandage rimmed her neck; two more were tucked beneath her arms. Rhiannan could not hear her breathe nor see the rising and falling of her chest. For one horrible moment she thought that Mary had rattled out her last gasp of a breath and died.

But Kiel was there to reassure her. "She's in a deep, deep sleep and resting easily now."

The three of them sat by Mary's bedside all through the night. Rhiannan knew when morning had come because the white-coated figures changed shifts.

Morning, and Mary still hadn't moved, hadn't whimpered.

"Donald?"

All three of them started when the sweet voice tentatively came out in a soft whisper.

Her eyes were open. They were clear and focused if somewhat confused as they fell on Donald's bowed head.

"Mary!" he exclaimed. He was wide awake and the tears were running down his cheeks again.

Kiel stood and touched Rhiannan's shoulder. "I'm getting Trenton," he told her swiftly.

A moment later Trenton was at the bedside. As he had dozens of times already, he examined Mary, checked her chest, her throat, her eyes, her forehead. A broad smile slowly formed on his face. "Young lady," he told Mary. "You are on the road to recovery."

Rhiannan wondered then if Mary had ever really known just how sick she had been. She offered them all a tremulous smile, then looked at Donald with new confusion, threading her thin white fingers through his hair.

"Donald?" she queried with awe. "Do you . . . do you really want to marry me?"

"Yes, Mary, yes. With all my heart. If you . . . if you don't feel you'd be saddled with an old man."

Mary laughed, and the sound was so loving and wonderful that Rhiannan felt tremors of warmth through her whole body.

"Oh, Donald! You're going to be the one saddled with a

problem. I'm never going to know how to be rich. I'm always so afraid I'll embarrass you in front of your friends!"

"You're looking at my two best friends," Donald told her. "And, Mary, you could never embarrass me. Never in a thousand years."

Mary closed her eyes with contented exhaustion. "All I want is a lifetime, Donald. Just a lifetime."

Kiel tapped Rhiannan on the shoulder, then placed his arm around her. Together they tiptoed away, then strode out of the infirmary.

Why, Rhiannan wondered, did she suddenly feel so awkward in Kiel's presence. She had been waiting now for days for a chance to be alone with him when they were both awake. But now, in her moment of truth, she was nervous. The world was a beautiful place as they came up on deck and saw a shimmering sun begin a brilliant climb to a crystal blue sky.

Mary had made it, and with her survival Rhiannan knew that the plague had met its death. Her mind was filled with Mary, with Donald's happiness, with the knowledge that golden miracles could occur . . . and that Kiel was leading her to the cabin they had come to share.

"You haven't had any sleep again," she murmured as he turned the key in the lock and ushered her inside. "Will someone come and wake you up as soon as you hit your pillow?"

"No, I doubt it," Kiel replied with a shrug. "The emergency is all over now. We've passed the crucial period."

He paused in the center of the room, smiling with a grateful wonder. "We didn't lose a single soul, Rhiannan. Not a single soul. We all survived." He turned and smiled ruefully at her. "Trenton is the real hero—and Picard and Trivitt, of course— but I feel a bit like Rocky. If we were in Philadelphia, I'd be tempted to run up the steps of the capitol, shaking my fists in the air."

Rhiannan had started to smile in return, but Kiel's mention of Glen Trivitt drained the smile from her face, reminding her starkly of the conversation she had overheard that morning.

"Oh, Kiel! I forgot! I was so worried about Mary all day!"

He was pulling his shirt over his head but he was frowning at her as he pulled the knit from his arms and his face appeared.

"Forgot what?" he asked her cautiously.

"Kiel," Rhiannan said urgently, approaching him and placing her hands on his bare chest with a sudden vehemence, "you know how I keep telling you that something just isn't right about Joan Kendrick and Dr. Trivitt."

"Yes," he said, suspiciously, his eyes narrowing at her. "What about it?"

"I was right: Something is up. Something serious. I overheard them talking together this morning. I think that Trivitt was threatening Joan. He didn't want her near you and Joan was saying that she would do what she pleased, that her sex life wasn't part of the 'deal.' Kiel, it was frightening. They sounded so deadly and so serious! Joan Kendrick is involved in some—"

"Rhiannan!"

She was startled into a pained gasp when he gripped her upper arms forcefully and gave her a shake. "Stop it!" he told her. "Forget about Trivitt and Joan. You probably heard them wrong. It's been a strenuous few days. The plague has unnerved you. You're creating situations that don't exist."

"I am *not!*" Rhiannan protested furiously. "Kiel, I do not make things up and I do not have faulty hearing! I'm telling you that something is going on between those two. Something dangerous."

"And I'm telling you to forget it! Quit running around, trying to play cloak and dagger. Just drop it."

"Kiel—"

"Rhiannan!" he snapped in return, despising himself for his tone but determined not to let her know that yes, something sure as hell was going on. He knew that he sounded like a bastard; she was bright and she knew exactly what she was talking about. At the moment, though, he couldn't afford to have her know too much; he couldn't afford to have her involved, have her come too close to the truth. And he was terribly afraid that if she came too close, she might do something dangerous. He was just going to have to keep sounding like a real bastard. "We've been up the whole damned night again. You need to get some sleep and so do I."

She was amazed when he walked away from her, drew the drapes so that the cabin fell into darkness, and calmly sank to the bed to remove his shoes and socks. She was still standing in the middle of the room when he stood again, dropped his pants, kicked them out of the way, and crawled beneath the covers.

A stark and explosive silence reigned for a moment, then Kiel rasped out, "Oh, for God's sake, Rhiannan, will you please get into the damned bed!"

"No, I will not!" Rhiannan thundered. "Damn you, Kiel Whellen, why won't you pay attention—"

Her words were cut off as he pounced from the bed with smooth, swift agility and came toward her purposefully. Instinctively she backed away, putting her hands defensively before her.

"Kiel, I am not getting into that bed with you when you refuse to acknowledge the fact that I am not a blithering idiot!"

He ignored her comment, sweeping her off her feet and into his arms despite her enraged flailing against him.

"Want to take your own clothes off?" he asked her. "Or shall I?"

"Kiel, you bastard, I am not going to . . . to fall into your arms when you—"

"I'm not asking you to fall into my arms. I'm asking you to get into bed and stop letting your imagination run away with you so that we can get some sleep."

The action was futile, but she struggled against him anyway. She gave up when the steel bands that were his arms refused to yield, and went rigidly still before meeting his hard and unyielding eyes.

"If you wish to get some sleep, Congressman, I'll be happy to allow you to. But I think I'll prefer going to my own cabin."

"That isn't possible."

"Why?"

"Your cabin is occupied now by one of the men from Disease Control."

With that last comment he literally dumped her on the bed and grasped one of her legs to haul off her shoe.

She tried to kick him with her other foot, then realized belatedly that he was naked and might easily assume that she had a far more vicious intent than her desire to escape him in her anger. She missed, but her thoughts had run along the right vein. He looked at her with a touch of murderousness in his eyes, and before she knew quite what had happened, he had pounced on top of her and his naked weight was pinning her to the bed.

"Rhiannan, so help me God, don't push this. Not now. And don't expect me to feel like a macho brute for making you get some sleep in the same bed you've been sleeping in for nights. The outrage just won't work. I'm going to tell you this one more time: Forget about Trivitt and Joan. Just forget it. There isn't a damn thing you can do about anything anyway. Just stay away from them. And don't get up again! I am at zero patience level, and if I get up to come after you one more time, I won't be responsible for the consequences. Get it?"

Her chin rose belligerently, but she compressed her lips and bit into them to keep herself from snapping back in reply.

Kiel was clearly in a dangerous state; she wasn't fool enough not to recognize it or the fact that he indeed meant what he was saying. She had never felt such a shimmering tension about him—never seen his muscles so bunched and taut. There was an explosiveness about him that warned her to exercise good sense rather than press the issue that she was right.

He stared at her threateningly for another moment, then released his hold and rolled from her onto his side. Rhiannan stared up at the ceiling, seething with anger, an anger that doubled and tripled when she heard his muffled but still commanding voice again: "Take off your clothes and settle down!"

It was on the tip of her tongue to tell him he could go to hell on a fast train, but she forced herself to refrain. She didn't want to get into another scuffle with him. It was too nerve-racking to have him over her when he was naked. No matter how angry she was, she discovered too quickly that she couldn't breathe, that she couldn't keep her mind on her thoughts or her eyes locked with his.

Silently she sat up and threw off her remaining shoe. She glanced his way as she drew her shirt over her head and tossed it to the floor, but his back was still to her.

She finished stripping and crawled beneath the covers, turning her back to him. But although her fatigue lay about her like an extra blanket, her eyes refused to close. Why had they wound up fighting like this? She had wanted nothing more than to crawl into his arms. She had to fight him when he refused to take her seriously.

"Rhiannan?"

For a moment she wondered if she had imagined the soft, husky drawl of his voice, but it came again.

"Rhiannan?"

"What?" she choked out, knowing that a breathy quality dominated her own voice.

"I'm sorry," he said quietly.

"You're sorry," she said bitterly, "but you still don't believe me."

"I didn't say that I didn't believe you."

"No, you said that my imagination was enhancing a normal conversation."

He was strangely silent, but despite her curiosity, Rhiannan couldn't allow herself to turn around. She kept her back directed at him.

He rolled toward her. She started quivering, hoping she wasn't going to cry, when his fingers, firm but gentle, began to stroke her hair, brushing her cheek and then her bare fingers.

"Rhiannan, I do believe you. So all right, Dr. Trivitt and Joan Kendrick have something, some kind of a deal, going on between them. What can be done about it? I can hardly go and demand to know what goes on privately between them. Neither of them would give me an answer. So forget it and stay away from both of them. Okay?"

No, it's not okay, she thought. *If you don't care, Kiel Whellen, I do. And I am going to find out what's going on.*

"Okay," she said stiffly.

He hovered over her a moment longer, as if loath to leave her. But she still couldn't bring herself to turn to him.

He sighed softly. "Okay. I'll let you get to sleep."

He rolled away from her, no longer touching her. His back was to her back once again.

For a long, long time she lay there, fighting an inward battle. She was angry with him, but she still loved him and still wanted him.

"Kiel?"

"What?"

At last she turned, edging closer to him and staring at the rugged planes and angles of his profile over his shoulder.

"I . . . I don't want to go to sleep."

He turned to study her eyes for a moment, then smiled broadly. "Well, then, Mrs. Collins, do come here!" He threw up the sheets, encircling her in his arms and sweeping her slender form on top of his.

Her eyes widened with surprise and wonder as her thighs met with the hardened potency of his naked desire. And she had thought that he had been lying beside her, unaffected. . . .

A rich smile appeared on his face as he stared up at her. "Want to 'use' me again, eh?"

Now . . . now was her chance to tell him how much he had come to mean to her. Three small words, whispered softly.

"If you don't mind," she murmured, demurely casting her eyes down.

His fingers threaded firmly through her hair on either side of her face, but his touch was not painful, merely exultant.

"Be my guest, my love. Be my guest."

"Kiel . . ." she pleaded softly.

He drew her face down to his, holding it a scant distance away as he searched her eyes. Then he cradled her head to pull her closer and touch her lips with his. The kiss was slow at first. Just a brush. A tantalizing teasing with his taste and scent.

The tip of his tongue rippled lightly over her lips, then plunged between them, ran along her teeth, and sought demandingly. Rhiannan moaned softly deep in her throat, and betrayed her own hunger as she met and matched the hunger of his kiss, returning the velvety thrust of his tongue with the silken ravaging of her own. Her arms encircled him and her fingers dug into his hair. Thick. Male. Invigorating to touch.

His hands, with gentle but firm pressure, raked over her shoulders, over her ribs, and down to her buttocks, enjoying the soft flesh, questing and pleasuring. They moved over and over again, creating waves of delicious heat until all of her ached for that touch of rough magic.

With a swift, abrupt movement he broke the kiss and swung her onto her back and rolled onto his side. He smiled lazily at her and brushed her lips with a quick kiss, savoring the moistness of her mouth.

Then he watched his own hand as he stroked her slowly, eliciting an expectant quiver as his fingers grazed her collarbone, fascinated by the shadows on her skin. He cupped her breast, then circled it lazily over and over, yet never touching the nipple. He dipped his head, as if he had saved that luxury for his tongue. At that first warm, moist contact Rhiannan whimpered and arched, offering the pink crest that had been so taunted and deprived despite her wanton need.

She was to be deprived no longer. He played on her with his mouth, nipping lightly with his teeth, soothing that touch with a sweet, savoring suction.

Wildly she dug her fingers into his hair, vaguely wondering how he could set her on fire so quickly, then too delirious with sensation to care anymore.

As his lips and teeth and tongue administered to the tempting tip of her nipple, his hand continued to wander, his knuckles grazing the soft, vulnerable flesh of her belly, his palms running along her hip, seeking her, glorying in the feel of her. There was nothing, Kiel thought with a fierce pleasure, that could excite a man more than free and abandoned desire of the woman he loved. She wasn't just beautiful; she was motion. Fluid grace. Exotic in the arching and writhing of her body, volatile and almost unbearably evocative with each rhythmic twist of her sleek hips and legs.

And the taste and scent of her . . . it would forever be with him. As clean and fragrant as the sky and sun yet wickedly feminine. With simple gratitude for all that she was, he rested his head beneath her breasts for a moment, watching the large bronze back of his hand as he ran the calloused tips of his fingers over the soft, creamy flesh of her inner thigh. To his delight he watched as her long leg quivered.

"Kiel . . ." she whispered, starting to twist toward him, lifting her knee with sudden modesty.

"Rhiannan . . ." he uttered in a long husky breath, burying his face against the slope of her belly, then teasing her navel with his tongue. He shifted his body, forcing her legs to give completely and fitting his strength between them.

Her soft moans were the melody of a wild and sweet desire as he indulged himself in wanting all of her, in finding all the secret, vulnerable places that were intimately female, intimately her. It was a form of the most erotic torture, because just touching her had sent him spiraling to the brink of a magical madness. He felt the pulse of his own blood, the thunder of his heart, the thunder within his sex, aching to thrust into her embrace.

"Oh, please, Kiel! I can't stand any more!"

"Neither can I," he admitted hoarsely, the warm whisper of

his breath and the dampness of his flesh adding to the wonderful sensations that were invading her blood until she felt as if she were a volcano, flaming lava on the verge of total eruption. She knew nothing but the desperate heat, and yet, she knew every nuance of his touch.

"Please, Kiel!" Her nails dug into his shoulders, then her fingers tugged at his hair. "Oh, Kiel. I'm using you, remember? Let me use you, let me touch you, too. . . ."

He came to her, delighted by her husky words, by the longing within them. His lips caught hers again and ravaged them with a sudden force of need. Still, she was there to meet him, and her mouth moved breathlessly from his, showering his face with the delectable moistness of the tip of her tongue, biting softly at his earlobe, finding the hollows of his throat. She pressed gently at him to push him away, and then allowed her own passion free reign.

"My turn . . ." she cried softly, and her hands and lips roamed feverishly over his chest. Her body rubbed excitingly over his as she moved alongside him, her legs entwined with his as she savored the sinews of his chest with her taunting fingers and the hungered caress of her lips.

The world spun a vibrant shade of crimson for Kiel as she made heated love to him. Momentarily stunned by the savage beauty of her passion, he lay still as she adored him with a finesse born of elemental sensuality. Each subtle twist and touch started his blood raging anew until he could take no more himself.

"Rhiannan . . ." he protested huskily.

But she ignored him, and he shuddered as a massive wave of searing fever stabbed him through and through and she took him as thoroughly as he had taken her, a gentle, feathery touch of moistness. Then the demand grew and grew, carrying him to the point where he would explode out of control. . . .

"Now!" he raged suddenly, tensely, and his arms swept powerfully around her, dragging her down beside him. His knee parted her legs with a forceful thrust, and as his eyes met hers he saw them shining and glazed with the thrill of her own power. He smiled as he lowered himself over her.

"Trying to drive me insane with desire for you, love? You do it well. So damned well. . . ."

He entered her as he spoke, filling her with a heat and strength so volatile that it was in itself a shattering, exulting shock.

"Kiel . . ." she moaned, locking her arms about his neck.

He fit his hands beneath the smooth firmness of her buttocks and met her in another shattering thrust. She cried out softly, then pulled his mouth to hers. His tongue stroked her mouth as his body surrendered to hers.

Never had he felt so completely embraced, so absorbed, by a woman. So consumed within her, a part of her, that he was detached from the world with the blinding, rhythmic need that brought him ever closer to a burst of heaven. Yet, completely, totally, aware of—immersed in—her. His passion continued to soar in desperation. In a primitively, elementally male way, he was determined to leave his mark on her, on her soul, on her memory. She would never even think of making love with another man. Ever. Ever again.

His fierce desire flew ever higher, bringing her to wave after wave of quivering culmination. It was his heart that he poured into her as he shuddered, his heart and his soul. As he collapsed against her, fingers entangling in a fierce caress in her hair, he cried out her name with the greatest pleasure and the greatest anguish. "Rhiannan!"

She pressed her face against his shoulder as if she were somewhat embarrassed with her free abandon, now that their raging desires had been so fully satiated. She didn't say anything as she lay next to him, but she curled against him, and he was gratified that she needed him still. She came for comfort now, for a strong shelter in which to indulge in the bliss of the languid aftermath.

He shifted his weight and held her close, lightly stroking her bare shoulder, and a minute later he was smiling ruefully.

It seemed it had taken her barely seconds to fall asleep. He closed his eyes and savored the feel of her beside him. She had trusted him with all her vulnerabilities, and knowing that enhanced the depth of the love he felt for her. *Ah, my Queen of Hearts, I am your Ace,* he thought firmly. *When the game is over, I promise that you will be mine to hold, to love, every night.*

For a long time he lay awake, his body and mind filled with the wonder of the strength of the bond between them. Then slowly the seeds of worry rose above those of wonder. Chills trailed along his spine and he held her closer, as if the fierce movement could protect her.

The plague isn't over! he told himself angrily; and Rhiannan wasn't a liar, nor was she letting her imagination run away with her. He knew damned well that she had heard something. He had known damned well since he came on the ship that something . . .

You're not a psychic! he raged mentally. But on this voyage he was. He had known that something was wrong. Very wrong. Not just the plague. Trivitt . . . and Joan. . . .

His fists clenched at his sides. Why didn't it all mesh? Why was he haunted by these feelings, yet unable to make them crystallize?

Why? Why had he been so convinced that Trivitt. . . . That Dr. Trivitt what? Why had he been arguing with Joan?

Kiel forced himself to expel a long breath. Wait . . . and watch. That was all that he could do. And be ready. For what he didn't know. He only knew that this time he was going to be the one on top. He would tear another human being apart with his bare hands to keep the piece of heaven he had found now.

Come on, he thought ruthlessly. *Come on and get me. I'm ready for you. I dare you, take me on. . . .*

But they were futile thoughts. You couldn't challenge an invisible enemy.

Fourteen

"You really should marry me," Kiel said laconically, staring up at the brilliant blue sky. "I really can use a hostess, and it looks like Donald won't be needing one once this cruise is over."

Although they weren't touching, Kiel felt Rhiannan stiffen beside him. Damn! He wanted to kick himself, but he hadn't been able to keep the sarcasm out of his voice. He was flippant because he was afraid of losing her. He just didn't seem to be able to handle his feelings except by attempting a caustic deal.

In the four days since the plague had hit its crisis point and then receded, she had been his, but only in the magic of the night. With the passengers allowed to move about the ship, they had both been constantly busy. And so they had met in the darkness as lovers only, and neither had spoken much except for whispered words of passion. Maybe they were both afraid to break the magic.

Kiel knew that she was still angry because he had refused to listen to her; he also knew that he didn't dare tell her that he felt there just might be something to worry about. He didn't want to frighten her.

As the days passed, it all seemed more and more absurd anyway. Everything was going well. They were going to be allowed to come into port in another two weeks; the delay was only for safety's sake.

Somberness was no longer a part of the trip. The infirmary was still full, but only so that the patients could recover their strength. The worst was definitely over, and things were in full swing. Meetings went on daily; the cruise directors were back in business, even if business had changed slightly. All activities had to take place on the ship, unless some enterprising and active soul decided to take one of the *Seafire*'s rowboats out for a spin.

Which was what he had talked Rhiannan into doing this morning. They had rowed out some distance, done a little useless snorkling, since the water was too deep to offer much in interesting viewing, and come back to dry off lazily on the flat stretch of deck bowside of the mainmast.

He felt her movement as she sat up and looked about, hugging her knees. He began to wonder if he had even spoken aloud, when at last she answered him.

"That was quite a declaration, Congressman," she said coolly. "One day, if you grow up to be President, I'll be able to gather my nieces and nephews around my rocker and tell them how the great Kiel Whellen fell to his knees, overcome with emotion, and asked me to be his wife."

Rhiannan knew she sounded excessively tart, but she couldn't help the way the words came out. What was he *really* doing with her? she wondered. When he had spoken, he had been so nonchalant that she was certain he was laughing at her. *Was* he being serious? Maybe he was the one still hung up on the past. Maybe he felt he would never truly forget Ellen and that she would make as good a figurehead as a wife as anyone else.

The little chills that caused the blackness, the wall, about her struck again. If he was serious, what about her? She loved him, but the love hurt. The fear of loss was always there. And he would want children. . . .

"I'm very serious, Rhiannan," she heard Kiel drawl, and she started when he ran his fingers along her spine where the dip of her bathing suit left it bare. "I told you once before, I can't begin to pay the wages Donald does, but it could make for an interesting life. There's a fair amount of excitement in D.C. I think that you'd like it."

She turned to stare down at his heavy-lidded eyes, noting
that only a glint of silver returned her stare.

"Marry yourself a hostess—get her cheap?"

He shrugged.

"What a wonderful deal. But as I asked you before, what
do I get out of it?"

"A home and a family."

"I don't want a damned home and a family."

"I think you're lying."

She had been wrong to think him languid beneath the rays
of the sun. He remained flat against the towel on the deck,
but she could see the tension of his now extremely bronzed
shoulders as his muscles rippled in a slight, irritated adjust-
ment. She had the feeling that he was about to pounce with
full force.

"I'm not—"

"You do want children and you do want a home. You were
born to be a wife and mother. You're just a coward."

"All right!" Rhiannan snapped. "I am a coward. But I do
not ever, *ever,* want children again."

He swung up so quickly that she would have run from him
if she had had the slightest chance. His arm encircled her waist
and the silver steel of his eyes darkened to a smoldering gray
as he challenged her with a heated hiss. "Really? That's a
strange tone of confidence from a woman who's been sharing
some rather reckless nights. We're not talking about a single
occasion here anymore. Unless, by chance, one of our residen
physicians came aboard with a prescription for you."

Rhiannan felt the blood drain from her face. She *had* been
reckless. Crazy. Insane. But she had wonderful excuses—the
plague, the fatigue, the fear, the need for someone during the
trauma.

Great excuses, but they didn't change the facts. She had
been behaving like an ostrich with its head in the sand.

She blinked, regaining composure she hardly felt. "No, Con
gressman. Your sarcasm is amusing but not necessary. I have

no worries; in the great physical scheme of things, this is just the wrong time."

He smiled tightly. "Sure of yourself, aren't you?"

"I told you, I'm not having—"

"Let's be hypothetical here. What if . . . ? *If!*"

"There are no *if's*—"

"Oh, yes there are."

"Damnit," she said, "I told you I will not have children again."

"You'd have an abortion?"

Rhiannan tore her eyes from his and stared out to sea. She didn't dare speak, so she nodded. Was she lying? she wondered. Or was she telling the truth? Or was she still keeping her head in the sand, determined that it couldn't be. The odds were with her. Weren't they?

His fingers suddenly crawled around the back of her neck as his voice seared her ear with its vehemence. "Not *my* child, you won't."

The cruelty of his hold was bringing tears to her eyes. She fought his grip and twisted to see him out of the corner of her eye.

"You'd better get back to Washington and study the law, Congressman . . ." she began, trailing into silence as his hold tightened.

"This may just be one time when the law doesn't mean a hell of a lot to me," he warned her.

"Let go of me. We were talking hypothetically. The whole matter is irrelevant."

"Not any more it isn't—"

Kiel broke off instantly as another, nervous voice suddenly interrupted him. "Ah . . . excuse me, Congressman."

Tony Vinton, the ship's purser, was standing before them, blushing and shifting his weight from foot to foot. The pall that had come over Rhiannan was washed away in a flood of crimson as she realized that the purser had been discreetly trying to interrupt them for some time.

"What is it, Tony?" Kiel asked evenly. Only Rhiannan could sense the raw annoyance in his tone.

"This was left for you on my desk." Tony withdrew a sealed envelope from his breast pocket and presented it to Kiel. "I don't know who brought it, but it has your name on it, sir, with URGENT printed on it. I hate to bother you, but with the way things have been . . ."

"It's all right, Tony. Thank you," Kiel said.

Tony smiled a bit awkwardly at them both and then hurried away. Kiel frowned at the envelope a second, then ripped it open.

Rhiannan watched Kiel, her own brow furrowing, as she saw his features go taut and his lips compress into a line.

"What is it?" she asked tensely, struck by chills that surpassed any sense of alarm she had ever felt.

"What?" He tore his eyes from the paper to look at her; it was as if he had forgotten that she was there.

"What is it?" she persisted.

Kiel stood up, refolding the letter. "Nothing."

Rhiannan jumped to her feet and grabbed his arm. "Kiel—"

"Leave me be, Rhiannan!" he ordered sharply, turning away from her and starting across the deck toward the pilothouse.

Truly alarmed, she started to follow after him, clutching at his arm again. "Kiel, where are you going? Tell me what's wrong."

He shook off her arm rudely. "Nothing is wrong. Go finish sunning."

"I don't want to finish sunning."

"Then go play cards. Read a book. Go back to work. Just leave me alone!"

"But where are you going?"

He gave her his full attention at last, running cruel, assessive eyes over her. "To see if I can't pick up a more amiable date for dinner," he lied coldly.

She froze and stared at him, stunned, not quite able to hide the hurt that clouded the green of her eyes.

"Will you excuse me now, *please*," he mocked her, dipping his head in an exaggerated bow.

She released him without another word and spun about to glide gracefully across the deck, her head held high as she moved blindly toward the bow.

Oh, God! Kiel thought, waves of agony seeming to cascade down upon him. He would never forget the way she had looked at him, but he'd *had* to get away from her. The invisible enemy he had prayed he was imagining had at last struck—with deadly intent. Far more deadly than he had envisioned with all his irrational fears.

He strode purposefully to the bow and the small office that had become his in the last week. Letting himself in, he locked the door behind him. He picked up the ship-to-shore phone and waited for the radio engineer.

"Whatever you hear," Kiel warned the competent young man, "you keep silent. I mean *silent*. Do you understand me?"

"Yes, sir," the voice assured him. Kiel trusted the man, who had handled all past communications with commendable calm. But not even that trust could offer him the least relaxation.

His call went through to the White House easily: The *Seafire* still had direct access. Kiel tensely demanded that the top men all be present. He could almost imagine the scene. It would be just as it had been the day that the 747 went down, except that he wouldn't be there.

He was here. In charge. And he was going to stay in charge. He was going to give the orders and call the shots. And, God help him, he was going to win this time.

"We're ready here, Kiel," the President told him. Kiel knew from the President's tone of voice that he was already worried sick: He knew Kiel would not have made such demands unless a situation was crucial.

Kiel began to read his note:

To the various heads of state, through the care of Congressman Kiel Whellen:

The recent outbreak of bubonic plague aboard the clipper ship was not an act of God. We, the members of the Red Liberation Army, take full responsibility for its creation.

We did not wish to kill, nor do we now. The plague was set loose as a warning and as proof that we do mean and can carry out the threat we now make. If certain missile sites listed below—and certain experimental centers for agents of germ and chemical warfare—are not dismantled and disbanded within the next 96 hours, we, the members of the Red Liberation Army, will set loose aboard the *Seafire* a new plague, gentlemen, the likes of which you have never seen.

This plague is called the AZ strain, and is virile in its action. Its degree of infectiousness is 99.5 percent. There is no vaccine for this virus. No antibodies are known to have any effect whatsoever; there is no cure. That, gentlemen, might leave you with one person alive aboard this ship. If you do not believe in the existence of the AZ strain, please feel free to check with your own experts. We believe that they will confirm all that we claim. The virus was taken from one of your own centers.

In addition to the dismantlement listed below, we demand a ransom of $25 million to be delivered to the ship via one *unarmed* helicopter on the morning of the fourth day. Bear in mind that the first show of disrespect to the terms of this letter will immediately set our virus into action.

Some of the strongest voices in international government are aboard this vessel. We suggest that all countries involved remember this when considering what action to take.

In a dull monotone Kiel went on to list the centers described in the demands. He read through the final paragraph.

Congressman Whellen will relay any messages you wish brought to our attention. We will await his reply in the

Pirate's Cove each midnight. Gentlemen, you have four days. Any attempt on Mr. Whellen's part to light the lounge or to apprehend us in any way will result in the instant circulation of the virus. Please don't gamble.

Kiel stared at the signature at the bottom of the page for a moment before saying it out loud: "Lee Hawk."

The silence on the other end lasted so long that Kiel began to think that the lines of communication had been broken. "Is there anyone there?" he asked tensely.

"My God!" someone hissed. "He's alive! Red Hawk *did* survive the plane crash!"

"Yes, yes, we're here, Congressman." It was the President's voice. "Hold just a minute, please . . ."

Kiel heard mumblings, then the President's voice again. "We've, ah, contacted one of our head scientists at Disease Control, Kiel. I . . . uh . . . I'm afraid that the AZ does exist . . ."

"Son of a bitch!" Kiel was certain that the expression of outrage came from the secretary of state. "These people— these . . . *rabble!*—think that they can force us all to our knees with their terror tactics. I say *no!* I say—"

Someone hushed him up, but not before Kiel was forced to realize fully the fear that had gripped him as soon as he had read the note. The demands *were* preposterous. They would never get that many countries together; they would never get the international agreement that they needed. And rather than risk a plague that could eradicate the civilized world, it was very possible that some enterprising power would decide to blow the *Seafire* right out of the sea.

"We all need to be calm and handle this like rational men," the President began, but Kiel realized that the voice interrupting him was his own, harsh and grating.

"That's fine, sir. You stay calm. None of you are on this bloody ship! Well, I'm telling the lot of you something too: not again. I will not lose to this man again! You can sit up there in your ivory tower and plot and plan all you like, but come up with something reasonable."

"We're going to need time, Kiel."

"I'll stall for all the damned time I can. But I'm not going to be a sitting duck."

"Kiel," the President said quietly, sending shivers of dread down the congressman's spine, "you must realize that . . . that . . ."

"That the AZ strain is deadly and can't be allowed to spread? Yes, sir." He exhaled slowly. "Yes, sir, I do. I realize exactly what you're saying. But you want time. . . . *I* want time."

"You've got your time, Congressman."

The conversation continued. Kiel was promised that a meeting would be called with representatives from all the countries mentioned, and then there was nothing more to say.

At last Kiel sat down in the chair, entirely alone. He covered his face wearily with shaking hands. Lee Hawk had survived; he was alive and on the ship. Ellen was dead. Rhiannan's husband was dead. Her children. Scores of other innocent people. And Lee Hawk had the audacity to be alive.

"Four days," Kiel murmured aloud. And then, if the demands were not met, Lee Hawk would release his virus. After witnessing the effects of the bubonic plague, Kiel couldn't find much reason to hope that Hawk might be bluffing. And if it came to that—if a deadly disease spread like wildfire through the ship—the government would be forced to eliminate the *Seafire* and all who were aboard her. It would matter little, because if what the letter said was true, they would all be corpses by that time anyway.

"Oh, God," Kiel groaned. Four days. Four days to think, to try desperately to plan something. A way out. But what? What could possibly save them? Kiel sat back and remembered his luncheon with Picard, before the plague. A germ could be spread in many fashions—filtered through food, through an air-conditioning system, through water, from person to person.

And a virus such as this AZ strain would catch like ignited tinder and devour men, women, and children.

The phone buzzed at his side. Anxiously Kiel picked it up. It was the Vice-President.

"Kiel, I have some curious information for you that just might shed some light on the situation."

"Go ahead, please!"

"Well, about that Dr. Trivitt you were so concerned about: We dug a little more thoroughly. As I told you before, his records are letter perfect. But the thing is, no one seems to remember him. None of the professors at Johns Hopkins, and he was listed as a resident at Mercy in Miami from 1979 to 1983. No one can remember him there, either. His name is on their records, but no one can remember a face."

Kiel wasn't hearing the Vice-President's voice anymore because his head was spinning. He knew what it was, what had nagged at him ever since he had first come aboard the ship, what had irritated his almost photographic memory. A memory with a distorted picture. That very first night when he had gone to seek out Rhiannan in the casino, he had passed a familiar face, and he had looked again, his memory jarred. But it had just been the ship's doctor, a man he had met earlier on deck and who was, of course, familiar. No, familiar from *before. From long ago.* A face that had changed drastically, but still, the structure . . . the eyes . . . Lee Hawk had probably been burned and scarred and mangled in the plane crash, but he had survived, and then gone through all kinds of reconstructive plastic surgery, changing himself . . . but not quite completely.

The angle of his profile, those strange eyes, the way he held his head . . . all those things had struck a chord somewhere in the mysterious regions of Kiel's mind. A picture had been imprinted, hovering over and now, at last, merging with the picture that had been on the cover page of newspapers the world over. And now—only now!—was it all making sense!

"Congressman Whellen, are you there?"

"Yes, yes, I'm here." Kiel laughed suddenly, a dry, bitter crackling sound. "Yes, I'm here. And now we know who the enemy is. *Trivitt* is Lee Hawk. I can go out and face him, but I'm still walking blind, sir. He could have that virus anywhere On his person. Hidden anywhere in his cabin. Hidden any where aboard the whole damned ship—maybe even timed to enter the water system or air-conditioning!"

"Congressman—"

"Don't bother, sir," Kiel interrupted with a rude and weary sigh. "I'm just running off a bit here. I know you're not per sonally responsible. You all just make sure you don't hit any panic buttons up there, you hear me? You give me my full four days to work on this thing."

Give us a chance, he prayed silently. *Just give us a fighting chance. . . .*

"Congressman," the Vice-President protested indignantly "we do not panic, sir! You will have your time, and we have all the faith in the world in you. You just make sure you keep the ship's passengers from panicking."

"No one is going to know, except those whom I have to involve: Flaherty, Trenton, and Picard."

"Good. Make sure you do keep it quiet or we will have another mess on our hands. . . ."

Another mess? As far as Kiel was concerned, they were already working at a disaster level. . . .

Rhiannan was sitting on the bed when he walked into his cabin. Her eyes were hard and brilliant as she looked at him He hadn't done much of a job of fooling her. He couldn't stay around her because he didn't trust himself. His entire nervous system had been savaged. If he came too near to her, he would want to confide in her, pour out his heart and mind, or else attack her with a half-mad desperation. Four days. They only had four days left. They couldn't waste them. He wanted her He wanted to have her again and again, to lose his soul to her, to forget. He wanted the hot fire of her sweet passion before the cold, black chill of death descended on the ship. . . .

"Kiel, would you quit this bull and tell me what the hell is going on?" she demanded succinctly.

He forced a cruel grin to slash across his features. "No bull, 'Annan. I'm just ready to move on."

"I don't believe you."

He raised a brow mockingly. "Honey, you're good in bed, but once you open your mouth for conversation, you've got more thorns than a damned rosebush. I'm tired of the battle."

He saw her flinch, and then he saw fury leap into her eyes. She hurtled across the room at him so fast that not even his primed reflexes could ward off the stinging blow she sent flying across his cheek. The crack of flesh against flesh was sharp and clear, echoing and resounding about them as they stared at one another.

Kiel instinctively brought his fingers to his face, absently rubbing his reddening cheek. He shrugged, then turned from her abruptly. "Excuse me," he told her tonelessly with his back to her as he headed to the bathroom.

Rhiannan stared incredulously at his retreating shoulders. No! He couldn't mean it! Something *had* happened. Something was wrong. He hadn't fallen out of love with her in a matter of minutes. . . . But maybe he had never been in love with her, she told herself bitterly. Maybe it had all been the thrill of conquest, the idea of having the unobtainable. He had wanted her. He had had her. He had asked her to marry him! Because he wanted a hostess. But that couldn't be true. It was simply too ridiculous. But he could have easily wanted her without loving her. He had never mentioned love. . . .

No! Her soul cried out in silent anguish. Tears started to form in her eyes, but she brushed them away impatiently. No! She didn't believe him. She didn't accept what he'd said for one minute.

Something *was* wrong. Drastically wrong. Worse than before. She should have been frightened. Instead she was deter-

mined, very determined, ready to plot, plan, and connive. Anything to understand what was happening.

From the bathroom she could hear the vigorous stream of
the shower as it pounded against the tiles. Walking to the door,
she hesitated for just a second, then slipped smoothly and
soundlessly inside. The steam immediately engulfed her. She
stood still for a minute, wondering if he had heard her or
sensed her presence. Apparently he hadn't. The water just kept
pounding.

He was too enmeshed in his own dilemma to suspect that
she would trail after him like a tenacious bird dog. He had
been angry with her before the note—angry, but not *aloof*. If
she could just find the note. . . . She didn't feel a bit bad
about snooping. Her main concern was that she find the note
while the water was running and Kiel remained wrapped in
his mist of heat and steam.

It was there, folded and placed beneath his watch on the
vanity. She slipped the watch aside, careful that the metal band
didn't scrape against the marble. Silently she unfolded it and
the words, in bold standard type, swam before her eyes. Like
an ostrich again, she refused to allow them to make sense. But
then she saw the signature, and it was as if she had journeyed
back in time, back to another world, laughing with Paul, worrying about fresh vegetables and dip, walking up the stairs,
kissing the children, thinking of how lucky she was. . . .

Walking across the lawn on a moonlit evening, when the
velvet green grass was suddenly rent into flames and a peaceful stillness became a shattering thunder. . . .

Lee Hawk. The man who had killed her family. The man
who had caused the destruction of everything she loved. The
man who had stripped her heart and soul naked and left her
nothing but a shell of pain.

Then there was Kiel. The man who had given her love again.
Who had fought Hawk once and was now forced to fight him
again. Kiel . . . saddled with responsibility again. Kiel, fight-

ing so very hard, somehow retaining his heart and soul. Striving again with silent courage.

Her fingers trembled. For a moment she thought she would scream with the pure anguish of her memories. She doubled over, clutching her stomach, containing the sound. Seconds ticked by. Seconds of blackness. Slowly the mist returned. Slowly the sound of the shower encompassed her again, and with it came a startling calm.

Rhiannan straightened. She carefully refolded the note and placed it back beneath Kiel's watch. Silently she eased out of the bathroom, closing the door with hardly a click.

When Kiel emerged moments later, she had slipped beneath the covers of the bed and lay with her back to him. She felt his hesitation and knew that he was puzzled to see her lying there.

"I'm going out."

His voice was harsh.

She was glad that she was turned away from him because her lips twisted into a sad smile and tears stung her eyes. She knew where he was going: to meet with Donald, Trenton, and Picard; to share the responsibility with them because he had to, because they just might be able to help.

But she knew he would shoulder the rest, and he would do his damnedest to keep the rest of the ship from knowing.

And after he met with Donald and the others, he would go after Joan, because he knew as well as Rhiannan did that Glen Trivitt had to be Lee Hawk. He had believed her when she told him that something was going on between them. He just hadn't known what it was . . . until now.

"Go on out," she told him, muffling her voice in the pillow.

Again she sensed his hesitation and his surprise. "You're going to stay here?"

"Yes," she told him. "Yes," she repeated softly. "I'm going to be here."

She closed her eyes and heard him moving about the cabin, drawing his clothing from drawers and from the closet. The bed shifted beneath his weight as he sat to pull on his socks and shoes. She felt him again, hovering near, as if he longed to reach out and touch her but could not.

At the cabin door he broke somewhat, and she had never loved him so much as at that moment. His voice betrayed his strain. It was tense and husky . . . and wistful. "I'm glad you're going to be here."

The door closed with a soft click behind him.

Rhiannan turned about in the bed, staring at the door. Luckily she was still calm, deadly calm, and determined. *You are strong, Kiel,* she thought, torn between tears she couldn't shed and the urge to smile with a loving pride. *And you may just be the only person who can possibly trick Joan but you can't handle Hawk as well as I can. Lee Hawk has dealt with governments, men with minds like iron fists, but he has never had to deal with a woman from whom he has taken everything. . . .*

Rhiannan waited an hour, barely moving. It was four o'clock when she rose and dressed, her plan fully formed in her mind.

Fifteen

"If he is carrying the AZ strain, it would be possible for him to do almost anything," Michael Trenton said with a dismal shrug. "He could arrange to send the germ through the air-conditioning system, through the water . . . hell, *anything*."

"But how would he be carrying it?" Kiel demanded. "And for that matter, how did he carry the bubonic plague?"

Trenton shrugged again. "A number of ways. Isolated in a small vial. Maybe he even had a damned rat caged up somewhere, although I don't see that. You see, Congressman, for all of our wonderful electronic devices, it's impossible for any type of a detector to discover germs! Tiny little microscopic life that can bring down elephants, tigers—and man."

Kiel walked around the desk in the office where he had been sitting and perched on the edge of the oak desktop, facing Trenton. Picard and Donald also sat in the room. But during Kiel's long monologue regarding the new situation and his personal opinions, they had spoken little.

Donald still looked as if he were in shock, and Picard merely wore the sad eyes of doom.

"What I want to know, Michael," he told Trenton, "is how you think Lee Hawk is carrying this . . . this AZ thing."

"What do I think?" Michael asked.

"As you said before, Michael, in some type of lab vial," Picard answered with a certain assurance.

Trenton turned to Picard, then slowly agreed. "Yes . . . yes,

Picard, I think you are right!" He turned back to face Kiel. "It is unlikely that he has made prior arrangements with this plague, such as setting it within the air or water systems with a timed release. The virus is too dangerous. Where it is . . . studied"—Kiel noted Trenton pause and search for a verb— "the isolation of the germ and all those working with it is severe. Room to room to room, et cetera. Lee Hawk would have to handle it almost as he would a gun with a rusty safety. You just can't trust it. He must keep it with him at all times— upon his person—"

"And—" The interruption came from Donald so suddenly that Kiel started and almost slid from the desk. "—if he does have an accomplice, as Kiel assumes, his security against being caught with it on him is the fact that another of his terrorists is aboard."

"More than possible. More than possible," Michael Trenton agreed.

Kiel took a deep breath, wishing desperately that he could stop feeling so jittery. It was going to be the gamble of a lifetime. The house was playing with all the cards. He had to come up with the winning hand.

"In other words, Dr. Trenton, Dr. Picard, you believe that we have two people walking around the ship with small vials in their pockets or whatever, ready at any time to infect the person nearest them and so spread the AZ through contact."

"Precisely."

"So we do have a chance."

"I don't see how," Donald murmured. He was calm but as white as a sheet.

Kiel smiled grimly. "We have to have a chance. One by one. We know who they are and they don't know that we do. All that we have to do is lull them to a feeling of safety."

Trenton was shaking his head. "I just don't understand it. It would be impossible for someone to steal the AZ strain. It was too well guarded. Most of the personnel at the center didn't even know that it existed."

"Well," Kiel said softly, "apparently someone you all didn't check out thoroughly did know."

Trenton kept shaking his head. Donald looked at Kiel. "What are you planning?"

"One by one," Kiel repeated with a grimace. "And you strike at the most vulnerable first."

"Joan?"

"Joan."

"And what are you going to do, monsieur?" Picard asked.

"Be charming and lulling," Kiel said flatly. "Well, gentlemen, if you'll excuse me, it's time that the first half of the battle got under way." Then he left the office.

Rhiannan glanced toward the bow as she slipped from Kiel's cabin. A few sailors lurked idly about, and a number of the passengers lined the rail, but no one she knew intimately. No one who would wonder why she was hurrying below to reach her cabin.

She felt like a stranger in her own quarters, and her fingers were shaking so badly that she had to go through her drawers twice before finding what she wanted—the pistol Paul had bought for her shortly after their marriage. Pearl-handled, it was a weapon so small that it fit in the palm of her hand or into the pocket of her Windbreaker.

She had never used it. She wasn't sure that she would know how. When Paul had purchased it, he told her that it wasn't accurate at long range but it was deadly up to ten feet away. All she had to do was hold her hand steady. When she had asked him why he had bought her the gun, he had told her that women alone were easy prey and he wanted her and the children protected when he wasn't home.

Tears stung her eyes and she brushed them away. She slid the elegant little pistol into her pocket and left the cabin.

It wasn't difficult for Rhiannan to find Glen: He was, for once, seated at his desk in the small doctor's office on the promenade deck. To her amazement she wasn't shaking; she wasn't even nervous. It was almost as if another person had taken over her body and her own soul had been pushed away to become a shadowed observer. Mata Hari in action, she told herself with dry humor.

There was no wondering what could come of her action—no worry about repercussions. If she could just get him off the ship. . . .

Then where did she go from there? It didn't matter. That eventuality was shrouded in darkness, like the blackness that fell over her when she thought of life without Kiel.

But she couldn't think about Kiel now. She had to keep her concentration on the task of getting Trivitt away with her.

"Glen, I'm so glad to find you here!"

He glanced up after she entered, obviously startled to see her. But Rhiannan's warm, friendly facade quickly assured him, he greeted her with lazy pleasure. "Rhiannan, how nice. I thought you had forsaken old friends."

"Oh, hardly forsaken, Glen." She smiled, perching on the edge of his desk. "This has been a hectic cruise, a terrible strain . . ." she added softly, purposely trailing her voice into a weary whisper.

"Yes, but clear sailing ahead soon, isn't it?"

You bastard, she thought. She saw the way that he looked at her, sitting in his pivoting chair, relaxed, his eyes like a hawk's. A bird of prey . . . carnivorous. Deadly.

She wanted to reach across the desk and rip him into tiny pieces and then stamp on them until his blood could cleanse away the loss that was forever in her heart. She smiled sweetly. "Clear sailing ahead, Doctor."

He smiled. She had reassured him. To his mind only the congressman knew that there was a terrorist aboard, threatening devastation, and not even Kiel knew who that terrorist was. Glen Trivitt was still a laid-back physician, the type of man you would embrace. A snake in the grass, as yet undiscovered

"Where's Whellen?" Glen asked, his voice quietly joking. "He must be off someplace if you've dropped in to see me."

"Glen, how can you say that!" Rhiannan protested with another brilliant smile.

His eyes fell over her warmly, and with a certain regret? *Might it be,* she wondered fleetingly, *that you are going to be sorry to kill me with the others, but are resigned to the fact?*

"Just asking," he said laughingly.

"Well, actually, Glen," Rhiannan murmured, studying her nails before meeting his eyes again, "I have this horrible headache—"

"Ah—ha! You want something from me! That's the way it is with all the beautiful women!" He sat back with a dejected moan and then chuckled. Then he stood and picked up her hand, making Rhiannan ready to scream in revulsion and horror and a fury that seemed to blacken her heart and blood as it writhed and boiled within her.

She didn't jerk her hand away; she just kept smiling and gazing at him with expectant curiosity.

"All right, Your Majesty!" He dropped gallantly to one knee. "For the Queen of Hearts, my very best aspirin."

He turned around and headed for a spotless cabinet with glass shelving and rummaged around for a minute.

Rhiannan stared at his back. Was he really carrying the virus around? Or was she crazy in her assumption. She didn't know a damn thing about germs. But she had to be right. She had to be. . . .

A trickle of chills crept up along her spine. *Am I planning a suicide mission?* she asked herself in horror. She had a gun, but Glen had the virus. He could probably manage to infect her before she could aim the gun. Was she being suicidal? Definitely not. Until the *Seafire,* she hadn't known how very, very badly she wanted to live. Not until Kiel had she known. Kiel was life—a storm, a tempest, and a safe, calm harbor. He was a fighter and he had made her into one.

She didn't intend to kill Lee Hawk, alias Glen Trivitt, just make him believe that she would. But would she if it came to that? Right now she thought that she would gladly see him drawn and quartered. Skinned alive. The man had caused the death of her children. . . .

She shouldn't be doing this because she wouldn't stay calm for long. She would break, torn between a conscience that told her it was wrong to kill and the heartfelt belief that the man didn't deserve to live. . . .

There was no other way. Strangely enough, she was stronger than Kiel. She was the only one in the world who could possibly con Glen Trivitt—or Lee Hawk. It had nothing to do with suicide. It had everything to do with the desire to live. And there was no alternative.

"Here we go: two aspirin, and a paper cup of water."

Rhiannan smiled her thanks and took the aspirins from his hand and swallowed them down quickly. She handed him back the empty paper cup. "Thanks, Glen."

He was standing too close to her. She jumped off the desk and started wandering around the small office.

"Do you know what I really think it is?" she murmured without expecting an answer and hurrying on. "The tension is getting to me badly now. Oh, I realize that it's all over but, well, as Donald's hostess, I'm always supposed to be cool and calm. And I'm supposed to entertain everyone else so that they don't worry about what's going on. I just wish I could forget it all for an hour. Just an hour. It would make me feel so much better." She sighed softly.

Glen watched her as she moved about his office. She didn't dare look at him and try to decipher what emotion lurked in his off-color eyes.

"Why don't you get your congressman to take you out in one of the rowboats for a while."

"My congressman? Oh—Kiel." She manipulated her voice so that she sounded as if she were attempting not to seem irritated, but allowed the irritation to show through. "Kiel has been . . . busy." She laughed dryly. "I'm not sure with what."

Suddenly she spun about to face him. "Oh, Glen! Aren't you tired of being cooped up on this ship? I'd love to get away in one of the rowboats! I know this is an imposition, but would you mind coming with me? You can tell me about the sails again and I can pretend that they are all unfurled and that the *Seafire* is about to crest the westward waves!"

Rhiannan noted every movement that he made with an acuteness that was painful. He glanced at his watch, but just barely. He touched his left pant pocket, but just barely.

"Sure, 'Annan," he murmured. "I'll take you out for an hour. When?"

"Now!" *Don't call me 'Annan,* she thought, the black fury touching her heart again. *My brother can call me 'Annan. Donald can call me 'Annan. Kiel can call me 'Annan . . . just as Paul did. But not you.*

"Don't you want to get anything—"

"No, no! I wore my jeans and Windbreaker, hoping that I could beg you into a reprieve! Let's just go. Please, Glen?"

She touched his arm. She had expected it to feel slimy. Foolish. He was just a man, nothing more. Human with human weaknesses. They just had to be found and exploited.

She forced another dazzling smile to her lips, hoping that they would not turn to plastic and break. They wouldn't. She was human, too.

"How about dinner, gorgeous?"

Joan Kendrick swung around in surprise as Kiel pinioned her to the guardrail with his arms. She stared at him with wide, curious, and skeptical eyes.

She raised a delicate brow at him. "Dinner again, Congressman? What's with you and our black widow? Our dear, dear Mrs. Collins."

Kiel scowled but decided that he needn't put on much of an act. Joan liked things brash and straight. "Rhiannan and I are not quite hitting it off."

"Why not?" Joan demanded.

"Is it any of your business?"

"Yes, I think so. Because the way you've come to me, I think you're after more than dinner. I'd like a lot more myself. But before I hop into bed with you, I want the truth."

Kiel shrugged. "That sounds fair enough. Why aren't Rhiannan and I hitting it off? Because I don't like substituting for a corpse. When we turn the lights off, I feel as if she imagines a dead man's face in place of mine."

Joan kept staring at him, then nodded thoughtfully. "That can be a bit of a drag, I would think." She stared at him a moment longer. Kiel kept his eyes fixed evenly with hers.

"All right," she said at last.

"All right, what?"

"All right, I'll go with you. But not to dinner yet. We'll head to your cabin first."

"Let's make it *your* cabin."

"I'd prefer—"

"I'd rather have different surroundings, if you don't mind. And if you're into muscle, Joan, you have to give way to it some." It couldn't be his cabin. If she had meant what she had said about waiting for him, Rhiannan would be in his cabin.

Joan hesitated for a moment. "All right," she told him again with a shrug and a feline smile. "My cabin."

Kiel took her arm and started to lead her to the stairs. One deck below and they would come at long last to the moment of truth.

It was twilight. The sun set in a sheet of orange and crimson all about them and bathed the proud masts of the *Seafire* in a splendid dazzle of gold to match her name.

A half-mile away from the gently listing ship, Rhiannan turned back to watch her, aware that the time had come when she would pitch eternally into the blackness or rise above it.

"When the sails are all unfurled, filled with the wind and flying proud, the one to first touch the sky is the topgallant. Then there is the—" Glen turned to her and his discourse suddenly broke off.

It must have been in her eyes, a clear portrayal of all that she knew—a reflection of horror, of anguish, of incredulous wonderment, of hate.

He stared at her in silence for a moment, then asked quietly, "How long have you known?"

"That you are Lee Hawk? I'm not sure," Rhiannan replied. "Only for certain since today."

"You're judging me wrong, you know."

"You're a murderer."

"No I'm not. I just see far beyond the range of most men. They talk, they dawdle, they threaten, they plead, they compromise. And while they do all that, science and technology bring us ever closer to the extinction of the human race. Can't you understand that?"

Rhiannan smiled at him. "Yes. I do understand that but I also understand that every human being's life is precious. You killed my husband, Lee Hawk. And my son. A little boy so full of life and trusting that he embraced the world with a beautiful vigor. And my baby. . . ."

Her fingers, shoved into the pocket of her Windbreaker, began to shake. She couldn't allow them to. "An infant, Lee Hawk. Tiny, sweet, precious. Totally vulnerable. Innocent. Mine. You destroyed their lives. And God alone knows how many others."

"You're wrong, Rhiannan. I didn't kill your family. A foolhardy F.B.I. man caused all those deaths aboard that plane. He just had to be a hero."

"Is that what happened in those few minutes?" Rhiannan demanded, her voice absurdly light.

"He pulled a gun and started firing. He blew the whole plane."

"But you lived."

He shrugged. "I was in the tail section. It broke off, it was cushioned by the forest. Of course, I was broken and bloodied and a mess, but that proved to be a blessing. A plastic surgeon was able to put me back together looking entirely different."

"Yes," Rhiannan murmured dryly. "What a blessing."

"I never wish to kill," Lee Hawk told her. "Only to save humanity from itself. And I . . . I never intended to allow you to die."

"Oh? You were going to order the virus to pass me by?"

"I can take you away from the ship right now."

She shook her head.

"Whellen isn't a bad guy. He's just a patsy."

Rhiannan lifted a brow. "A patsy?" she inquired politely.

"He thought he knew what was up. But they didn't tell him about the F.B.I. agents. When I finally told him, it was too late. Who knows? He might have been able to talk some sense into those half-baked heroes. Too much of a half-baked hero himself. He figured they'd made the best decisions that they could, but they were wrong. They should have given him the full score. Whellen . . . he's a government man, all right."

Rhiannan was silently fighting bitter tears. No, Kiel never would cast the blame on others. There was no blame. They were imperfect, but damn! They fought, and they tried. . . .

"And Whellen knows that I'm right. He knows the chemicals, the germs, and the nuclear weapons have to be stopped. He tries, I'll grant you that. He pushes sane legislation. He can rally more countries together in reasonable debate than any other man living. But it just isn't enough."

Rhiannan's mouth curved into a sad, wistful smile. "You're the one who is wrong, Hawk," she said softly. "Kiel knows that men cannot—will not—be run by terror tactics. And he also has the compassion to realize that each and every life on this earth is unique and precious."

Hawk didn't say anything for a minute. He turned to stare back at the *Seafire*. "Ah, but that ship is a gallant beauty. She comes from a noble age. From a time when man met the ele ments and accepted them. The sky, the sun, the sea. It is an age gone by." He turned back to her once more. "I can't bring you back to the ship, Rhiannan."

A coldness settled over her with his words, a fear that struck her bones like a painful ague.

"You know who I am," he continued pleasantly, his eyes on her with a trace of sadness. "I'd like to save you; I'd like to believe that I could trust you eventually."

"And what would you do with me?" she inquired politely.

He laughed. "I had no intention of staying aboard a doomed ship, Rhiannan. If the ransom had been met, I would have slipped away at night. They wouldn't have dared to try to stop me. I could have opened my Pandora's box at any time. It would have been easy to leave the vial where it would have been crushed and the germs released into the air. But as I was saying: There's a yacht waiting for me not five miles from here. I could take you, except that you would always be a threat. A knife against my spine."

"You killed my children. What do you expect?"

He shrugged. "It's unfortunate that you feel that way."

He started to move. Rhiannan deftly pulled the pistol from her pocket and he paused, sitting back and smiling once again.

"I don't think you're capable of using that."

Rhiannan started to laugh.

"Look, you can't even hold it steady. You're not capable of killing, Rhiannan."

She forced herself to stop laughing. "Normally, no. But don't you understand this, Lee Hawk: *You killed my family.*"

"You still can't kill."

Rhiannan flicked back the safety and aimed the gun at him. "Watch me," she whispered softly. *Don't,* something warned inside of her. *Don't let yourself try to be God and judge and jury. Shoot to stop him, not to kill him, even though he should die. He is more of a disease than his virus. . . .*

" 'Annan . . ." He started to move once again.

She aimed and squeezed the trigger. Nothing happened. No bang, no blast. The pistol had jammed. It had lain idle too long.

Rhiannan saw Lee Hawk's slow smile. She stood, rocking the small rowboat precariously. Her only escape might be a desperate dive into the twilit sea. . . .

"You can't escape, 'Annan. But I loved you, you know. I'll bring you gently into night."

The world started to blur on her. She stared beyond him, paralyzed for a moment as sheer terror ripped its way through her backbone. Shadows and darkness were all about.

Lee Hawk was stooped and stalking her as the rowboat swayed, and behind him it seemed as if even the sea were rising in shadow. A form, a dark form, was coming from the sea. Rising . . .

The Devil himself, Rhiannan thought fleetingly, arising to aid and abet his henchman. She broke her paralysis with a scream of terror and dived into the sea.

Joan slid from Kiel's arm and kicked off her shoes when she and Kiel walked into her cabin. Then she turned to face him once more, rubbing her chest against his and planting a moist kiss against his lips. She started to move away from him. "Make yourself at home, Congressman," she told him huskily, "and I'll be right out."

He caught her arm and crushed her back to him. "No . . ."

"I have to undress."

"I want to see you."

"I . . . I . . . uh . . ."

You need to hide the death that you're carrying, Kiel thought fleetingly. *I can't afford that.*

He pressed her more fully against him and nibbled at her earlobe, breathing heatedly. "I want to watch you," he hissed with passionate demand.

She stiffened, then moaned softly as he trailed rough kisses along her neck. Was she relenting? Convinced that he was a man torn by desperate trouble and lost in a heated desire to ease his body and soul?

"Please . . ." he whispered, moving his hands hungrily over her voluptuous curves and slender waist. "Please, Joan, give to me. I need you. All of you. . . ."

He began fingering the buttons of her blouse. She stiffened once more, but didn't fight him. A second later the blouse fell to the floor. He pulled the zipper of her denim skirt and allowed that, too, to fall.

She stepped away from him, smiling as she unfastened her bra and stepped gracefully from sheer lace panties.

Kiel sustained his hungry smile as he watched her dispassionately.

She was beautiful, slim, lushly curved. Her features were lovely, her skin flawless. She had grown up with every advantage in the world. What had happened?

"Kiel . . ." she whispered, opening her arms to him.

He stepped toward her, enveloping her in his caress and bearing her down to the floor ostensibly in passion. She seemed to trust him fully, for she sighed with smug satisfaction as she arched her bare flesh against his still clothed body, enjoying the rough touch of the fabric of his suit.

Kiel slid his left fingers into her hair and locked her head against his as his lips took hers in a savage kiss. Her eyes were closed; his wide open and fixed on his right hand as he deftly riffled through the clothing she had shed. Nothing in her blouse pockets. Nothing in her skirt pockets. Where? Where?

He held her in his embrace as he desperately continued his search. Then it occurred to him that he must have truly been hit by a brick, as Donald had told him. Joan was beautiful but he felt nothing. Nothing at all. She was not Rhiannan; she did not have Rhiannan's velvet and ebony hair, nor did her flesh feel like the finest Chinese silk. He would have smiled were he not so desperate. Being so in love was a sweetness that bound him heart and soul and body. . . .

His fingers kept combing through her skirt and at last hit upon something small and hard in a fold of the fabric. He kept delving around it and at last found a slit. He inserted his forefinger and touched the coolness of glass. He broke the kiss abruptly, straddled over Joan's body, and shoved the vial beneath her nose with a clenched fist.

Her eyes were on him like fire. She hissed and tried to fight him, to no avail. Finally she lay still, just staring at him in furious defiance.

"Why, Joan?" he demanded hoarsely.

"Why?" she retorted.

"You had everything."

She shrugged beneath him. "I had a boring life." She smiled with hard eyes. "Lee Hawk is power, Congressman. Pure power."

"Power?" Kiel repeated incredulously.

"Lee can bring governments to their knees, Congressman. And it's the greatest high in the world. It will get you higher than the best drug in the world."

"You're wrong, Joan. Lee doesn't have the government on its knees. A terrorist can never be anything but a snake in the grass, striking the unwary but always forced to hide out himself. Always beaten in the end."

"He isn't beaten!" She chuckled huskily. "And you haven't a damned thing, Congressman. You have me and *one* vial. Hawk has more. In fact, Congressman, they could be all over this ship."

He smiled grimly at her in return. "But you know if there are more or not, don't you, Joan?"

"Of course. But I'll never tell you."

"I think you will."

"Congressman! Violence against a prisoner is against the law!"

"Is it?" He released her arms for a moment and carefully tossed the germ vial on the padding of the bed. She started to flail at him, but he secured her wrists with one hand and reached into his jacket pocket with the other, producing a jackknife.

"I'm willing to die for my cause, Congressman," she told him, but he sensed the fear in her voice and knew he had to play on it.

"Are you, Joan? Maybe you are willing to die. But death is too easy. You know," he continued pleasantly, "I was in all kinds of war protests when I was a kid in college. Then I got drafted. Can you imagine that? But it turned out to be very educational. You have a beautiful face, Joan. A really beautiful face." He touched the blade of his knife to her cheek. "I can cut it to ribbons, Joan. I can make it into a bloody pulp. I can rip your fingernails out one by one. Break your arms and your legs. And then allow you to live."

"You!" she shrieked, squirming. "You the great congressman, the great lawmaker, the—"

He laughed, cutting her off. "Joan, this isn't a game one plays by the rules. I'm anxious to live, and there are another two hundred people aboard this ship who are anxious to live. If you think I'll refrain from violence or any trick in the book at this point, you're sadly mistaken. I could cut you up so fast, you might not even feel all of the pain."

To prove his point he pressed the blade down with greater force.

"Stop!" Joan screamed hysterically. "Stop! There are no more vials aboard except the one Hawk is carrying. I swear it, I swear it!"

"I don't believe you."

Tears were streaming down her cheeks, soaking his knife. "It's true—oh, God, I swear it. Please don't cut me! Please don't cut me! Please! I swear I'll tell you anything you want to know. It won't matter, because Hawk will break that vial as soon as he knows that things are going wrong."

"Maybe." Kiel stood up, releasing her. He turned about to pocket the vial.

She jumped after him like a cat, screaming, spitting, and

clawing. "You're going to die, Congressman, do you know that? You're going to—"

Dragging her with him, Kiel went to the cabin door and threw it open. Dr. Trenton and two of the security men were standing outside, waiting.

Kiel tossed Joan toward the security men and handed Trenton the vial. He inclined his head toward Joan. "She needs to be bound and gagged and guarded by at least three men. We can't afford any escape attempt."

The security men were good at their jobs. One of them had already covered her with his jacket and slipped cuffs around her wrists. The other was trying to still her flying feet to cuff them, too.

Kiel closed the cabin door on the stream of curses she was shouting at him.

"I'm going to get on this right away," Trenton said.

" 'On it'?" Kiel queried, lifting a brow in confusion.

"Thanks to the plague, I've the equipment aboard to do a safe analysis. Listen, Congressman, we've a bit of a problem. It seems Hawk is off the ship. While we were plotting away, Rhiannan conned him into taking her out in one of the rowboats. They were gone before we knew about it: The crew had no reason to stop them. What do we do now? Think they'll sail on back?"

"Oh, God!" Kiel leaned hard against the paneled hallway, bereft of breath, as if someone had stabbed his gut with a rusty razor and then slowly twisted it.

"She knows," he murmured in a daze of horror. "She must know. She must have decided that she could take him on. . . ."

The world began to spin dangerously. His life raced through a mental vision in a meaningless jumble as if he were drowning.

He *was* drowning, because his life would be without purpose if something were to happen to her. It was terrifying, because he knew to lose her would be unbearable, and knowing that, he understood the pain that she had lived with for so long, the pain that would make her determined to take on Lee Hawk no matter what the odds or danger to her.

"Kiel!" Michael snapped sharply. He gripped the other man's shoulders and shook him.

Kiel's eyes focused on the doctor. A rigidness settled over him, not because he was calm, but because time and chances were running out, and he had to do something before he lost her.

"Where's Donald and the rest of them?"

"Here, Kiel. Right here."

Donald, with Picard and a security man in tow, was coming down the hallway.

"Okay," Kiel said quickly. "Exactly where are they?"

"Not half a mile out."

"I need a dark wetsuit—black, preferably. And tanks. No, wait, I take that back: no tanks. Too cumbersome. Just a mask and a snorkel."

Donald started snapping out orders.

Fifteen minutes later Dr. Michael Trenton had disappeared into a makeshift laboratory with the virus.

And Kiel was diving from the bow of the *Seafire* into the evening sea.

Rhiannan stared at the sea as the dark waves loomed before her. But behind her she could hear Lee Hawk. She jumped from the rowboat, hurtling through the water. It wrapped around her like a wall of blackness. She kicked her legs hard and the blackness became murkier, then grew clearer and clearer as she neared the surface. The sun had almost set, but a new moon was rising. She broke the surface and gasped for air.

Swim! she told herself. *Swim! He'll be coming after you. He'll dive right after you and drag you back to the sea, to that horrible embrace of total blackness . . . eternal blackness. . . .*

She started to swim, gasping and gulping, expecting a crash

behind her at any second. None came. Instead she heard a
shout.

"Don't come any closer, Whellen. I'll break the vial—I
swear I will."

Whellen! Kiel had come. Rhiannan halted, still gasping
wildly for air, and strained to see the rowboat behind her. Kiel
had slipped aboard. He had been her "shadow" from the sea.
He was poised, balancing low on his knees, ready to pounce
on Hawk. His stance was deadly. The moonlight reflected the
knife he held in his left hand. *And you called him a patsy,
Lee Hawk!* Rhiannan thought with wistful pride. *You can't begin to understand all the courage that makes up that man. . . .*

"Oh, God!"

She heard the scream and realized that the sound was coming from herself.

Kiel had stalked his prey and leaped. The two men were
grappling in a desperate fight aboard the madly listing rowboat. In the growing darkness she couldn't tell who was who.
One of them suddenly flew overboard.

"Kiel?" Rhiannan called out tremulously.

"Rhiannan! Swim back to the *Seafire*. Swim as hard and
fast as you can."

"Kiel, I'll come to you!"

"No! No!" There was silence from the darkness for a second. "Rhiannan, Hawk is in the water somewhere. I have to
go after him. And he . . . he managed to open the vial. Get
back to the *Seafire*."

"Kiel!" It was a scream of anguish that tore from her throat.

"Go back! Please, 'Annan, go back. . . ."

Sixteen

Absurd as it was, Rhiannan hesitated only because she knew that Kiel would yell at her, but even that hesitation was slight. Rational thinking did not come into play.

She loved him. He had risked his life to save hers. She couldn't swim away from him. She couldn't think about the future or dread the days, or perhaps the hours, to come. She had to reach him. That was all. She had to be with him, and then, no matter what came, they would be together. Rhiannan began to swim toward the rowboat.

Kiel turned away from Rhiannan with a dull pain thudding heavily in his heart. *I will never hold her again,* he thought dully. *Never know the sweet touch of her lips, the loving fever of her supple form. I'll never hear her whisper, see her eyes light up like green magic. . . .*

Hawk, he reminded himself. Lee Hawk was somewhere in the water. He had to be stopped and dragged back to the rowboat.

The vial had broken after Lee Hawk had gone overboard, so he probably wasn't infected. But he was dangerous to the world. He had to be stopped before he could cause more devastation—or perhaps the final devastation.

Kiel strained to see across the water and at last discerned movement. Hawk hadn't gotten so terribly far.

"Help!"

The call came to him loud and clear, then sounded again with a choked gasp.

"Whellen . . . help me. *Help!* The damn thing is stinging me all over. . . ."

"Where are you, Hawk? I can't see you anymore."

"Here . . . I'm caught. It's a—oh, God! The pain! A jelly-fish . . . something . . . tentacles . . . all over me. . . ."

Kiel hesitated, then picked up the oars. He would pick up Lee Hawk, and then the two of them could sit it out in the rowboat until they died and someone came along to burn away the terrible threat of disease.

"Hawk?"

"Help! Oh, hel—" The words were cut off by a final, gurgling sound.

The sea was silent.

Kiel sat morosely with the oars in his hands, then started violently as a hand came over the bow and a voice softly called "Kiel?"

"Rhiannan! No—"

Her drenched form fell awkwardly into the boat as she pulled herself over with a strained effort.

" 'Annan . . . no!" he whispered sickly, tears stinging his lids.

She struggled to right herself.

It was too late, too late. The vial had broken and its contents had been sprayed all over the boat. She was as outcast and as doomed as he.

Kiel reached for her tenderly, stooping low in the boat and sweeping her into his arms.

" 'Annan . . . 'Annan . . . why didn't you listen to me? Why didn't you go back?" He covered her face with kisses and tasted the salt of the sea and that of her tears.

"I love you, Kiel," she whispered to him.

"Oh, my sweetest darling, I love you, too."

For long moments he held her, cherishing the touch, the soft pounding of her heart, the beauty of a love that was destined to be denied.

"I didn't want you to be here," he told her brokenly. "Oh, Annan, why, oh, why didn't you swim back to the ship?"

"You came to save my life," she whispered, touched by the sweet anguish in his voice. He had loved her all along, fought for her, given to her.

"So, you decided to sacrifice your own," he murmured despairingly, resting his cheek against the top of her head as he held her tenderly against him.

"Kiel, that wasn't it. I just had to come to you. I couldn't leave you."

"But—"

"I understand, Kiel. The vial is broken. What will happen now?"

"I don't know, exactly," he murmured. "I . . . I don't know how this virus works. We'll . . . get sick. . . ."

"And then?"

She pulled away to meet his eyes openly in the moonlight. He drew in a deep breath, unable to answer her.

She lowered her lashes. "They can't take any chances, can they? They'll have to blast or burn this boat."

"Rhiannan . . ."

"Hold me very tightly, Kiel. Please."

He crushed her to him.

"I was ready to marry you, Kiel," she said softly. "That is, if you meant—"

"I meant," he assured her tenderly.

"Would we have lived in D.C.?"

"Yes," he whispered, then drew back as they both stared up at the moonlight. He spoke softly, weaving dreams as they waited for night to fall.

"D.C., or maybe Alexandria. We would have found a Colonial house. An old one, in excellent condition. Two stories, or maybe three. A modest dwelling, though, with great dignity. One with a long, graceful porch and rolling, sloping lawns. . . ."

"And an attic that could be made into a playroom."

"A playroom?"

"For our children," she said quietly. "A boy and a girl. Or maybe two boys. But I . . . I would have dearly loved a baby girl again."

"Oh, Rhiannan," he groaned, burying his face into her damp hair.

"Kiel, please don't. I would have wanted her only if . . . if she could have been your baby. Not without you. You came and gave me strength and you let me love again."

He had no reply for her. He embraced her in silence.

"Kiel . . ." She was interrupted by the sound of lapping water and a sudden flare of brilliant light. Kiel gently shoved her from him to leap to his feet. The rowboat began to pitch and toss, and he waved his arms madly at the newcomer.

"Go! Go back! The vial broke! You have to get away—"

"Kiel!"

The voice shouting was Donald's.

"Donald, you idiot, don't you hear me? Get away from here. Listen to me! Hawk's vial broke—"

"Where is Hawk?"

"Dead, but listen—"

"You killed him?"

"No, a jellyfish did. What difference does that make? Will you stop coming closer! I don't know how far this thing can carry!"

"I'm not that close, Kiel!" Donald shouted. "And you listen to me: Trenton analyzed that other vial. It was water, Kiel. Nothing in it but water."

"Water!" Rhiannan gasped behind Kiel.

"Water, 'Annan!" Donald called out.

"Oh, Kiel, it was water! It was a bluff!"

Kiel turned carefully to take her into his arms and stare tensely into her eyes. "Wait," he said quietly, turning back to Don and speaking painfully. "Donald, all right, we know now that Joan's vial was a bluff. But . . . maybe Hawk's wasn't."

"I . . . uh . . . know," Donald said unhappily.

"Oh, God!" Rhiannan covered her face with her hands. It

was too cruel. Hope had come and then been viciously torn away.

Kiel embraced her tenderly, running his hands along her back. He started to speak, but Donald called out first. "Oh, 'Annan, don't cry! Please don't cry! There's a good chance— See, Trenton knows how this thing works. If you don't have symptoms by morning, then there was no virus. And, 'Annan, Trenton still believes it would have been impossible for anyone to have gotten to that virus at the Center. We . . . just have to wait."

"Till morning," Rhiannan whispered.

A strained silence settled between the three of them. It was as if they stood within the eye of a storm, wondering from which direction the wind would blow next.

Donald cleared his throat. It seemed funny to Rhiannan that she could hear him, because he seemed so far away across the dark waves. "There's water and blankets and some kind of emergency food in the little cabinets beneath the seats," Donald said. "Uh, Trenton suggested that you row out a little farther and cast your anchor, just in case. But he's really convinced," Donald added hastily, "that you're going to be all right."

"Thanks, Donald," Kiel said quietly. "Now, will you please row back before you get any closer."

"I'm going," Donald promised, but still he hesitated. "Oh, guys, I don't know what to say. I love you both. I'll be praying. The whole ship will be praying."

"Donald, for God's sake, please don't go on! We know all that. Hopefully we'll all be having dinner together tomorrow night."

"Yeah," Donald said thickly. "Yeah."

At last he turned the rowboat and started away. Kiel and Rhiannan watched him; then Kiel sat in the center seat to pick up the oars. Rhiannan sat opposite him as he put more distance between them and the *Seafire*.

After a while he stopped and nimbly climbed to the bow. He tossed the anchor over the side, muttering something about hoping that the weight would keep them from drifting in the night. Then he stooped and went through the cabinets, producing canteens, blankets, and some kind of meat sticks in cellophane wrappers.

He carried it all back to the center of the craft, arranging the blankets in a little cocoon between the seats. He sat on the floor where he could lean against the center seat and patted the space beside him. He looked at Rhiannan with a dry grin. "How about dinner, Mrs. Collins? It isn't exactly candlelight and roses, but . . ."

She smiled, hoping she wouldn't cry again. "We've the silver of the moon, Congressman, and the shimmer of the sea. What more could we ask?"

Rhiannan rose and joined him. He wrapped his arm and the blanket around her shoulder, drawing her close as he offered her the canteen. Rhiannan took a long sip of the water and handed it back to him.

In the moonlight she watched his profile. Handsome, strong, a sculpture in reflected bronze glory. Whatever came, she would be grateful for this night.

"I'm going to hold you to everything you said," he told her gravely, unwrapping a meat stick.

Rhiannan took a bite of the meat. It was tasteless, but she studiously chewed it anyway. "Hold me to what?" she murmured.

"Two kids. If they're both boys, we try again for a girl. A Colonial home. A large German shepherd. Maybe a Belgian shepherd. A couple of cats. And a bird. I always wanted a parrot."

"Just like Long John Silver, huh?"

"Yup."

"If we make it," Rhiannan whispered. She turned against him suddenly, almost violently.

"Kiel," she whispered, "make love to me tonight. Please. I want to believe— I want to lose myself in magic, feel the world spin once more in the shelter of your arms."

He stared into her eyes, wide, green, shimmering, beautiful with the depths of her love. He leaned to capture her lips in tender devotion, exploring their beauty with the tip of his tongue, tasting again the salt of her tears and the welcoming hunger she gave to him.

He clutched her to him in a fierce and ardent demand, trembling as the rampant thunder of their hearts joined together. His kiss deepened, his tongue forcing entry to sweetly duel with hers. The moonlight seemed to invade them. There was no fear in their embrace, just need and beauty. Together they could wait until morning.

He broke the kiss with a rueful grin. "There's no subtle, sexy way out of a wetsuit. But don't go anywhere: I'll be right with you."

He stood carefully. Rhiannan watched as he peeled away the dark suit. He might have been a bronzed ocean god as he stood beneath the moonlight, baring his chest, his muscles rippling, his skin gleaming. Rhiannan stared up at him, smiling as he shed his wet trunks and slipped back down beside her. The power of suggestion had a potent effect on him. Unashamed, she reached out and touched him, meeting his eyes as her fingers stroked in tantalizing pleasure.

"I wonder if we're being lascivious and decadent?" she whispered with a little catch.

"If so," he said softly, embracing her and burying his face against her shoulder, "please let's not quit. . . ."

A moment later he groaned and set her on her feet, kneeling in the tight space before her. She shivered as his fingers found the snap of her jeans and tugged on the zipper. She had to grip his shoulders as he worked the wet denim from her hips, balancing against him as he finally pulled away each leg.

"Take off the Windbreaker," he murmured huskily.

It was a strange feeling to strip in the open. The cool night breeze caressed her bare flesh as she discarded the nylon jacket and then the T-shirt she had worn beneath it. She felt a bit like a goddess herself, ridiculously like a mermaid granted a night of life. She stood against the velvet night sky, illuminated by the moonlight, framed by the deep indigo waves.

Kiel placed his hands on her hips, watching as her drying hair was picked up and softly tossed about by the breeze. She was so straight, so proud, so beautifully sculpted in cream beneath the moon. She was shadowed in mystery yet bathed in the silvery mist of the heavens. Her breasts were full, her legs long and wickedly supple and shapely.

"Never," he told her with reverent ardor, pressing his lips tenderly against the softness of her belly, "have I seen a woman as lovely as you."

He stared up into her eyes as she looked down at him. A soft smile touched her lips as she idly ran her fingers through his hair.

"You're a practiced flatterer, Congressman," she said lightly. "But may I return the compliment? You're absolutely the most perfect man. . . ." Her voice trailed away and she bit her lip suddenly. "Kiel?"

"Yes, my love?"

"How did you get to Joan? I . . . I knew you would go for her first. Did you . . . make love to her? I'll understand. . . ."

He smiled. "No, I didn't make love to her. Things didn't have to go that far."

"But you had to get to her clothing, didn't you?"

"Yes," he answered honestly.

Rhiannan smiled ruefully. "I imagine she is perfect."

"No, you're the perfect one."

"And you're a liar, but I love you for it."

He laughed. "I am not—"

"You are—probably in both instances. But it doesn't matter—truly it doesn't, Kiel. I love you and I want you."

There were tears in her voice. He didn't want her to cry. Audaciously he slid his fingers abruptly along her thigh, delving into her womanhood with a possessive yet tender stroke that made her gasp and shiver with the sudden delight.

"You are the perfect one," he murmured, firmly cupping her

buttocks with his free hand and nipping gently at the line of her hip, then showering her with intimate kisses. "And don't dare dispute me again."

She couldn't dispute him. She could barely breathe, barely stand. Ecstasy swept through her in wave after wave until she cried out, terrified that she would faint with the delight and topple over him.

"Kiel . . . please, no more . . . no more. . . ."

Carefully he rose to stand before her, wrapping her in his arms, taking her weight off her trembling legs. He sought out her lips again, passionately exploiting them, loving her with reckless fever. Then he lowered them gently together, sitting on the hard wood himself, bringing her legs around him. He guided her, holding her as he brought himself into her, then shuddering as she smoothly embraced him with her womanhood.

Beneath the silver sheath of the moon, they loved one another with a wild passion that was still somehow infinitely tender, infinitely caring. Time stood still; the night stood still. Only beauty surrounded them. Night breezes swept by to whisper a gentle melody; the sea rocked them in a tempo to contrast the heated rhythm of their soaring desire.

They might have reached for the moon, for the silver that held them in that timeless wonder. Cries escaped them, cries of wonder, cries of joy. Cries of wild and wonderful fulfillment. Cries of love.

And when it was over, they began again, touching, whispering about each other, the beauty of the moon, the wonder of the night.

When he wasn't within her, he was beside her, holding her, sheltering her with the heat of his body and that of the blanket.

When the moon rode high in the night sky, she slipped into a light sleep beside him, and Kiel continued to hold her. He couldn't sleep. He just kept watching the moon. *Until morning comes,* he kept reminding himself, and he turned his eyes to the east, wondering if he would welcome or dread the dawn.

He felt fine. Just fine. He couldn't be ill.

At last the moon began to slip from the sky. Far to the east, crimson streaks could be seen across the sky. He started to flex his arm. It was stiff. His throat, he noted with sinking despair, was sore. *No, God,* he prayed silently. *Please, God, make us be fine. Make us be whole with the morning. . . .*

The crimson streak became stronger. The moon hovered, but it was distant and pale. The sun was coming.

She was still sleeping cramped between the seats, and curled into his chest and the crook of his arm.

Was he crazy or was he sick? Or was he simply cramped and stiff and sore because he had kept his long body folded between the seats all night?

He didn't want to awaken her, so he reached carefully for the canteen and took a long, long sip of the water. His throat felt better. He didn't feel feverish. Not at all. After he swallowed a few times, his throat felt fine.

Kiel gently placed his hand on Rhiannan's forehead. It was cool, as cool as the breeze that had caressed them through the night.

He closed his eyes. *We've made it. I think we've made it. God in heaven, thank you, bless you, oh, thank you!*

"Well, I suppose I should have expected this totally indecent display!"

Kiel opened his eyes with a start as the laughter came to him across the water. He squinted against a sudden burst of pure golden sunlight.

Donald was rowing right up to them.

"Idiot!" Kiel laughed, hurriedly trying to cover more of their nakedness with the blanket. "What are you doing? You didn't even ask me how I felt yet! I could be burning up with fever!"

"You're perfectly okay!" Donald said, allowing his boat to collide with theirs.

"How the hell do you know?"

Donald sobered for a moment. "Because Trenton said you'd be dead by now if you had contracted the AZ strain. I didn't want to tell you that last night because . . . well, because—oh, hell! Kiel! That's obvious!"

Kiel looked up to the sun and began to laugh. Rhiannan stirred against him. Her green eyes opened. He kissed her lips quickly and jubilantly. "We've made it! Oh, my love, we've made it!"

He hugged her, then stood up, jumping in a rush of enthusiasm that made the boat rock.

Don smiled indulgently as Kiel dived into the water, relishing its coolness on his body.

"Bit of an idiot, don't you think?" he told Rhiannan with a broad grin. "Jumping around stark naked, skinny-dipping at dawn."

Rhiannan stared at Donald a long time, perplexity clouding her eyes, which was then replaced by comprehension as clear and startling as the sunlight.

"Donald?" Her voice quivered only slightly.

"It's over, 'Annan. You're well. It was all a hoax, played out well and to the final hand. There never was an AZ plague strain aboard the ship."

She closed her eyes tightly. She was going to live. Kiel was going to live. No, *they* were going to live.

Morning had brought blue skies, a brilliant sun, calm seas—and life.

She looked at Donald again, incredulous joy in her eyes. They looked over to where Kiel was diving and surfacing, throwing the water about him to cascade downward like crystals beneath the sun.

She laughed and shrugged. "An idiot, is he? Well, then, Mr. Flagherty, just call us a pair of imbeciles!"

Still laughing, she stood, mindless of Donald and the *Seafire* in the distance as she shrugged off her blanket and dived into the sea. The water was cold, a shock to her system. It was good to feel the shock, wonderful to taste the salt, to feel it sting her eyes. Suddenly she was feeling something else, slightly rough, very tender: Kiel's arm encircling her.

They surfaced together, laughing and almost crying.

"We did make it, Kiel!" Rhiannan whispered.

"We're going to live."

"For a full lifetime."

"And have two sons!"

"And a daughter!"

"And a Colonial house!"

"Don't forget the parrot!"

"Or the Belgian shepherd!"

"Don't you two think you could do some of this planning back aboard the ship?" Donald cut in laconically.

Kiel ignored him. He kept kicking strenuously against the water as he embraced Rhiannan and met her lips in a long but very salty kiss.

"All right, I give up," Donald muttered. "I'm rowing back. We'll have the celebration as soon as you two can make it back. I'm throwing a pile of clothes into your boat. For heaven's sake, get dressed soon. Kiel, you're not much of a bargain, but Rhiannan could cause a mutiny among the crew!"

He hesitated a moment before picking up the oars. Lost in their embrace of shattering joy, Rhiannan and Kiel barely noticed.

"Mary and I were going to have the captain marry us today. If you're interested in a double wedding, I'm sure it could be arranged."

Kiel at last drew away from Rhiannan. She was so surprised to lose the power of his kicks that she slid beneath the surface. Kiel hauled her back up absently by the hair, ignoring her sputters.

"Married, huh? Today? That sounds good to me. Rhiannan?" He laughed as he saw her indignant eyes. "Well?"

"Well, of course it sounds wonderful to me too! But mention marriage to a man and he's dragging you around by the hair!"

Kiel laughed again and tucked an arm about her, swimming steadily toward the rowboat with her in tow.

Blackjack, Rhiannan thought suddenly. Kiel could always

come up with twenty-one. His Ace had taken the Queen of Hearts, and the Queen had gladly fallen, and they had set their chips flat on the table, playing out against terror, standing firm against a bluff.

Donald turned his back to them with a "See you soon" as they reached the boat and started to climb out of the water. Kiel leaped aboard first and turned to help her, pulling her into his arms once more.

"We really won," she said softly.

"Uh-huh," he said, his eyes silver as they rested tenderly on her. "Lee Hawk was the power behind the Red Hawks. They'll fade into history now. We can both put the past behind us and look to the future."

"He didn't have the right cards up his sleeve!" Rhiannan murmured. She was glad the man was gone for good, yet somehow also glad that nature had taken him.

She smiled suddenly. "He just never knew that a royal flush beats anything."

Kiel glanced at her with a frown.

"Together," she told Kiel softly. "You and me . . . Trenton, Picard, and Donald. A royal straight flush!"

He laughed, then sobered suddenly. "Are you really ready for marriage?"

"Really."

"For a new lifetime of love and commitment?"

"Definitely."

"Damn, do I love you!" he whispered fiercely, pulling her to his chest.

Rhiannan accepted his embrace with wondrous gratitude. In the shadow of his arms she felt tears sting her eyes and knew it would be for the last time. She would never forget Paul or the children they had created and loved together. She would never stop missing them or wondering what they would be like as each year passed if they had been able to grow and live.

But Kiel had taken her from darkness to light, just as the sun had risen that morning, bringing life.

"Let's get back," she whispered. "I'd hate to be late for my own wedding."

He kissed her one last time in the listing rowboat. "My love, we will *not* be late for our wedding!"

They dressed hurriedly.

The sun continued to rise, high and brilliant, as they rowed back to the *Seafire* and the future that awaited them.

Epilogue

Congressman Kiel Whellen's steps were long and staccato as he hurried down the corridors of the White House to the Oval Office. He was alone as he walked, his features drawn into a light frown of curiosity and perplexity, and admittedly, more than a little nervousness chilled his system.

Three years ago this night he had been summoned to this office, and on that occasion. . . . He didn't want to think back. A reign of terror had begun, and now at last it appeared that it had all ended. And in between it all, he had gained something infinitely precious.

The President was alone as he sat at his desk. He stood at Kiel's entrance, a small grin curving his mouth and easing the strain of office from his features. "Congressman, sit down, please."

Kiel, more baffled than ever by the summons, took the chair pulled up before the President's desk.

The President kept smiling as he pushed a button on his call box. "Congressman Whellen is with me now, if you'll send the cart in, please."

Kiel almost laughed aloud as a silver serving set was wheeled in. He was not a member of the President's political party, but it appeared that he had been casually invited to tea.

Well, not just to tea. As they were both served, Kiel watched the President. He was anxious for them to be alone.

Moments later the doors closed and they were alone again.

"First on the agenda, Congressman, is my heartiest congratulations."

"Thank you, sir," Kiel replied.

"When is the baby due?"

"The beginning of March."

"Wonderful, wonderful," the President said jovially. "The first lady and I will both be delighted to welcome a young one to the capital. Ah, they grow so fast."

"Yes, sir," Kiel replied politely. He appreciated the presidential concern, but he would rather be on his way home.

It appeared that the President might have been reading his mind, as he chuckled softly. "I do have another piece of news for you, Kiel."

"Yes?" Kiel set down his teacup, suddenly and tensely alert.

"Nothing bad, Congressman, just a final wrap-up on the Lee Hawk affair." He hesitated for just a moment. "A group of salvage divers came up with some bones out in the Atlantic, near St. Thomas, about a week ago. We've just made an identification."

"Lee Hawk?"

"Yes." The President stared down at his hands for a moment. "I just thought you would want to know."

"Yes, I appreciate your telling me."

The President paused, then smiled again. "You can go on home now, Congressman."

Kiel, to the President's surprise, flushed. "Sir—"

"You're not being rude. From what I've heard, Congressman, you've every reason to want to rush on home. I'm looking forward to meeting your wife myself. She has this whole town buzzing, you know."

Kiel laughed. "That's exactly why we've steered clear of D.C. for the time being, Mr. President."

"Ah, yes, newlyweds do need their time alone. Well, Congressman, when you two do start doing the social scene, I'd very much enjoy it if you would have dinner with the First Lady and me."

"Certainly, sir."

"Good night, Congressman."

"Good night, Mr. President."

Kiel stood and walked toward the door.

The President called him back. "Mr. Whellen, may I say that I'm awfully glad that you're still a bit too young to wind up on the opposing ticket?"

Kiel laughed, "Thanks, sir. I take that as one hell of a compliment."

His steps were long and hurried and staccato once more as he left the White House and headed for his car.

SEPTEMBER 22, 7:30 P.M.
ALEXANDRIA, VIRGINIA

Rhiannan set the dog's dish down and threw open the back screen door.

"Jack! Jack Daniel's! Leave that poor rabbit alone and get in here!"

Out on the sloping green velvet lawn, a huge black Belgian skidded to a halt, barked, wagged its tail, and began a new breakneck race to the house.

"You jump on me, you overgrown monster, and I'll hide every chew stick you own!" Rhiannan admonished the animal as he rushed at her.

He jumped on her anyway.

"Jack, you're just going to have to learn some manners!" Rhiannan wailed.

"Jack Daniel's is a bad dog. Jack is a bad dog. Bad dog."

Rhiannan spun around to see the macaw, Old Abe, flaring its colorful feathers and screeching at the top of his lungs.

"Kiel just had to have a bird!" she moaned with exasperation.

"Pretty bird. Pretty bird," Old Abe replied.

"You're a pretty noisy bird, if you ask me," she retorted.

Jack Daniel's made a lunge for his dog food, almost knocking Rhiannan over. "Okay, guys, the kitchen just isn't big enough for the three of us. Or rather," she added softly, "the four of us. I'm leaving!"

Patting Jack on the head, she skirted around the island range and stepped out into the magnificent living room. She smiled as she ran a practiced eye over the room. The first floor of her home was large and airy, decorated in warm earth tones. A grand piano stood near the rear French doors, which hinted of a bygone era, while the stereo equipment that lined the paneled walls gave the residence a contemporary flair. Everything was as neat as a pin.

Her smile turned to a soft, wistful frown as she gazed up the curving stairway. Her feet seemed to lead her to it of their own accord. She placed a hand on the banister and slowly walked up. She bypassed the master bedroom and moved down the darkened hall. She placed her hand on a doorknob, twisted, and walked into the room.

Three years ago this night she had come to a room prepared just like this one. She had bent over a crib, and had touched soft flesh.

There was a rocker near the crib. An old rocker, painted white.

Rhiannan picked up the teddy bear that had sat as if waiting in the crib.

Absently she sat in the rocker, hugging the teddy bear. For a moment the old grief was strong, so strong that she felt dizzy. But the pain began to fade, and she smiled softly.

She looked at the button-nosed teddy bear and straightened the yellow ribbon about its neck. "I'll never forget them," she whispered to the bear. "Never. Not if I should live to be one hundred. But I'm so glad about this baby, little bear. So very glad. I can't wait to hold him, to share him with Kiel. . . . And I'm not going to be overprotective. I have to promise myself that I won't be." She hugged the teddy bear to her and stood rocking.

"Rhiannan?"

She stopped rocking and looked to the door. Kiel was standing there, so handsome and distinguished in his fall tweed three-piece suit. But his eyes were dark with concern; he whispered her name almost hesitantly.

She leaped from the chair and rushed to him, throwing her arms around him. He embraced her gently, smoothing her hair back as she rested her head against the pleasantly rough lapel of his jacket.

"Are you okay?" he asked her softly.

She pulled away from him to meet his gaze.

"Yes. Oh, Kiel! It's never going to be easy for me . . . but, Kiel, it is so much better now. With you. I . . . I love you so very much. And I'm so anxious for our baby to be born!"

Kiel smiled, grazing his knuckles across her cheek. "Don't be so anxious, my love. We've a half-year to go!"

"Not quite," Rhiannan protested. "Five and a half months."

"Five and a half months," Kiel granted her tenderly. He slipped an arm around her shoulder and led her casually from the nursery.

"Do you think the father of this child has come home too late to beg some dinner?"

"You'll never be too late for dinner," Rhiannan promised, leaning against him as they ambled back down the stairs. She tilted her head and grinned mischievously. "I'm the perfect wife."

"I told you long ago that you were perfect."

She stood on tiptoe to kiss him, then frowned. "Why are you so late?"

"A presidential summons," he told her with a grin. "I received some very official congratulations."

"How nice."

"Hm. But aren't you glad now that we were married on the ship?"

Rhiannan gazed at him in confusion for a moment, then laughed. "Because our child will probably arrive nine months to the day? Yes, I suppose I'm glad. This way, all the gossips will have to wonder!" She sobered suddenly and lowered her eyes. Concerned again, Kiel reached for her chin and tilted her head up to his. He was glad to see a brave little smile cross her face.

"This may seem strange, Kiel, but I like to think that this child was conceived on that day we knew that Mary had made it through the illness. It makes me feel as if two lives were given to us: Mary's and our son's."

Kiel smiled and folded her back to his chest, his words a whisper against her forehead. "It doesn't seem strange to me at all, my love. What does seem strange is that you're so sure we're having a son."

She pulled away from him smugly and whirled toward the kitchen, calling over her shoulder. "Oh, I know it's a boy."

Kiel followed her, planting his hands on his hips and following her every movement as she efficiently drew a casserole from the refrigerator and stuck it into the oven.

"How do you know?"

"Because I had an amniocentesis this morning."

"A what?"

"Amniocentesis."

"Without telling me?" Two strides brought him across the room, and he gripped her shoulders. Luckily the casserole made it into the oven. "Rhiannan! I should have been there. I—"

"Kiel, I was a little worried because of the plague and the vaccines. I didn't mean to go against you in any way; I just had to be sure."

"And . . . ?" She had never seen his eyes smolder darker, but she smiled, knowing that it was a gray storm of concern.

"And everything is fine. We're definitely having a boy."

He laughed and hugged her to him. "Great! A little King of Hearts!"

"No!" Rhiannan protested, laughing, too, as she felt his hands begin to wander. "His father is definitely the King of Hearts."

"Uh-uh. I'm the Ace, my darling. Always remember that, should you feel a little rowdy."

"Hmph!" Rhiannan sniffed indignantly.

"Hmph, yourself. But oh, sweetheart! I know you want your little girl, and I would have gladly welcomed a daughter, but I have to admit that I think a boy first will be great. And remember, we'll try again."

"And again?"

They smiled at one another, identical grins slowly curving their mouths in soft laughter. Simultaneously they spoke. "Royal straight flush!"

Laughing harder, they embraced again. Kiel's hold on her was fierce. Slowly he released her, and she saw a new smoldering in his eyes.

"How long does that casserole take?"

"About an hour."

The words were barely out before be swept her into his arms and turned purposely from the kitchen.

"Kiel—"

"An hour is plenty of—ouch! Jack Daniel's! Will you get out of my way?"

The shepherd whined, wagged its tail, and trotted over to the cool tiles by the screen door.

Kiel shook his head in mock exasperation. "This gallant bit is difficult when you trip over the dog."

"Hey, *you* wanted the dog."

"And the bird," Kiel agreed pleasantly.

"That bird is half crazy, you know."

"That's okay." He grinned. "You're the one who wants a half-dozen kids."

"You were the one who wanted all those kids and I'm already pregnant!"

"We don't want to get out of practice."

"Oh."

"Any objections?"

She smiled at him, her eyes a beautiful, dazzling green. She looped her arms securely about his neck as he started up the stairway once again.

"No. I can't think of a single one."

More Women's Fiction From Kensington